ISBN: 979-8-9875529-0-2 (paperback)

ISBN: 979-8-9875529-2-6 (hardback)

ISBN: 979-8-9875529-1-9 (ebook)

Library of Congress Control Number: 2023913111

Cover designed by MiblArt.

 Created with Vellum

THE
PRINCE
OF
TERRANA

HAYLEY TURNER

THE PRINCE OF TERRANA

THE HEIRS OF ESRAN
BOOK ONE

HAYLEY TURNER

Hayley Turner

Author ✦ Composer

CONTENT WARNINGS

This book contains depictions of physical abuse, torture, suicide, blood/gore/violence, and a brief reference to miscarriage.

To all the kids who grew up and still love fairytales.

CONTENTS

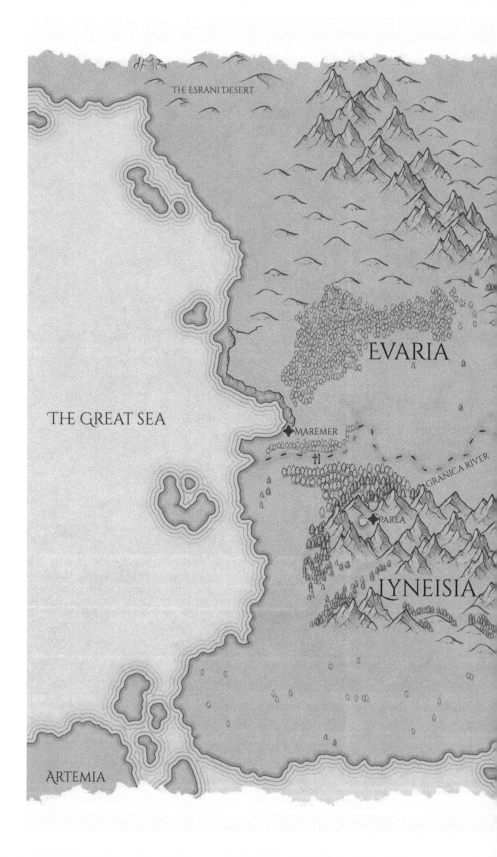

THE ESRANI DESERT

EVARIA

THE GREAT SEA

MAREMER

GRANICA RIVER

PAREA

LYNEISIA

ARTEMIA

ESRAN

CRESTFALL

RIVENDYA

ELLYR

RYOS

THE CASPIAN FOREST

GRANICA RIVER

TERRANA

PERMARE

IUES

GRANGERTON

INMEDIO RIVER

BARLEO

THE BLACKWOOD FOREST

The Gods of Esran

THE ESCAPE

The prince ran.

With sparks of pain shooting up his right leg, he ran as fast as he'd ever run in his life. Cold air burned his throat and lungs, and the metallic taste of blood crept into his mouth as he pushed himself harder, ignoring the remnants of dark magic lashing through his body.

If they caught him, it was over—he'd never have another chance to escape.

His bare feet slapped against the obsidian floor louder than he'd have preferred, but speed was more important than stealth now that two priests of Calixtos were dead, their bodies certain to be discovered at any moment. Indeed, shouts and barked orders barreled down the corridor in a terrifying echo. But the prince had planned for this and was almost to the place he sought...

There.

Just ahead was the end of the corridor, a torch set in the center of the wall. He slowed his run to avoid smacking into it and removed the torch before holding the flame against a stone to its left. A pattern of rectangles appeared, one dark red. The prince found the stone the symbols indicated on the wall and pushed.

It took some extra effort, made more challenging by the sweat on his hands as the voices grew more frantic and footsteps became audible, but the wall finally gave way and began to open before him. This ancient, secret door would lead him to his freedom.

The moment it opened wide enough for him to fit through, he slipped inside, torch in hand, and shoved the stone back in place to reseal it. Slowly, painstakingly, the door shut behind him, and he took off down the secret passage.

Minutes later, the prince burst out of a trapdoor in the stables, hay flying and horses startling. He scrambled for the wooden barrels nearby and reached into one containing clothing he'd stashed two weeks prior. With a thundering heart and shaking hands he yanked off the tattered shirt and trousers he'd been wearing three days ago after he purposely botched a mission that would have changed the fate of the continent. His father had never been in such a rage, and the prince had paid for his defiance in pain and blood.

He threw the old clothes back into the barrel and yanked on the boots, wincing at the deep, freshly inflicted gashes in his right leg, back, and arms. They weren't bleeding freely anymore, but they would pose a problem if he didn't keep them clean over the next few days.

Later. Worry about that later.

Shouts sounded from just outside the stables, and the prince vaulted over a nearby door, hiding by an unperturbed horse snacking away at some hay. After the voices faded, he peeked out to ensure no one was around before clambering back over the stall door. He crept down to another stall, where he knew a fully saddled horse was waiting for him, courtesy of a paid-off stable boy, who was now also conspicuously absent, as instructed.

The prince mounted up and left the stables at a gallop, heading to the south where no gate stood in his way—it wasn't needed when the River Inmedio provided enough defense on its own. He brought the horse to a stop several yards from the short cliff's edge, and after ensuring he had his weapons and supplies, sent her off, back toward the Keep.

The prince sensed the whizzing of the arrow in almost the same instant it found its mark in his right shoulder blade, the tip exiting cleanly through the flesh just below his collarbone. He cried out, the momentum of it sending him to his hands and knees, and an instant later another arrow lodged itself into his thigh.

"We've got him!"

No.

The prince tried to stand, and another arrow hit him in his calf, sending him back to the ground. With a growl, he snapped off the arrowheads and began to crawl for the cliff's edge.

"Stop him, now!"

Horses were approaching. He was two feet from the cliff. Another arrow to the other leg. He screamed, dragging himself forward, then rolled off the edge of the cliff and into the river below.

KING GABRIEL LaGUARDE stood on his balcony at the top of the Obsidian Keep, pondering the rushing river in the distance. His son, it had been reported, disappeared into the Inmedio three days ago after being shot more than four times. The boy had mettle; if only he weren't so weak-minded and empathetic, they could join their power together and achieve Gabriel's dream to unite Esran, ruling over it all without the risk of anyone opposing them. But his son had never embraced the darkness, and it was Gabriel's greatest disappointment that his heir was so *soft.*

Gabriel had tried for almost a decade to beat that softness out of his son and had thought he'd been getting somewhere recently with the priests. Alas, he had been mistaken—a rare occurrence. How was he supposed to create and maintain an empire when he couldn't even control his own blood? It was his divine right to rule, placed upon him by Calixtos himself—why else would the LaGuarde line have had the god's dark power bestowed upon them when their dynasty began three hundred years prior?

A knock sounded behind him. The captain of the guard entered the king's chambers and, with shaking hands, removed his helmet.

"You sent for me, Your Grace?"

The hem of King Gabriel's emerald cloak fluttered in the breeze as he slid his gaze from the river and the darkening horizon. He stepped away from the balcony's edge and closer to the trembling man before him. "Tell me, Ronan, why my son has not yet been found."

"W-well you see, Your Grace, w-we tracked him to—"

"Because I seem to recall you, several days ago now, insisting that we need not use the Terranian Elite to 'track and subdue an unruly eighteen-year-old boy.' You told me that your men would have him home in a matter of hours."

"We...I..."

"I will not tolerate such incompetence. Go fetch the assassins, and if you return quickly, I may even consider sparing your life."

"Yes, Your Grace."

The king sat by his obsidian fireplace, his knuckles white on the arm of his chair. He'd go after the boy himself, were it not for that godsdamned prophecy. He must move carefully, strategically—the healer-advisor in his court was a dull man, but Gabriel followed his counsel without question. Leaving Terrana without all elements under his control could bring about his own demise.

Ronan returned before the king had time to get comfortable. The king smiled as two of his favored assassins entered the room alongside the captain of the guard. With a nod of his head, one of them buried a knife deep into Ronan's heart. He slumped to the floor in a bloody heap, eyes wide. King Gabriel looked at him with disgust, then addressed his assassins.

"Do not disappoint me as he did."

The two assassins bowed and then left, swift as shadows. King Gabriel settled once more into a chair by the fire, frowning at the flames.

PART ONE

CHAPTER 1

A CHANCE ENCOUNTER

THREE YEARS LATER

Dust flew up around Relaina as she hit the ground with a *thud*, the taste of blood and wounded pride in her mouth. With a huff, she leapt to her feet and faced her opponent, a spindly man, the first to give her a real challenge today. He raised his arms to the crowd, which offered equal amounts of cheers and hisses, and Relaina dove, sending them both careening to the ground of the fighting ring. He was slippery, but Relaina overpowered him as they grappled. A horn wailed and the crowd erupted.

Relaina stood, grinning as cheers thundered around the underground fighting ring, but as she bowed gratefully, her eyes caught the nearby clock on the dimly lit limestone. *Shit.*

She grabbed the winner's coin bag from the ring master and dashed up the steps of the stands two at a time, grabbing at the mask over her mouth to ensure it was still intact. She slipped behind a stall selling black-market jewelry and into a tunnel that led from beneath the city of Parea into a secret passage within Castle Alterna, ignoring the growing stitch in her side as the minutes ticked by. The collection of bruises on her legs and abdomen nagged at her as she forced herself up the final ladder that would lead her into the castle's kitchens. Once she'd made it to the top, she displaced the trapdoor with an expert hand and crawled through, ignoring the impulse to lie down on the stone floor to catch her breath. On another day, she might've had time for rest.

Relaina replaced the trapdoor and hopped over the stray bags of flour strewn about the pantry before darting out into the kitchens. If the workers saw her as she ran past, none of them said a word.

When she arrived at the end of the corridor at the lift, Relaina flipped the corresponding levers to inform the operator on the first floor where to send it and waited impatiently for it to arrive. She stepped inside, flipped the lever for the eleventh floor, and breathed a sigh of relief as it began the climb. During the few minutes it took to make the trip, however, her newly acquired aches and bruises began to throb more insistently; it would take a good amount of acting for her to hide her pain during the council meeting.

Back in her chambers, she tossed the bag of coins into her wardrobe's false bottom, peeled off her boots, dirty trousers, and shirt, and undid the braid that contained and disguised the dark curls for which she was well known. If she had time to try and tame them a bit after changing, she would.

A knock came at her door, making her jump. She tossed on a robe and scurried to the door.

"Relaina, it's me. One of the maids saw you sprinting through the kitchen again, and I figured you'd need help dressing."

"Oh, Victoria, thank the gods," Relaina said, inviting her in and closing the door behind her. "I was about to start panicking."

"Don't you worry, dear, I'm always here to—gods above, Relaina, have you been in the fighting rings again?" She pointed to Relaina's fresh bruises, the deep reddish-purple stark against the princess's fair skin. When Relaina didn't answer, looking at the wall, Victoria flicked her nose. "One of these days someone is going to bruise your face, and your father will flog everyone involved—you included."

"There's a rule against strikes above the neck. And besides, I'm careful enough to avoid it anyway."

"I understand a bit of adventure is fun and healthy for everybody.

But gods, why not just go explore the part of the city that's above ground?"

"You know I do that too. In fact, I plan to do that this evening."

"Ah, to be young," Victoria sighed, flipping her ash-blond hair over her pale shoulder. "This evening I'll go home, have some wine with my husband, and go to sleep."

"That doesn't sound all bad." Relaina grabbed at the skirt of her scarlet gown to smooth it out while Victoria fastened a golden necklace at the back of her neck.

"Oh, dear, I wasn't complaining. That's my ideal night these days." She laughed.

A few minutes later Relaina entered the small council chamber on the thirteenth floor, a few doors down from her father's study. She'd taken the lift up, not trusting herself to brave two flights of stairs without tripping on her hem. Her hair was piled on her head in an elegant twist with several ringlets hanging loose that tickled her neck.

The room was quiet—the men and women of the council either conspiring with the person beside them or silently twiddling their thumbs. They sat around a large oak table with eight chairs. The one at the far end was covered in pale blue velvet with silver trim, with the Lyneisian sigil—the lynx—sewn masterfully with silver thread into the fabric of the chair's back. The cunning mountain cat looked as if it were prowling, waiting, observing the world with its keen eyes and pointed ears.

The members of the council stood, and Relaina took her seat to the right of that magnificent, empty chair, studying those present.

With her usual tight bun and high-necked gown, Misenia, the Keeper of Law, sat two seats down from Relaina. The muted purple of her attire complemented the older woman's silvery hair and brown skin, and she stared at one of the eight stained-glass windows as though she could burn a hole in it if she concentrated hard enough. Torrence Doldren, the Keeper of Records, oozed insincerity as he lauded Misenia's gown, but the woman's dismissive hum told Relaina enough about her opinion of the man.

Relaina's uncle and the Lyneisian Captain of the Guard, Jeremiah, entered the chamber and took his seat to her right. His pale blue guard's uniform was pristine, but the stubble usually adorning his chin had grown wiry, and his graying bronze hair stuck out in several places. Dark circles beneath his eyes stood prominent against his fair complexion. Despite his impressive height and status, his presence hardly changed the atmosphere of the room, and most of the council members ignored him.

"Morning, Relaina." He exhaled slowly, rubbing his eyes. They were bloodshot around his dark brown irises.

"Long night?"

"Very. Twelve of my newest recruits were found in an unauthorized brothel. The workers there weren't paid."

"Gods."

"The gods were nowhere near that place, believe me. Especially after I arrived. The workers are being sent home or offered places in authorized establishments, and the proprietors are all dead. Four of the recruits are packing their bags as we speak."

"Just four?"

"They claimed they didn't know it was unauthorized, so I gave them the choice of extended training for six weeks followed by waste duty for their first two months in the Lynx Guard, or they could leave for home. Eight of them chose honor; the rest chose shame."

"They all chose shame when they went to a place like that. Why not go to a reputable parlor? Madame Faulkin's is respectable."

"Money, I expect. Still no exc—how do you know about Madame Faulkin's?"

Relaina raised an eyebrow. Jeremiah nodded.

"Ah. Aronn."

"He's not exactly modest about it."

Another council member entered the room—Archan Conclave, cousin of Zarias Conclave, one of her brother's friends. Archan was not the pig that Zarias was—his respectful demeanor and kind nature had once been enough for Relaina to consider him as a potential consort until he'd married a woman from his home in Lamina. They both lived in Parea now, in one of the large manor houses close to the base of the castle.

At last, King Stephan Gienty arrived, sweeping through the double oak doors. Everyone stood from their chairs and bowed as he walked to his place at the head of the table, silver cloak rippling behind him like shimmering water. He sat and adjusted his silver crown, sunlight catching the intricate metal engravings and the aquamarine stone in the center. Relaina stared at the crown atop her father's auburn hair. She didn't want to think about the fact that she would be the one wearing the weight of it after he died, or the fact that she would likely be married with children when that time eventually came.

"I proclaim this meeting of the king's council commenced," the king said, the others watching him with their full attention. "There are several things I wish to discuss today, but I have a meeting in one hour with a visiting noble family. Firstly, there is the matter of Lord Henry Swanson. Archan, if you will explain."

Archan, the Keeper of Coin, cleared his throat and leaned forward as all eyes turned to him, his voice quiet but clear.

"In order to keep trade agreements pleasant, I would suggest making his stay as hospitable as possible. He is incredibly wealthy, and his grain-rich lands could be instrumental in buffering our food stores this winter."

"What sort of expenses are we expecting with his stay?" Torrence asked, his beady eyes narrowing.

"Our source has told me the young lord is quite particular. He is rather fond of roses and always has his rooms in Rivendya filled with them, freshly cut twice a week. His cousin, Lady Hemington, is accompanying him, along with a small group of servants. We will need to ensure the placement of roses on the floor where he will be housed for his stay, and—"

"He's staying in the castle?" Relaina asked. "Rather unusual for a visiting minor noble to be granted rooms in Castle Alterna."

"Indeed," Archan said, and Relaina tried her best to ignore her father's glare. "But as I said, Lord Swanson is rich in both gold and fertile farmland, and we wish to please him. We know nothing of his character and how he intends to rule his small bit of this world, so it is, in my opinion, best to give more and risk being overbearing than to give less and risk offense."

For the next half hour, the council discussed Lord Swanson's

upcoming arrival, which they expected in a fortnight. Archan and
Torrence argued back and forth, only occasionally interrupted by the
king or the high priestess, an aging woman with jet-black hair, who
inquired about Swanson's devotion to the gods. Old Edamir, the Keeper
of War, had fallen asleep five minutes into the meeting, snoring softly
with his chin on his chest. Relaina fought the urge to rest her elbows on
the table and fall asleep herself.

"Excellent. Now that Lord Swanson's visit is settled, there is another
matter which I fear we must discuss, as it is of great importance."
Relaina's attention snapped into place once more as her father spoke.
"This information was brought to me by a trusted source, whose identity will, for now, remain a secret for their safety. For the foreseeable
future, no one besides Lord Swanson will be allowed to enter or leave
the city. My source tells me there is a very good chance the Prince of
Terrana is currently in Parea."

The chamber was utterly silent for a single breath, and then—

"We must find him!"

"Did he not disappear a few years ago?"

"He must be caught."

"By the gods, I thought he was dead..."

Relaina and her uncle exchanged a glance, his eyes thoughtful. He
either didn't have an opinion on the matter, or he agreed with Relaina
—this was a disaster. King Stephan held up a hand, and the room
quieted.

"Your Majesty, we *must* capture him as soon as possible," Archan
said. "If this is another plot like that foolishness twenty years ago—"

"Terrana has always been secretive; you've seen those patrols at the
border crossings—"

"This could be the answer to unveiling Terrana's mysteries—"

"The Tyrant King will come for us all!"

"*If* you capture him," Relaina said, "what do you intend to do?
Torture him for information? If the prince grew up with the Tyrant
King as his father, don't you think he's suffered enough? Why not reach
out diplomatically?"

"Lyneisians' safety and well-being is always my first priority," the
king said, throwing a sidelong glance at his daughter. "We know little of

this prince beside the fact that he left Terrana, and we must assume he is highly dangerous. If we can glean information that could potentially save innocent lives, I will gladly do whatever is necessary." There were several murmurs of assent and Relaina opened her mouth to argue, but her father cut her off. "That's enough for now, Relaina."

For the remainder of the meeting, Relaina sat seething in silence, her irritation written plainly on her face.

After adjourning the meeting, her father placed a hand on hers.

"Relaina, we need to talk."

His face was drawn, as if someone had wrung him out. It was the first time she'd really looked at him in a while, and her heart softened toward him somewhat, knowing that feeling of exhaustion all too well.

"I know you want to offer your voice to the conversation, but until you are queen, it is not your place," he said.

"Then why bother having me in the room at all? If I'm just supposed to be a silent statue, what is the point?"

"You are there as a reminder that you will be their sovereign one day. You are an extension of me. You cannot argue with me in front of council members—it will be seen as dissent within the family, and those who would seek to harm us or break us apart will take advantage of any perceived weakness."

Relaina looked at her hands on the table, clenching them.

"You have to know I don't mean to disrespect you. But how am I supposed to learn to be queen if all I am is an extension of you?"

"Wisdom will come with time. You still have much to learn, and you have many years to learn it."

Her father dismissed her, and she left, glad the meeting was over.

"Princess Relaina!" Relaina turned toward the voice just as her right foot lifted, ready to take another step down the immense stone staircase.

"Princess?" she asked with a snort as she descended to the floor where a young man stood, his arms crossed over his chest. "Since when have you called me that?"

Bracken Averatt grinned with a familiar sparkle of mischief in his blue-gray eyes. He joined Relaina as they continued downward, passing through a shaft of light that briefly cast a golden hue upon his brown hair and made his ivory skin almost glow. "I hear Lucinda is looking for you."

"Oh, gods in hell. Now?"

"Well, you know, the Harvest Festival is in a week, and it usually takes a while to make a dress—"

"She's just..." Relaina wrinkled her nose.

"The faster you go meet with her, the faster you can get out of there."

Relaina exhaled and punched him in the shoulder.

"Ouch, Laines. Save that for the fighting rings."

"I was there this morning."

"Of course you were."

Relaina grinned. "I'll see you later, *Lord* Averatt." Bracken made a retching sound, a few freckles on his nose disappearing as he scrunched it in disgust.

"Not for many, *many* years."

Relaina laughed and continued down the stairs, a little slower now. Her destination was only another floor down. Her plans to go visit Maurice, the only farmer in the city of Parea, were now on hold.

DARREN CURSED SILENTLY as he stood before the crowded entrance hall and corridor beyond. The first floor of Castle Alterna was bustling with people, maids and servants and nobles alike, all preparing for the Harvest Festival that would take place in a week's time. Maurice had sent him here to find a woman named Victoria—he needed to determine what kind of flowers and how much food would be needed for the festival, but thus far he had been unsuccessful in his search. Any time he asked a servant, they either dismissed him after a moment or ignored him completely. Finally, after approaching a dozen different people, one of them responded half-coherently.

"Eleventh floor," the man mumbled, not breaking concentration on the piece of paper in front of his nose. It was a list of some sort, but Darren didn't get a close look at it before the man walked away, muttering to himself. Darren turned toward the servants' lift, but there was a very long line of people waiting, carrying various heavy loads. He sighed, pushing his hair back from his forehead—the blond strands in his eyes reminding him that he really ought to trim it soon—and began to look for the nearest staircase.

It was easy enough to find, situated just outside the entrance hall and winding right through the center of the seventeen-floor castle. Maurice had told Darren a little about what to expect: ballrooms and banquet halls on the higher floors, kitchens and servants' quarters on the lower floors. As Darren began his climb, he expected he'd find out exactly what was on floors two through eleven today.

Darren indeed passed by the servants' quarters and a laundry room filled with smells reminiscent of both wet dog and fresh linen. He could certainly smell the fifth floor before he reached it. The staircase traveled through a small room with chairs and couches to lounge on, and though the doors beyond that room were closed, the kitchens must lie behind them. As Darren trekked past the next few floors—which only revealed long corridors and closed doors—he began to develop a new respect for the kitchen workers who would have to deliver the prepared food from the fifth floor to the banquet halls on the higher floors, even with the lift.

By the time he reached the eleventh floor landing, Darren's thighs were burning and his lungs ached for air. He took a moment to catch his breath and swore again, as before him was a long corridor lined with identical doors. With a great sigh, he opened the first, and his jaw nearly dropped.

It was a magnificent room, with high ceilings and windows that allowed sunlight to bathe the floor. Directly ahead of him, two glass doors opened to a balcony, accented by flowering vines and gossamer curtains that danced placidly in the breeze. To his right was a large bed, decorated in the light blue, white, and silver colors of the Gienty family. To his left was a large wardrobe, vanity, and an open door leading to a washroom that certainly had running water—even the poorest of houses in Parea had that luxury.

"Who the fuck are you?"

Darren jumped, his hand flying out of instinct toward the figure that had appeared behind him. She ducked, grabbed his arm, and shoved him against the corridor wall beside the door, her arm at his throat.

Gods in fucking hell.

He was almost nose-to-nose with Princess Relaina Gienty. She scowled at him before her eyes widened.

"You," she said. "You're Maurice's apprentice."

"I..." Darren stared at her, dumbstruck.

"You'd better be glad a guard didn't see you almost strike me. Did Zarias send you up here?"

Darren shook his head to clear it. "Who—? I...no, no—sorry, Princess, er, Your Highness, I just...I got lost."

"And you thought going through my room would help you find your way?"

"Yes—I mean, no!" He choked a little and coughed. "Could you please take your arm off my throat? It's a bit inhibiting."

Princess Relaina removed her arm but not her steely gaze, her green eyes striking against the red flush of anger in her cheeks. Her tense, defensive stance made him feel small, though he was slightly taller.

"You have ten seconds to explain yourself."

"I asked someone for directions, but I suppose I was given incorrect information. I came across your room, and I admit I got distracted. My deepest apologies for almost grabbing you."

"You've intentionally avoided me ever since you started working for Maurice, so I don't *really* know you. Am I supposed to take you at your word?"

"You think Maurice would hire someone untrustworthy?"

"Hmm." Relaina narrowed her eyes and looked him over. He tried to stand with relaxed confidence so she wouldn't think he was lying, but it was difficult to do anything when she had him frozen in place with those viper eyes.

"What's your name again?"

"Darren."

"And where were you *actually* trying to get to in the castle?"

"I was trying to find Victoria. A servant downstairs told me she'd be on the eleventh floor."

"Well, for starters, she's on the tenth floor. And secondly, Victoria isn't even here right now. She left earlier to visit a neighboring village to set up some things regarding the Harvest Festival."

"That's unfortunate." Darren's mood deflated even further.

"It is indeed. Now, if you wouldn't mind, I'm trying to avoid the dressmaker."

Darren bowed and headed for the stairs again. He glanced over his shoulder, meeting Princess Relaina's eyes just before she shut her door. As he descended to the bottom of the castle once more, he sighed, dreading the trip back to Maurice's, flower cart in tow.

RELAINA DIDN'T SEE the farmer's apprentice, Darren, at all during the next five days. She wanted to find out more about him—she'd been curious ever since he came to Parea a year ago, but he was aloof and cold each time he'd encountered her. Yet when she'd seen him around other city dwellers and citizens of Parea's outer village, he was friendly and warm. He'd never been unkind, but he always had an excuse to avoid her.

Despite Relaina's desire to solve the mystery of this strange man, she was pulled in other directions leading up to the Harvest Festival, by servants and Lucinda and her mother and father. The evening before the festival, exhausted by the excessive planning of the past week, Relaina was relieved to spend some time with her sister as the sun was setting.

"What color is the dress you're wearing to the festival?" Annalise asked, joining Relaina on her balcony and balancing the cup of hot tea in her delicate pink hands as she sat.

"Dark green," Relaina said. "It's rather lovely, actually."

"She chose silver for me again." Annalise sighed.

"That's not a bad thing. You look lovely in silver."

Annalise blew the rising steam from the hot tea in her hands. "I just wish for once we could all wear whatever color we like. I would wear yellow, and you could wear that pretty lavender color you like so much."

"That would be nice. You'd look like the sun, and I'd look like...the sky."

"The sky is blue, Relaina."

Relaina laughed. "I mean in the early morning, before dawn breaks."

"You could be a poet." Annalise reached for a small pastry on the table between them.

"Maybe I should just renounce my title and go travel Esran as a bard."

Annalise set her teacup down a little too forcefully, horrified.

"I'm joking, Anna." Relaina tucked a strand of her sister's hair behind her ear and lightly tapped her round nose. Annalise took more after their mother than Relaina did, with her gently curling golden hair, blue eyes, and full figure. Relaina's hair was far curlier, the dark brown allegedly identical to her grandmother's. Relaina had never met her maternal grandmother, since she lived in the northeast of Evaria and her health did not allow her to travel, and her other grandparents had died before she was born. Their brother Aronn's hair was auburn—the eighteen-year-old prince was the spitting image of King Stephan.

"Good," Annalise said. "I don't know what I'd do here without you."

"You'd be stuck with Aronn."

Annalise grimaced. "But he doesn't like talking about dresses or handsome knights and lords or flowers."

Relaina smiled at her sister. She didn't really care to talk about those things either.

"He'll grow out of this phase eventually. And then you can talk to him, and I can live in peace."

"His friends all flock around you because you're so pretty." It was common knowledge that some of Aronn's friends, namely Zarias, practically stalked Relaina around the castle whenever they were on the grounds. "I wish I looked like you."

Relaina raised an eyebrow. "Those boys flock around me because they're power-hungry pigs with no sense of boundaries. Besides, I am five years older than you. That just means I look more grown up. It doesn't mean I'm prettier than you."

Annalise raised an eyebrow and shook her head.

"Beauty isn't everything," Relaina said, recalling her own insecurities from when she was Annalise's age. "But if it makes you feel better, I'll tell you this: the entire kingdom sings praises of Mother's beauty, and you look just like her."

"You really think so?"

"Without a doubt. Now, Victoria will be cross with you if you're too late to the greenhouses. She won't chastise you like Lucinda but she does need to know which flowers you'd like for the festival decorations."

Annalise frowned and stood from her cushioned chair on the balcony, pausing for a moment to gaze at Lake Alterna's sparkling green-blue waters. Relaina joined her, breathing in the mountain air and hugging her sister from the side.

"Are you coming as well?" Annalise asked.

"In a little while. She had more questions for you."

Annalise nodded and hurried off. It was probably a good thing that Annalise was last in line for the crown—her temperament was gentler than Relaina's or Aronn's, her priorities focused on suitors and marriage. Relaina's own search for a husband would forestall any betrothal for her sister, and once she herself was married she could help find her a suitor that would see Annalise as more than just a stepping stone on their way to more power and a higher title.

In Relaina's regard, it was clear that her father was more concerned about finding a politically smart, economically advantageous match than a man of exemplary moral character. An arranged marriage with some high lord would keep the kingdom together and maintain peace, and Relaina had long ago come to terms with the idea of an arranged marriage. But the prospect of marrying any of the lords she had met thus far was exceedingly depressing. Relaina still shuddered when she thought about the situation with Lord Mirnoff from last summer—her father had liked him especially, and it had been difficult to ward off his insistence on that particular match without explaining that Mirnoff had found Relaina kissing one of his guards in a closet.

While the memory of it still made Relaina want to shrivel up like a date in the sun, it certainly wasn't as disastrous as it could have been. Mirnoff had burst out laughing, admitted that he found Aronn more attractive than Relaina, and left amicably the next day when he discovered Aronn was not, in fact, of the same disposition when it came to attraction.

As the sun went down, Relaina's thoughts drifted to her encounter with Darren five days ago. She hoped he would be at the festival in the castle tomorrow, if only so she could find out more about him.

The day had been overcast and foggy, but the sky cleared as the sun set, and the flickering lamps from the city below appeared once more. She watched the lights for a while longer and then headed down to the tenth floor to find Victoria and Annalise. Before she entered the greenhouse, Annalise's excited voice carried out, and she smiled, putting her hand on the doorknob. Before she could enter, someone pulled the door open from the other side, yanking her forward. She hit the stone floor hard, scraping her left forearm and elbow.

"Oh, gods in hell, are you all right?"

She looked up, dazed, and discovered Darren standing over her, his face riddled with concern. She ignored his efforts to help her up and stood upright herself, wincing at the scrapes as her face flushed with embarrassment.

"I'm so sorry, I didn't think anyone would be on the other side—"

"Well perhaps next time you should be more careful," Relaina snapped. His face went blank with shock, and she immediately regretted her outburst. He straightened himself.

"Apologies," he said, all warmth in his brown eyes gone. "I'll take my leave. Goodnight Victoria, Princess Annalise."

He bowed and left, leaving the door wide open behind him.

"Relaina!" Annalise said. "What is *wrong* with you? He was so nice, and you nearly bit his head off."

Relaina frowned as cold shame washed over her. It didn't entirely douse the spark of irritation—she still felt that in her stinging arm.

"That's the second time he's been in the wrong place at the wrong time with me," Relaina said, shaking her head.

"Oh, he meant no harm," Victoria said, flipping her short, silvery hair as she set down a bouquet of flowers and walked over to Relaina. "He came here to meet with me for Maurice and ended up telling Annalise the secret meaning of different types of flowers. Even I learned a few things."

"He was *so* nice!" Annalise said. For some reason, the fact that he'd interacted with her sister irritated Relaina even more.

"It doesn't matter," Relaina said. "Now, show me the flowers you picked out."

Annalise had chosen bright yellow lilies, which signified happiness and friendship, according to Darren. Relaina tried not to roll her eyes and instead praised how beautiful they were. After Annalise left, yawning, Victoria pulled Relaina aside.

"Let's go have a cup of wine, shall we?"

They sat on the seventh floor by the fire, lounging in plush blue chairs and sipping red wine from Barleo. It was the perfect night in Parea; the mountain air retained a chill even at the height of summer, and the heat of the fire mixed deliciously with the cool breeze coming in from nearby open windows.

"So," Victoria said, "tell me more about Lord Daldnor."

Relaina nearly spit out wine as she snorted.

"He was dreadful. When he arrived, he looked scared out of his wits to even be here. Getting him to talk was exhausting, and when he did open his mouth, not a single interesting thing came out. Thank the gods he left two days earlier than anticipated. If he'd stayed the whole week, I might've gone mad."

Victoria cackled, sloshing some of her wine onto the floor.

"The poor man. He was probably just as miserable as you."

"It wasn't even endearing, Victoria. I just felt sorry for him."

"Well, he's gone now. Cross another off the list. How many does that leave? Two? Three?"

"Gods, I don't know. But I'm running out of options. I've turned down so many men that my mother asked me last week if I wanted her to add women to the list of suitors."

Victoria cackled again. "Your mother is kind. She only wants what's best for you."

"Unfortunately, what's best for me doesn't seem to be any nobleman in Esran." Relaina took another sip of wine. Victoria leaned over to rest a hand on her knee.

"Let's talk about something else, then. That boy Darren..."

"If you're going to reprimand me for snapping at him—"

"Who do you think I am—Lucinda? No, no, of course not. I just found him interesting. Before today I'd never met the boy. I've heard a great deal about him from Maurice. He kept to himself for a while, but he's a hard worker, from what the man says. He's the only young man to stay with Maurice for more than a few months. I think he just wants a sound future and stable pay like anyone else."

"Sounds like Darren's got everything figured out."

"Quite...and he's not bad to look at either."

Relaina glanced at her sidelong, trying not to picture Darren's flushed face when she'd pushed him against the wall a few days ago, or the shift in his eyes tonight after she'd told him off. "Hmm."

"Oh, come now, Relaina. He might've started off on the wrong foot with you, but he did his best to amuse Annalise when she pounced on him up there. And I've never seen *you* look so dumbstruck by a man in my entire life."

"I'd just fallen right in front of him because he yanked open the door! Of course I looked dumbstruck."

"All right, all right." Victoria set down her empty wineglass. "Maybe I just thought I saw something that wasn't really there. You know I just want you to be happy, Relaina."

Relaina smiled gently at her. "I know."

CHAPTER 2

THE HARVEST FESTIVAL

"Busy evening ahead, eh?" Bracken said. He came forward and climbed onto the rampart beside Relaina, his hands trembling as he did so. Relaina smirked at him.

"You don't have to sit up here if you don't want to."

"No, no, it's fine. I must find out for myself this magical feeling you get when you sit on the edge of a four-hundred-foot-tall castle."

"In the fifteen years you've lived here, you're only just now getting the urge to do so?"

"I'm trying to take a risk, here. As my best friend you are required to support me in my effort to challenge myself."

Relaina laughed.

"Just don't think about the fact that it's *eight* hundred feet above the lake on the south side."

"Wonderful." Bracken grimaced, finally situating himself. He wasn't from Parea originally—he had been born in Barleo, the only town through which the Inmedio River flowed in Lyneisia, right before it emptied into the sea. As Relaina's twenty-first birthday drew nearer and her father had grown more desperate to marry her off, he'd even once suggested Bracken despite the Averatts' lack of real wealth, and to Relaina's eternal relief, her friend had declined.

Relaina's eyes shifted from the castle grounds to the north, the outer edge of the city, where Maurice's apple orchards were located. "Bracken, have you met Maurice's apprentice?"

Bracken thought for a moment and snapped his fingers.

"I have! His name is Darren, right? Nice fellow. Although, I thought I noticed Jacquelyn being awfully friendly toward him once. She told me I was a fool."

Relaina laughed at him.

"You *are* a fool."

"Well, I'm a fool in love." He batted his eyelashes at her, and Relaina rolled her eyes.

"Sometimes I feel depressed that I've never been in love, but a lot of the time I wonder if it's even worth the fuss."

"Just wait, Relaina. When you fall in love, you'll be far more insufferable than me. I'm nauseated just thinking about it."

"Whatever you say."

"So, why'd you ask about Darren?"

Relaina ignored the heat that crept into her cheeks as she relayed their encounters.

"I feel bad for him now," Bracken said, laughing. "Poor fellow first got manhandled by you and then you snapped at him for something he didn't do on purpose."

"I should probably apologize." Relaina glanced down at her arm, which had scabbed over and was already mostly healed.

Bracken studied her for a moment.

"I'll ask Jacquelyn if she can contact him. And I'll have her invite him to the castle festivities tonight."

Relaina looked at the surrounding mountains, the breeze blowing her hair out of her face. "I'm not looking forward to any of it. You're lucky you can disappear to the city or the outer village."

"It's certainly less pressure. I can get piss drunk and nobody's noble father stares down his nose at me."

Relaina grinned and nudged him with her elbow, and he reached out in a flash to grip the stone beside him.

"Gods, Relaina, I didn't plan for shitting my pants today. Now I'll have to change."

Relaina snorted. "I'm sorry, I didn't mean to ruin your day."

"I ought to go, anyway. I'll see you later, Laines."

Relaina bid him goodbye and breathed in deeply, gazing at the winding city streets below. Was the Prince of Terrana truly somewhere within Parea? It was unlikely she'd ever find him before her father did, and even so, she wouldn't know what to do about it.

Today, though, she would place those worries aside for the festival. The sun was just past its peak, so, in keeping with personal tradition, she ventured out of the castle for some lucrative fun before she was trapped with all the nobles tonight.

"ARE you telling me that Princess Relaina has specifically requested that Darren attend the festival in the castle tonight?" Maurice asked the red-haired, doe-eyed woman in his flower shop, glancing between her and his apprentice. Darren could hardly believe it himself.

"She told Bracken Averatt that she'd like for him to come, and he relayed the message to me," Jacquelyn said, shaking her fiery hair out of her fair, freckled face. "Although...I wouldn't mention it to Princess Relaina. She's quite proud."

Darren coughed, and Maurice shot him a withering look. He forced the smile from his face and busied himself with a nearby half-finished flower arrangement.

"Princess Relaina is a dear friend," Maurice said to Jacquelyn. "I'm familiar with her temperament."

"Why does she want me to come, anyway?" Darren asked.

"You'll just have to come and find out, won't you?" Jacquelyn said, grinning.

A few minutes after Jacquelyn left, Darren was staring at the trunk in the corner of his modest room, as if trying to will proper attire for the festival into existence. He hadn't worn any fine clothes in years and didn't have a single stitch of it with him. There were plenty of shops around Parea that would sell something appropriate, but he'd have to find a way to scrounge up enough money to pay for it. Asking Maurice or his wife, Camille, was out of the question—they made enough money to support themselves and to generously keep Darren, and he would not burden them with anything else.

He took a deep breath and reached for a set of dark clothing in his trunk, donning a black shirt, gray trousers, and black hood. To complete the ensemble he pulled on a black mask, letting it rest beneath his chin for now.

There was one way to make some quick coin, and though he'd thus far avoided it, now it seemed his only option.

Darren stole out of his room and down the back hallway, avoiding his caretakers' gazes and slipping outside before his absence was noted. He walked down back alleys and side streets of the city until he came across a smoke shop that smelled sickly sweet, making him fight the urge to cough the moment he stepped inside. He slapped a silver piece on the counter and the clerk swiped it up before jerking her head toward the back of the shop. Darren pulled up his mask and opened a door that revealed a dark, narrow staircase made of stone. With as deep a breath as he could take in the shop, he began to descend.

Halfway down the stairs, Darren stopped, leaning on the stone wall for support. He pulled the mask down from his nose and mouth and took several measured breaths, trying to slow his racing heart.

You're fine. It's just underground.

The smell of rich spices wafted up the staircase, further grounding him. He allowed it to flood his senses and pulled his mask up once more, finishing his descent into the Parean underside.

He hadn't been down here in a few months and had only come in the past to find seeds and fertilizer for Maurice when there was a shortage in legal markets. Last time, he had given into curiosity and peeked at the fighters for a while, so he knew where to go—all he had to do was weave around shoppers and stalls in the torchlight, following the loud cheering. He stepped through a ratty black curtain, the volume of the cheers increasing the deeper he ventured into the stands. The crowd was shrouded in dimness, but the ring in the pit of the cavernous room was well-lit by bright lanterns. Two people fought in the ring: a large man with great strength but little agility, and a woman with a long, dark braid and quick feet. Her speed and flexibility outperformed the man's brute force in mere minutes—she had him on the ground after some well-timed kicks to his legs and abdomen.

Darren had seen her fight before. She was the only person in the ring who hid her face when fighting, and he wondered why. Perhaps she, too, needed to conceal her identity for personal protection.

As the crowd cheered for her victory, Darren headed for the ring entrance, calming himself with each step downward. The ring master had his employees help the large man out of the ring, and Darren stepped up to the seedy-looking man, holding out a handful of silver coins as his entrance fee. The man's eyes gleamed with greed, and he smiled a toothy smile.

"Enter at your own risk," he said, and Darren checked his hood and mask before entering the ring, ensuring both were secure. The woman standing at the other end was catching her breath, hands on her hips. When she saw him, she stopped short, and his heart leapt into his throat —did she recognize him? He thought for a moment she might say something, but then the bell rang, and she was on him.

Darren prepared himself to hold back but found he didn't need to. She was lightning fast with solid technique. As they twisted and whirled kicks and punches at one another, Darren was almost out of breath from quiet laughter.

"What the hell is so funny?" she hissed, right as she landed a blow to his ribs. He winced and coughed.

"Nothing's funny. Just haven't done this in a long time. You're good."

"I know." She lunged at him again, aiming to kick him. This time he blocked her and twisted his arms around her leg, flipping her onto her back. She hit the dirt with an *oof,* and Darren straddled her, pinning her legs down at her thighs and grabbing the arm that wasn't moving too much for him to work into a hold.

"You held back," she accused, as the crowd's cheering died down. Her eyes seared into him, and he faltered. *Those eyes...*

His moment of distraction cost him; she took advantage of his weakening hold and jabbed him in the center of his ribs with her free hand. Pain clouded his vision, and she wiggled out from under him.

Darren exhaled and got to his feet, realizing that his hood had been displaced. Even with the mask still intact, he needed to end this quickly.

He caught her foot midair between his forearms and yanked her forward, twisting her around and locking her into a hold around her chest and neck. Before she could try to kick him, he brought them both down to the ground and wrapped a leg around both of hers, pinning her successfully.

"Fuck," she said, and Darren laughed.

"Sorry, Princess," he said in her ear, and Relaina flinched in his grasp. "Don't worry, I won't tell."

In a way, she was paying for him to come to the event she'd asked him to attend.

And though Darren didn't consider himself a particularly vengeful person, it was satisfying to win against her after being the object of her vitriol twice now. It shouldn't surprise him that someone with her temper would be found in the fighting ring, but her talent for combat was unexpected for a Lyneisian princess.

Darren released her after he'd been deemed the victor, and Princess Relaina strode out of the ring with haste, eager to get away from him. Darren stared after her—his heart beat faster as she fixed him with that look again, her eyes sharp and distrustful. Warmth that had nothing to do with physical exertion crept up the back of his neck as she stalked up the steps and left the loud, dusty chaos of the fighting ring.

NIGHT WAS FALLING FAST, the last glimpses of sunlight kissing the ballroom windows and casting a warm light on the golden-thread flowers adorning Relaina's emerald gown. It was one of her favorites Lucinda had made. The silhouette was elegant and flattering to her figure, the neckline plunged low between her breasts, and the color made her eyes striking.

Two hours after the festival began, after smiling and nodding politely and enduring every noble's suggestion for marriage, she was standing alone, far away from the dancing. It was the time of the evening when she expected she'd be asked to dance, but with no one else approaching her, she took the opportunity to glide past the musicians' dais and perch behind a row of statues. As she looked through the high windows out into the gardens, she took a deep breath and winced—that man in the fighting ring earlier had given her some wicked bruises, and she'd scraped her cheek on the rough dirt. Lucinda had turned so blue in the face with rage that Relaina thought she'd faint, but there wasn't much to be done. Relaina was far more concerned that someone had recognized her in the ring, and if her father heard even a whisper of her exploits, that would be the end of that.

Down the row of statues, toward the entrance to the gardens, a servant held a tray of wine. Relaina aimed her steps in his direction.

"If you would prefer a finer drink, Princess, I'll go back to the kitchens—"

"Is this wine?"

"Y-yes?"

"Then it's fine enough, thank you."

Relaina searched for Bracken, hoping he hadn't left to attend the outer village festivities yet, though she wouldn't blame him if he had. The servant sauntered off, offering wine to others, and Relaina slipped into the gardens, the music drifting outside with her. Relaina attributed her reprieve from prying questions and not-so-subtle marriage suggestions to this popular tune. "The Farmer's Dance," as it was called, was a tradition at the Harvest Festival.

Outside, candles and lanterns lined the garden path, and a few guests strolled through, pointing at flowers and fountains they found particularly beautiful. Relaina was glad for the darkness—she was not as easily recognizable in the lamplight. She made her way to the fountain that bloomed out of the northwest corner of the gardens. The nearby stone railing was still warm from the day's sunlight, and Relaina ran her hand along its smooth surface, taking a moment to breathe. Far below, the city was just as lively as the festival in the castle, with dancing torches and large bonfires and the sound of merriment finding its way up to the fifteenth floor. Relaina smiled and laughed to herself, wishing she were down there dancing drunkenly around a fire and eating her fill instead of walking around in a tight dress that aggravated her sore spots. She took a sip of the wine and cringed—her least favorite kind. Frustration built as she swirled it around, and then she tossed it over the railing. It shattered on the side of a rock face twenty feet below.

"Good thinking, white wine is disgusting."

Relaina turned and beheld Darren with his hands clasped behind his back, the sleeves on his deep red jacket cuffed halfway up his arms. The jacket complemented his brown eyes and fit his muscular yet slender frame perfectly. His black trousers were tucked neatly into polished leather boots. He'd even trimmed his hair, the ash-blond strands no longer falling in his eyes, revealing dark, expressive eyebrows against his tan skin. Relaina tried to say something, but words failed her.

"I don't mean to intrude," he said, walking forward with his hands out. Though he wasn't significantly taller, Relaina suddenly felt very small next to him, and her face flushed. *Gods, he's beautiful.* "But I wanted to apologize again for, uh, intruding. And almost hitting you. And for the door incident."

Relaina blinked, still ogling him. "Thank you. I mean, no need to apologize for the second incident. I was already frustrated that day and I took it out on you, and I'm sorry for that."

The corners of Darren's mouth lifted slightly.

"Apology accepted. Are you coming to the outer village later? It's far more relaxed down there."

"I wish I could. But if I went missing tonight, my father would likely kill me."

Darren laughed, and the sound was familiar somehow.

"I understand. In any case, I'm glad I found you here. A man spotted me at the entrance and led me up here before leaving."

"Bracken. He's my close friend."

"I got the sense that he didn't like me much."

Relaina tried not to laugh.

"It takes some time to get him to warm up to you."

"I'll keep that in mind. And if you don't mind, I'm going to head back down to the village."

"I hope it is significantly more enjoyable than this." Relaina gestured to their general surroundings, and Darren smiled.

"I can get you another glass of wine before I go, if you'd like." He glanced over the edge of the railing and grimaced. "I'll make sure it's red."

Relaina fought a smile again. "That would be greatly appreciated. I'd like to avoid being accosted by more nobles for as long as possible."

Darren nodded, his face unreadable, and headed for the ballroom. Relaina stared after him, wondering at his unexpected kindness.

"Ah, *there* you are, Relaina."

Gods damn it. Zarias Conclave approached, his band of sycophants close behind. They were the worst of the highborns in Lyneisia, and some of their relatives had even hinted at marriage between them and her. Relaina's scowl would have settled that matter if those relatives were present now.

"I've been looking for you all night," Zarias said, brushing his long, black hair out of his face, revealing fully his square jaw and smooth, bronze skin. Relaina wasn't sure how someone could smile so arrogantly, but Zarias managed to do so every time she saw him. The man was attractive—and he knew it.

"Do not presume to address me with such familiarity, Zarias," Relaina said, heat rising in her cheeks. "We are not friends."

"You wound me, Princess." He pouted, placing a hand on his heart. He was dressed much like the other highborn men at the festival, in a jacket representing his family's colors. His was deep violet.

"My apologies, I had forgotten that it is my aspiration in life to please you and smother you with praise."

"Now, that's more like it," Zarias said, grinning and running a hand through his hair again.

Relaina glared at him for a moment. She could put him in his place, or she could save her breath and find a better use of her energy. But Zarias followed her as she walked away.

"Oh, come now, Princess. It's not exactly a secret that our parents intend to betroth us."

Relaina froze, the fountain beside them loud in her ears. Her mouth twisted into a snarl that made the noblemen behind Zarias recoil.

"Never, in any existence of hell or otherwise, would I marry you."

"This appears to be an enticing conversation."

Darren reappeared, holding two glasses of wine. He handed one to

Relaina and she took it, grateful for anything that might keep her from lunging at Zarias.

"And just who are *you*?" Zarias asked.

"Unimportant," Darren said, shrugging. "But you, you look like the sort of man that's talented in the art of distasteful advances. It took you, what, two minutes to make her want to murder you in your sleep? Truly impressive, sir."

One of Zarias's cronies, Laviath, stifled a laugh, and Zarias jerked his head around. Laviath lapsed into obedient silence once more, his brow furrowing in submission.

"So, *this* is the reason you deny me?" Zarias said to Relaina, his eyes darting back and forth between the wineglass she held and Darren. "Oh-ho, I know you. Aren't you the farmer's boy?"

His followers erupted into derisive laughter. Relaina's self-control dwindled.

"You're assuming quite a bit about matters that are none of your concern, Zarias," she said through clenched teeth.

"Oh, my, it appears I've touched a nerve. All right, you go and have your fun, Princess, as is your prerogative," Zarias said, snickering. He lowered his voice, but not enough that Relaina couldn't hear what he said to his companions. "Gods above, what would King Stephan say if he found out his heir was sleeping with a baseborn *farmhand?*"

Relaina's cheeks flushed again, and she handed her wineglass to Darren. Zarias was still laughing when her fist made contact with his face.

He tumbled backwards, landing in the fountain. He thrashed around for a moment, water running down his face and jacket, accompanied by a stream of blood from his nose. "What the *fuck*—"

His friends scrambled to the fountain to help, and Relaina wrung her hand as Darren turned to her, his eyes bright with mischief.

"Self-important ass," she said, stalking off in no direction in particular. Darren hurried after her. "He always says horrible things like that and gets away with it. He's a spoiled, depraved *child* who thinks he can just go around—"

"Princess—"

"—insulting you, implying that the only reason I deny him is because of another man—"

"Uh, Princess Relaina—"

She turned to face Darren while still walking in the opposite direction.

"As if I'd *ever* consider binding myself to that *pig*. I hope his nose bleeds all over that stupid purple jacket of his—ack!"

Darren grabbed her arm just before she fell into a rosebush, steadying her. Relaina stared at his hand, at the contraction of the muscle in his forearm, and part of her wished he'd just drop her so she could disappear into the bushes. He released her, clearing his throat.

"Sorry," he said. "I didn't want you to fall."

Relaina took too long to respond.

"It's all right. Thank you."

"So you won't call the guards on me?"

Relaina rolled her eyes. "Just so you know, I'm normally very coordinated."

"I'll believe it when I see it."

"You saw it when I shoved you against a wall."

"And a few days later you fell when I opened a door."

Relaina snorted and waved her hand dismissively, but it bumped his chest as he moved forward at the same time, and he grunted in pain.

"What in...? Are you made of parchment?"

"Sore spot." He winced as he rubbed his sternum. Relaina stared at him for a moment, and then her eyes widened. His hair and eyes were the same as—

"You?"

"*Relaina!*"

Relaina nearly fell into the bushes again at the sound of her father's furious voice. *Shit.*

Everyone in the surrounding area stared at Relaina as King Stephan marched toward them, his anger growing with every step. His sweeping blue cloak fluttered in the evening breeze as he came to a stop before them, and Relaina's mother stood behind him with pursed lips. Beside Relaina, Darren knelt, his head bowed.

"Relaina, what is this I hear about you breaking someone's nose?"

King Stephan demanded. Relaina tucked her reddening hand behind her back.

"I broke Zarias's nose," she said, determined to remain calm. It was not in anyone's best interest for her to get into a shouting match with her father right now.

"May I ask what possessed you to do such a thing?" The king's voice carried despite his efforts to keep it down.

"He insulted me."

"So you broke his nose?"

"He insulted me greatly."

Her father took a deep breath and ran his hand through his hair.

"Relaina, I would appreciate it if you would join me in my study."

Christine came forward, placing a gentle hand on her husband's arm and speaking softly.

"Stephan, is that really necessary?" The king waved her off, and she stepped back, taciturn once more.

"Relaina, meet me in my study promptly."

"Your Grace, if I may speak on Princess Relaina's behalf, the young lord intentionally antagonized her."

Fear shot up Relaina's throat. Knives would have flown from her eyes if it were possible as she looked down at Darren. *Stop talking. Please stop talking.*

King Stephan's eyes darted to Darren.

"Who is this?"

Darren glanced at her from the ground, and Relaina cleared her throat.

"No one. A guest."

"A noble?"

Relaina didn't answer, kicking herself. Why hadn't she thought of a lie before now?

"Gods in hell," her father said. "Get this boy out of here. Guards!"

Two guards appeared and grabbed Darren by the arms. He looked to Relaina, panicked, but she avoided his gaze, turning away as they removed him from the grounds. The king left just as Aronn and Annalise appeared, her sister accompanied by friends straining to hear what had happened. Everyone nearby whispered and stared as Relaina seethed. She wrung out her hand again and set off through the gardens at a brisk pace, head held high.

DARREN PULLED at the fabric of his fine clothes as he strode through the castle's Northern Gate, adjusting the heavy wrinkles inflicted by the castle guards that had shoved him through the doors moments before. Why hadn't Relaina said anything to stop them? And why had she invited him in the first place if lowborn guests weren't allowed?

"Oi, farmhand!"

Darren turned; Zarias approached him, his jacket still damp and indeed stained with blood, his nose slightly off-center. His cronies were nowhere to be seen.

"Let's make something clear." Zarias stopped in front of Darren in the middle of the path, taking advantage of his height by looming over him with stiffened shoulders. "You don't belong here, and you never will. Stay away from Relaina."

"So those attempts to demean me and shame the princess were just to soothe your own flimsy pride?"

Zarias got in his face, and Darren mastered the impulse to shove him. Getting into a fight with this fool would do him no favors.

Except, perhaps, with the princess.

"I'll tell you this once, and I better not have to tell you again: Relaina belongs to me."

Darren cringed. "She's not a possession."

"I don't care what you think. I'm going to marry her."

"She just broke your nose. If you're too stubborn to realize that won't make for a good marriage, I can't help you. Now, if you'll excuse me." Darren turned and walked off before Zarias could reply.

CHAPTER 3

THE OUTER VILLAGE

When Relaina arrived at her father's study, he was sitting at a small table by the fireplace, pinching the bridge of his nose with his fingers. She relaxed a bit—if he meant to shout at her more, he'd be standing at the fireplace with his arms crossed.

"What were you thinking tonight?" he asked.

"Have you told the Conclaves that I will marry Zarias?"

"The subject has been discussed."

"He said that it wasn't a secret that you and his parents are planning to betroth us. A secret to me, it would seem."

"Relaina, you haven't exactly been cooperative with this whole ordeal. I'll make the decision for you if I must."

"You will *not!*" Relaina's voice lashed out like a whip as she took several steps forward. "Zarias is *foul*. How could you possibly agree to marry me to someone like that? To allow someone like that to be my consort?"

"His family is wealthy and his bloodline is strong, one of the oldest in the kingdom. You're more than capable of quelling his more distasteful behaviors, as you exhibited tonight."

"So you *want* me to punch him when he's an ass?"

"That's not what I said."

Relaina huffed through her nose and rolled her eyes. "I'm going to bed."

"Very well. Get your emotions under control, Relaina. No more public displays of vulgarity."

Relaina swept from the room, blood boiling. *Fuck it.* Her father had just excused her absence from the castle festivities. She'd go join the others at the outer village.

RELAINA FLEW through the city streets on horseback, led by the faint glow of a large bonfire on a hill in the distance. Silhouettes stood out against the flames, talking and singing and laughing. Relaina dismounted and tied her horse, Amariah, next to the other horses in an open stable with a water trough. She hurried along the stone path, smiling as two figures branched out from the crowd and approached her.

"Relaina!"

"Bracken! Jacquelyn!"

"Hello, Relaina," Jacquelyn said, her face pink and her eyes serene. The smell of the fire conjured autumnal nostalgia.

"Where's the wine?"

"I'll go get more," Bracken said. He narrowed his eyes. "Perhaps two for you, Relaina."

She sat on a log by the fire, and as Bracken handed her a drink, Darren appeared on the other side of the flames, no longer wearing fine clothes as he laughed with friends. His eye caught hers and his smile faded.

"Shit."

"What?" Bracken asked.

"I may or may not have let Darren get thrown out of the castle tonight."

"Gods, Relaina..."

Relaina started to panic as Darren got up and walked behind the circle of people, apparently headed in their direction. To Relaina's bewilderment, he sat beside her.

"Evening, Princess."

Relaina raised an eyebrow. "Have you been drinking?"

"I may have had a few horns of ale." He shrugged and threw her a lopsided grin. Relaina stared at him, trying and failing not to smile.

"By the way, no hard feelings about tossing me out of the castle. I'll just leave you alone and we'll all be happier."

The fire dancing near them was no match for Relaina's scowl.

"You nearly struck me the first time we met. You're lucky I didn't mention that."

"I thank you for your mercy, Princess." Darren stood up and bowed. "Your kindness is unmatched."

Relaina got close to his face.

"You're drunk and foolish."

"I'm drunk and honest."

"Isn't tonight just *lovely*?" Jacquelyn squeezed between them and placed a hand on each of their shoulders. She leaned toward Relaina, red hair glowing in the light of the fire. "Let's go watch that lad over there doing acrobatic tricks next to some of my friends. Bracken, join us?"

Jacquelyn elbowed Darren in the ribs as he started to say something else, and she grinned and steered Relaina away from him.

"I thought you were going to fight," Bracken said. "Or maybe kiss, it was hard to tell."

Relaina choked. "I would *not—*"

"*Gather round, my fellow Pareans!*"

A young woman silenced the musicians nearby and beckoned to those in attendance.

"The time has come for a tale...a tale of darkness, of power and fear."

The woman's voice transported Relaina back in time, sending shivers of excitement down her spine as she, Bracken, and Jacquelyn hurried to find a place to sit and listen. It had been too long since she'd heard a story told by firelight.

"Long ago, there lived a young man with darkness in his soul. He lived each day with a power he was unsure how to control; how would he learn to tame it? He walked among his fellows and none of them knew his pain, his fight, his envy of the light. The other magic wielders healed, and he could only harm, or so he thought.

"An old woman appeared one day in their dwelling, their village in the hills. They welcomed her as they did any traveler, with food and drink and shelter, and that night as they all gathered to eat, the young man spoke to her. Immediately she knew of his power, could feel it, and she told him so. Frightened, he lied and denied. *I know not of what you speak,* he said. *I am unremarkable; I am weak.* The woman merely smiled. *I will come to your house this night at the darkest hour,* she said. *I will knock three times, and I will reveal to you your power.*"

Relaina studied the faces of others as they listened, turning away from the fire for a moment to cool her face. A few feet away, Darren sat in the grass, his arms crossed over his knees and his eyebrows scrunched together as he stared at the flames. The storyteller swiped a piece of wood from the ground and knocked on it three times, drawing Relaina back into the tale.

"The night was moonless when the young man opened his door to let the old traveler woman inside. What he didn't expect was her companion, another man from the village, his neighbor. Even so, he led them inside and locked the door behind them, afraid others might have seen. They sat together at a table, where the woman explained the nature of her power, the young man's power.

"*You can take hold of others,* she said, *you can bend them to your will.*"

Relaina shuddered. The name of those with this dark power evaded her, but she remembered this story and others like it now.

"Before the young man's eyes, a shadow, a black vapor appeared to seep from his fellow's skin. His neighbor let out a cry as the darkness relinquished its control of him, and he stood from the table, screaming, *Evil! Evil!* The young man was frozen with fear. The woman laughed and sent her shadow to the other man once more; his eyes turned into voids for a moment, the woman's mirroring them, and then he was calm once more, seated at the table.

"*Tenebrae, we are called,* the old woman said. *The tenebrae are powerful, but even stronger when combined. Join me, young one, and feel the freedom of your strength.* The young man stared at his neighbor, who sat across from him with a placid smile. He stood and shook his head. *No! No, I won't! This isn't right, I won't!*"

The storyteller chuckled, and Relaina shivered again.

"*Then I'll take you anyway,* the woman said, and *HA—*"

The storyteller jumped forward and clapped her hands together, eliciting several yelps from the crowd.

"The woman took him by the neck, her aging hands strong as she pulled the darkness from him, and with it, took his life.

"Do not forget that shadows lurk,
    they creep among us still;
    don't walk alone without the moon,
    or they will take your will."

The crackling of the fire was the only sound in the moments of silence after the story concluded. Dread hung over them all until a woman across the circle from Relaina put her hands on her hips.

"Gods in hell, Pauline, that one almost made me shit myself."

Laughter filled the circle of villagers, Relaina and Jacquelyn included. A jaunty tune soon filled the air again, and people danced around the fire. Relaina insisted she was fine sitting by herself as Jacquelyn begged Bracken to dance, but when a song Relaina particularly liked began to play, she couldn't help but sing along. It was slower than the others, the fiddle soaring and heartbreaking as it played the introduction.

In the heart of our land,
With the mountains and the seas,
There's a place that we call home;
It's a place where you and I can be free,
Always together,
Watching the water lilies bloom.

After a short flute and fiddle interlude, many others joined in. Relaina grinned as her voice melded with theirs.

In the soul of the stars,
You can hear a song,
It rings loud and clear and true.
From the heavens it sounds,
And though here we are bound,
We can sit here forever,
Watching the water lilies bloom.

In the voice of a child,
You can hear the truth,
Which will always stay in your heart.
And though pain is along the journey,
Love will prevail,
And we can go on forever,
Watching the water lilies bloom.

After the song ended, some people continued dancing to a livelier tune, and others sat back and watched by the fire. The younger crowd started up a drinking game where the last two people to finish their cup of ale or wine had to kiss each other. A gaggle of girls surrounded Darren, grinning.

"Darren, come on." One of the girls tried to drag him over after he'd declined to participate. "You know you'll win, so what's the trouble?"

Darren forced a laugh and removed his arm from the girl's grip with surprising patience. "Sorry, Catherine, you'll just have to play without me."

Relaina watched this exchange and wondered at his reluctance to participate. But Bracken and Jacquelyn and several of their friends reclaimed her attention, all flushed from dancing and laughing.

When the fire was nothing but glowing embers, Relaina started to leave, sobered and ready for bed. She said goodbye to Bracken and Jacquelyn and traipsed toward the stable, her boots clacking on the stone path. Darren fell in step beside her.

"What do you want?"

"I live at Maurice's. You happen to be going in the same direction."

"I'm getting my horse."

"And you'd rather walk alone?"

"Yes."

"In the dark. Past midnight."

Relaina exhaled, glad they were close to the stable.

"Afraid a tenebrae will possess me?" She expected him to laugh at her, but his silence drew her gaze to the concern on his face. "I'm joking. You can't seriously believe shadows are popping out of nowhere to possess people."

Still staring at the path ahead, Darren lifted a hand to his chest, absently brushing his fingers over his heart. "I believe darkness follows us more closely than we realize."

Relaina chewed on that for a moment, her irritation dissolving. "I thought you said you were going to leave me alone."

Darren chuckled. They'd reached the stable now, and Amariah was the only remaining horse. Darren watched as Relaina prepared to depart.

"So you managed to sneak out of the castle?" he asked.

"Yes." Relaina patted Amariah's neck as she untied her reins from the wood above the trough. "I do that often. It's how I met Maurice."

"He and Camille seem very fond of you." Darren leaned against the stable wall, his arms crossed.

"I'm very fond of them." She stared at him for a moment. "They seem to like you as well."

"It's almost as if I'm a likable person."

"Well, those drunk girls certainly thought so."

"They try to get me to play their games every time."

"And you never do?"

"I'm not a fan of drinking games. Or kissing five different people in one night."

"Hmm." Relaina frowned, studying him. Amariah nuzzled her shoulder, and she patted her silky nose. "Can I ask you something?"

"I might not answer, but you're welcome to ask."

"Was it you in the fighting ring earlier?"

"What if it was?"

Relaina exhaled. "I just want to make sure you're not going to tell anyone about that."

"I told you I wouldn't."

"Even after tonight?"

Understanding dawned on his face. "I'm not so petty that I'd reveal what is likely a well-kept and important secret of yours because of that, even if it was humiliating." Relaina's stomach turned. "And I would appreciate it if you'd return that courtesy."

Relaina studied him further, looking into his eyes in the darkness. They were a dynamic shade of brown, rich ochre by the fire but dark and alluring in the moonlight.

"I won't say anything," she said, and he inclined his head in thanks. "And I'm sorry about you getting kicked out."

He shrugged. "Perhaps I enjoy humiliation."

Relaina snorted. "Some people do."

"Not my flavor." Darren laughed. Relaina wondered for an instant what he *did* like and turned violently red. The last thing she wanted to be thinking about was Darren's sexual proclivities.

"Sorry. It wasn't my intention to scandalize you."

"I'm fine. I've heard worse from my brother's friends."

Darren wrinkled his nose.

"If Zarias is a representation of the rest of them, then I'm sorry you have to deal with that. He deserved that broken nose."

Relaina smirked. "Perhaps you are likable, Flower Boy."

"That's a new one." Darren rolled his eyes.

"Really? You must have boring friends."

"I'm not sure I have any friends."

"But you're so *likable.*"

"Doesn't mean *I* like other people."

Relaina, despite herself, grinned as she stepped into a stirrup and swung her leg over, mounting her horse in one swift movement.

"Well, I'll let you get back to having no friends."

"Does that mean I do have a friend while you're around?"

"Don't push your luck."

Darren laughed again, and Relaina's stomach flipped in a strange, new way that she'd have to decipher later.

"Relaina!"

Bracken approached, wheezing as he hurried toward them.

"It's Aronn. Again."

Relaina exhaled and groaned. "Where?"

ARONN KNEW he ought to stop drinking when the room began spinning. But Zarias was there, and the rest of his friends, and there were beautiful women about who kept handing him tankard after tankard. So he drank another, and then another.

When the door slammed open and raucous calls went out around him, directed at whoever had just entered the underground tavern, he blinked slowly at the dregs of his most recent tankard of beer. How many had he had?

"Out of my way, you bootlicking fucks!" His sister appeared through the fog of his drunkenness, assessing just how angry she ought to be. He opened his mouth to attempt an apology and vomited on the floor near her boots. Relaina glared at him.

"Come on, Aronn."

He was vaguely aware of Relaina and some other person helping him from the stool, of her draping his arms over their shoulders and helping guide him out of the tavern, of her spitting scathing words at his companions as they passed. Somehow, they made their way through the city's underside and back above ground, emerging in a narrow alleyway just minutes from Castle Alterna.

"I've got it from here, Bracken."

"You sure?"

"Yes. Thanks for your help."

They managed to stumble through the castle gates, but instead of heading to the entrance hall, Relaina led him to the secret passage in the main armory.

"Relaina," Aronn grimaced at the taste of his own mouth, "I think I —*hic*—drank too much."

Relaina removed the ancient battle axe and the wall shifted aside. "You don't say?"

Aronn groaned as they followed the passage, which grew progressively steeper until they reached a ladder.

"I can't carry you up the ladder, so you go first, and I'll make sure you don't fall on your ass." He nodded once and focused all his energy on putting one hand in front of the other, then one foot in front of the other, then another hand, left, right, left, right...

After what felt like an eternity, he reached the trapdoor above and unlatched it with fumbling fingers. He emerged into the greenhouse and flopped to the floor beside a few flowerpots as Relaina closed the door and ensured it was hidden again. Aronn closed his eyes.

"Oh, no you don't."

She gripped the front of his tunic and pulled him upright.

"You can't fall asleep here, Aronn. I'm going to take you to your rooms and then find a servant to stay with you tonight."

"Get Yolan, please." He was the least judgmental of Aronn's castle servants.

"All right."

"I'll have Victoria bring you a drinking tonic tonight and tomorrow morning." How did they reach his rooms so quickly? He didn't recall walking up any stairs. "Drink the tonics with lots of water. Keep a goblet by your bed."

"I've been ill from drinking before, Relaina."

"Yes, I know, but the goal is to *not* be ill."

She guided him to a plush red couch in front of a lit fireplace and plopped him down. He blinked and looked up at his sister, whose lips were pursed as she surveyed him.

"Just say it."

"Those men you associate with are nothing but leeches."

"They're my friends."

"If they were your friends, they wouldn't have brought you to that tavern only to put drink after drink in your hand to loosen your tongue and your pockets. Did you pay for all of them?"

Aronn didn't answer.

"Zarias is the worst of them. The air he breathes reeks of arrogance."

Aronn recalled Relaina's parting words to his companions as they left the tavern.

Touch me or my brother and you'll have a broken jaw to go with your nose, Zarias.

"Relaina?" He was met with silence and realized he'd closed his eyes. He opened them, blinked a few times, and found his sister waiting for him to ask his question. "Did you really break Zarias's nose?"

Relaina's mouth twisted. She held up her hand so he could see her bruised knuckles. Aronn smirked.

"I have to admit that's funny."

"We need to talk about your choice of friends. But you're in no state for it now, and we both need sleep. I'll go fetch Yolan and Victoria. Get some rest, Aronn."

"Mhmm." Aronn's eyes were already closed again. He was asleep before his door clicked shut.

ON THE QUIET streets of Parea, Darren stared at the dying bonfire in a daze, not ready to go to Maurice's shop for the night. The fire was nothing but a black heap now, and the circle of logs was empty. The story from earlier echoed in his mind.

...A black vapor appeared to seep from his fellow's skin.

Darren shuddered. Perhaps it was time to head back.

As he walked, nearby whinnying captured his attention—in the stable, Relaina's horse was still tethered, distraught that her person had left her. Darren walked over and patted the mare's neck.

"I'm a fool, aren't I?" She shook her head at him, pawing at the ground. He sighed. "I'll take you back."

He untied the horse's reins and mounted up, heading down the empty street toward Castle Alterna. The gates to the castle were still wide open and manned by guards, but none of them stopped him. He brought Relaina's horse to the castle stables, handed her over to a young stable boy, and began his trek back to Maurice's. When he returned to the farmer's home, he was surprised to find Camille sipping tea by the dim glow of the fire, her graying hair in a loose plait. She set her cup down.

"Sit." She motioned to the chair across from her. He sat, and she pushed a cup of tea across the table for him. For a while they drank in silence by the small, crackling fire.

"You look miserable," Camille said, and Darren dropped his gaze to the table, rubbing his face in his hands.

"I'm just a fool."

Camille's face gave away nothing as she nodded.

"We've all felt that way. Did you have fun tonight?"

Damn the smile that threatened his lips. "A bit."

"Who all came?"

"The usual crowd."

"Hmm. And the usual crowd made you feel like a fool?"

"Princess Relaina was there."

"Ah, I see."

"You've known her a long time, yes?"

Camille nodded. "She's...a force, as I'm sure you've noticed. But she is also kind."

Darren mumbled, thinking. Or, rather, trying *not* to think about the way Relaina's face twisted when they'd spoken at the fire or the way her dark curls fluttered when she laughed.

"Did you two get into a row at the bonfire?"

"Not quite. But I may have prodded her a bit."

"You *are* a fool," Camille chuckled. Darren smirked.

"It doesn't matter, anyway. Thank you for the tea, Camille. I'm going to bed."

"Sleep well, dear. Try not to worry too much."

Darren trudged down the back hall and entered the last door on the right. His bed was unmade in the corner, the quilts disheveled and faded with age. A worn rug lay in the center of the room, faded and dusty, covering a small part of the creaky wooden floor. There was a basin beneath the lone window, and Darren thanked the gods every day that even the buildings on the outskirts of Parea had the luxury of indoor plumbing.

He washed his face and hands in the water basin and looked outside as he hung a towel on the basin's edge. Two men had appeared in the square, engrossed in conversation by a lantern. One man was pale, with unkempt brown hair and strange eyes, eyes that held years of violence and malice. Darren froze, staring at him. No, it was impossible.

He scrambled backward, tripping on the rug and crashing to the floor. He clenched his teeth against the rising panic in his chest.

"Darren?"

Camille and Maurice appeared in his doorway.

"What's wrong?" Maurice asked. Camille came forward and knelt by Darren. He trembled, his breath uneven, and gestured toward the window. Maurice sauntered over, peering outside.

"Darren," Camille said, her voice soft. "Breathe."

He nodded, grounding himself in his surroundings to quiet the terror in his mind; Camille's hand on his shoulder, the towel on the basin, the roughness of the rug beneath him...his heart began to slow.

"The man with the Lyneisian guard knows you?" Maurice asked.

Darren took another breath. "His name is Xavier. He was a Terranian assassin when I knew him."

"Gods in hell. Nasty scar down his neck, though. Your doing?"

Darren nodded. "He's not a man to cross."

Maurice grunted. "He looks like the sort of man that'd gut you for serving him the wrong drink."

"Why is he here?" Camille asked. "Surely he doesn't know..."

Darren shook his head. "I don't know."

"We'll keep you out of sight," Camille assured him.

"That we will." Maurice shut the curtains to Darren's window. "He and the guard are gone. We'll just have to be careful."

"I'm sorry," Darren whispered.

"For what? Helping me run my farm? Wanting to live peacefully? Nonsense."

"We'll take extra precautions, tonight especially." Camille helped Darren stand. "Please try and rest, dear."

Darren was grateful for them both as he climbed into bed, comforted by the weight of the quilt and the candle lit on the nearby table. But even as he slept, fear crept in that darkness had found him yet again.

CHAPTER 4

THE FARMER'S HOUSE

Relaina looked over the edge of her balcony, savoring the touch of the midmorning breeze on her face. Thunderclouds gathered in the western sky. Past the peak of Mount Noble, one of the smaller surrounding mountains, lightning flashed, but the resulting thunder was a low rumble, distant and almost gentle. The sky's activity made her restless. The guards in training would have the day off following the festival, so perhaps her uncle would be available for an impromptu spar. Training and fighting always cleared her head better than anything, and after the council meeting last week and the events of the previous night, dozens of worries clanged around her skull.

Relaina donned her training gear: a black tunic, a protective leather vest, a pair of fitted, comfortable pants, and her favorite worn leather boots. She braided her hair back and headed down to the sixth floor, crossing the open sparring space to the black door tucked away in the corner that went unnoticed by most—exactly as her uncle preferred. Relaina knocked.

"Come in."

Jeremiah was in his study, a room with all four walls lined with bookshelves. His feet were propped up on the table in front of him and a book was in his hands.

"Up for some training today?" he asked. Relaina nodded, and he placed his book facedown on the desk. He walked to a chest beneath a dusty window and unlocked it, pulling out two practice swords with blunted edges.

A light rain had begun to fall, and the breeze blowing throughout the windowless stone columns of the sparring area made Relaina shiver. No matter—she'd be sweating soon enough. Jeremiah threw her one of the blunted swords and she caught it deftly, the grip familiar in her hands. He circled her, and she mirrored his steps. He swung and she parried. As he drew back, she struck and narrowly dodged his immediate counterattack. A full-blown storm gathered and then raged outside while they sparred, the minutes passing by quickly as Relaina threw all of her frustration and anger into her strikes.

Jeremiah blocked another attack and stood at ease. "Good. Now, let's see how well you have mastered the attack we've been working on these past few weeks. Whenever you're ready."

Relaina blew a stray hair out of her face and lunged at him, feinting to the right before whirling around to attack him on the left, making Jeremiah's defense for the initial attack much less effective. She moved to disarm him, but a loud whistle floated through the space from behind her, followed by unintelligible jeering. Relaina whipped around. Her brother dragged one of his distasteful friends toward the next flight of stairs. His friend, clearly inebriated, stumbled and pushed Aronn off, grinning at Relaina as Aronn muttered something through his teeth.

Jeremiah handed her his sword and strode toward the two young men. Aronn grabbed his friend's sleeve and yanked, and Relaina caught a bit of what her brother said this time.

"...captain of the guard...let's *go*."

"Aronn," Jeremiah said, his deep voice echoing against the stone.

"Oh no, you're in trouble, Prince Aronn." The boy's smile disappeared as Jeremiah grabbed his collar.

"Mind your tongue, you insufferable child. Consider this a generous warning, and know your sister will hear of your disrespect toward the family she's sworn to protect. Now get the hell out of here."

Aronn's friend scampered down the stairs.

"Keep your friends in line or keep them out of the castle," Jeremiah said. Aronn winced and started toward the stairs himself, but Jeremiah blocked his path. "You're a prince, Aronn. Start acting like it."

Jeremiah stepped aside and Aronn skulked off, disappearing down the stairs. Relaina's uncle returned to her, seething.

"His sister is a guard?"

"Indeed, and a damn good one." He nodded as Relaina handed back his sword. "She'll straighten him out quickly when she hears of this."

"I told Aronn his friends are shit."

Jeremiah snorted, and Relaina grinned. They reset to practice her new technique again; only a few more tries and she executed it to near perfection.

"Some council meeting last week, eh?" Jeremiah asked as they entered his study once more, putting the practice swords back in their trunk.

"I'm worried."

Jeremiah raised an eyebrow.

"Worried for the Prince of Terrana?"

"Worried my father is going to start a war." Relaina shook her head. "I don't believe it's right to capture the prince. He's not doing anything to harm our kingdom."

"Some would disagree with you."

"I know. But I stand by what I said before. The poor man's probably suffered enough. From the sound of it, my father wants him captured and tortured for information, and that is not something I will support. Is he not thinking of the Tyrant King's reaction? This would be the perfect excuse to attack us, regardless of whether he truly cares about his son."

Normally when Relaina complained about her father to her uncle, Jeremiah did not respond.

"He's always been a stubborn man, ever since I've known him. But he is the king, and he's trying his best to protect his people, and we must accept him for who he is and do our best to support him."

Relaina turned, a response already on her lips, but found Jeremiah holding a long wooden box, polished to perfection. He placed it on the desk and unlatched the sides as she walked back to him, curious.

Relaina stared as Jeremiah lifted a sword carefully from its velvet bed and handed it to her. The blade was thin and light but wide and sharp enough to cut through both flesh and bone. The balance was perfect. The golden pommel and crossguard shone just as brightly as the steel of the blade, inlaid with deep sapphires and minuscule text that read,

Fearless, I rise eternal
Lifted in great heavenly truth

"Do you like the feel of it?" Jeremiah asked. Relaina tore her eyes away from the sword and looked at him, nodding. "Good. It's an early birthday present."

Relaina's jaw nearly dropped. "It's mine? But...my birthday isn't for another three months."

Jeremiah grinned, a rare sight indeed. "I know, but the best blacksmith in the city has been working on it for weeks, and she finished it much earlier than I anticipated. It is yours."

"What do these words mean?"

"They are from an old, proud house. The family existed long before the three kingdoms of Esran were founded. I read about this in an old history tome and thought they were fitting for such a fine blade."

Relaina grinned. "Thank you, Uncle."

"Sharpen it regularly. And take care not to kill anyone you don't fully intend to kill."

Relaina laughed as she placed the steel back into the box, next to the sheath that had been made for it.

"It's magnificent, Uncle. I can't thank you enough."

After clasping the box shut, Relaina threw her arms around Jeremiah. He was startled at first, but then he chuckled softly and held her close.

"Keep out of trouble, Relaina. And don't make a habit of breaking people's noses."

"You heard about that?"

"Of course I did. Your mother told me about it this morning. She could barely get the words out between fits of mirth. But don't tell her I told you that."

Relaina grinned. "I won't."

"Do be careful, though. I could tell during training today that you were in pain. How hard did you fall?"

Relaina stared at him for a moment too long. "Oh! Yes. I, uh, fell and landed on my ribs. Quite embarrassing. I have a bruise."

"Hmm." Jeremiah studied her. "Just be careful, as I said."

"I will be."

She told him goodbye and headed back to her room, the sword box tucked under her arm.

After bathing and dressing, Relaina paced around her room for a few minutes, still restless. She glanced at the sky, at the rain that had abated for now. If she left soon, she could get to Maurice's place without getting soaked. She grabbed her cloak and stole down the stairs, flying toward the stables.

How wrong Relaina had been about the rain.

She'd found Amariah in her usual place toward the back of the stables, kicking herself for forgetting her in the outer village amidst Aronn's foolishness. Darren had brought her back, according to the stableboy, and Relaina marveled at his unexpected kindness yet again.

Amariah was a Nocturian mare, black as night with a magnificent wavy mane. The horses were highly sought-after, prized beyond all others for their intellect and bravery. And now, unfortunately, Amariah was smart enough to be miffed at Relaina for taking her out and getting them stuck in a downpour.

On horseback it didn't take long to get to Maurice's place, even if it was on the outer edge of Parea. The winding cobblestone streets were almost empty and made her journey even faster than usual. Shops were crowded as the people of Parea took shelter from the storm, but Relaina only caught short glimpses of the cozy merriment within the various taverns, tea shops, and boutiques as she rode through the rain.

When she arrived at Maurice's shop entrance, she remembered that she might run into Darren there and almost didn't knock. But the rain wasn't going to let up anytime soon, and she'd come all that way. Thunder echoed her knocks on the door.

Maurice answered and grinned, the wind blowing what remained of his gray hair out of his aging face. "Who in the world would be out in this weather besides Relaina Gienty?"

Relaina walked inside and wrung out her hair, the smell of flowers a familiar comfort. "You know I hate staying in the castle on rainy days. It's far lovelier here, where I can see more than just stone."

"I know, I'm just teasin' ya," the farmer laughed. "What brings you all the way out here, though?"

"I meant to visit last week, but festival preparations got in the way."

"Oh, I see...royal matters are more important than little old me..."

"Oh, stop it, Maurice." Camille walked into the room, wiping her hands on a rag. "You know Relaina would spend time here every day if she could."

Maurice just chortled. "How else am I supposed to have fun around here?"

"Hello, Relaina." Camille started to hug her but drew back. "Goodness, you're soaked. I'll bring you a towel and get you some tea."

A few minutes later, Relaina was seated in a wooden chair by the shop counter, sipping hot tea.

"You won't believe what we spoke about in the council meeting last week. My father informed us that there is a strong possibility that the Prince of Terrana is in Parea."

Camille nearly dropped the tea kettle she was holding, looking first at Relaina and then exchanging a glance with Maurice.

"Is that why they've closed the gates?" Maurice asked.

"It is."

"Are they trying to find him?"

Relaina opened her mouth to explain when the shop door flew open, letting in a fraction of the torrent.

"Maurice, I thought you said that the rain would hold off until I finished tying the—oh, shit."

Darren wrung out his shirt, which he'd just pulled over his head in the doorway to reveal a chiseled abdomen and toned chest, and Relaina inadvertently inhaled some of her tea. Camille looked down at her with concern and Relaina waved her off, eyes watering as heat crept up her neck. Darren went into another room and returned with fresh clothes on, either oblivious to Relaina's reaction or kind enough to ignore it. There was something curious she'd glimpsed on his chest, though—a large, X-shaped scar that crossed over his heart.

"Tie down all the saplings?" Maurice asked.

"Every one." Darren took the towel Camille handed him and dried his hair, which was so wet it looked more brown than blond. He hung the towel on a hook by the door and walked over to the shop counter as Maurice handed him some tea as well. He hoisted himself onto the counter and sat there, shivering as he took a sip.

"Relaina was just telling us that there are suspicions that the Terranian prince is in Parea," Camille said, going behind the counter. It was Darren's turn to almost spit out his tea.

"No one will enter or leave Parea without express permission," Relaina said. "I tried to talk some sense into the council, but they wouldn't hear of it. I just don't understand why we need to capture a man who cut ties with King Gabriel."

"How do you know he's cut ties with the king?" Darren challenged.

"I don't, and that's the point. What do we know of Terrana? That King Gabriel is a shit human that lusts for power and rules with fear? We don't even know the prince's name."

Darren stared at her. "So you truly don't think he should be caught?"

"If he was raised by Gabriel LaGuarde, I think he's probably suffered enough. Not to mention, capturing him would give King Gabriel the perfect excuse to declare war on Lyneisia, which we cannot afford right now. My father is being stubborn and single-minded in this."

"Even if the prince *isn't* a horrible monster like his father," Maurice said, "I suppose King Stephan would want to find him anyway to get information on the Tyrant King."

Relaina sighed. "I know what they intend to do if they find him, and I don't approve."

"You have a kind heart, Relaina, but you don't know if he's truly innocent," Camille said. "There's always the possibility that this is all a ruse and the prince is supposed to be spying on Lyneisian nobles."

"Maybe." Relaina wasn't convinced. She *was* convinced that Gabriel was one of the cruelest men in the world, and anyone who was able to escape his grasp and remain alive was cunning, resourceful, and courageous to the point of stupidity. She looked at Darren again, expecting him to agree with Camille, but he just gave Relaina a strange look, something akin to skepticism. She fought the impulse to snap at him. Did he think she was being naïve? She may have a kind heart, but she wasn't a fool.

"Well, enough talk about the Tyrant King and his son," Camille said, heaving a great sigh. Maurice set to organizing the shelves behind his counter. "I have to go tell Lonnie that we won't have the roses she wanted for next week. Since Lord Swanson is arriving tomorrow, we'll need all the roses we can get."

Any thought pertaining to the Prince of Terrana vanished from Relaina's mind. Maurice hit his head on one of the shelves above him, and Darren set down his cup of tea. All three of them spoke at once.

"Gods help me," Relaina said.

"Lord Swanson?" Darren asked.

"What does he need roses for?" Maurice grimaced, massaging his head.

"He's a young lord of the Evarian lowlands. His father, Reginald, died about two years ago, passing his lands and title to his son, Henry." Camille looked to Relaina. "Your father invited him to stay at the castle while he's visiting Lyneisia?"

Relaina's mood plummeted as she nodded. Camille turned to her husband.

"Apparently, he is fond of having roses fill his chambers," she said. "I think he enjoys the fragrance. You know these lord types that just *must* have everything they want. Queen Christine sent word earlier today and has asked us to provide the roses. Which is why I need to go tell Lonnie that she'll have to wait on them for a while."

As Camille left the shop, clutching her cloak around her to keep as dry as possible, reality came crashing down on Relaina once more. If she rejected Swanson, her father was likely to push her marriage to Zarias. She stood and walked outside, angry tears already blurring her vision.

"Relaina?"

She ignored Maurice, stepping out into the rain, eyes stinging. At least it was raining, so if she did cry, it wouldn't be quite so apparent. A hand touched her shoulder.

"It's raining too hard for you to leave just yet, m'dear," Maurice said. "Come have another cup of tea."

She nodded, and he headed back inside. Relaina took another moment to gather herself before she followed, taking a seat again and holding her cup of tea with both hands.

"So Darren," she said, clearing her throat. "Where are you from?"

"A small town called Ellyr. It's right on the border of Evaria and Terrana," Darren said.

"Te vochae Evari?" *You speak Evarian?*

"Ne vrai na erha i'is." *Not much since I came here.*

His Evarian was good, but he spoke with an accent she couldn't place. She continued speaking it. "Your speech doesn't sound like a typical east-Lyneisian accent."

Darren narrowed his eyes. "What is that supposed to mean?"

"Exactly what I said."

"It sounds like you're suggesting that being from an east-Lyneisian town means I'm uneducated."

"No, I think you sound very educated. Which is not typical of dwellers in the east."

"That sounds awfully elitist of you, Princess."

"All right now, you two, I don't know what you're saying, but it certainly doesn't sound friendly," Maurice said. "Darren, go get some yeast from the back room. Camille will want to make bread later."

Darren jumped down from the counter and left the room. Relaina didn't expect he'd return any time soon. Fine by her.

"How dare he call me elitist?" she said. Maurice exhaled and continued stocking shelves. "I am always the one reminding my father of the people whenever I get the chance."

"You're going to have to catch me up, dear, I've forgotten all the Evarian I learned as a boy."

Relaina recounted their conversation as he stood and stretched.

"Relaina, you know that I know you have a good heart. And I know you've worked hard to see the world through the eyes of others, but it sounds like you were looking for ways to mistrust him just then. His father worked in a noble house and Darren received a quality education because of it."

Oh.

"What about his mother?"

"Ellyr was raided by Terranian soldiers years ago. You were too young to remember, I'd wager. Those who weren't killed became slaves in Terrana. Darren's been on his own for a long time now."

Relaina's stomach lurched. "Was he a slave?" she whispered.

Maurice smiled sadly. "It's not my place to speak of his past."

Yet another reason to despise the Tyrant King: the legality of slavery in Terrana. Relaina shuddered.

"I should get going," she said. "The rain's let up now."

"Very well. Glad to have you visit today. Come back soon."

"I will. Tell Camille I'll be back for some of her bread."

"If I tell her that, she'll make four loaves."

"Perfect."

CHAPTER 5

THE MANHUNT

It was nearly midday, and Darren's eyes were heavy and dry from the sleep he'd lost the previous night. He hadn't seen Xavier since the night of the Harvest Festival, but Relaina's visit yesterday nagged at his memory and his conscience—she was in danger, and she had no idea. And telling her that would attract questions he could not answer.

"Darren, get your head out of your arse, we've got a customer coming!"

Darren shook his head and opened the door. A man dressed in a gray tunic and black trousers emerged from a grand carriage and strutted inside, his haughty air permeating the room almost as thoroughly as the smell of flowers. There was an older woman who remained in the carriage, and a handful of servants carrying bags and leading mules packed with supplies. One servant took the man's gloves off for him and fixed his windblown blond hair.

"Hello, good sirs," the man drawled, nodding to Maurice and frowning slightly at Darren's dirty shirt and worn trousers. "I am Lord Henry Swanson. I would like to have a flower arrangement delivered to the castle this afternoon."

"Oh, yes, of course." Maurice bowed. "What kind of flowers would you like?"

"Oh, I don't have a preference. Just whatever is the most extravagant arrangement you can come up with. I hear roses have nearly filled the castle to the brim, but those are for my benefit, I suppose, so you can just use whatever's left for this arrangement."

The farmer and Darren exchanged glances.

"Might I ask to whom I should deliver these flowers?" Darren asked. The young lord turned to Darren, making eye contact with him for the first time, and snorted.

"The princess, of course. Although I do regret that someone of your...disposition must be the one to take them to her."

Darren stared at the man, unsure whether he wanted to laugh or throttle him.

"Right," Swanson said, turning back to Maurice and ignoring Darren once more. He gave Maurice a sack of coins. "I want them delivered to her rooms as soon as possible. Make an arrangement that really captures my presence—something she won't be able to ignore. And put this note with it."

He laid the note on the counter, turned on his well-polished heel, and left the floral shop, his servant following closely behind him.

"So that farmer's louse is the one Zarias told me about," the lord said to his servant as the door shut behind them, unaware that Darren could still hear him. "He was seen with her at the Lyneisian Harvest Festival, you know."

"He hardly seems like much of a threat to my lord."

"Indeed. But he's one of those strong, rugged types that women are inexplicably drawn to. Best watch out for him in the future."

"Of course, my lord." Their voices faded away, and a pleasant sensation tugged at Darren's insides. Zarias and the other nobles saw him as a threat. Perhaps it was simply his being in Relaina's presence that had irritated them, but it was hard to forget her eyes roving over him a bit too long at the festival, and her flushed face when he'd caught her as she stumbled.

"Sometimes I wish you could just...I don't know, give men like that a good walloping," Maurice said, rolling his eyes. "Strike some fear into their hearts, the cowardly, pompous fools. They'd never know what hit them."

"Mhmm."

"Darren."

"What? Oh, right. Well, attacking a lord in the middle of the street is not wise. Especially not now."

The farmer sighed. "I know." He set about picking a bundle of beautiful flowers from the shop, mixing lilies and carnations and irises.

"I don't know if I want to see roses ever again."

"At this rate you probably won't." Maurice put some finishing touches on the arrangement. "We delivered nearly every one we'd grown this year to the castle."

Once the arrangement was complete, Darren donned a hooded cloak, saddled up the horse, and loaded a bundle of flowers onto the cart to sell as he rode through town. Camille ensured his face was obscured before he set off. The rain from yesterday had cleared away and the sun glittered in the rushing water of the aqueducts, warming the cobblestones and rooftops of Parea. At least a dozen citygoers stopped Darren to buy flowers. They all admired the arrangement intended for the princess, and Darren forced his face into a smile, agreeing that it was indeed beautiful. His heart stopped any time a city guard appeared, but so far Xavier had not been among them.

He reached the castle with his flower supply greatly depleted and his moneybag much heavier. The guards by the doors greeted him warmly; one offered a quiet apology for the night of the Harvest Festival, and Darren nodded his thanks.

He craned his neck to see over the enormous arrangement as he made for the lift, narrowly dodging other servants as he went. Luck was on his side—there were no others waiting for it today. He stepped inside and told the operator where to direct it.

Soon the first floor disappeared, and Darren watched as each floor passed in turn, separated by thick stone. The man at the crank pulled the lever once more when the lift reached the tenth floor, and the doors unlocked. Darren pushed them open with his shoulder and stepped onto the landing. He turned a corner and Victoria appeared, striding out of the castle greenhouse.

"Victoria!" She turned, allowing him to catch up. "These are for Princess Relaina from Lord Swanson."

"Oh! I'm sorry dear, I've just been called to take care of some mishap with the roses in the guest chambers." She wrung her hands. "Would you mind bringing them to her chambers for me?"

"Oh...of course." It was only a floor up.

He passed by a guard stationed at the stairwell landing, nodding as he headed down the corridor. Relaina's door was already ajar, and he nudged it open with his foot, trying to keep his balance. He set the massive arrangement down on a table close to the door and left the note the man had asked for beside it. Just as he was about to leave, he glanced in her vanity mirror and found that Relaina was still in bed, fast asleep. Had no one woken her?

Shit. It wasn't his problem. But her father would be irate, and empathy held Darren in place. Surely there was a way to wake her that wouldn't require him to get close to her. He pulled a yellow lily out of the flower arrangement and braced himself to bolt from the room as he tossed it toward Relaina's exposed shoulder. It flopped against the mattress and fell to the floor. *Fuck me.*

Against his instincts of self-preservation, he walked to her bed and gently shook her shoulder.

"Princess Relaina." She stirred, her eyelids fluttering open.

"Darren?" She breathed in deeply and stretched. Gods, she was wearing a *very* thin nightgown. A heartbeat later, her eyes widened.

"Shit!"

Relaina flew out of bed, almost knocking him over as she scrambled to her wardrobe. She grabbed wads of fabric and disappeared into her washroom for a few seconds before returning fully dressed in a blue gown, rifling through an ornate box on her vanity.

"Help me, will you?"

She held out a pendant in one hand and pushed her curls aside with the other. Darren took the necklace and clasped it around her neck, hardly daring to breathe as his fingers brushed her skin.

Relaina scurried from the room, calling, "Thank you!" as she disappeared into the corridor, and resolve settled in the pit of his stomach.

That infuriating, beautiful woman—who defended the Prince of Terrana—was in the same city as a ruthless Terranian assassin. He had to do *something.*

"Darren!" Bracken walked toward him as he exited the castle, his hair windswept from riding. "You look like you've seen a ghost, mate. Where are you headed?"

"I..." Darren paused. Where *was* he going? What was he going to do?

But here was the answer was right in front of him; Bracken was around Relaina more frequently than anyone. Darren checked their surroundings and lowered his voice.

"Bracken, can I trust you?"

"Oh...uh, sure? I mean, yes, of course."

"There's a man working with the Lyneisian Guard. His name is Xavier, and he's Terranian."

"What? Why would King Stephan have a Terranian man working with his guard?"

"My guess is that he's having him help with the manhunt." Darren glanced around again. "Listen—make sure Princess Relaina stays away from him."

Bracken blinked. "Why?"

"Please just trust me. Keep him away from her."

Bracken narrowed his eyes but nodded.

"All right."

Darren sighed. "Thank you." He replaced his hood, got on his horse, and disappeared into the city streets.

"Relaina, you have turned away *every last suitor* I have brought to this castle! What do you expect me to do? Conjure up a perfect man based on your mood that day?" King Stephan demanded as he paced his study, his face white with rage. Relaina clenched her fists.

"It wasn't my intention to miss Lord Swanson's arrival, and how dare you reduce my decisions to fickleness? Can you honestly say that *any* of them would make a decent husband and consort?"

"You cannot waste more time, Relaina! You must choose someone. You *will* be married by the end of this year."

"What is the *rush*? I won't be queen for years to come; why can't I take my time choosing the right person?"

"You know why, Relaina. You must provide an heir. You must be an example to the people."

"I would sooner pitch myself from the castle roof than bear a child by Zarias or any man like him."

"Gods damn it, Relaina, *enough!*"

Relaina turned to leave, but two guards blocked her path. The air in her lungs smoldered as she pivoted to face her father.

"You will *listen* to me," he said, his voice low and dangerous. "You are not to leave this castle anymore. You will remain within the boundaries of its walls. I will give you the list of men who have come here seeking your hand, and you *will* choose one of them before your twenty-first birthday, or I will choose one for you."

The king swept past her and left his study, doors shutting behind him with finality. Relaina stared at the empty desk before her, unmoving. She blinked a few times and walked into the hall.

"Princess, there you are!"

Relaina froze on the landing of the eleventh floor, her insides prickling. Just past her doorway, Zarias stood next to a man with dark eyes and a tan complexion. His hair was honey-blond and fell just past his angular chin.

"Princess, this is Henry Swanson, a dear friend of mine," Zarias said, and Swanson bowed, smirking. Of course he was friends with Zarias. "We were just about to enjoy refreshments in Aronn's chambers, if you'd care to join us."

"Thank you, but I'm busy." Relaina's dress billowed behind her as she approached her room.

"Oh!" Zarias palmed his forehead. "I forgot. You're more interested in lowborn farmers. My mistake."

"What woman wouldn't be interested in a man who's good with his hands?" Relaina grinned at Zarias's scowl and Swanson's widened eyes. She slammed her door shut before they had time to reply.

❧

RELAINA HAD NEARLY HACKED a straw dummy to shreds when Bracken found her in the sparring hall late that afternoon.

"I think he's dead, Laines."

She huffed a laugh and plopped down on the floor, wiping her sweaty forehead. Bracken sat next to her.

"Want to tell me about it?"

Relaina caught her breath and relayed her father's ultimatum, digging the tip of her practice sword into the stone.

"So you have to pick someone to marry in less than three months, or your father will pick him for you? And you've been confined to the castle?" Relaina nodded. "Oh, Laines, that's...that's horseshit."

Relaina, despite herself, laughed.

"Oh, speaking of horrible men, I saw Darren a while ago," Bracken said. Relaina recalled Darren's flustered face from earlier, and the brush of his hands against her neck, and cleared her throat.

"I didn't think you felt so strongly about him," she said.

"No, no, not that *he's* the horrible man. He told me about a man working with the Lyneisian guard, Xavier. Says he's Terranian and not to be trusted."

"What? How does he know that? How does he know him?"

Bracken hesitated a moment. "I think he's—"

"Bracken Averatt."

Relaina and Bracken stood as three figures strode into the hall, one of whom was her uncle. Bracken threw her a confused look, and she shrugged. Jeremiah looked at his niece with regret and then nodded toward Bracken, and the two soldiers on either side of him seized her friend, pinning his arms behind his back. Relaina yelped a curse, and Bracken stared at Jeremiah in bewilderment.

"Uncle, what is the meaning of this?"

Jeremiah extracted a piece of parchment from his lapel and began to read.

"Bracken Averatt, you have been accused of high treason to the Lyneisian Crown. In accordance with the law, you will be imprisoned, and the King of Lyneisia will decide how you will be judged. Should his royal majesty see fit to allow you a trial, it is your choice as to whether you wish to plead your innocence or confess your crimes and hang."

"*Hang?* For what? I've committed no treason!" Bracken yelped.

"What false source gave this accusation?" Relaina demanded.

"I'm sorry, Relaina," Jeremiah said. "But we have received evidence from a trusted source that he has been passing information about the Lyneisian royal family to King Gabriel LaGuarde and that he has been trying to sabotage our efforts to locate the Terranian prince."

"*What?*" Bracken and Relaina said in unison. Jeremiah nodded to his men, and they began to drag Bracken off.

"Stop!" Relaina hurried after them. The guards ignored her. "Bracken, I'll fix this, I promise!"

In utter disbelief, she watched the two soldiers take Bracken away. Once the doors shut behind them, she whirled around to face Jeremiah.

"Uncle, there *must* be some mistake."

"I sincerely hope there is, Relaina. But we must act in accordance with the law. I do not doubt your father will offer him a fair trial, and that the truth of this will be found out."

Her uncle followed his men and her friend into the corridor, and a hard, leaden feeling settled in Relaina's stomach. Bracken would *never*. Who would accuse him of such a crime?

Without another thought, Relaina raced up the stairs, wheezing as she reached the tenth floor. She dashed through the ballroom and out into the gardens where she wrenched open the trapdoor that would lead into the passageway below, her father's orders be damned. She climbed down the long flight of stairs and entered the tunnels, walking in the dim light for what seemed like hours, until she emerged by a tea and spice stall in the Parean underground. Curious looks followed her as she sprinted past the entrance to the fighting ring and up the winding stairs nearby. The smoke shop owner didn't question her as she passed through. She waved the smoke out of her face as she stepped into the street and headed to Maurice's shop.

When she arrived, she ran to the back door, pounding on it. Moments later, Darren appeared, wielding a knife.

"Gods in fucking *hell*, Darren!" Relaina jumped back.

"Princess Relaina?" He lowered the knife.

"Who is this man, Xavier?"

"What?"

"Xavier." Relaina stepped around him to enter the shop's back hallway, and Darren shut the door. "Bracken told me about him, and how he's helping find the Terranian prince. He's been arrested."

"The prince has been arrested?" Darren asked, bewildered.

"No—Bracken. They say he's been passing information about the royal family to Gabriel LaGuarde, which I know is a lie, and that he tried to sabotage the Lyneisian Guard's efforts to find and capture the Prince of Terrana."

"That's...quite an accusation. Do they have any proof?"

"No!" Relaina strode up the hallway and into the shop itself; Darren followed her, tucking his knife away. Camille and Maurice weren't around. "I have to find a way to get him released. What do you know about Xavier? Bracken tried to warn me about him moments before he was arrested."

Darren hesitated.

"Tell me, damn you!" Unbidden tears sprang into her eyes. "If it can help free Bracken, then tell me."

"He—he's a Terranian assassin." Relaina blanched.

"Then what in Ashima's name is he doing here? Why does my father trust him?"

Darren shook his head. "I have no idea. But he's dangerous. If he's here, it's not for any good reason."

"How do you know him?"

Darren took a while to answer. "He tried to capture me after I'd escaped enslavement in Terrana."

Relaina's blood ran cold. Her hands shook as she looked at him, the room, the windows.

"Are you proficient with a sword?"

"Am I...?"

"A sword, a bow, anything? I know you can fight hand to hand, but can you wield a weapon?"

Darren's brow furrowed. "Yes."

"Good. Then will you keep an eye on him?"

"On Xavier?"

"Yes. I'm going to try and find out what evidence they think they have against Bracken, and you can keep watch on Xavier to make sure he doesn't hurt anyone or do anything suspicious."

"I can do that."

Relaina opened her mouth again but hesitated. It was her instinct to mention the secret passageways and tunnels, but should she? He stood before her with confidence and resolve, and she threw caution to the wind.

"If anything goes awry, there's a secret passage you can reach through the tunnels in the city's underside," she said. "The entrance is in the alley behind the tea and spice stall. Take no turns and you'll end up by the hydrangeas in the castle gardens, on the tenth floor."

Darren nodded. "Does Xavier know of this passage?"

"He might. Most guards do." Relaina bit her lip. "Please don't tell anyone else."

"You have my word."

"Good. And one more thing."

"Yes?"

"You can call me 'Relaina.'" With that, she left the shop.

DARREN EXTINGUISHED the fire in the shop, his resolve hardening by the minute. He'd become complacent in his contentedness here, and that was at an end unless he did something about it. He'd either need to break the vow he'd made to himself when he'd first come to Parea, or he'd risk his own safety, and Relaina's.

Perhaps there was another way.

He went into his bedroom, removing the clothes he'd worked in that day. It was completely dark out now, but he was familiar enough with the locations of his few belongings that he didn't bother lighting a candle. He opened the trunk at the foot of his bed and extracted the same dark clothing he'd worn to fight Relaina and pulled it on quickly. As he left the shop, he took his black cloak off the nearby hook and locked the door behind him. Maurice and Camille were at a friend's place and wouldn't be back until the wee hours of the morning, so he had plenty of time to get back before they did and avoid raising suspicions.

The city guard quarters weren't far—the large stone building was about halfway between the edge of the city and the castle, with many amenities. Guards with family usually chose to live at home, but the temporary soldiers or unmarried young guards and trainees lived here. The building loomed before Darren against the night sky, but he was not afraid of what he would find there. After a breath and a prayer, he darted for the wall, avoiding the gaze of a guard nearby, and sprang toward a windowsill. His fingers found purchase on the stone easily; seconds later he'd scaled the wall to the second floor, vaulted onto a balcony, and picked the poorly-designed lock on the doors entirely unnoticed.

A fire crackled at the end of the dining hall, but the long table was empty. It was past curfew for day-patrollers, so Darren counted on them to be sleeping. He walked quietly to the end of the hall and crept through the doors, emerging onto a plush red carpet. Directly in front of him was a common area complete with couch and chairs. There were many doors on either side, and at the very end of the wide hall was a particularly large one—cherry wood carved with intricate swirls surrounding the Gienty crest. This was why he'd come. Without making a sound, he slipped inside.

The room was devoid of occupants, as he'd expected. A single desk stood in a stream of moonlight, and after a few minutes of rifling through papers strewn about, Darren found what he was looking for. He studied the map of the city and castle grounds before replacing them on the desk, just as they were. The guards' routes were easy enough to remember. Darren unlatched the nearby window and stole outside, pulling himself onto the roof. Ahead, Castle Alterna rose toward the stars, beckoning.

He followed the guards' route along the rooftops, slipping past one man as he sleepily watched the street below. Cobblestones were briefly illuminated as someone opened the door to a pub. The route led to the north gate of the castle, and Darren leapt from a nearby rooftop onto the castle's perimeter wall. He landed almost soundlessly and crouched low, finding a place that allowed him to see just inside the grounds. Now, he waited.

Only a few minutes passed before Darren caught sight of Xavier, who was walking with Captain Andovier, Relaina's uncle. Two guards stood at attention by the north gate as they approached, torches lighting their faces.

"...And make sure when he's brought to the throne room that—"

"I know how to escort a prisoner, sir," the captain said. "Thank you for your information and input. King Stephan is very grateful."

Xavier bowed. "I'll return in the morning for the trial."

Every muscle in Darren's body tensed as Xavier walked through the gate and out into the city. He jumped down from the wall and followed until Xavier turned down a small, dark street. Darren drew a dagger from his belt. Now was his chance.

Darren clapped a hand over Xavier's mouth and held the dagger to his throat. Xavier struggled for only a moment and then stilled as he felt the cold metal against his jugular. Just a flick of the wrist and he'd be dead, but Darren stayed his hand.

"Don't move or call for help if you want to live." He removed his hand from Xavier's mouth. "Know this: if you so much as glance in Princess Relaina's direction, you'll wish I'd ended you now, with a quick death. Understand?"

"Who are you?"

"No one of import." For another heartbeat, Darren considered killing him, but two figures rounded the corner, and he threw Xavier to the ground and vanished. The Terranian assassin massaged his throat as two guards approached him, offering aid. But Xavier ignored them, searching wildly for the man who attacked him.

There was nothing but the dark.

CHAPTER 6

THE TRIAL AND THE TRUTH

Bells tolled in the distance, marking that the hour was midday. It was time.

With as much poise and composure as she could muster, Relaina swallowed her panic and walked out of her room, and once in the lift began the long descent to the Hall of Judgment. Two servants whom she did not know had come to assist her with her gown and hair this morning, and Relaina had been miserable throughout the entire process, wishing that Victoria was there. She had discovered from the servants that Victoria was at home with her husband, who had caught some terrible sickness.

As Relaina descended the final few floors in the lift, she muttered prayers to every god she could think of, throwing in a prayer to Iros for Victoria's husband's health. Relaina stepped out of the lift, her black and silver gown sweeping the floor as she approached the seldom-used hall. Many others were headed in the same direction, talking lightheartedly. Relaina's stomach churned. The tiara woven into her intricately braided hair dug into her scalp.

The hall was packed with both nobles and city dwellers and surrounded on three sides by guards spaced along the walls and by the doors. Two mahogany chairs were situated to the right of the two permanent thrones at the front of the room, all upon a dais. Relaina's father sat on his throne, also wearing black as a symbol of solemnity and impartiality. Still wearing a mask of calm, Relaina walked to the front of the room to take her seat in the chair closest to the thrones as the crowd buzzed with hushed chatter. Misenia sat on her right, expressionless as ever. The queen perched on her throne and watched Relaina silently, her golden tresses pulled away from her face in an intricate, braided knot. Aronn and Annalise arrived shortly after Relaina sat, taking seated positions at the front of the crowd that had gathered. They each gave Relaina a small, encouraging nod.

The hall filled steadily until the only remaining space was a path through the middle, to make way for the accused. Icy dread settled in Relaina's stomach, but she assured herself that it would be all right. She'd spent the rest of the previous day in the castle library with Aronn and Annalise, going through every legal book they could find, and she had read enough to know that if the trial seemed to be going badly, she could save Bracken with a last resort.

The crowd in the Hall of Judgment erupted. Bracken had been brought up from the dungeons. People hurled insults at him as he was led up the center by a guard holding his chains. Annalise recoiled as they passed by her, and Relaina couldn't blame her gentle-hearted sister. She herself was disturbed by her people's apparent lust for blood. Bracken came clearly into view at the base of the dais and Relaina ground her teeth together to keep from hurling insults right back at the crowd. Her friend had only been in the dungeon for a day, but he was haggard and pale, the light in his eyes diminished. King Stephan stood and held up a hand to silence the crowd, and the noise died down.

"Bracken Averatt, you come before your king today to stand trial and plead your innocence."

"I do, Your Grace." Several people in the crowd hissed. Relaina ignored the heat rising in her stomach. *Stay calm. Be composed.*

"You have been accused of the following acts of treason: passing secret information about the Gienty family to King Gabriel LaGuarde of Terrana, and plotting to inhibit the search for King Gabriel's son, the Prince of Terrana. Do you deny these accusations?"

"I deny the first," Bracken said, holding his head a bit higher, "but not the second."

Relaina felt as if her lungs had been punctured. The crowd erupted once more.

"Let him hang!"

"Traitor!"

"*Scum*! Hang him!"

Relaina's ears continued to ring long after the king silenced the crowd. *Bracken...what are you doing?*

"Very well," the king said. "You will have a chance to explain, but first I call forth the source of these accusations, Xavier Carel."

Relaina blinked, returning to her senses. A murmur wove through the room as Xavier walked forward, garbed in a Lynx Guard uniform. Relaina glared at the man. He had dark brown hair and a pallid complexion, and there was something unsettling about his eyes. Relaina distrusted him even without Darren's warning. She didn't see Darren here but hoped he was watching the man from the shadows, as she'd asked.

Xavier stood at the front and addressed the room.

"Being a former Terranian soldier," Xavier said, and a subtle ripple went through the crowd, "I have special access to certain information that could have easily been lost or overlooked by Lyneisian forces. Averatt is a name I had seen and heard many times in Terrana. If you need proof," he extracted parchment from his cloak, "I have letters here, with the boy's signature on them.

"As for the other accusation, this boy began following me yesterday, asking me questions about the hunt for the Terranian prince. And if that were not evidence enough," Xavier pointed to Bracken, "last night, I was attacked in the city streets by one of his lackeys and told that if I continued my search, I would be killed."

The cry of outrage was shorter this time but just as wild. Furious indignation burned behind Bracken's eyes. But Relaina remained calm. She had an idea.

"Thank you, Xavier," the king said. Before he could go on, Relaina stood. Her father gave her a stern look, but when he saw her collected expression, he allowed her to proceed.

"Let me see those letters."

Xavier walked up the steps, and Relaina glared at him as he handed her the paper. She unfolded it and scanned through most of the content. There was no mistaking that the information must have come from someone inside the castle, and seeing her own movements tracked in such a tangible way was disconcerting. But a glaring detail caught her eye that could be used to her advantage.

"This is not Bracken's handwriting," Relaina said. Xavier kept his face unreadable other than a slight twitch at the corner of his mouth. A dull murmur rippled through the crowd, and Relaina felt a twinge of irritation. Why was it that hordes of people were always so eager for bloodshed?

"I can prove it isn't his handwriting," she continued, her voice stronger, more confident now. "Annalise, will you go up to my chambers and retrieve one of the notes from Bracken?"

"I will accompany her," Misenia said, standing.

Her sister nodded, and she and Misenia left the room. Relaina would have sent a servant, but Annalise looked like she needed a reprieve from the atmosphere of the room, and her sister knew exactly where Relaina kept Bracken's notes.

"Is there a particular reason why Your Highness has notes from Bracken Averatt in her chambers?" Xavier asked, raising an eyebrow. Relaina hoped he saw the loathing in her eyes as her gaze settled upon him.

"I would remind you that I am not the one on trial here. Bracken Averatt has lived here since we were both children, and it is common knowledge that we are close friends. If anyone in here wishes to put me on trial for sending notes to a friend, by all counts, I would be found guilty."

There was an appreciative chortle from the crowd, and Relaina took it as a victory. At least she had them somewhat reined in now—better to have them laughing than screaming for blood. Relaina looked down at Bracken, who gave her an appreciative smile. She couldn't bring herself to return it.

Annalise and Misenia reentered the room, holding several small pieces of paper. Misenia brought them up to Relaina, and Annalise sat down as Relaina unfolded the notes.

"As you can see," she put the papers right below Xavier's nose, "the handwriting on each of these is the same, and the script on those letters is quite different."

"It is not so far-fetched to consider the idea that he can change what his handwriting looks like," Xavier said.

"Then it is not so far-fetched to suggest that someone else could have penned these letters and signed Bracken's name to them," Relaina said. Xavier glowered at her but had no rebuttal.

"Very well," the king said, and Xavier stepped down and took his seat. "Bracken, what say you about the second accusation?"

Bracken shifted on his feet, attempting to straighten his posture.

"I was indeed observing Xavier upon my return yesterday because I do not believe that he is trustworthy. I also do not believe the Prince of Terrana is a threat to our kingdom. Capturing him and holding him prisoner would only incite war with Terrana."

The crowd was restless but promptly silenced by the king.

"I see," the king said, his eyes narrowing. He looked away from Bracken and addressed the room. "Subverting the laws of the land cannot go unpunished. With this confession in mind, I declare that Bracken Averatt be sent to Maremer, far from Barleo and Parea, to be held prisoner by Fabian, King of Evaria."

"*What*?" Relaina's cry was drowned out by the buzzing that had started up in the room. She felt a ringing in her ears—there would be no vote by the judges. Bracken would live, at least, but she had no way of stopping him from being exiled to Evaria.

"Should the prisoner in question be found innocent regarding the first accusation, he will be allowed to return to Lyneisia, though no longer as a guest of the Gienty house. If found guilty by association, he will remain forever banished from our land."

Relaina's heart seemed to have stopped working.

"Does the accused have anything further to say?"

Bracken looked up at King Stephan, his face downcast. He then turned to Relaina.

"Relaina, you stay away from that one," Bracken said, gesturing with shackled hands to Xavier. "He's nothing but evil—"

The crowd roared again, and Relaina stood.

"*Silence!*" Whether out of shock or respect, the crowd obeyed Relaina immediately. She looked to her father, waiting for him to end the trial.

"Let the judgment be carried out." King Stephan said.

It was over. Relaina ran down the stairs and grabbed Bracken's upper arm as he was guided from the room. He turned just as she embraced him.

"I'll free you. I promise."

Bracken said something Relaina didn't hear, and then he was pulled away from her through the roaring crowd. Her heartbeat throbbed in her ears and the surrounding voices threatened to suffocate her if she didn't escape that room. She swept past her siblings and parents and exited through a back door that led to the servant's staircase.

As soon as the door to Relaina's chambers clicked shut, she threw the tiara in her hair at the wall with a scream of rage devolving into despair. She crumpled to the ground and began to cry.

Relaina was gazing numbly at a wilted yellow lily on the floor when the world jerked as someone hauled her upright by her hair, clapping a hand over her mouth to muffle her cry. She struggled but stilled as cold, wickedly sharp metal touched her throat. She hadn't even heard her door open.

"You're mine, Princess," Xavier said.

DARREN WAITED OUTSIDE THE CASTLE, ignoring the anxiety prickling up and down his spine as he watched Pareans file out of the trial viewing. Several of them groaned about the verdict, and a few looked relieved, but Darren's attention was directed at the guards that filed out, heading for their barracks. Xavier was not among them.

Darren left his hiding place by a tailor's shop and walked through the gates of Castle Alterna undetected. He ventured to the Hall of Judgment on the entrance floor and glanced around. Stragglers carried on hushed conversations, but still no sign of Xavier. Cold crept into his chest. Relaina. He needed to check on Relaina first.

The lift was vacant, so he gathered himself and requested the eleventh floor. The slow climb only heightened his anxiety, and when it finally stopped at the correct floor, he was half hoping to be manhandled and thrown out of the castle again for intruding.

But when he arrived at Relaina's room and found the door flung wide open, his heart stopped.

Not a single piece of furniture was out of place, but droplets of blood left a trail from the entrance. Every inch of his skin was alive with alarm as he followed the traces of blood to their starting point. A small piece of parchment was pinned to Relaina's vanity chair by a knife.

Long live the King of Terrana

Darren crumpled the note in his hand as his breath shuddered out of him, studying the marks on the floor. They led him out of Relaina's room, but it was impossible to see any blood on the red carpet of the corridor. Now that he was paying attention, though, there were places where fibers had been displaced or rubbed off completely, as if someone had dug the heel of their boot into it. It led right back to where he'd come from—the lift.

He would have seen Xavier if he'd left the castle from the main entrance, but there were other exits. Relaina's voice drifted into his mind.

Hydrangeas in the castle gardens.

That was only one floor down. Darren sprinted down the corridor and banged on a door he knew to be another of the Gienty children's chambers. Aronn answered the door. *Thank the gods.*

"What is it? I...Who are you?"

"My name is Darren. Prince Aronn, your sister is in trouble. I'm going into the passageway that leads to the castle gardens, but tell your uncle to send guards into the underside and the tunnels to head them off in the other direction."

Prince Aronn paled but nodded. Darren took off, passing the lift and bounding down the stairs instead. He burst through the massive ballroom doors, which were also already ajar, and out into the gardens, looking around wildly for the blue blooms that would lead him to Relaina and Xavier. He located them quickly and hauled the trapdoor up, hastening down the stairs.

For a few minutes, Darren crept along silently but swiftly, entering the tunnels through a narrow archway. He drew two long, curved daggers as he went, his face shrouded by the darkness and the hood on his head. If it weren't for the intermittent torches, it would have been impossible to see. A small part of Darren realized he hadn't felt a bit of hesitation when heading into the underground passage. Perhaps his determination to find Relaina had burned the fear away, at least for now.

Voices began echoing from ahead. It was difficult to make out what was being said, but the tone was hostile. He sped his pace.

"Stop...struggling...you little rat!"

Relaina swore at Xavier, and he growled, "I ought to gag you."

"You lied...Bracken...King Gabriel!"

A chuckle echoed off the stones, and Darren quieted his footsteps even more. He could now hear them clearly.

"Ah, yes. A bit of the truth with the lie," Xavier grunted. Darren could just make out his and Relaina's silhouettes against the lanterns lining the walls. "He was trying to thwart me. But *I* am working for King Gabriel, and I couldn't have your meddling lapdog of a boy get in my way."

Relaina swore at him again, this time in Terranian, and Xavier threw her to the ground as Darren rounded a curve and both of them came into view.

"How *dare* you befoul the language of my king with your unworthy tongue!" Xavier lifted her from the ground by her throat, slamming her against the stone wall of the tunnel. Darren mastered himself, though his hands ached to end Xavier there and then. Relaina's life was at stake if he exposed himself too quickly.

"You'll never leave Parea alive," Relaina said as he gripped his knife tightly in the hand that wasn't at her throat. Xavier bared his teeth in fury and lifted his knife, aiming for her chest. Darren moved.

Xavier yelped and leapt back to nurse his hand as one of Darren's smaller knives flew out of the dark and slashed his knuckles. Relaina broke free of him and looked down the tunnel in the direction from which the knife had come.

Her expression was hard to distinguish, but Darren imagined what he must look like coming out of the darkness, holding two daggers and wearing a hood that shrouded his face. Xavier regained his composure and drew his sword.

"Touch her again and you die," Darren said, walking forward and brandishing the daggers. He passed by a lantern, and Relaina's eyes lit up in recognition. Xavier smiled.

"Ah, Darren," he said, "don't tell me you've gotten attached to the Lyneisian princess? How terribly ironic." Darren took a moment to toss his cloak to the ground, and then their lethal dance began. He went to a cold, calculating place within himself that he had not accessed for many months. The light from the torches glinted on metal as blow after blow was dealt and blocked. Xavier drew a knife with his left hand and swiped at Darren, who hissed as the blade grazed his arm, but he did not falter. As the fight wore on, each of them barely scratching the other, Relaina moved uncertainly, as if trying to figure out a way to help. The answer came in the form of one of Darren's daggers flying out of his hand and landing at her feet. He readjusted his technique swiftly, and as he and Xavier remained engrossed in their battle, Relaina bent to retrieve Darren's dagger, using it to slice through the rope binding her wrists.

Darren narrowly avoided another slice to the arm, noticing Relaina's new position as he ducked. She flipped the dagger in her hand and lunged for Xavier's unprotected back, but the gown made her slow, and Xavier turned just in time to block her attack. Darren doubled down on him with his remaining dagger and Xavier was forced to turn again, giving Relaina an opening. She sprang and managed to get an arm around his neck, holding the blade at his throat. He froze, sword suspended where it had last clashed with Darren's blade. Darren looked at Xavier and then Relaina, breathing heavily.

"Drop the sword," Relaina said. Darren's eyes blazed as Xavier let the blade slip from his hand, landing on the stones with a *clang*. Xavier began to laugh softly.

"Letting your guard down so soon?" Like the strike of an asp, a knife appeared from Xavier's sleeve and he plunged it backward. Relaina moved, but the blade found its mark in her abdomen. She gasped and grabbed the hilt with shaking hands, dropping Darren's dagger and sinking to the ground.

"*No!*" Darren dove, retrieving his second blade. He rolled out of the way to avoid Xavier's newly recovered sword and slashed one of his daggers across Xavier's leg as he came to his feet. Xavier roared in pain and grasped at the gash in his thigh, falling into a kneel, and Darren disarmed him. Xavier got to his feet, trembling as he leaned against the wall of the tunnel. Darren held one of his daggers to Xavier's throat.

"You fight well, boy," Xavier said. "That's twice now that you've bested me. Perhaps you do have that mercilessness your father always thought you lacked."

"I am merciful." Before Xavier could say another word, Darren buried his dagger between the man's ribs. "But you don't deserve it."

Xavier's eyes went wide as dark blood trickled down the side of his mouth. Darren removed his dagger and let Xavier slump to the ground before running over to Relaina. He ripped a shred of fabric from his discarded cloak and wrapped it around her middle, trying to stanch the flow of blood. Relaina cried out, reaching for the hilt of the blade again. Darren grabbed her hands gently.

"Don't take it out. I know it hurts, but you could bleed out."

Relaina huffed, her face contorting in pain as she nodded.

"I'm sorry," he said, his voice breaking. "Relaina, I'm so sorry." She blinked at him.

"You..." Her eyes rolled back into her head as she fainted. Darren kept pressure on her wound around the knife, even as shouts ran down the tunnel from the opposite direction. There was a cut on Relaina's arm, too—presumably what had been the source of the blood in her room, but it was far less serious than the wound in her abdomen.

Footsteps thundered closer, and soon Lyneisian guards surrounded them. Two of them came forward for Relaina, following orders from Captain Andovier.

On Darren's right, a wheezing, rasping sound shot fear through his heart.

"Captain," Xavier said. He coughed, blood splattering, and then spoke again, damning Darren with his last breath.

"He...is...the Prince of Terrana."

Xavier's head lolled to the side, and it was only then that Darren felt the man's life slip away, a final untethering. It had been so long since he'd felt death's cold kiss in his chest that he hadn't thought to ensure that Xavier was truly dead. Jeremiah Andovier stared at the dead man and then turned his gaze to Darren, who was still kneeling by Relaina, his hands pressed to her wound.

"Take him," the captain said.

A part of Darren had expected this, had been ready to accept it when he went after Relaina in the passageway. Yet, as three guards came forward with fear and hatred in their eyes, he realized he'd allowed himself to hope for a different reaction, a different outcome.

"Step away from the princess."

Darren didn't move.

"She's bleeding a great deal. Someone needs to keep pressure on her wound."

"I said, *step away*."

"Not until one of you comes to take over." His heart's thundering pace opposed the steadiness of his voice, a fist beating against his ribcage, threatening to expose how afraid he was. But he kept calm outwardly. Begging and weeping did little to sway the decisions of those in power.

The guard that spoke came forward and jabbed him in the sternum with the butt of his spear, and the air whipped out of Darren's lungs as he fell backward. Tears squeezed themselves out of his eyes as one guard rolled him onto his stomach, digging a knee into his spine as they shackled his wrists together. They hauled Darren to his feet to face the captain. He didn't resist.

"Do what he said and put pressure on her wound," Jeremiah Andovier said. "Farrin, Oswold, get her to the healers, quickly." The guards shuffled around to do as they were told. Captain Andovier stepped forward, and Darren blinked the blurriness in his vision away as the man examined him with suspicious curiosity.

"I don't trust you," the captain said.

"You have no reason to."

"Except, perhaps, that you had my nephew inform me that you all were down here. So you're either trustworthy or incredibly foolish."

"Probably both."

"Hmm." The captain studied him further, not amused. "Take him to the king."

Darren fought the impulse to free himself of the guards' grip—it would be useless to try and escape in such a narrow corridor, and he was, despite it all, unwilling to kill them.

They led Darren through the tunnels and the secret passageway, back the way he'd come. King Stephan was already in the throne room when they arrived, his face wild with expectation. Darren suppressed a cry when they forced him to his knees on the cold marble.

"Ease up," Captain Andovier said, his voice low and sharp.

The doors to the throne room shut behind them, and Darren forced himself to breathe as King Stephan looked down at him.

"I've seen you before," the king said, stepping down from the dais. Darren exhaled and let his head fall. "Look at me, boy!"

Breathe. It's not him.

King Stephan was not King Gabriel—Darren wouldn't have been allowed the few extra moments it took him to gather the courage to look up.

Stephan had reddish-brown hair with gray at the roots that matched his shrewd, yet not unkind, gray eyes. He was dressed in exquisite finery, but not as lavishly as Darren's father had always dressed.

"What is your name?"

"Darren."

The jarring sting in his cheek as the king backhanded him *was* reminiscent of his experience with his own father, as was the taste of blood in his mouth.

"Your full name."

Darren spat blood onto the marble. "Darren LaGuarde."

"You admit to this freely?"

"I do. In the hopes that I might speak to you man-to-man, rather than endure pointless torture."

King Stephan smirked, now, all kindness in his eyes gone.

"You're not a man, though. You're a grasping claw of the Tyrant King. Your father has tried for years to have my daughter and heir murdered, and I've had reports that this task was given to none other than you, his son. There is nothing for us to speak on."

Darren's stomach turned.

"I will get the information I require from you." King Stephan turned and walked back up to the dais. "And then I will dispose of you."

The king's words fell on Darren's ears as if he were in a fog, slow and muddled. Darren had endured years of abuse at his father's hands—had even wished for death on some occasions—yet he'd never truly believed he'd be killed.

This, though. This was revenge, justified and swift.

"Take him to the dungeons. And say nothing of any of this until I decide how to move forward."

They lifted Darren to his feet once more and all but dragged him from the room. Darren hardly noticed when they arrived at the first floor of the castle and took a stairwell behind the lift that he'd never seen before. Captain Andovier shadowed them as they descended deeper and deeper, and Darren had to place all of his focus on not allowing the torrent of panic in his chest to rise to the surface. When they reached a door that led to a corridor with no windows, Darren flinched, pulling against the guards' hold on him. One of them elbowed him in the side and he went down. The other grabbed his hair by the roots.

"Enough!" Captain Andovier looked down at Darren, who was panting.

"Please, not there," Darren said. "Not the dark."

Captain Andovier studied him a moment and then looked to his guards.

"One more floor down."

Darren choked down a sob. But when they arrived at the next floor down, moonlight was shining on the floor of the corridor, through barred windows high on the walls. The two guards tossed him into a cell and left him lying on the ground. Captain Andovier stood at the bars, looking at Darren as his two men left.

"I'm sorry," he said, and then he, too, was gone.

Darren grasped at the straw on the hard stone floor, hugged his knees to his chest, and wept.

CHAPTER 7

THE HEIR OF LYNEISIA

Relaina awoke to light. She tried to sit up, but a gentle hand held her down.

"Only a bit longer, child," a quiet, warm voice said. "We cannot heal you properly if you don't remain still."

"Where am I?" It took a moment, but her eyes focused on the woman speaking to her. She had blue eyes as clear as fresh spring water, but some sort of headdress hid the rest of her face. She squinted in a way that made Relaina think she was smiling as she held up a glowing hand.

"Who are you?"

"You're in the Healers' Sanctuary, and my name is Ericka." The healer placed her hand on Relaina's forehead, and some of the fogginess in her brain vanished. "Your uncle sent you here."

"Why? What happened?"

"You were attacked, dear one." Other healers stood around her, their glowing hands mending her injuries. She closed her eyes. Her body ached. "Your uncle and the other guards found you injured in a tunnel. A Terranian assassin was caught trying to flee the scene."

"Xavier? But he's dead..."

"No, no, that wasn't the name. It was—"

"Darren." Relaina's eyes flew open again. She sat up, startling the other healers. Her wet hair fell limply over her shoulders, and she wore only her undergarments. After assessing her abdomen for a moment and finding that her wound had all but disappeared, Relaina looked at the blue-eyed healer to her right. "What happened to him?"

"He was arrested."

"Where is he now?"

"Down in the dungeons, I expect. He's to be executed for what happened in the tunnels."

"*What*? But he helped me!" Relaina looked around at the healers, but they weren't the ones she needed to convince. She leapt off the table and searched frantically around the room for her clothes until she remembered that she'd been wearing a gown that was ripped and covered in blood.

"There are clothes in the chest over there," Ericka said. Relaina started in the direction she'd indicated and stopped short. The entire cavernous room was made of white marble, even the floor. Tall stained-glass windows depicted various forms of Iros, playing the lyre, holding a lily in his hand. In the golden light of the setting sun, rainbow colors danced across the floor. The veiled healers watched her with mild curiosity.

Relaina shook her head to clear it, located the chest, and scrambled over to it, extracting a wad of fabric. It was all healer's garb—loose bone-white shirts with flowing sleeves that tightened after they passed the elbow, dark-blue trousers that stayed on by lacing them at the waist, leather open-toed sandals, and dark blue scarves used to cover their faces. Relaina pulled on the clothes, grumbling to herself about their impracticality and pausing briefly before deciding to put a scarf around her neck for warmth.

"How far is it back to the castle?" she asked the healers as she studied the insignia on the front of her shirt—an island lily embroidered in the same dark blue as the pants and scarf. She adjusted the scarf so it fell over the emblem.

"Not far on horseback," Ericka said. "You should arrive there in an hour."

"How long have I been here?"

"A little over a day."

"A *day*?" Relaina shivered as she pulled on the sandals. "Why so long?"

"Your internal injuries were extensive. We kept you sedated so you wouldn't feel any pain as we healed you."

Relaina barely heard her. "When is the execution supposed to take place?"

"Tomorrow at midday."

Relaina paled.

Darren, the Terranian assassin. Or at least that was the story the masses had heard. Pieces of Darren's exchange with Xavier floated through her mind.

Perhaps you do have that mercilessness your father always thought you lacked.

Dread settled in Relaina's gut. She had to get back to the castle and find out the truth of things.

"If you intend to save him," Ericka said, "I would leave now, and swiftly. We have horses out back."

Relaina nodded. "Thank you."

The Healers' Sanctuary was past the northern edge of Parea, hidden in the mountainous forest that surrounded the Lyneisian capital. Relaina bolted outside into the chilled air, wishing that she had her own warm clothes—it was as if autumn had come overnight. She wasted no time in clambering onto the first horse she reached in the nearby stable and racing off down the forest path. Relaina barely felt the cold as it whipped her cheeks, focusing solely on getting back to the castle while casting glances at the sun, gauging how much time she had and what she was going to do. Did her father know Darren had saved her life? Did everyone know that Xavier had tried to capture and kill her? Did they truly believe Darren was a Terranian assassin? If they did, Relaina was certain they'd spare him no pain in interrogations. Damned fools, all of them.

She arrived at the castle shortly after dark, entering through the deserted western gate. As quietly as she could manage, she dismounted her horse and tied the reins to the wood-rotted, two-horse stable nearby. This side of the castle grounds had been desolate for years—once the northern gate had been built, the western gate was mostly unused.

Relaina only saw two guards as she darted through the shadows toward the castle entrance.

"Relaina?"

Her heart stopped. "Father."

He came to a halt before her in the entrance hall.

"I've been waiting for your return," he said. "I know you must be tired, Relaina, but we need to talk."

Relaina nodded and followed him up the stairs, her heart thumping so loudly in her chest she wondered if her father could hear it.

They entered the king's study on the thirteenth floor, Relaina trying very hard to hide her uneasiness. She waited for him to say something, eager for him to get it over with so she could leave and gather her thoughts.

"I need to know everything that happened in the tunnels," he said, threading his fingers together on the table. "What do you remember from the attack?"

Relaina spoke carefully, trying to ignore her sweaty palms. "Xavier attacked me in my rooms. He brought me down into the secret passageway, but before we'd made it to the city, Darren found us and fought against Xavier."

Her father nodded and mumbled vaguely.

"He was trying to protect me."

The king scoffed. "I'm sure he was. So he could take you back to King Gabriel himself, taking the glory meant for Xavier. I don't know why I ever trusted that man."

"Darren saved my life. When Xavier wounded me, he tried to stop the bleeding. He doesn't deserve to be locked up. He doesn't deserve to die."

"Ah. I feared that this would happen."

"That what would happen?"

"That you would sympathize with him. I know he's part of the crowd you're friendly with in the city. Trust me, Relaina, he is not on our side."

"He isn't working for King Gabriel. He had countless opportunities to kill me or capture me if he wanted to. He tried to warn Bracken and me about Xavier."

"Oh? And how did he know Xavier?"

"I...he said Xavier was an assassin charged with hunting him down after he escaped enslavement." She faltered in her resolve some; she wasn't so sure about the truth of that, but that didn't change the fact that she was certain Darren had not intended to hurt her.

"Be that as it may," the king drummed his fingers on his desk, "he still failed to come forward with the information about Xavier. If he is not here for nefarious reasons, then why would he not immediately inform the royal family of Xavier's identity?"

"Perhaps he was afraid."

The king laughed once without humor. "We shall see. I received word shortly before your arrival that some new information has come to light amidst...interrogations. You should go get some rest, as you'll be expected at the execution proceedings tomorrow."

Relaina paled. "What have you done to him?"

"I've done nothing." The king walked to his fireplace. "But the prison guards have had him since yesterday. I'll be sending a healer down before he dies tomorrow."

Relaina gripped the armrest of her chair, her knuckles going white.

"First Bracken," she said, furious at the lump in her throat. "And now this."

Her father came striding back. She looked up at him from where she sat, disgust plain on her face.

"Gabriel LaGuarde will stop at *nothing* to destroy our family," King Stephan said. "He has sown seeds of betrayal and deceit among us for years. I am only doing what is best for our safety."

Relaina stood. "Bracken has nothing to do with King Gabriel, and you are so blinded by your hatred that you have exiled my dearest friend. He was like a son to you!"

"You're too naïve to know about these things, Relaina."

"I am *not!*" Relaina was shaking, her rage boiling over. "All you see when you look at me is some silly, innocent child who can't think for herself. I pay attention more than you know. I have always taken my birthright seriously and you have *never* acknowledged that. Maybe you think I'm a fool, but believe it or not, I am able to differentiate between authenticity and deception."

Her father's face turned deep red. "You put far too much faith in your own judge of character, Relaina."

"And you're too blinded by your own prejudice to see that Darren, Terranian or not, could be a good person. He saved my life!"

Stephan pounded a fist against the table. "You will not speak to me with such insolence, Relaina. Now sit down and listen to what I say or so help me I will forbid you from leaving not only the castle but your own chambers."

Relaina sat, glowering.

"The execution is commencing tomorrow. And I expect that while you are there you will keep your mouth shut and your emotions under control."

Relaina looked up slowly, her face smoothed over into a glassy mask of apathy, resolve settling into her bones.

"Fine." *I'm going to free him.*

"Good. Now, there *is* one more matter I wish to discuss."

Relaina remained silent, her face devoid of emotion.

"I spoke with the Conclaves. They have assured me that Zarias is still very willing to marry you and take on the responsibility as prince consort, despite the embarrassing display at the Harvest Festival. I'm glad to know you take your birthright seriously, because I told them that we accept this offer. You will be married within the fortnight."

Relaina stared at the wall behind her father's desk.

"I understand." *Go to hell.*

"Good. You may go. I will send for you in the morning when it is time."

Relaina stood from the chair once more and left the room swiftly.

BACK IN HER ROOM, Relaina flitted around, grabbing two cloaks and some old fabric that could be used to bandage wounds if needed, shoved it all down into a bag that went over her shoulder, and changed from the healer's sandals into her leather boots. Despite her earlier disdain for the clothing, she kept the healer's garb on, even pulling her hair back so she could don the face-obscuring scarf as the healers wore it. In the reflection of her mirror, she looked nothing like herself, and that was what she wanted.

She grabbed the sword Jeremiah had given her and the small bag of gold coins stashed in her wardrobe's false bottom. She ruefully fastened it to her belt; she'd intended to take it to the orphanage in the city as she usually did, but now she needed it herself. With one last look at her room, she shut the door, headed for Aronn's chambers. He answered the door after her first knock, and she pulled the scarf down so he could see her face.

"Relaina, when did—?"

"Shh!" She walked inside and shut his door.

"Aronn, listen to me." He looked at her expectantly, and her throat constricted. She bit her lip and stepped away from the door a little.

"I need you to do something for me. Can you get to the city's outer gate without being seen?"

"I...yes."

"Good. I need it opened at midnight."

Aronn stared at her.

"Relaina, what are you going to do?"

She looked him directly in the eye as she said, "I'm going to leave Parea. And before I go, I'm going to free Darren from the dungeons."

"Are you *mad?*"

"I've made my decision."

"You'll be judged a traitor! And then you'll *both* be locked up in the dungeon."

"That's partly why I'm planning on leaving tonight." Relaina's voice broke, her words hanging in the air as Aronn let them sink in. "After tonight, one way or another, I won't be the future queen of Lyneisia. You will be Lyneisia's new heir."

Aronn's face turned white.

"You...you can't...but I—"

Relaina took his shoulders in her hands gently but firmly.

"Listen to me," she said, forcing herself to hold back her tears. "Surround yourself with better friends. You have a mind for strategy and diplomacy, and though you hide it, I know you have a good heart."

Relaina pulled him into an embrace. "I'm not going to tell you where I'm going, but if I can send you a message, I will."

Relaina stepped back and pulled the scarf over her face, so only her eyes were visible. Her brother stood speechless, staring at her as she held out two pieces of folded parchment, which she'd hastily penned back in her rooms only minutes before.

"One of these is for you. Don't let anyone else read it. As for the other, give it to Mother after I'm gone."

Just as she was about to leave, Aronn looked up at her.

"What brought this on?"

Relaina smiled sadly.

"Everything is explained in the note." She now had one hand on the door, steeling herself for what was to come. "Goodbye, Aronn."

She slipped into the dark corridor, leaving her brother standing there, clutching the notes she'd given him. A knot formed in her throat as she glanced down the hallway toward Annalise's chambers, but she turned away and sprinted toward the lift. She couldn't explain all of this to her sister in such a short time, and she couldn't bear to see her face when she found out Relaina was leaving.

Twelve floors below, Relaina entered the underground dungeon after convincing two guards she was there to heal Darren before his trial. She shivered in the dank, chilly air and drew her cloak around her. Down she climbed, until she reached a guarded door. The woman stopped her when she approached.

"What is your business here?"

"The king has sent me to tend to the wounds of the Terranian assassin, so he might look presentable for his execution tomorrow."

"Oh, I thought you wouldn't get here until morning."

Relaina shrugged. "I was in the city already." The guard muttered something under her breath and moved to take out her keys. Relaina tried to stay calm and patient while she fiddled with them, extracted the right one, and led her down the corridor.

There were five cells on this level: the floors above and below held darker, smaller cells that hadn't been used in decades. As Relaina followed the guard inside, angry voices echoed down the hall. She braced herself.

"Last cell," the guard said, and then she turned and strode back to her post. Relaina approached slowly, listening.

"What is your name?"

"You already—"

A dull thud and a terrible cry followed, and Relaina hesitated, swallowing the bile in her throat. The smell of burnt flesh entered her nose, and she nearly retched. She composed herself—only a few more feet until she reached the cell. Fire flickered from within, casting shadows onto the hard, stone floor.

"*What is your name?*" the interrogator demanded again.

Relaina appeared at the bars, and Darren spoke the words that confirmed what she'd suspected since he'd fought Xavier in the tunnels.

"LaGuarde," he said, sweat and tears pouring down his face. "My name is Darren LaGuarde."

Relaina's breath swept from her lungs.

"And *what* are you?"

Darren sobbed. "A former assassin."

"You are *scum*. That is what you are."

Darren's wrists were chained to the ceiling of the cell. A freely bleeding gash went from below his left eye to his ear; his other eye was black and puffy, and there were bruises blossoming all over his arms, his neck, and any other visible surface of his skin. Pieces of bloodstained fabric hung from his arms and waist where his shirt had been ripped open.

"What are you doing here?" one of two interrogators sneered at Relaina, noticing her presence. He stepped up to the cell bars. She tried to keep the trembling from her voice.

"I...I was sent by the king," Relaina said. Darren's dull eyes found hers, and something irreparable snapped inside her.

"Piss off," the other interrogator said. "It's not even midnight, and we haven't finished questioning him." He patted Darren's back, and Darren cried out sharply. Relaina's vision blurred in fury. She spoke through gritted teeth, her voice unwavering.

"Unlock the cell."

He turned to smile at his companion. "Woman, we just told you—"

Relaina grabbed him, yanking the fabric of his collar through the bars, the point of her blade pressed to his spine.

"If you call for help, I will bury this knife in his back," Relaina said, and the guard by Darren paled and nodded. "You're going to answer a few questions first, and then you're going to unlock the fucking cell." The guard at her mercy made a tiny choking sound, and Darren's deadened eyes widened.

"Does the king know of his identity yet?" she asked.

"Y-yes."

Relaina's jaw tightened. "So you've known what his name is for how long?"

"Since before he was sent down."

"And you still tortured him since yesterday?"

"The king told us to just make sure he was presentable by morning."

Relaina looked at Darren, bleeding and bruised with his arms chained above his head.

"Is there to be a change of shift?"

"No."

"Good. Unlock the cell. *Now*."

The other guard scrambled to do so. Relaina slammed the first guard's head into the iron bars and stepped inside, avoiding his slumped form. She bent down and picked up an iron rod that looked as though it had been singed on the end, and the second guard lunged at her. She dodged and swung the iron rod at his head, knocking him out next to his companion.

She pulled the keys out of the door's lock, located the smallest one, and walked behind Darren, wincing when she saw the burns covering his back. She reached up and unlocked the chains. He fell, and she was unable to catch him before he hit the ground. She knelt beside him and pulled out the fabric she'd brought along with her. If she didn't get those burns bandaged, it would be impossible to get him out of here without him passing out from the pain, and she would risk the wounds getting dirty in the passageway. She cursed herself for not asking for healing supplies when she was at the sanctuary.

"I need you to sit up, if you can."

Darren nodded, breathing hard, and sat up slowly, allowing Relaina

to reach the burns on his back. She clenched her teeth and held in a cry
—it looked as though they'd pressed the hot iron rod to his skin. As
carefully as possible, Relaina wrapped the bandages around his torso,
gently covering each burn until she ran out of material. She tied it off at
his side, hoping that it was good enough to last until they could get him
to the healers.

"Can you stand?"

"I can try."

Relaina held out a hand and he took it as he struggled to his feet. As
soon as he was upright, his right knee gave out and Relaina caught him
before he hit the ground again. With great effort she draped his arm over
her shoulders, trying her best to avoid touching the burns, and slowly,
silently, they walked out of the cell. Relaina led him to the opposite end
of the corridor from where she had come. At the end of the hall, they
reached a cold stone wall, and Darren watched as Relaina fidgeted with
the different stones until she found the one that pushed in. It disappeared, and with a scraping sound that made Relaina cringe, the wall
moved aside, and they stepped into the secret passage. Once the wall
moved back into place, Relaina exhaled, thanking the gods that Darren's
cell had been on this level.

"Why are you helping me?" Darren asked, his voice rough.

"I'm getting you out of here." Relaina tried not to show how
much she was struggling under his weight. "Isn't that enough for
now?"

"Who...who are you?"

Relaina took him down a few more steps before answering.

"How disappointing. I thought you'd recognize my voice by now."

Silence. Then—

"Relaina. You...you're healed."

"I am. The healers told me what happened to you."

"And what...do you expect your father...will say about this...daring
rescue?"

"My father can do whatever the hell he likes, as long as he never
speaks to me again."

"Relaina—"

"If you're trying to convince me to take you back there and let you die at the hands of my deluded father, I swear I will knock you out right here and drag you down the rest of these stairs."

"Then what...exactly...is your plan?"

"Well, first," they reached the bottom of the staircase, "I'm taking you to the healers. Once you're able to travel, we are getting the hell out of Lyneisia. You can do what you like from there."

Darren took a while to respond. "We?"

"Do you really think I plan to stay here after freeing the Prince of Terrana? Besides, I recently discovered that I'm to wed Zarias shortly after your execution. So yes, *we* are leaving. With any luck, we can reach the Evarian border before my father's guards catch up to us."

Relaina removed a torch on the right side of the wall. The holster made a clicking sound, and the wall gave way as it had back in the dungeon. They stepped outside into the night air, and Relaina gently set Darren down on a large rock to give them both a reprieve. She looked over the steep slope only a few feet in front of them, catching her breath as she beheld the rocky bank of Lake Alterna, a hundred feet below, and then looked back at the moonlit cliff that rose behind them to meet the foundation of Castle Alterna.

Darren's injuries were even more pronounced outside. It hurt Relaina to watch him struggling to breathe, his entire body sweltering with fever.

"We'll have to get there on horseback," she said, kneeling in front of him. "You ought to ride behind me so nothing touches your back."

Darren nodded, wincing. Relaina helped him stand again.

"Ahead there's a path to the left that leads to the western gate. We need to move."

Darren gritted his teeth and nodded again. Relaina guided him up the path as quickly as possible, Darren clenching his jaw to contain the cries of pain seeking to escape. He was hurting far more than he was letting on, but they both knew that if they slowed their pace and were caught, it was all over.

The narrow, steep path led them away from the cliff and up through a thinly wooded area that smelled of pine trees. Relaina occasionally stopped their progress to listen, to make sure they weren't being watched or followed. Though the guard had said the next shift change didn't happen for another four hours, she was sure her father had other guards walking through to ensure the security of the prince, and Relaina didn't know how much time they had before Darren's absence was discovered.

They stood at the edge of the trees now, looking at the western gate from outside the castle walls. Relaina's eyes darted around, making sure no guards were present.

"Amariah is around the corner in the stables," Relaina said. Darren's face had grown considerably paler, his eyes unfocused. She had to move him quickly. Still supporting most of his weight, Relaina led him forward. The gate was still open, which meant that they hadn't realized Darren was missing yet.

Just as they turned toward the stables, they came face-to-face with a guard, his hand resting on the hilt of his sword, ready to draw it in an instant.

"Who goes there?"

Oh, gods. Relaina took a timid step forward into the moonlight, her eyes wide in appeal. Before she could speak, however, Darren lost consciousness, forcing her to bear all his weight. She staggered, and the man came forward. Relaina looked up at him in desperation.

"Uncle, please…"

Jeremiah looked between her and Darren, his eyes widening.

"Relaina, do you realize what you are doing?"

"I can't let him die, Uncle." Her voice broke on the last word. Leaving Aronn was hard enough, but Jeremiah was the single person that might reason with her to stay, and she couldn't allow that to happen. "If you try and stop me, I'll fight you with everything I have."

Jeremiah stared at her for a few more seconds.

"You would betray your kingdom and family to save the Prince of Terrana?"

It was more complicated than that, but she had no time to explain. "Yes."

Darren's breathing was ragged in her ear as she waited for Jeremiah's response.

"I'll help you get on the horse. But I can promise you no more."

Relaina could have broken down from relief right there, but they weren't out of danger yet. Jeremiah retrieved Amariah and helped Relaina with Darren's unconscious form, seating him in front of her. She removed the healer's scarf from her neck and secured Darren's waist to the horn of the saddle, taking hold of the reins in one hand and holding him firmly to her chest with the other. Blood seeped from the bandages on his back, staining her shirt. Perhaps it was best that he wasn't awake for this journey.

"Thank you, Uncle," she said, her voice catching.

"Get out of here quickly, Relaina. And don't get caught."

Relaina nodded, her face set. With a quick kick to Amariah's side, they were off, racing down the road that cut through the center of the city. Several of the Pareans looked on curiously as they flew past, but they were moving too quickly to be recognized. Just as they reached the edge of Parea, Relaina heard far-off shouts and turned her head. Numerous lights were flaring up in the castle windows. Fires blazed at the two guard towers by the northern gate, signaling a search for an escaped prisoner. The city gate was still shut in the distance. *Come on, Aronn.*

Just as they approached, the portcullis rose, clearing their way to freedom. Relaina sobbed. She sent a silent thanks to her brother and held tightly to Darren as they rode onward, praying for speed as they made for the Healers' Sanctuary.

CHAPTER 8

THE NORTHERN ROAD

By the time they reached the Healers' Sanctuary, the moon was high in the sky, bathing the tall stone structure in eerie light. As soon as Relaina reached the bottom of the steps, a woman appeared outside.

"Ericka," Relaina said as she dismounted, urgency in her eyes. The old woman said nothing, studying Darren for a moment before fetching other healers. Three of them hastened down the steps and helped get Darren off the horse. Relaina started forward to help but stopped— though all three were fairly small women, they weren't struggling under his weight as she had. Relaina followed them inside and watched as they took him to one of several stone tables within the large main room. Ericka stood beside Relaina and placed a hand on her shoulder. A single tear cascaded down Relaina's cheek, but otherwise, her face remained stoic and set, as if carved by stone.

"It will be all right."

Relaina took a shuddering breath. "How long?"

"It's hard to say. We don't know the extent of his injuries. If they are all topical, it will only take a few hours. With my help, maybe sooner. You are welcome to sleep, if you wish."

"I don't think I could if I tried."

"You may remain here then, but you must not interfere while we work."

Relaina nodded and sat in a small wooden chair by a window. The minutes ticked by with painful lethargy, and she watched numbly as they worked to heal Darren, their glowing hands gliding over his numerous injuries. Emotion built inside her like waves, growing and dissipating, for Relaina did not have the energy to hold on to all the rage, hurt, fear, and grief that threatened to swallow her if she dwelled on them for too long.

After a few hours of working, Ericka left the table and came to sit by Relaina.

"He's going to be fine," she said. "Most everything was external, save for the cracked ribs." Relaina's face went bone white. "I healed those and the other minor lacerations, and they're working on those burns now. They will finish soon, and once he wakes, he'll be wholly mended."

Relaina took her hand without looking at her.

"Thank you."

"You two. I sense that you are connected."

Relaina turned to her.

"What do you mean?"

"It's difficult to explain to a non-healer. But when we heal someone, we get a sense of their entire being, and there are certain similarities between the two of you."

Relaina looked over at Darren, an unknown feeling taking root inside of her.

"I don't understand," she said, but when she turned, Ericka was gone.

As dawn approached, Relaina found herself nodding off and forced her tired eyes to stay open. She managed to fall asleep, and when she awoke, the healers had all gone. She rubbed the sleep out of her eyes and walked over to Darren. They'd given him a fresh shirt, a healer's tunic, and he already looked whole, but still resting. Relaina looked down at his sleeping face, frowning. How could he be the son of Gabriel LaGuarde?

She bent down, putting her forehead on the side of the stone table, taking a deep breath and clasping her hands together. Was she a fool to trust him? She had seen him fight Xavier, and he had been arrested trying to protect her. He had even tried to reason with her when she broke him out of the dungeon, tried to ensure her well-being when he was weak and injured and facing the gallows. Relaina lifted her head from the table so she could see him again. His face was troubled, even in sleep.

"This is the Lynx Guard, open up!"

Relaina jumped so violently she slammed her knuckles into the stone, crying out. Darren bolted upright, reaching for a weapon that wasn't there. Ericka, carrying wads of fabric, hastened over to them with speed and agility that did not belong to an old woman.

"There's no time. Put these on."

Relaina and Darren pulled on the healer scarves, adjusting them over their faces as they dashed in the direction Ericka pointed them.

"Open this door!"

Relaina shut the door behind them as they ran into the living quarters, but before she could run straight for the door on the opposite side, one healer approached her.

"We took your horse around back. Take these as well." Through the door behind them, Ericka spoke calmly to the guard at the door.

"Well, I saw two riders headed down the *eastern* road, about two hours ago..."

The healer before them handed Relaina and Darren each an ornate dagger and sheath, and before she had time to utter any kind of gratitude, other healers ushered her and Darren toward the door at the other end, passing beds and water basins and chamber pots as they went. They burst out of the back door and found another healer waiting for them with Amariah and another saddled horse, holding a finger over his scarf to signal them to be as quiet as possible. Relaina vaulted onto Amariah and sped off down the path to the north, Darren not far behind. The forest was dark and cool in the pre-dawn of the morning, the purple sky still littered with stars.

Relaina had no idea where they were headed or how far this path would take them, but she was determined to put as much distance between them and the Lyneisian guards as possible. If the guards had taken the false lead Ericka had given them, that would give Relaina and Darren the extra time they needed to lose them.

IT HAD BEEN a long time since Darren made a distant journey on horseback, and it showed in his aching back and legs. Severe fatigue crept in as the hours passed and the sun climbed higher, and he and Relaina both removed their healer veils as the temperature rose.

"Do you think we'll be safe to take it slow for a while?" Relaina asked as they slowed to a walk, glancing behind them as he rode alongside her.

"Should be." His mouth was so dry he wondered how he'd managed to speak.

"Good." Relaina dismounted and lead Amariah to a nearby stream. Darren did the same with his horse, himself bending to drink. He stared at his cupped palms as he dipped them in the stream for the third time, the water rippling in his shaking hands. He let the water fall and sat back, clutching his knees to his chest as panic shredded his insides. He tried to breathe, tried to calm the trembling, but he couldn't focus on anything but the spiral of dread within.

Relaina spoke, but he didn't comprehend it until she drew closer, sitting beside him. "Can I do something I think will help?"

He closed his eyes and nodded. Relaina wrapped her arms around him from behind, and he reached to grasp her forearm as she squeezed him across his chest. Some of the turmoil subsided at her touch, and for a minute or two they remained there as Darren found his way back to clarity.

"Better?"

"Yes," he said, his heart slow and steady again. Relaina released him and moved a safe distance away. "How did you do that?"

"I used to have episodes like that as a child. The pressure of someone's arms around my chest and back always helped."

Darren exhaled. "Thank you."

"Before we go on, I need you to answer some questions."

Part of him ached to run, to flee and hide before she could ask him anything. But she gazed at him now with determination, not hatred, and answering her questions was the least he could do. He nodded.

"You are the Prince of Terrana."

"Yes."

"When did you leave Terrana?"

"Three years ago."

"Why?"

"That...is a long story."

"Shorten it."

Darren sighed.

"King Gabriel is every bit the monster the world believes him to be, and more," Darren said. He couldn't hold her gaze, so he looked at his hands. "He keeps a highly trained group of assassins in the city of Lues, any of them ready to travel anywhere in Esran to do his bidding. They are shadows...many of them are...well, I'll get to that later. The Terranian Elite are the deadliest assassins in Esran, and my father forced me to become one of them."

"And Xavier was one of them?"

"Yes."

"How early did you begin your training?"

"I was eight." He met Relaina's eyes again, and her horrified expression was oddly comforting.

"How did you escape?"

"I broke out of the catacombs beneath the Obsidian Keep and took a horse before anyone noticed. Archers caught up to me and I was shot about four times but escaped over a cliff into the Inmedio. I was found downriver by villagers who didn't recognize me, and they took me in until my injuries healed. My father sent two assassins after me. Xavier caught up with me months later, and I injured him badly enough that he lost my trail. I heard the other assassin was killed out of vengeance."

Relaina stood, looking at the trees on the other side of the stream. A chill breeze sent her flyaway curls dancing around her face.

"And how do I know you're telling me the truth?"

"You don't."

Relaina returned his gaze. Her hand shifted toward the dagger the healers had given her, and Darren's mouth twitched.

"I'd advise against that."

She scowled. "Oh?"

"If the last time we fought was any indication, you'd be on the ground before your fingers closed around the hilt."

Relaina rolled her eyes and went to retrieve a canteen from her saddlebag. "A suggestion for earning my trust: don't threaten me."

"Don't you think I would've killed you by now if I were going to?"

"I don't know. I can't read your mind."

"Then why did you rescue me?"

Relaina stopped as she braced herself to mount up again. She looked back at him.

"Because it felt like the right thing to do."

They were both quiet for a while as they returned to the path, horses watered and reenergized. Darren had never appreciated the smell of the forest, of pine trees and earth, so much as he did now. It was the smell of freedom, and riding beside him was a woman who'd given him that freedom...a woman who found him insufferable one moment and likable the next.

Surely the gods were mocking him.

"What happened in the tunnels?" Relaina asked, drawing him out of his reverie. "After I passed out."

As Darren explained, her frown deepened.

"Why not just fight your way out?"

"What?"

"I've fought you. I saw the way you fought Xavier. You could've killed those guards easily."

Darren's hands began trembling again. "I'm not a monster."

"You killed Xavier."

"He was trying to kill you. And he's killed countless others."

"And you haven't?"

Darren stopped his horse, and Relaina mirrored him, startled. "What I did under the influence of my father haunts me every fucking day of my life. If you are so determined to paint me as a villain in all of this, then you should have saved us all some trouble and let your father kill me."

He pushed onward, his palms sweaty and his pulse racing. He was so tired. Would he ever be able to defend himself without part of him feeling like he deserved the scorn of others?

"Thank you."

The shift in her voice brought him back to the present. She shifted in her saddle, her mouth twisting.

"For saving my life," she finished.

Darren blinked, staring at the trees ahead, and nodded.

Another hour passed, and the sun shone from directly overhead. Their path cut through the heart of the forest and between sheer walls of stone, shielding them from its light.

"No one has ever come to my rescue before," Darren said. Relaina looked at him. "Thank you for beating the hell out of those guards and saving my life."

She smiled grimly. "They deserved it."

They lapsed back into silence as their horses carried on down the mountain path.

"Oh!" Relaina's outburst made him nearly leap out of his saddle. "I've just remembered my mother grew up as a ward in Maremer, and that's where they've taken Bracken."

"Maremer? Why would Bracken be in the Evarian capital?"

Relaina's face fell. "He was sent there to live in exile under the charge of King Fabian."

"What? Why?"

"He admitted to trying to thwart the hunt for the pr—for you. He was also accused of selling my family's secrets to King Gabriel, but I knew the evidence was unreliable and proved that it wasn't enough to execute him. For my father, though, it wasn't enough to acquit him. The people in the Hall of Judgment were not pleased with me for robbing them of their macabre entertainment."

"No, I expect they weren't. Not when he was accused of such treason. What was the evidence against him?"

"Letters with his signature. It was clearly forged. I read those letters, and they certainly had information that only someone living in the castle would have, but Bracken would never sell my family out to King Gabriel."

"Well, if nothing else, you've saved two lives in the past four days."

Relaina's mouth morphed into a small smile. "I suppose that's something worth celebrating. Though we aren't in the clear yet. I won't feel at ease until we've crossed the border into Evaria."

For the rest of the day, they alternated taking the path at a slow pace and galloping. They were still in the heart of the mountains, and the northern road was almost devoid of villages or cities. Once or twice, it branched off in different directions, but the main path remained wide, and they kept north by stealing glances at the sun whenever the trees thinned. Relaina constantly looked over her shoulder, worried they would encounter other travelers.

"Even if we do," Darren said when she voiced this concern, "it's highly unlikely that they'd recognize either of us. We're both dressed as healers."

When dusk fell, they found a small clearing a little way off the path and settled down for the night, tying their horses to low tree branches so they could graze. Relaina helped him get a fire started so they would be warm, gathering kindling twigs and watching with curiosity as he used two of them to create enough friction that a glowing ember appeared. It was a modest but adequate fire, offering a decent amount of warmth. The autumn snows would begin in the highlands of Lyneisia in a week or so, and Darren said a silent prayer of thanks that they wouldn't have to travel in that weather.

A few hours later, Darren was dozing against a fallen tree, one of the cloaks Relaina had brought pulled around him for extra warmth. Each time he opened his eyes Relaina was in the same place, seated before the fire. She shivered in the chilly night air and drew her own cloak around her, gazing up at the star-smattered sky.

"Can't sleep?" Darren asked, sitting down beside her.

"Especially not now."

Darren bit his tongue—her petty venom was somehow soothing after the events of the past two days. "You know, I'm trying to be friendly."

Relaina sighed. "We don't have to be friends."

"You quite literally hugged me out of a nervous episode earlier. We're definitely friends."

Warmth crept through him as Relaina struggled not to smile. Her tongue was sharp, but that gods-damned smile.

"How much farther is it to the Lyneisian border?"

Darren cleared his throat, kicking himself mentally. "I can't say for sure. But we've probably got at least two more days ahead of us."

Relaina groaned.

"Oh, don't be such a princess."

"Remember that you have to sleep near me."

"Is that a threat?"

"That's up for interpretation."

Darren laughed and settled down right where he was, on a soft patch of grass by the fire. After a moment of consideration, Relaina lay down beside him. She shivered as a breeze passed through the clearing, her teeth chattering. Darren propped himself up on his elbow.

"Are you cold?"

Relaina looked over her shoulder.

"A little. But I'll be fine. We don't have any other cloaks."

"You can move closer to me, if you want. I don't mind."

He settled down again, facing away from her, and hoped he hadn't made her uncomfortable. His heart picked up speed as she shifted closer to him until her back was against his. He stared at the dark forest from the ground, awestruck by this pleasant internal warmth that had nothing to do with the fire.

RELAINA'S EYES FLEW OPEN, her instincts pulling her violently out of her deep slumber. Darren was asleep behind her, his back moving against hers with steady, slow breathing, but something wasn't right. She sat up, looking toward the forest path. A small, blurry ball of light, a lantern perhaps, bobbed around. Voices drifted over from the light.

"We are not stealing from innocent travelers!" said a treble voice.

"But they can't catch us if they don't have horses," said another voice, deep and rough.

"We have a cart."

"With another horse we'd make it out of here much faster. The

Lynx Guard won't be more than a few hours behind us, and even though they aren't after us, they could easily decide to take us back to Parea with them for interrogation."

"But we didn't even help the prince escape!"

"It doesn't matter. They'll be suspicious of anyone leaving Parea at a time like this."

As they continued their argument, Relaina got up and quietly shook Darren awake. By the path stood two silhouettes and a horse-drawn cart with a lantern attached to the side. Relaina approached the clearing's edge, unafraid that they would see her. She'd be damned if she and Darren got caught by the Lynx Guard because two travelers stole their horses in the night, and she'd gut anyone that tried to take Amariah anyway. Taking a deep breath, she reached for the knife she'd shoved into her boot back at the castle, then hid behind a tree just off the main path. Darren darted behind a tree on her left, listening.

"Would you rather inconvenience a couple of travelers or get caught by the Lynx Guard?"

"They could die out here if we rob them of their only means of travel!"

"Walking is certainly an option."

"We are *trying* to get out of here without getting into trouble." Now that they were closer, Relaina thought she sounded oddly familiar. "And stealing two well-bred horses is not the way to remain undetected. What if they're important people?"

"Important people wouldn't sleep in the woods."

Relaina looked to Darren, ready to end the argument herself. He nodded and they both dashed out, grabbing them from behind. Relaina held the knife up to the man's throat and Darren wrapped his arm around the woman's neck. She and Relaina locked eyes at the same time.

"Relaina?"

"Jacquelyn?"

Darren released her. "Wha—what are you doing out here?" Jacquelyn asked.

"Oi! Jacquelyn! I have a knife at my throat!"

Relaina released her captive, and he staggered away, moving to stand by Jacquelyn. He was of average height and lean, with short red hair and eyes the same dark brown as Jacquelyn's. His most distinguishing feature, however, was the scar on his face that went from his left temple across the bridge of his nose to the right side of his chin. Both of them sported numerous freckles that peppered their fair skin, visible even in the lantern light.

"Fancy seeing you here, Darren," said the man with the scar. "Thought you were still back in Parea."

"Not exactly," Darren said, grimacing.

"Are you Jacquelyn's brother?" Relaina asked. Jacquelyn had mentioned him a few times, but he worked the night shift on the aqueducts and hadn't made an appearance in city gatherings while Relaina was present.

"I am. My name is Connor. How do you do?" he asked, his scar splitting as he grinned.

"Where are you two headed?" Relaina asked.

"We're trying to get to Evaria," Jacquelyn said, her voice a little thick. "To be close to Bracken. We weren't sure when to leave, but then the news came of the prince's escape, and we figured what with all the chaos that our absence wouldn't be noticed."

Relaina studied her in the lamplight, her red hair giving off the illusion of fire. Even in her tired state she was striking.

"Wait, wait, wait," Connor said. "So...you're Princess Relaina?"

Relaina looked at him. "Yes."

"But why would you be out here? With the Terranian prince on the loose, isn't that a bit dangerous?" Jacquelyn asked. Relaina raised her eyebrows and stared at her, and Jacquelyn looked to Darren, then back to Relaina, her quizzical expression slowly morphing into understanding. Her mouth fell open and she looked back and forth between the two of them a few more times before she spoke.

"You? But...no. *How*?"

"Long story," Darren said. "Which I've already recounted once today." Behind Jacquelyn, Connor gawked at him, catching on.

"So...so you're...?"

"Darren LaGuarde."

Jacquelyn was the first to recover.

"I suppose that means you're the two riders that people saw galloping through the streets last night?"

Relaina nodded. "When did you two leave Parea?"

"A few hours after the announcement had been made that the Prince of Terrana had escaped," Jacquelyn said. "Connor works at the aqueducts on the mountain when they need repair, and news travels fast there—it was common knowledge that the prince escaped with the aid of some girl by the time we left. No one suspected it was you, though."

Relaina contemplated for a moment and decided that it didn't matter if or when people found out that she'd freed Darren LaGuarde. From the sound of it, most people didn't even know the prince's name, much less that it was the Darren they all knew from Parea. Perhaps they had been planning to expose his identity at the execution. That she'd robbed them of such a dramatic reveal gave Relaina no shortage of vindictive satisfaction.

"Do you have weapons?" she asked.

"I have a couple of swords and a spear," Connor said. "Oh, and a bow as well, though neither of us are that good of a shot."

"I am," Darren and Relaina said together.

Connor grinned. "Excellent."

"You take it," Relaina said, nodding to Darren. "I've got my sword."

Connor walked over to the empty cart, and after struggling for a moment he pulled up the wood on the floor, revealing a secret compartment. He tossed Darren a quiver of arrows and a bow made from dark cherry wood. Darren plucked the bowstring to test its tautness and slung the quiver over his shoulder. Jacquelyn took the spear.

"Interesting weapon of choice," Relaina said, impressed. She'd never been able to get used to a spear.

"My father is a fisherman."

"Our father didn't teach you how to *fish* with that."

"You said the Lynx Guard wasn't terribly far behind you," Relaina said, her mind on the pressing matter at hand. "If that's the case, we need to move."

"Indeed, we do," Connor said. Jacquelyn looked at him, paused, and shoved him with one hand.

"You see? They *were* important people! How would you feel if you'd been responsible for their capture?"

Connor scratched the back of his head. "Right. Sorry about almost stealing your horses. I got a bit carried away with trying to get out of here as quickly as possible."

"Just don't try it again, or next time I won't be so forgiving," Relaina said, grinning. Jacquelyn laughed.

"I'd tread lightly, Connor."

Once all of them were satisfied with their weapons—Relaina still had her sword at her hip, plus the dagger the healers had given her—they prepared to depart. They agreed that it would be safer traveling together. Darren walked toward his horse, and Jacquelyn opted to ride in the cart. Relaina mounted her horse and let Darren take the lead, since he was the only one out of them all who'd traveled this road before. Relaina rode beside Connor, whose face was thrown into relief by the lantern on the cart. It made his scar all the more pronounced.

"I'll tell you the story about it," Connor said, gesturing to the scar. "If you tell me why you freed Darren LaGuarde."

Relaina appraised him, embarrassed that he'd caught her staring at his face but intrigued by his forwardness.

"He didn't deserve to be imprisoned," she said. "I decided to take matters into my own hands."

"That's noble of you. And from what I hear, your actions at Bracken's trial were noble as well. I thought Jacquelyn was going to pass out while we waited for the news, but she agreed that staying away from the trial was the right decision. Jacquelyn might not tell you this herself, but she will be forever grateful to you for saving Bracken's life. I don't know what she'd have done if they'd hanged him."

"I don't know what I'd have done either."

They were both quiet for a moment.

"Climbing accident."

"What?"

"The scar. I was about ten, and my father, Jacquelyn, and I were climbing up to one of the fishing ponds we used to go to. It's in a remote location in the mountains south of Parea. It was a weeklong trek, and halfway there, I stepped onto a loose bit of rock and fell quite a ways onto a small ledge below us. Tore my face up, broken bones. My father rushed me to a nearby village to find a healer. She was a novice so the scar never fully faded, but it weren't for that woman, I'd be dead."

Relaina shuddered. "That had to be terrifying."

Connor shrugged.

"More so for my family than myself. I was unconscious for the most part, and I was a fearless bastard back then."

From the back of the cart, Jacquelyn called, "You're still a fearless bastard!"

Relaina laughed as Connor yelled something sarcastic back at his sister, but a strange ache built in her chest. Aronn had made some poor decisions, complicit in his friends' treatment of her, but she still missed him. She pushed her horse forward so she was riding just behind Darren and didn't speak for the remainder of the night. The sky lightened by infinitesimal degrees, heralding the dawn. Relaina's mind drifted back to her conversation with Annalise just before the Harvest Festival.

...the sky in the early morning, before dawn breaks...

Regret pooled in the pit of her stomach. Regret that she'd left her sister and brother, regret that she'd been unable to protect Bracken, and frustration that she hadn't known from the beginning who Darren was. Perhaps then she could've avoided all of this—Bracken's exile, Xavier's attempt to capture her, and Darren's imprisonment.

But even so, she had saved Bracken's life, and Darren's. And that was worth something.

The day waned as they traveled along the forest road, everyone taking turns napping in the cart. The temperature climbed as they went, which, if nothing else, indicated they were making progress. Relaina wondered if they would ever get out of the forest.

"It does end," Darren said. "The trees start thinning out and before you know it, they're gone entirely, and right ahead is the Granica River."

"The border. Thank the gods."

"Since we aren't having to stop as much to sleep now, we should get there very soon."

Relaina looked at Darren from where she sat in the cart. She'd intended to let Jacquelyn ride Amariah, but the finicky horse resisted, wanting to stay nearer to Relaina, and only allowed Darren into her saddle. Relaina could have sworn that Amariah looked rather pleased with herself as she trotted along.

"I've never seen the Granica," Relaina said, yawning. "I've seen a small portion of the Inmedio around Barleo, but that's it."

"Have you ever seen the Great Sea?"

"Once, from a distance. But even from there, it was beautiful. I've always had a sort of fascination with water."

"Not surprising, considering you grew up around those massive aqueducts in Parea."

"Mm." Relaina's eyelids drooped. As soon as she lay down flat, she slipped into unconsciousness.

They collectively decided against stopping that night since they were all taking shifts to sleep, but the next night they were all so fatigued that they decided to camp in a clearing. They had put a reasonable enough distance behind them that Relaina's concerns were minimal.

Relaina, though tired, sat with her back against a tree at the edge of the clearing, watching the dying fire crackle as the others slept. Connor and Jacquelyn slumbered by the cart, snoring steadily. Darren was closer to Relaina, just a few feet away on the soft grass. She'd gotten some sleep during the daytime, but it was fitful and plagued by nightmares. She didn't remember them when she awoke, but a gut-wrenching fear gripped her for a few seconds whenever she opened her eyes. Her eyes were dry and heavy now, and knowing she ought to at least try and sleep, she moved to the grassier area. Darren sat up, startling her.

"Have you slept?"

"No."

"Neither have I."

Relaina could think of nothing to say, and Darren didn't try to break the silence. They both stared into the fire for a while until Relaina lay down and closed her eyes.

"Relaina?"

She looked over her shoulder at him.

"You don't have to be afraid of me." Shadows danced across his face in the firelight.

"I'm not afraid of you, Darren LaGuarde."

And it was the truth, she realized, as she closed her eyes once more.

CHAPTER 9

THE GRANICA RIVER

The morning dawned crisp and chilly, but not so cold as it would have been back in the mountains. The Granica River border was close now, and soon they would reach Evaria and be out of the realm where Lyneisian soldiers could lawfully arrest them.

This agreement between the three kingdoms had always seemed strange to Darren. Preventing cross-border extradition had created some hostility in the past when certain criminals had crossed into another kingdom, but he had been thankful for it the past three years as he did his best to avoid capture himself. It hadn't prevented Gabriel's assassins from pursuing him, but as far as he knew, neither King Fabian nor King Stephan had any intention of delivering him back to Terrana. King Stephan simply wanted to kill him.

Darren could only hope that King Fabian would continue to abide by this agreement and not give him or Relaina up to King Stephan. He glanced her way as they rode on, taking it slowly for the time being, and caught her staring at him. Relaina looked away quickly, studying a random tree with great interest, and that same warmth he'd felt that first night in the clearing filled his chest.

"How much farther is it?" Connor asked from behind. He sat on the front of the cart while Jacquelyn rode comfortably inside.

"We should make the border in about an hour," Darren said.

"Excellent," Connor said, stretching. "And then we'll be able to stay in an inn and eat some real food on our way to Maremer."

Relaina's stomach growled audibly, and Darren smirked.

"Hungry?"

"I'm fine," Relaina said, cheeks flushing.

"It's all right. When you're used to three meals a day, traveling like this can be difficult."

"I don't want to complain."

Darren patted his horse's neck and gazed at the path ahead. "Complain all you want. Eating gamey rabbits is fucking awful."

"Agreed!" Connor said. "Hunt us a boar, Darren, for Iros's sake!"

Relaina giggled, and Darren grinned in return.

The trees around them began to thin, and the path led out of the forest. Before them was open land, sweeping plains of tall grass that stretched for miles on either side and would soon lead them to the Granica.

"How wide is the river?" Relaina asked.

"Too wide to swim," Darren said. "But the northern road leads directly to the West Bridge. It shouldn't be too far from here."

They trudged on, Darren keeping an eye out for a glimmer of sunlight on the river. The day grew warmer as the sun climbed higher in the sky, allowing them to shed their cloaks and toss them into the cart. Darren inhaled slowly, taking in their surroundings with an air of calm he hadn't felt in weeks. The sky was deep blue, the grass around them swayed lazily in the breeze, and in a matter of minutes, they would catch a glimpse of the Granica River.

"I see it!" Relaina called out. With bright excitement in her eyes, Relaina looked at Darren and then kicked her horse, galloping for the bank. Darren took off after her. Moments later they were neck and neck, racing to the river, and Relaina turned her head and smirked at him. She spurred Amariah onward and flew past him once more, barreling toward the riverbank. Before either of them could slow down, their horses went hurtling into the river's shallow edge. Relaina dismounted, knee-deep in the water by the bank and gazing out at the shimmering blue before them. Darren followed and, propelled by playful impulse, splashed Relaina with a considerable amount of water. He gazed nonchalantly in the opposite direction as Relaina glared at him, mouth agape. She splashed him back, soaking him through, and Darren laughed as Relaina tackled him, sending them both careening into the riverbed.

"You bastard," she said, laughing.

They grappled for a moment, disrupting the gravel and mud, but froze when they heard urgent shouting from behind them. Connor and Jacquelyn rode to them with incredible speed. The horse that had been attached to the cart now carried the two of them toward the river, with no cart in sight.

"Five members of the Lyneisian Guard!" Connor said. Jacquelyn was pale and tearful behind him. Relaina released her grip on Darren's arm, and they mounted their horses, scanning the field. The five guards surrounded the cart only a small distance away. At least three of them were already headed toward the river.

"Head west," Darren said. "Toward the bridge."

They rode onto the bank once again and raced parallel to the river, pushing their horses as fast as they could go. Darren chanced a glance over his shoulder at the Lyneisian soldiers. They were still far behind them across the large expanse of open field, but they were slowly gaining speed.

"They're going to catch up to us!" Relaina said. Darren glanced between her and Connor and Jacquelyn, took a steeling breath, and veered to the left, turning his horse around and halting it. He pulled out his borrowed bow and nocked an arrow into place.

"You two ride ahead and find the bridge!" Relaina said, turning around as well. "We'll catch up to you!"

Darren took aim and fired, sending one man sprawling into the grass as his horse reared and cantered off in the opposite direction, the arrow in its left flank. Relaina appeared in Darren's periphery, sword drawn. He took aim again as the soldiers continued to approach at an alarming speed and loosed another arrow. It ricocheted off a soldier's chest armor but hit him with enough force that he went flying off his horse.

"Try not to shoot me." Relaina raced off before he had time to protest. She met them head on, using the flat side of her sword to knock one to the ground. The guard stood up and drew his sword as Relaina wheeled around and dismounted. Darren trained his arrow on him, ready to shoot in an instant, but then the soldier whose horse he'd shot appeared out of the grass behind her, yelling something unintelligible. Darren's next arrow lodged itself in his shoulder.

"Argghh!"

Darren kicked his horse into motion and rode up behind Relaina, another arrow aimed at the guard in warning. Relaina turned her attention to the other man, who looked terrified at her approach but stood his ground. Darren's grip tightened on the bow, almost firing the arrow, but Relaina brandished her sword and he held steady, ready to help if she needed it. She lunged at the guard, her sword clashing with his, the sound echoing in Darren's bones as he watched from horseback. Her apparent adeptness at fighting was impressive, but he couldn't fully ignore the pangs of fear each time the guard nearly landed a hit. But his worry was short-lived. Relaina disarmed the guard quickly and grabbed him by the front of his armor.

"You and your fellows are going to ride back to Parea and tell my father that I'm in Evaria. Tell him that he has lost any hope of earning my forgiveness."

She threw the soldier away from her, and he scrambled on the ground, retrieving his sword. Darren lowered his bow as the other man tried to get up and failed, clutching at his shoulder. Relaina sheathed her sword and mounted her horse again.

"Are you hurt?" he asked, and Relaina shook her head. Connor and Jacquelyn were waiting ahead of them by a long stone bridge that led across the river. Relaina led Amariah to one of the other horses, who was drinking by the river's edge, and took the beast's reins, calling Connor and Jacquelyn over.

"Now we each have a horse," Relaina said, and Jacquelyn dismounted quickly, nodding her thanks as she climbed onto the guard's horse.

"Shit, we need to move," Darren said. Yet another guard appeared, galloping in the direction his fallen comrades indicated. Relaina cursed.

They all took off, their horses' hooves clacking on the stone beneath them. The bridge was narrow and forced them to cross one after the other. Relaina somehow ended up at the back, and as Darren reached the other side, he whipped around just in time to see the guard's horse and Amariah stumble over one another and go tumbling off the side of the bridge.

Time halted as Darren gazed in horror at the place where they'd disappeared into the river, but moments later air rushed into his lungs as Relaina broke the surface again, shortly followed by Amariah and the guard's horse.

The guard flailed as his horse swam for the opposite bank. Relaina swam to meet him, dragging him along by the sleeve on his leather armor. Darren scrambled down from his horse and followed their progress as Relaina, struggling under the guard's weight, made her way to Amariah. Relaina grabbed her mane while the mare swam toward the Evarian border, her strong legs pulling them out of the current. Jacquelyn and Connor rode up behind Darren as he helped Relaina drag the guard out of the water, dropping his limp form to the muddy bank. Relaina slumped to the ground, breathing heavily.

"I'm fine," she said, trying to catch her breath. Darren could only stare at her, rattled by how terrified he'd been those few moments she'd vanished beneath the water. She closed her eyes, exhaling slowly, and then sat up. With another reassuring glance at Darren, she got back on her horse, still dripping wet, and Darren followed suit.

"Let's get out of here," Connor said, his voice hard. When Darren looked back as they rode off, the guard Relaina had saved from the river was staring after them.

ARONN'S FATHER paced in front of the fire on the seventh floor of Castle Alterna, bristling, while his mother sat in one of the plush blue chairs. Christine was exhausted and clearly wanted nothing more than to sleep, but Aronn knew she would wait until they heard news of Relaina. He also knew that his father wanted nothing more than for a guard to burst into this room with Relaina and the Terranian prince in tow.

Someone knocked, and they all froze.

"Come in," Christine said. The doors opened and Jeremiah entered.

"I have news of Relaina, Your Grace. Four of the soldiers from the band you sent have returned."

"Four? I thought we sent out five."

"One is gravely injured, I'm afraid." The king stared at Jeremiah.

"Send them in."

Two soldiers entered the room as Jeremiah left, both bowing to the king, queen, and prince. The larger of the two spoke first.

"We caught up with them right at the border, Your Majesty. They were traveling with two villagers from Parea. I tried to stop them from crossing the border, but the princess and I fell from the bridge into the river. I lost them as they rode into Evaria."

King Stephan looked to the other man.

"Would you care to explain how five members of the Lynx Guard were defeated by a twenty-year-old girl, a farmhand, and two common villagers?"

"Strictly speaking, he isn't a farmhand, Your Grace—"

"Answer the question."

"We were pursuing them on horseback when the prince doubled back and started firing arrows. He injured Samet's horse and shot Trystan right off his. The princess rode to meet us as well and knocked me from my horse. She attacked me and I...surrendered." The guard cleared his throat. "Your daughter told me to pass on a message. To you, Your Grace."

"And?"

"She said to tell you that...that she is in Evaria, and that you've lost any chance of earning her f-forgiveness."

Stephan turned away from him, his nostrils flaring. Aronn and his mother could sense the imminent eruption.

"Stephan, let us speak alone," his mother said, her quiet voice cutting. The king glanced at her, considering, and nodded stiffly.

"Leave us," Stephan said.

There was a quick shuffling of feet, and then the guards were gone.

"Stephan," Christine said, approaching her husband and placing a hand on his face. "You have already asked one favor of King Fabian—

you have no power in Evaria. Relaina is gone. Despite your best efforts to stop her, she has managed to evade you. You cannot chase her all over Esran."

"This isn't about Relaina," Stephan said, shrugging off his wife's hand and turning to pace some more. "This is about justice for what has happened."

"I thought the whole purpose of this hunt for the Terranian prince was to ensure Relaina's safety." Aronn blinked at his mother's tone. "His capture proved fruitless."

"Her safety? She is *with* the prince now, who has seriously injured one of my best men, and you think she's *safe*? The very thing we've fought against for all these years has come to pass!"

Aronn's brow furrowed. "What are you talking about?"

His parents didn't hear him, still arguing.

"This is all your brother's fault. If he hadn't been training Relaina in combat—"

"Don't you *dare* blame Jeremiah for this."

"I'll blame whoever I want—"

"This is *your* fault, and no one else's," Aronn said, and both of his parents turned to look at him. Aronn focused on his mother. "Did he tell you he was going to force her into marriage as punishment before the fortnight was out?"

Christine's eyes widened with a fury he'd seldom seen his mother wield.

"Marriage to *whom*?"

"Zarias Conclave," Aronn said for his father. Christine blinked.

"Who *are* you, Stephan?" She walked around him, headed for the door. Just before leaving, she turned to face the king again. "Relaina saw an injustice and sought to fix it, to fight for what she thought was right. You once did the same."

The king had no response. The queen exhaled and swept from the room, allowing the door to slam behind her.

CHAPTER 10

THE HAPPY STUMP

"Are you sure about this place?" Jacquelyn asked.

The inn was small and a little dingy, but it was the only one they'd come across in two days, and Darren was as desperate as the rest of them to sleep in a bed. It was settled in a tiny village by a small brook, the sign above the door swinging and creaking, reading, "The Happy Stump."

"If you want to stay outside while we get cozy rooms, be my guest," Connor said, riding for the stable. Jacquelyn sighed and hurried after him.

Relaina and Darren followed them silently. Relaina had been distant since they'd crossed the Granica, hardly speaking to anyone, and Darren hadn't had a chance to privately check on her. Jacquelyn and Connor, on the other hand, had been exceedingly talkative since the guards' attack. Perhaps tonight Darren would have a chance to speak to Relaina uninterrupted by the others.

As soon as they walked through the doors, they were enveloped by warmth and the smell of freshly baked bread. There were a few travelers at the tables in the dining area, but most were quiet as they ate their food, speaking in hushed voices amongst themselves. Connor led the way up to the innkeep's counter. Relaina and Darren both had their healer veils pulled in front of their faces, though Darren suspected they were attracting more stares than they would have if they'd been in normal attire.

"Evening," Connor said to the wizened innkeep. "What rooms do you have available?"

"Got two rooms left," the old man said, rather louder than necessary. "Let's see here, this one's more expensive, see, it's got a bathing room and all."

"Perfect, we'll take them." Connor thumped the counter, and Relaina handed over a gold coin from her bag. "Will this cover the rooms and a hot meal for all of us?"

"Oh, yes." The innkeep's old eyes grew wide as he snatched the coin from Connor's fingers. "Is there anything else I can do for you lot?"

"Just make sure our horses don't get stolen. We've got four in the stable."

"Ah, of course." The man squeezed the gold coin in his small fist; Darren had the distinct impression that if anyone tried to pry it open, they would be unsuccessful. Relaina pulled out another gold coin.

"Could you also have some fresh clothes brought into the rooms? And hot baths drawn?" It was the first full sentence she'd spoken in two days. The old man's eyes nearly popped out of his skull as he swiped the second coin out of her hand.

"Most certainly, miss! Glad to be of service."

Connor took the keys the old man handed him and gave one to Relaina.

"We're both on the second floor," Connor said. The second floor was, as it happened, the highest floor. They walked up the stairs and took a left, wooden planks creaking beneath their feet, and found that their rooms were right beside one another. Relaina unlocked the door, and Darren felt all the blood rush to his face.

There was only one bed in this room.

Relaina pushed past Darren, putting her bag and sword down on the bed before removing the scarf from her face, appearing wholly unbothered by the sleeping arrangements. Her eyes were unfocused as she sat and faced the door.

"I know this is a stupid question," Darren said, and she looked up at him. "But are you all right?"

Relaina blinked once.

"You're right. That is a stupid question."

Her response cut him more than he expected, and Darren fought the urge to snap at her, taking a deep breath as he removed his own healer's veil.

"All right, I'll stop bothering you with my presence."

"I have a lot on my mind right now."

"We *all* have a lot on our minds right now, Relaina. Connor and Jacquelyn had no idea what they were getting into by joining us; I'm still recovering from the fact that I killed someone after swearing an oath to never do that again and nearly being executed myself. And you've freed the second-most-hated man in Esran and abandoned your home all in one fell swoop. It's all shit, and we're all an absolute mess, but that's just it—*all* of us are a wreck right now. Fucking gods, just cut my heart out right here if you're going to keep snapping at me for existing nearby."

He breathed heavily as Relaina stared at him, the sides of her mouth twitching.

"Are you done?" she asked, suppressed laughter in her voice.

Darren exhaled. "I think so."

"No one's ever talked to me like that before."

Cold shame washed over him, the fire fizzling out.

"I'm sorry. You do need to take some time to process what's happened, and that's fine. But...just don't forget that we're all doing the same thing, and you biting my head off isn't fair."

"Drinks!" Connor burst into the room, carrying a large mug overflowing with wine, his arm around a blushing tavern girl holding a pile of fresh clothes. Jacquelyn was behind them, fingers pinching the bridge of her nose. "Evarian wine is the best in Esran, I'm telling you. Oh—sorry, am I interrupting something?"

"No," Darren said, looking at Relaina. She gazed back at him unflinchingly.

"Well come on, then, you two," Connor said, grabbing the clothes from the tavern girl and tossing them to Relaina and Darren. "There's two bathing rooms on this floor in addition to the one you have in here. So, wash up, get dressed, and let's go drink, eat, and drink some more."

Connor, with the blushing tavern girl and irritated Jacquelyn, left the room. Relaina frowned after them.

"You can use the bathing room in here," Darren said. "I'll go to the shared one."

After scrubbing himself clean with the lavender soap the inn provided, Darren climbed out of the tub and wrapped one of the rough towels around his body. A dirty, freestanding mirror stood beside a water basin, and Darren examined his scars as he dried himself off. Many of them had faded, but the one that crossed his heart in the shape of an X still stood out plain as day three years after it was first inflicted. *Cursed thing.* He looked away and pulled on the clothes the inn had supplied, surprised they fit so well. The shirt was an earthy green that would blend in nicely with the forest, and the pants were a worn-looking tawny color. He tied the crisscrossed laces at the top of the shirt and took a deep, cleansing breath. His stomach growled.

Raucous laughter and merriment greeted him when he reached the first floor. Connor had succeeded in spreading his gaiety to the other travelers, and the previously sober room had erupted into a scene of drinking games, pink-faced patrons, and toasts that rang out at random. Darren found the table in the center of it all where Relaina, Connor, and Jacquelyn sat, and shortly after taking a seat, a petite girl, no older than twelve, brought them hot food. They ate amidst the chaos, the toasts going on for quite some time until one man recited an ode to a healer who had cured his unsightly toenail fungus. After that, the workers in the inn kept their distance, and everyone went back to telling stories amongst themselves. Connor, however, had attracted an audience of women, who now surrounded their table with giggles and flirtatious eyelash batting. Jacquelyn rolled her eyes at her brother and drank heavily. Several of them made advances toward Darren, and he tried to politely decline, but they were persistent.

"And then the tiger jumped at me, raking one of its claws right down my face, and that's how I got this scar here," Connor said, eliciting a chorus of renewed interest from the women around him.

"I swear to Praelia," Jacquelyn muttered as they watched him act out his tale. "If Connor thinks I'll sit in the hall while he brings a woman into our room, I'll throw his mattress out the window." He stood and made a lunging motion at an imaginary enemy but lost his footing and fell, taking his chair and one of the girls with him. Relaina snorted into her drink and tears squeezed themselves out of Darren's eyes as he choked and laughed simultaneously. Jacquelyn glared at Connor across the table as he regained his seat, all the girls giggling at him. He winked at one girl, and she blushed.

"Connor, if you even think about it—"

"You didn't tell me you had a lady, Connor," one of the girls complained, cutting Jacquelyn off.

"Ah, sweet Beatrice. I didn't tell you that because Jacquelyn here is only my sister."

Beatrice smiled and the other girls giggled again. Jacquelyn's knuckles were white on her cup, her eyes full of murder. Darren started to say something, but another woman blocked his view. She leaned on the table, her raven hair falling over her shoulder and her face far closer to Darren's than he would have liked.

"What about you, handsome, is she *your* sister?" the girl asked, jerking her chin toward Relaina, who glowered at her. Darren set down the drink he had to his lips and looked at her with a placid smile.

"No. She is not my sister."

"Oh." The girl pouted, but she didn't move. "Is she your lady, then?"

Darren's eyes darted to Relaina of their own accord. Gods *damn* the blush that rushed up his neck and face.

"I—"

"Yes," Relaina said, flashing her teeth in a dangerous smile. Darren stared at her. "Now fuck off or I'll toss you into the brook outside."

Jacquelyn roared with laughter as the girl huffed and sauntered away. Beatrice left Connor's lap to join her rejected friend and several men at a nearby table. One of the other tavern workers, a tall, muscular man who was twirling a patron's hair as she showed him each of her bejeweled rings, turned to glare at their table as Beatrice whispered in his ear.

"Relaina, do you make a habit of scaring the hell out of beautiful women?" Connor asked. "Because if you do, you and I are going to have a serious problem."

"Connor, every one of those women would rob you blind," Darren said, finishing off his drink. "This isn't a tavern in a city. This is an inn in the middle of nowhere that makes extra money by hiring attractive people to flirt with patrons and swipe their money pouches. And jewelry." He nodded to the man beside Beatrice, who had gone back to wooing the woman with the rings.

Relaina caught Darren's eye as Connor grumbled and Jacquelyn launched into a lengthy diatribe of her brother's behavior. Their bickering grew louder, and Darren stood and headed for the door, keen to get out of the noise and incessant merrymaking.

The night was warm, unlike what it would be in Parea, and just around the corner of the inn was the brook with an old fence erected in front of it. Darren leaned on the lichen-covered wood, watching the water trickle along. The moon danced on the water's surface and cast its beams on a little orchard across the brook, and Darren breathed against the ache forming in his chest at the sight of it. What was happening in Parea now? He hoped that Maurice and Camille were safe; he hated that he hadn't had the chance to tell them goodbye, but they at least must have learned of his escape and now knew he was safe from the wrath of King Stephan. They'd risked their lives to house and protect him, and he would find a way to thank them someday.

Quiet footfalls approached from behind, and Relaina appeared in his periphery, leaning on the fence beside him. Moonlight settled on her dark curls.

"Sorry if I crossed a line in there," she said. "You looked like you needed rescuing from that woman."

Darren's heart picked up speed, and he kicked himself for staring at the way her lips moved when she spoke, for wishing she would cross the line further. "I did. I appreciate the intervention."

"I'm sorry for being rude earlier."

Darren let the silence between them deepen for a few moments, allowing his heart to slow.

"Has it occurred to you that I might be the one person who can truly empathize with what you're going through?"

Relaina frowned and looked at her hands. Even in the dark, Darren could see her lip quivering. *Gods in hell.*

"It's not easy, regardless of the reason you left," he said. Relaina turned away from him, but he still saw the shimmer of a tear as it cascaded down her cheek.

"I can't imagine what horrors you've been through."

"You don't want to imagine them. Trust me."

Relaina snorted and wiped her eyes. "And that's what I have to figure out, still." She turned and locked eyes with him. "Whether or not I'm going to trust you."

"I wish you would."

His breath stagnated as Relaina held him with her gaze for a few immeasurable moments. *Was that too much?* She stepped away from the fence, drumming her fingers on the edge.

"We'll see."

She trudged back to the inn, and Darren remained outside for a while longer, trying his best to slow down the swirling thoughts in his head. If he could only not *think* for a while, perhaps he'd feel less on edge.

A frog croaked nearby, startling him. He shook his head and walked back inside. Connor had reacquainted himself with several ladies at a different table, red-faced and guffawing, and Jacquelyn sat at the bar talking to the innkeep. Relaina was nowhere to be found—she must have gone to bed.

Darren weaved his way through the tables, nodding to Connor when he called out to him in greeting, and took the steps two at a time to the second floor. He hesitated outside the door to his and Relaina's room. *Don't be stupid.* He turned the knob and stepped inside.

But Relaina wasn't in bed. Darren looked around the room, peeking into the bathing room, and found no sign of her. He left their room and knocked on Connor and Jacquelyn's door before opening it. Also empty.

"Relaina?" he said, though he knew there was nowhere to hide in these rooms. No answer. *Fuck.* He'd go get his dagger, question a few people downstairs, and take Relaina's horse if he had to. She was faster than any other they'd brought along.

"Oof!"

In Darren's haste to turn away from Connor and Jacquelyn's door, he ran right into—

"You really need to break this habit of bumping into me."

"Relaina," Darren said, relief coloring his voice. She raised an eyebrow at him. A glance behind her told him she'd been in the shared washroom.

"Were you worried about me?"

"You... I..."

She tried and failed to hide a grin. It was infuriating.

"I was just in the washroom," she said. "The one in our room doesn't have candles."

"Oh. Are you going to bed?"

"Yes."

"Well, uh, goodnight."

Relaina stepped around him. "Goodnight, Darren."

Darren stared after her as she walked away down the hall.

"Relaina?"

She turned.

"I... nevermind." It wasn't a good time to bring that up. She nodded uncertainly and went into their room, closing the door behind her.

Darren lingered downstairs a while longer, hoping Relaina would already be asleep by the time he returned. He drank another ale in the bar with Jacquelyn before the two of them retired, leaving Connor to his wooing.

Jacquelyn bid him goodnight, and Darren stepped into his own room without hesitating this time. He could just make out Relaina's form in the bed, her middle rising and falling slowly as she slept. As quietly as he could manage, he crept toward the bed and sat, pulling his boots off. She moved, and Darren froze, but she was still fast asleep. He adjusted the blanket so it covered her shoulders and then slipped beneath it himself, reveling in the comfort it brought compared to the ground. Careful to stay on his side and not touch her, Darren closed his eyes and waited for sleep to take him.

∾

RELAINA WALKED through a forest unlike any she'd seen before.

Trees towered a hundred feet or more above her head, their bark black as night and leaves so light the green was almost silver. The path ahead wound through the forest, stones and fallen leaves scattered on the ground. Relaina breathed in deeply and blinked, finding herself in the room at the Happy Stump. She was close to Darren, her hand resting on his arm and her nose nearly touching his shoulder. The stubble on his jaw and above his mouth was prominent in the morning light, making him appear older and travel-worn, but no less attractive. Without thinking she breathed in again, and it wasn't the smell of the forest that flooded her senses, but a natural musk mixed with lingering hints of lavender soap.

A knock came at the door and Relaina pushed back, launching herself away from Darren. The bedcovers tangled in her legs and arms, and she landed on the floor with a thud, one foot still partially on the bed.

"Relaina! Darren! Hurry up and get moving so we can get out of here."

Connor's voice was muffled by the door but still jarring. How in hell was he so chipper when he'd had so much to drink the night before? Relaina groaned as Darren's head appeared over the edge of the bed, the trace of a smile on his face.

"Are you all right?"

Relaina flushed and looked at him from the floor, her foot still twisted in the bedcovers.

"Never better."

He glanced at her foot, then her face.

"Would you like some help?"

"If you don't mind."

He untangled her foot before offering her a hand. She took it and he brought her to her feet with slightly too much force—she bumped into his chest and he steadied her as she stumbled, her nose brushing against his neck and his breath tickling her ear as they reoriented themselves. Relaina leaned back and let her eyes linger on his for a moment too long, her pulse in her ears and her skin covered in chills where he'd touched her.

Relaina blinked and shook her head. They gathered their few things in silence, Relaina briefly going into the washroom to splash herself with cold water and braid her hair. Darren went in after her to run a bit of water through his hair as a means of taming it, and Relaina studied him as she hitched her bag onto her shoulder.

"How much farther to Maremer?" she asked.

Darren wiped some water out of his eyes. "About two more days. We'll need to take plenty of food and water with us in case there isn't another inn between here and there."

"And you're coming with us?"

Darren stopped short, draping a towel over the edge of the water basin.

"Would you rather I didn't?" He tried to hide it, but the dullness in his eyes betrayed his disappointment. Relaina's cheeks burned.

"I don't mind. I just wondered why."

Darren stepped out of the washroom.

"Well, I'm the only one of us who knows Maremer. I've been there before, and I figured I could help you find Bracken."

Relaina was speechless.

"And," he took a deep breath, "I don't have anywhere else to go."

Relaina opened her mouth to respond just as another knock pounded on the door.

"Connor, I swear to Ashima—"

Both Connor and Jacquelyn burst inside the room.

"Lyneisian guards," Jacquelyn said. "Across the road."

Relaina needed no further explanation. They all bounded down the stairs, and Connor led them to an alternate exit behind the bar.

"Leaving so soon?" the old innkeep asked, his long beard fluttering as they flew past him.

"Sorry, Roderick, we've got to go!" Connor said, and the four rushed outside to the stables, keeping low. Relaina chanced a glance across the road and located four Lyneisian guards mounted on horses, questioning a villager with a baby on her back and a basket of eggs in her arms.

"Do we wait and hide, or do we run?" Jacquelyn asked as they took cover behind a few barrels near the horses' stalls.

"It will be far too obvious if we go now," Darren said. "They would question our departure."

"Damn it all, we should've stayed at the inn," Connor said.

"The inn will be one of the first places they go to check," Darren said. "Just wait here and stay quiet. If we don't move around too much, they won't see us."

Relaina pulled the hood of her cloak up as an extra precaution, and Darren did the same. It wasn't until the guards walked farther down the road that she realized she'd been holding her breath. She exhaled and Darren's head turned in her periphery.

"We'll get out of here," he assured her.

They watched the guards ride off out of sight, and Relaina darted for her horse. The four of them rode out of the village, headed west for the coast.

"Well, I guess we're just going to have to rely on Darren's hunting for the next day or two," Connor said once they eventually slowed their pace.

"I'm afraid there will be little to eat," Darren said. "Game here is small and hard to come by. It will get worse the closer we get to the coast."

"How fast can we get there if we ride through the night?" Relaina asked. She didn't particularly want to do that, but if they were low on food, and low on water, they might not have a choice.

"We could probably be there before dark tomorrow if we don't stop to sleep," Darren said.

"We should do it," Jacquelyn said. "The city has to be safer anyway, and the guards will be less likely to catch up with us."

"I don't understand," Relaina said, shaking her head. "It's against the law for them to seize anyone in another kingdom."

"Perhaps they're traveling to Maremer to ask King Fabian for permission to take us," Darren said. "Or perhaps they're headed to Lyneisia."

"Maybe they were the guards that escorted Bracken to Maremer," Jacquelyn said, her face paling. "If they hurt him, I swear I'd ride back to find them and—"

"Stop worrying, Jacq," Connor said. "Bracken was friends with many of those guards. They had to do as the king commanded, but they'd never hurt him if they didn't have to."

Nausea settled in Relaina's stomach. She glanced sidelong at Darren, who stared determinedly at the path before them. He'd been friends with those guards too.

"Darren," she said, and he turned. "Would...would you mind, when we get to Maremer, I mean, would you be willing to teach me some of your fighting techniques? I want to know how to...well, after seeing you and Xavier, I want to learn..."

"How to fight a Terranian assassin?"

Relaina nodded, swallowing hard.

"It won't be easy. But yes, I'll teach you. We'll have to procure some weapons besides these."

"Maremer is one of the largest trading ports in the world."

"Then it should be no problem, with that gold purse of yours," he said, winking, and Relaina's insides warmed. "I'd like another set of daggers, if possible. I prefer to use two blades."

"I believe it. If I could fight like you did in the tunnels, I'd want to be armed to the teeth."

Darren chuckled. "Perhaps not to the teeth. Well...unless I knew I was going into a difficult fight."

Hours passed as they rode on, Darren halting their progress here and there when he thought he spied game, but each time, whatever it was scurried away too quickly to catch. They had a few rations left, and Connor had gathered several pieces of leftover bread from the inn's tables the previous night, but they would be quite hungry come tomorrow.

"I don't even remember grabbing these," Connor said as he passed out pieces of bread. It was hard, but Relaina's growling stomach cared little. She chewed slowly as they rode, hoping to make it last a little longer and stave off the aching hunger.

"I'm still astonished you woke up without vomiting this morning," Jacquelyn said.

"The secret is moderation, dear sister. 'Drink four ales an hour and you'll recover all your power!'"

"That makes no sense, who told you that?"

"No one. I came up with it myself."

It was close to sundown when Darren stopped them again, dismounting and drawing his bow. He stepped off the path and into the silty brush, letting two arrows fly in quick succession. He stood up straight and walked farther into the woods.

"What was it?" Connor asked, craning his neck from atop his horse.

Darren emerged again, holding a large bird of some sort by its legs. Its feathers were a lush brown color except the tip of the tail, where they turned bright blue.

"What the hell is that?" Jacquelyn asked.

"It's a wild kyter," Darren said. "This will feed us for two days, at least."

"Thank the gods," Connor said.

"How is our water supply?" Relaina asked. Connor checked the canteens attached to his horse.

"Enough for a day, maybe two if we stretch the supply," Connor said.

"We would be safe to stop for the night, then," Relaina said, squinting ahead at the setting sun. "If we wanted to."

"I'm eager to get to Maremer, but I'm also sore from being on this horse all day," Jacquelyn said. "I say we settle down off the path somewhere and start a fire."

An hour later, the four of them were settled in a small clearing a safe distance from the forest path, sitting around the fire as Jacquelyn cooked the bird. Darren had shown Relaina how to pluck the feathers and fillet the meat with the dagger the healers had given him.

"Do they have kyters in Terrana?" Relaina asked.

"A few as you go farther east," Darren said. "When I was on the run it was a rare blessing if I could find one. But I spent little time in eastern Terrana before crossing the border. They're more common in Evaria."

"How many places did you go when you were on the run?" Connor asked, resting his chin on his knees.

"It's hard to say since I mostly stayed out of large cities. But I went as far north as Maremer and as far south as the Inmedio."

"Kyter is done!" Jacquelyn said, passing sticks with meat on them around. Relaina took a bite and made a sound of contentment.

"This is far better than rabbit or goose," she said, and the others nodded in agreement. They sat and ate their fill, and Jacquelyn folded the remainder of the meat in a piece of leather from Connor's saddlebags.

"We're lucky there aren't wolves around here," Relaina said.

"Very true," Darren said, tossing his now-meatless stick over his shoulder. He looked at her. "Want to do some training?"

"Now?" she asked. "It's nearly dark."

"And assassins tend to strike at night."

Relaina raised her eyebrows and nodded. Connor and Jacquelyn saw to the horses as Relaina and Darren retrieved their weapons.

"Just the dagger to begin with," Darren said, stopping Relaina as she reached for her sword. She followed him to another part of the clearing away from Connor, Jacquelyn, and the horses, studying him in the firelight. He wasn't muscular in the way that some men were with large, bone-crushing arms. He was lean and proportionate, with granite hidden beneath his skin. Relaina swallowed against the sudden dryness in her mouth.

"Let me see your stance," Darren said, and Relaina faced him from the side, her feet planted on the ground, slightly more than shoulder-width apart. "Good. Now raise the dagger with your right hand, blade downward but facing me..."

~

"ARRRRRGGHHHH!"

Relaina was, for the third time, on the ground. She picked up her sword and stood again, wiping the blood from her lower lip and taking a defensive stance, ignoring the throbbing pain in her left palm. Darren, however, lowered the sword he'd borrowed from Connor, and the sound of Connor's laughter drifted over to where the two of them stood in the light of the fire. After doing some work with the dagger, they'd switched to swords, which Relaina had looked forward to...at first.

"Please don't make me continue to hurt you," Darren said. Relaina ignored him and took advantage of his lowered defenses to run at him again. He raised his sword just in time to block the blow she'd aimed at his side, and metal rang throughout the clearing. Relaina backed away a few steps, circling him.

"Don't take so much time between your attacks," he said. "Your instincts are good, and your blows easily have enough strength behind them to injure whoever you're fighting, but any hesitation could be fatal."

He lunged at her and she dodged, and before she could gather herself, he came at her again, knocking her blade from her hand. It hit the grass, and Darren held his sword to her throat, his face inches from hers.

"No hesitation, no mercy." He lowered his sword. "That's what they teach the Terranian Elite."

Relaina blew a stray curl out of her eye.

"If that's how Terranians fight, why don't they teach Lyneisians the same way?" she asked, retrieving her sword and returning it to its sheath. She brushed the dirt off her shirt and sat down on the grass, wiping sweat from her forehead and assessing the deep cut in her left palm—she'd caught herself before she slammed into the ground, but her hand had landed on a sharp rock. Darren sat down next to her.

"It's been years since the last conflict between Terrana and Lyneisia. Gabriel trains his soldiers and assassins to be the best in the world. Every person in Terrana that joins the guard or trains to be a soldier is required to learn to use a sword, bow, or other weapon of their choosing, and they must master it by the age of fifteen. Lyneisia, on the other hand, has seen no cause for training its soldiers in such a rigorous way, and their method of fighting is based on fighting in their homeland, where battles typically take place within forests."

Now that she thought about it, Relaina realized that the soldiers of the Lynx Guard were a little less skilled than she would've liked. Not to mention that she, Darren, Conner, and Jacquelyn had escaped five of them.

"Your hand," Darren said, noticing her cut. "I'll get a bandage."

He walked to Amariah, who bumped him with her nose as he reached into Relaina's bag. He gave her a pat, and Relaina could have sworn that Amariah looked at her.

Darren returned with a roll of bandages and a canteen, waving

Relaina off when she held out her hand for them. Relaina's insides warmed as he sat next to her and gently cleaned the cut, muttering apologies when she winced. After wrapping it and tying it off, he looked up at Relaina, and she watched the fire's reflection in his brown irises for a moment before realizing his hands still cradled her injured one. She looked down at them, a slow blush creeping across her cheeks.

"Relaina?"

"Darren?" She returned her gaze to him.

"Do you know why Xavier tried to take you?"

She blinked, her blush fading away rapidly.

"I...well, no. I never really thought about it until now."

Darren nodded and took a deep breath. "I don't want to scare you, but I think you should know."

Relaina's heart sank. "All right."

"I began defying my father's orders years ago. He didn't notice at first. I would find a way to make it appear as though the target had been assassinated, or pretend like I had failed. After a while, though, he began to suspect that I was failing intentionally. Each time I returned without confirmation of a death, he...he had me brought down to the catacombs of the Obsidian Keep, where the priests of Calixtos reside."

Relaina's blood ran cold. Gatherings of the priests of Calixtos were outlawed in Lyneisia due to their habit of sacrificing people to the god of darkness.

"To what end?"

"He had them perform rituals on me to make me stronger. To make me less merciful, less soft-hearted, as he described it. It was all nonsense."

Relaina glanced at his chest, remembering the scar she'd seen there.

"Anyway...Xavier. Before he hunted me, before I escaped, his task had been something else entirely. He was ordered by my father to go to Parea."

"Where his mission was...?"

Darren hesitated a moment. "Your capture and eventual murder."

Relaina took a steeling breath.

"How long ago was this?"

"Five years. Over the course of the next two years, he failed so many times that my father decided to pass the mission off to someone else."

Oh, gods. Darren's hands trembled around Relaina's as he gazed at the fire.

"He had me brought to his chambers and gave me the order. That's why your father was so determined to kill me—he must have known." Silence filled the clearing. Relaina looked at the fire, then at Connor and Jacquelyn's sleeping forms, and then at their hands.

"So, is this the part where you tell me I'm a trusting fool, whip out your dagger, and carry me off into the night with no one the wiser?"

Darren looked up at her, confusion and hope in his eyes.

"Well...if you're into that sort of thing."

Relaina coughed a laugh.

"I'm joking! I'm joking," Darren said, holding his palms up. "But in all seriousness...You trust me?"

Relaina took a moment. "Yes."

A smile tugged at the corners of Darren's mouth.

"My only question," she said, "is what does Gabriel want with me?"

"I never knew for certain. I overheard him talking about some sort of prophecy once. He has always been a superstitious and paranoid man."

"My father is paranoid as well. Perhaps it's a trait of kings."

"Perhaps it is. In that case, I'm glad I'll never be one."

The fire was beginning to die down, so Darren got up to tend to it as Relaina stood and stretched. She would be sore tomorrow after training with him.

"You did well today," Darren said as he returned. "Truly. You're a fast learner."

"You think I could take a Terranian assassin if I fought one today?" Quick as the strike of a snake, Darren closed his hand around her wrist, and a moment later she was pinned to the ground, almost nose to nose with him. Her heart shot into her throat.

"Not quite," he said, smirking. Relaina struggled for a moment before pushing him off, and he rolled over onto the grass, laughing. They sat up together, Relaina brushing the grass from her back. Darren pulled a few pieces out of her hair, and that damned blush spread across her cheeks again.

"Thank you," Relaina said. She hesitated as she watched the fire reflected in his eyes. "For teaching me. And for telling me the truth. And for enduring whatever horrors your father put you through for refusing to hurt me."

Darren reached for her hand again, studying the bandage on her palm.

"I'll teach you what I know. But should any of my father's assassins come for you again, they will not touch you, Relaina. I won't allow it."

Relaina held his gaze, eyes blazing as his vow settled into the air around them. That fire pulled at her, begging her to lean in, to close the space between them, to lift her chin that extra inch and press her lips to his. Resolve formed in Darren's eyes in response, and he began leaning in himself—

"Water!" She stood and almost knocked Darren over as she pulled her hand from his. "Amariah needs water."

"Oh." He blinked in the firelight. "All right."

Relaina scurried away, muttering, "*Fuck*," under her breath over and over again. Kissing Darren—the *Prince of Terrana*—in a forest on her way to a foreign city after abandoning her home should be the last thing on her mind.

Yet as she led Amariah to a nearby stream, where the mare just stared at her and swished her tail, Darren's warm brown eyes and smile appeared in her memory, and the iron casing around her heart shuddered and faltered. She plopped down by the water's edge.

"Fuck," she whispered again.

CHAPTER 11

BARMAIDS AND BLADES

"Would you two hurry up?" Connor asked. "I'd like to make it to Maremer before sundown!"

Relaina finished parrying a blow Darren sent her way and wiped her brow, breathing hard. They'd been training for about an hour while the four of them took a break by a small stream to water their horses. Relaina was used to a taciturn teacher after training with Jeremiah for years, but Darren gave new meaning to the word "distant." With a sinking feeling in the pit of her stomach and the overwhelming urge to scream, Relaina sheathed her sword as he walked toward his horse.

"Any suggestions?" she asked, jogging to keep up with him.

"None as of now." His smile didn't quite reach his eyes. "Just keep practicing."

Relaina frowned as he mounted up and trotted off after Connor and Jacquelyn. She looked at Amariah.

"I am a fool," Relaina said, and Amariah shook out her mane and pawed the ground as if to say, *I'm aware.*

The coast wasn't far, for the trees grew smaller and the soil siltier. The evergreens that covered the Lyneisian mountains were nowhere to be found along the road to Maremer. The trees here had begun changing from green to rich reds, yellows, and oranges. Though Relaina had always found a silent power in the Lyneisian pines, these boasted an undeniable beauty, and the colorful leaves swaying in the warm breeze put her mind at ease.

Darren rode ahead of her silently, face drawn, and she mastered the impulse to ride forward to take his hand. What in Saeva's name had this man done to make her so irrational?

"Is the Great Sea as big as everyone says it is?" Jacquelyn asked, falling back a little to direct her question at Darren.

"Bigger," Darren said. "As vast and endless as you could possibly imagine."

"You've sailed before?"

"Once. When I fled Terrana, I took a ship headed for the Bay of Trade. There's nothing like the wind on your face and the water shimmering in the sun for miles in every direction."

"So you've been to Maremer."

"Briefly. Terranian soldiers were waiting for me at the harbor, in disguise. It was all I could do to get out of the city. It didn't leave much time for exploration."

"No, I suppose it wouldn't." Jacquelyn rode on, catching up with Connor again. Relaina pushed Amariah forward until she was beside Darren.

"How did you manage it? Being on the run for so long?" Relaina asked.

Darren didn't look at her. "It was difficult. I was never able to stay in one place for too long, because Xavier would catch up with me. But I hadn't escaped Terrana for a lifetime on the run. So I fought Xavier and injured him badly enough that he could not continue following me for a few weeks. That was enough time to get as far away from him as I could and disappear. Parea was not the first place I lived, but it was the first place that felt like a kind of home." Darren paused, taking a breath. "I knew I would never truly belong there, but it was nice to have one place to sleep every night, and to have Camille and Maurice."

Relaina gazed at him, her brow furrowed, but he kept his eyes determinedly forward.

After a few hours, the coastal forest gave way to a grassy plain, its arrival pushing Relaina's whirlwind of worries aside. In the distance, a city sprawled for miles, running along the great bay in the west and leading northward to the perimeter wall of the Evarian palace, perched atop a rocky cliff. Relaina gazed at the sea in stunned silence. Lake Alterna was massive, but here... She almost couldn't tell where the sea ended and the sky began. Jacquelyn stopped alongside her, looking out on the water as gulls cawed above them. The setting sun danced in the blue waters, sending a streak of gold down the center.

"It's beautiful," Jacquelyn said.

"It's...magnificent," Relaina said.

"Yes, yes, it's big, it's blue, and we're wasting time!" Connor rode ahead of them. Jacquelyn broke out of her own stupor and clicked her tongue at him.

"Connor doesn't appreciate the simple pleasures in life the way he ought to," she said, turning to follow him. "But I expect we'll have time to gaze at the sea as much as we want while in the city, and soon it will be dark out."

Relaina tore her eyes away from the water and marched on after her companions. They followed the path through the tall grasses and approached the harbor settled into the massive bay, with countless ships, sailors, traders, goods, livestock, and every kind of food imaginable. Voices rang out along the docks as water lapped at the shore, and parents called children back within the city's walls before dusk fell. If the soft thudding of her horse's hooves had not changed to a clomping on wood, Relaina would not have noticed that she'd gone from the beach to the docks. The great bustle of the Bay of Trade was almost more mesmerizing than the sea, so unlike anything Relaina had ever seen before. As they approached the city gate, a small boy ran by them, weaving between their horses as his mother scolded him.

"Get in here, Nahan, you know you aren't supposed to be out after dark!"

She stopped as the four on horseback reached the gate, drawing her son closer to her and backing away. Relaina's heart jumped into her throat—did they recognize Darren? Or herself? She scanned the streets as they entered the city's walls. The guards didn't appear suspicious, but most city folks gave them a wide berth when they saw the little group of travelers.

"Why are they all afraid of us?" Relaina asked as they rode up the wide, cobbled main street.

"Maremer is highly trafficked by foreigners, and you never know who you can trust," Darren said.

"Is it that obvious that we're not from here?" Jacquelyn asked.

"We're wearing clothes made for cooler temperatures, and our horses look like they've been carrying us for days, which they have. Not to mention, we're clearly speaking Lyneisian right now."

"And people pay attention to those things?"

"The people of Maremer do, it would seem."

Relaina guided her horse to the side to avoid colliding with an old man steering a cart of apples, and then frowned.

"I thought you said you didn't stay in Maremer for long," she said.

"I didn't." Behind them, Connor jumped down to purchase a few apples, so they halted as well. "But being on my own taught me to think in a way that would keep me safest. It's how we'll need to think going forward if we want to remain out of harm's way."

"Oi! Jacq!" Connor said. "Do you have an extra copper? I'm short one!"

Jacquelyn rode back to where Connor was and purchased an apple for each of them. They munched contentedly as they rode on.

"So what now?" Relaina asked. "Do we look for an inn?"

"I suppose so," Jacquelyn said, tossing the apple core over her shoulder. "There has to be one around here somewhere."

Jacquelyn was right. After only trekking another minute down a wide street, they came across an inn called The Gnarled Root. The sign outside creaked and swung in the slight breeze, but inside there was light and warmth and chatter. The foursome dismounted, handed their horses off to a stable boy who approached them, and walked inside.

There were several dozen people inside, all eating, drinking, and talking boisterously. The high ceiling of the inn's main hall amplified the sounds of camaraderie and mingling. Relaina walked over to the bar counter, weaving her way through the many bodies holding beer, wine, and plates of food.

"Hello, sir," Relaina nearly shouted over the din, and the bartender put down the goblet he was cleaning. "Do you have room for four?"

"I do indeed," the innkeep said, his voice carrying over the noise. He was bald and incredibly tall, with dark brown skin and a bright smile. "Will you be needing food as well?"

"Yes," Relaina said. The man reached below the bar to retrieve two keys. "Do you have extra clothes?"

"For a price," he said. Relaina nodded, and he smiled again. "I'll have them brought to your rooms. Upstairs. Lynx room and panther room. Two beds in each. Washrooms are halfway down the hall."

Relaina took the keys, which were carved to look like the animals he'd mentioned. She slapped two gold pieces on the counter.

"Will this cover it?"

"Indeed."

Relaina stuffed her coin purse away. She didn't want any strangers knowing how much money she carried.

"I'll have four plates prepared," the bartender said. "You're welcome to sit anywhere you like."

"Many thanks to you."

It took a while for them to settle in. Relaina bathed herself thoroughly and changed into the garments provided by the inn. They were a little loose but did well enough. She soaked her other clothes in the soapy bathwater and carried them back to her room, hanging them over the posts at the foot of her bed. Darren's belongings and clothes were there, but he wasn't around. *At least we have separate beds.* She sighed at her reflection as she assessed her haphazard, hopelessly messy hair.

Relaina trudged downstairs, exhausted and wanting nothing but food and a good, long sleep now that she was clean. She scanned the room for the others and found Connor, Darren, and Jacquelyn sitting at a table in the center of everything, surrounded by women. This time, however, Darren was entertaining the women almost as much as Connor. He smiled at a redheaded girl as she laughed, twirling a piece of her hair around her finger, and the exhaustion disappeared from Relaina's body. She made her way over to the table, fluffing out her wind-flattened curls and tucking the hem of her oversized shirt into her trousers when she spied the redhead's flattering laced-up bodice.

Connor and Jacquelyn greeted Relaina as she sat down, but Darren hardly glanced at her. She ate in silence, seething as both Connor and

Darren chatted with the women around them. Jacquelyn looked nearly as annoyed as Relaina.

"If Connor is going to sleep with any of these women, he better have a plan that doesn't involve our room. I refuse to be kicked out and lose sleep because of this idiocy."

Relaina's stomach lurched. Darren wouldn't sneak off with one of these girls—would he?

"Why don't you two join us at the bar?" one girl asked Connor and Darren. "There are plenty of drinks and we can all sit together."

Relaina's knuckles turned white around her goblet as Darren and Connor got up and headed over to the bar, five girls in tow.

"Finally. Now we can drink in peace, eh?" Jacquelyn said. She caught sight of Relaina's expression, and her demeanor shifted. "What's wrong?"

Relaina shook her head, taking a long drink from her cup.

Jacquelyn hummed as Relaina wiped her mouth with her sleeve. "You've got feelings for Darren."

Relaina stifled a dry laugh. "Nope."

"You do."

"I don't."

"You look like you want to bite those girls' heads off. As much as I'd love to see you give them all a good walloping, I'd really like to sleep in a bed tonight, so don't get us kicked out of the inn."

Relaina sighed. "I'll try not to."

Jacquelyn drained her mug, patted her on the shoulder, and got up to locate the privy.

Relaina remained in her seat, sipping ale silently. A barman brought her another after she finished her first, and Relaina just frowned at the brown liquid, trying to tune out the sounds of merriment around her. A strident female laugh grated on Relaina's ears and, despite herself, she turned to look.

Darren was still talking with that redheaded girl, who apparently thought every-gods-damned-thing he said was wildly funny. Relaina was about to turn back to her ale when the girl locked eyes with her. She smiled, grabbed Darren by the front of his shirt, and kissed him full on the mouth.

Icy shock washed over Relaina. Several people around them wolf-whistled and cheered, and Darren and the girl broke apart. She giggled and bit her lip as Darren readjusted himself on the barstool, dumb-struck. Relaina didn't move as a dozen emotions roiled through her, each one fighting to come to the surface.

The sardonic smile the redhead threw at her made her want to shatter the mug in her hands.

Relaina stood and strode away from the table, cursing every god for the angry tears that filled her eyes as she went. She headed for the door and wrenched it open, stalking into the night and bracing her hands on a post that supported the wooden awning at the front of the inn. She gritted her teeth, trying to will the tears away. Her nails dug into the damp wood of the post, and she tried to focus on the light patter of rain and ignore the insistent little voice in her head.

It should have been me.

~

HE HADN'T WANTED her to kiss him.

The flirting, yes. Darren had flirted shamelessly with all the women who approached them during dinner, and though it had felt hollow, he'd still craved it.

He sighed. *Darren, you fool.* As he stared at the door leading out of the inn, his stomach turned.

"I'm sorry, I have to go," he said to Freda. Their conversation had been sufficiently distracting, but the kiss had been unexpected and unwanted. Relaina's rejection last night hadn't magically made his feel-ings for her disappear.

How strange to admit to himself that he cared for her, so much so that he had to make sure she was all right, even if she had let him in one moment and shoved him back out again the next.

Outside, Relaina stood by a post beneath the awning, almost in the rain. He ached to reach for her, to thread his fingers through her hair and kiss her.

"Relaina?"

She sniffled, a small curse flying past her lips. He came to stand beside her and she looked away.

"Why are you out here?" she asked.

"Because you left suddenly and I wanted to make sure you were all right."

"I'm fine."

"You don't sound fine."

She pushed herself off the railing and looked at him. "*Damn* it, Darren. I can't—I mean, seeing you in there with..." She stopped, closing her eyes.

"I did not want that to happen."

Relaina's eyes flew open again. "You didn't?"

"No. Not with her."

His heart thundered against his ribs as Relaina's icy stare melted into something soft and unguarded. It was the same look she'd given him last night.

"I..." Her eyes dulled again, and she wrapped her arms around herself. "It doesn't—*shouldn't* matter. My entire life has changed course in a matter of days and I'm...gods in hell. I can't do this."

Darren swallowed against the dryness in his throat, nodding. She swept past him, the door behind her closing with a dull *thud*.

Darren remained outside for quite some time, leaning against a wooden pillar and frowning at the rain. Somehow, gods knew how, Relaina Gienty had become more to him than just a foreign princess he refused to capture or kill for his father. She'd saved his life at great personal cost, but it was more than that. From the moment they'd met, Relaina had seemed immune to the fear and hatred that plagued him wherever he went, defending him before she knew him, a voice against all the prejudice toward the Prince of Terrana.

The door opened behind him, letting the sounds of merriment drift outside, but he didn't turn.

"Rough night?"

Jacquelyn appeared beside him.

"Not the best I've ever had."

"I take it you and Relaina didn't come out here to poetically confess your feelings for one another."

Darren's head whipped around. "I...what do you—"

"It's none of my business. But I can see it. Hell, *Connor* can see it, and he's about as perceptive as a fork. You hide it so poorly that it's honestly a wonder you were such a successful assassin."

"Most people rarely saw my face."

Jacquelyn shrugged. "And I'm certain if they did, they were dead soon after."

Silence grew between them as the rain picked up.

"Anyway, Relaina looked upset but didn't appear to be in a mood to talk about it. Just making sure I don't need to kick your ass."

Darren laughed and then grimaced. "One of the girls in there kissed me."

"*Shit.*"

"Quite."

Though Jacquelyn had said it was none of her business, she lingered as if waiting for him to elaborate. He, however, wasn't inclined to share, so she went back inside, leaving him to sulk. The rain had lessened again now, and the night was still warm. Darren fidgeted, restless. He needed to *do* something, go somewhere to expend his energy, but he had no money on him, and no desire to reenter the main tavern area after what had just transpired. He stepped out from under the awning to assess the exterior of the inn. It was made of rough stone, easy enough to climb, especially amidst the windows and railings. The room he and Relaina had been assigned would be on this side of the building, just to the left. After targeting the correct window, he searched for a sturdy foothold and, despite the rain, began to climb. He didn't want to walk back into the inn, but he couldn't go gallivanting around the city without a cloak and some coin.

After some effort and a near-slip at a windowsill, he jostled the glass panes at their room, loosening the old locking mechanism. It creaked and groaned in protest but gave way, and Darren pushed the window inward, climbing through carefully. He stood upright, water from his hair dripping down his back, and froze in place.

This was not his shared room with Relaina.

It was, in fact, a washroom, and a very large, very naked man was sitting in the bathing basin, staring at him.

"Oh f—"

"You try to steal from me, and I'll gut you."

"I don't doubt it, sir," Darren said, his voice cracking. He flew out of the room and into the hallway, his heartbeat pulsing in his ears as he walked down the hall and found the correct room...and discovered that it was locked. He let his head hit the door and closed his eyes.

"How did you get up here?"

Darren sighed.

"I scaled the wall and climbed through a window." He hadn't removed his forehead from the door.

"Not our window?" Relaina asked.

"Nope."

"Ah." The floor creaked and something small jingled by his face. "I'm guessing you'll be needing the key."

He held out his hand without a word and she dropped it into his palm. They both entered the room, Relaina sitting on her bed while Darren donned his cloak.

"Going somewhere?"

"Yes."

He put the hood of his cloak over his head, trying to avoid Relaina's gaze.

"Well...if you need any money, the gold is beneath the floorboard between our beds."

Darren turned to thank her, but she'd climbed in bed and rolled over, facing the window. He pried the floorboard up and took several gold pieces, tucking them in his boot before leaving.

BY THE TIME Darren returned to The Gnarled Root, the rain had abated. He'd found a little weaponry a few streets down and purchased a pair of fine white steel daggers and an extra quiver of arrows.

The tavern was empty besides a few late-night workers cleaning up and hoisting passed-out drunkards to their feet. Darren dodged a few of them and headed for the stairs, yawning.

"Well, where did you disappear to?"

Darren cursed silently as Freda approached him, hands on her hips. Her hair was bound now, the small apron on her front dirtied. He gave her a halfhearted smile and turned away.

Another barmaid with honey-blonde hair blocked his path. She smiled at him, and before Darren could ask her to move, she unsheathed a knife and buried it in his side.

His cry rang out through the tavern and the other workers began screaming, letting glasses fall and shatter as they scattered. Darren scrambled away from the girl, holding a hand firmly to his wound as she and Freda stalked closer to him, laughing. His vision blurred and he stumbled into a table as he backed away from them. When was the last time an opponent had surprised him so thoroughly? Gritting his teeth, he unsheathed one of the daggers he'd just purchased, the freshly honed blade gleaming sharp and wicked in the candlelight. Darren forced himself to breathe, to calm down, to *think*. Freda smiled, brandishing a curved shortsword. Her pupils began to expand until the whites of her eyes disappeared, leaving only an all-consuming void. The other girl's eyes looked the same.

Tenebrae.

They came at him with inhuman swiftness, taking advantage of his weakened state. He blocked most of their attacks but couldn't prevent the curved blade in Freda's hands from slicing his upper arm. Time was running out to get his wound stitched up by a healer before he lost too much blood.

The blonde barmaid dove at him and the two of them went tumbling to the ground, taking chairs with them. She kicked Darren's dagger out of reach and straddled him, plunging the knife toward his heart. He caught her wrist just before the tip pierced his skin.

"*You will pay for the death of our brother!*" Freda hissed.

Oh, gods.

They were avenging Xavier.

They were going to kill him.

The blonde shrieked, and he was free of her. She grappled on the floor beside him with another figure that knocked the knife from her hand before punching her with enough force to stun her. His rescuer pushed the woman off and scrambled to her feet. The tenebrae lunged, but the other figure twisted and elbowed her in the face to knock her out before grabbing Darren's discarded dagger and standing before him, blocking Freda's path.

Relaina, alone and holding a single blade.

"*Bitch*," Freda spat.

"Fuck you," Relaina said, panting.

Freda struck, and Relaina met the curved sword with the dagger. Sparks flew as Freda rained blow after blow down upon Relaina, illuminating their faces as they fought. Darren had never felt so useless in his life. He struggled to his feet just as two more figures barreled down the stairs, armed and panicked. Jacquelyn turned to Connor as Freda backed Relaina into a corner.

"Shoot her!"

Connor drew his bow and took aim. *Oh gods, please don't hit Relaina...* But Connor's arrow struck true, finding its mark in Freda's unprotected back. She screamed and went down, writhing. Darkness flooded out of her eyes, her mouth, her nose, and formed into a cloud right in front of a thunderstruck Relaina. The darkness lunged for her, and Darren, forgetting his injuries, ran.

"*No!*" The word tore from him as he reached Relaina too late. The darkness enveloped her, and he began rushing through the words in his head, the words that would free her, that would destroy the parasite.

But the moment the darkness touched her skin, it recoiled. With a horrible shriek it fractured and then dissipated into nothing, leaving them all to stare at the empty space, astonished.

Darren's pulse pounded against his skin, blood flowing freely out of his right side again, just below his ribcage. He put his hand against it, swaying, and Relaina dropped the dagger, rushing to catch him before he fell. The innkeep appeared from behind the bar, dressed in nothing but a pair of wrinkled trousers.

"Get a healer in here!" he said. Darren wasn't sure who left, and he didn't care. He squirmed in Relaina's embrace.

"I have to...get to the other woman..."

"She's unconscious, we can take care of her later," Relaina said.

"No, I have to do it *now.*"

Relaina steadied him and helped him hobble over to the blonde's limp form. Darren dropped to his knees, swearing, and Relaina helped him turn her onto her back. Relaina took over putting pressure on his wound while he placed his bloodied palms on either side of her head and spoke.

"*Apage.*"

Darren kept his eyes on the woman before him, trying not to think about what Relaina's reaction would be. Cold filled him as his eyes turned obsidian, and the woman lurched, her own eyes flying open. Relaina flinched.

"*Hear and obey, tenebrae,*" Darren said, his voice lower, rougher than usual. and the woman stilled. "*You are banished from our realm. I send you back to Calixtos.*"

The blonde writhed for a moment in his grip, but he held fast as the whites of her eyes returned to normal. Her breathing slowed, and with one long exhale the dark vapor appeared from her mouth, dissipating into the air much like the other had. Darren still couldn't fathom why the tenebrae had not taken Relaina, but he couldn't solve that mystery now. Not as he slumped against Relaina, who gently helped him to the ground with her hand still on his wound, mumbling a string of curses so filthy it could curdle fresh milk.

Quick feet approached them and a man appeared, wearing a city guard's uniform with a deep blue cloak. A healer-guard.

"I am Shojen," he said, his voice a balm after such chaos had erupted. Other guards entered the inn and, after conversing with the innkeep, surrounded the again-unconscious blonde barmaid a few feet away, putting shackles on her. "May I see the wound?"

Hours of healing later, Relaina, Connor, and Jacquelyn remained on guard in Relaina and Darren's shared room as Shojen stood and turned toward them. Dawn was just beginning to break over the bay, visible from their window.

"He will be weak for a day or so," the healer-guard said. "But his wound is closed and scabbed over." Shojen turned back to Darren, whose eyes were heavy. "Try not to reopen the wound. No combat or training, and no sudden movements."

Darren nodded. He exhaled and sat up, only to wince at the cut in his upper arm. The healer made quick work of it, bowed to them all, and was gone. Relaina whirled on Darren the moment the door clicked shut.

"What the gods-damned fuck happened down there?"

Connor and Jacquelyn exchanged a glance behind her, and Darren stared at them all for a long moment.

"They were tenebrae."

CHAPTER 12

THE KING OF SECRETS

It couldn't be true.

And yet, she'd seen them. Relaina had *seen* those shadows leave their hosts and vanish. She'd seen their speed and felt their brute strength.

Darren explained everything as if in a trance, how almost half of the Terranian Elite were tenebrae—shadow-beings that were thought to have died out over the millennia, little more than myths. The only magic that remained was that of the healers, or so Relaina thought. She couldn't even remember what the healers' race had originally been called, when they'd been powerful and mighty in ancient times.

"The Terranian royal family has always been connected to the tenebrae," Darren said. "Our secret histories warn the rulers of Terrana that to call upon their power for personal gain is to forfeit one's soul to the deepest part of Calixtos's realm for eternity."

"And yet your father..."

"My father damned himself and the rest of us. In his lust for power, he brought pain and death and darkness into the world."

Relaina's hands began trembling.

"Darren, what is he planning?"

He met her gaze with pain in his eyes. "I truly don't know."

"Do you think it's war?" Jacquelyn asked, stepping closer with her spear in her hand.

"Possibly," Darren said. The ice-cold hand of fear gripped Relaina's throat. "He once held ambitions to conquer all of Esran. It's likely he still does."

"Darren," Relaina said. "If he's planning to attack, and he has tenebrae—"

A knock startled them all. Jacquelyn trained her spear on the door as Connor drew his bow, and Relaina answered the knock. She drew the door open wide enough that their caller could see the weapons her companions wielded.

Before her stood a woman of exceptional beauty, with deep umber skin and black hair coiled tightly against her scalp. She was of small stature, but every bit of her radiated power as she stood there, the golden cloak fastened at the collar of her crimson, armor-reinforced dress swaying slightly. She gripped an ornate halberd that matched the etchings of her armored bodice. Her large, brown eyes lighted on Jacquelyn and Connor, unimpressed.

"Desiree Fontaine," the woman said by way of greeting. "Captain of the Seacastle Guard. I need you to come with me."

"Where?" Relaina asked.

"You can follow me of your own accord, or I can take you by force." Captain Fontaine tilted her head. Darren got to his feet behind Relaina, but she held out a hand to stop him. The last thing they needed was the Seacastle Guard knowing that the Prince of Terrana was in their city. Relaina looked at Darren and the others reassuringly.

"Very well," Relaina said, turning back to Captain Fontaine. "But one of them is coming with me." The captain nodded. Relaina motioned to Jacquelyn, who lowered her spear and followed. They walked toward a window at the end of the corridor, and then turned right, stepping through a door to a back stairwell. Only torches lit the dark space. Down they went for two, three flights of stairs until they came upon another door. Relaina paused and looked behind them, praying to whatever gods would listen that this wouldn't end in bloodshed. Jacquelyn gave her an encouraging nod.

She turned and followed Desiree again, stepping gingerly into a dimly lit cellar and gazing at the candles along the walls.

"Greetings, Princess Relaina."

The voice spoke from behind a large table. Candlelight danced across his dark brown complexion and the golden circlet resting atop his locs. He stood, and though he was indeed tall, it was his voice that made him a giant. Jacquelyn swore softly behind her.

"I am Fabian Thereux, and I would very much like to talk to you."

Relaina swallowed hard, now aware that there were four guards in the room: two just inside the cellar's entrance and two on either side of the king of Evaria, plus Captain Fontaine.

"How do you know who I am?" Relaina asked, her tongue easily forming the words in Evarian as her eyes darted to the weapons the guards held.

"I make it my business to know when important people enter my city. I knew it was unlikely that you'd accept an invitation to meet formally at the castle, given the fact that your father sent your friend here to be my prisoner." The king cocked his head to the side, and Relaina's insides caught fire. "So I came here when I heard of the incident that occurred during the night."

Relaina suddenly regretted the decision to bring Jacquelyn along. What if she'd put her in more danger?

"Don't be afraid," King Fabian said, walking around the table. He looked every bit like the king of a mighty nation, with his chiseled facial features and locs that fell halfway down his back. And his eyes, the fabled Thereux eyes, golden brown as they gazed at her, striking against his rich, brown skin and black hair.

"It's not my wish to interrogate you," King Fabian said, holding out his hand in offering. "But I do have some questions for you and your companions. If I tell you that your friend Bracken is staying in my Seacastle Palace and *not* being treated as a prisoner, would you agree to meet with me there?"

Relaina stared at him. Bracken was here, staying in Seacastle as a guest, not a prisoner, and King Fabian wanted to meet with her, Jacquelyn, Connor, and—

"Forgive me, Your Majesty," Relaina said, eyeing his extended hand that offered welcome. "But I must assume that if you know who I am, then you know the names of my companions as well."

King Fabian smiled and dropped his hand.

"I do. Jacquelyn of Parea." He inclined his head toward Jacquelyn. "And her brother Connor. And Darren LaGuarde, Prince of Terrana."

Relaina nodded once. "After what happened in Parea, I am hesitant to bring Darren into the palace of another king who might consider him an enemy."

The king considered for a moment.

"Would you believe me if I said I do not consider him my enemy?"

"I mean no disrespect, Your Majesty, but I would require more assurance than that. For his safety."

King Fabian swept forward and offered his hand again, and this time, Relaina took it. To her eternal surprise, he knelt, and the guards around him dropped as well. He raised his face to hers, his free hand over his heart.

"Princess Relaina Gienty, you have my word as King of Evaria that no harm will come to Darren LaGuarde while he is within the walls of my palace." Relaina stared at him. It was unspeakable for a king to kneel for anyone, let alone the disgraced princess of a neighboring kingdom. "I will not imprison him or put him in any danger. Will you accept my invitation to Seacastle Palace, to be treated as guests in exchange for speaking with me there?"

"I..." Relaina put her other hand on top of their clasped ones and glanced to Jacquelyn, who nodded, eyes wide. "I accept."

"Excellent." Fabian smiled again and stood. In a much more traditional gesture, he lifted her hand and touched her knuckles to his forehead. "I will have my guards escort you."

When they arrived back at their rented room, the guard remained posted in the hall. Connor and Darren converged on Relaina and Jacquelyn, Darren taking Relaina's shoulders into his hands.

"What happened?" Darren's face was set with concern as he examined her, carving another crack in the wall around her heart. *Damn him.*

"We're fine," Relaina said. The two men stood in shocked silence as Relaina recounted their experience in the cellar.

"You just accepted this man at his word?" Darren asked. "How do you even know he was really the king? What if it's all a trap and we show up tonight only to be imprisoned?"

"It was him," Relaina said. "He had the Thereux eyes. And I can't imagine we'd be surrounded by this many Seacastle Guards if he wasn't the king."

"He *knelt* before her," Jacquelyn said. Connor and Darren gawked at her. "He seemed sincere to me as well, and if he intended to imprison any of us he would've done so already. I think we should go."

"He's offered to let us stay at the palace," Relaina said.

"Then let's go now!" Connor said, stowing away his bow and beginning to scuttle around the room to gather belongings until he realized he wasn't in his own room.

"The guards are waiting to escort us to the palace," Relaina said. Jacquelyn and Connor left for their room, and Relaina gathered her things quickly and splashed water on her face using the basin beneath the window.

"Ah—!" Pain shot through the left side of her face where she'd touched it, just below her eye.

"What is it?"

Relaina blinked the water from her eyes and turned away from the window, lightly pressing on her cheekbone.

"One of the tenebrae hit me," she said, wincing. "I'd forgotten until just now." Darren sheathed his daggers and slung the bow across his back before approaching her.

"Can I?"

Relaina nodded, not daring to breathe as he examined her face, his touch impossibly gentle. He frowned.

"It's starting to swell. Hopefully they'll have a healer in the palace."

"They do." One of the guards appeared in the doorway, smiling. She had a square jaw and hazel eyes, with high cheekbones and black hair that fell in a curtain of night against her brown skin.

"My name is Saheer," she said. "If any of you need a healer, my sister Nadia works in the palace."

After packing their few belongings and thanking the innkeeper, the four companions rode through the streets of Maremer with their escort of two guards, heading toward the palace. Relaina breathed in deeply the smells of a bustling city that reminded her of home. A dull pang of sadness touched her heart, but so did warm familiarity and comfort—she'd always been at home in the vibrant buzzing and chatter of hundreds of strangers.

They rode down a wide, abandoned street, with lights flickering inside houses and signs creaking above the doorways of shops that hadn't yet opened for the day. The sun had fully risen when they reached the steep, winding path that led to the palace. It took only minutes to reach the top on horseback, and Relaina turned in her saddle to a sight that took her breath away. The bay shimmered turquoise in the morning light, framed by the city's western wall and colorful trees. To the right, far below was the eastern wall of Maremer, and beyond spanned grassy plains that fed into more autumnal forest.

Saheer called to the guards manning the perimeter wall of Seacastle, and they pulled a large lever, opening the massive, gold-gilded gate with a mighty groan.

The palace was wide and six stories tall, with high turrets and huge windows decorating most of the exterior. The corner of the left side, which faced the sea, was made entirely of glass, including the domed ceiling. As they passed through another wall and a second set of gates, also inlaid with gold, they entered gardens that put the majesty of Castle Alterna's garden to shame. Hundreds of flowers along the stone path lit their way through the gardens and to the great front doors. A figure strode out, silhouetted by the bright warmth from within, and Relaina's heart leapt. She would know that gangly frame anywhere.

"You all certainly didn't waste time getting here," Bracken said, grinning at them. Jacquelyn dropped her horse's reins and ran to him, nearly knocking him over with the force of her embrace. A strange ache thrummed in Relaina at their reunion. When Bracken released Jacquelyn, Relaina wrapped her arms around him, laughing even as tears filled her eyes.

"I'm so glad you're safe, Bracken," Relaina whispered. Bracken punched her arm gently and whistled.

"What happened to your eye?" He wrapped an arm around Jacquelyn's waist.

"Long story."

Darren came forward, and he and Bracken clasped arms.

"I'm glad to see you're alive," Bracken said.

"And I you."

"Xavier?"

"Dead." Bracken didn't have to ask who'd killed him.

"Good."

"Bracken, how did you end up as King Fabian's guest?" Connor asked, clapping him on the back. "We all expected to have to formulate a plan to break you out of here."

"We'll have to get into that later," Bracken said, nodding to the gate now far behind them, where two figures rode through. Desiree was arriving. She'd changed since their meeting earlier. In the light of the lanterns, the golden Evarian crest, a phoenix with wings expanded, skyward bound, gleamed on the front of her red tunic. The sigil stirred a memory that Relaina couldn't quite place.

Two of Desiree's men came to stand on either side of her with stoic faces and spears held at attention as she dismounted. Desiree was much shorter than they were, but her body language alone commanded their respect and obedience.

"Gaius, go fetch a healer," Desiree said, and the man on her right disappeared. "You all can follow me inside."

Relaina took a deep breath; they were all now in King Fabian's hands, and she hoped he was true to his word.

If Relaina had been impressed by the palace's exterior, it was nothing compared to the entrance hall. The ceiling was made entirely of glass. Hundreds of lanterns hung from it at different lengths, unlit in the daylight. Suits of armor and exquisitely carved statues lined the walls on either side, interrupted only by torches in gilded holsters every few feet, and inlaid within the walls themselves were thousands of seashells. The doors shutting behind them echoed off the walls and the tiled floor. A narrow red carpet ran the length of the room, leading to another set of tall, polished-wood doors.

The guard Gaius reappeared, along with a small-framed healer with a shaved head and green eyes outlined in kohl. The woman took one look at Relaina and came forward, her reddish-brown hands motioning in the air before her. Desiree motioned back, and the healer responded in turn.

"Nadia says it will take less than five minutes," Desiree said as the healer reached for Relaina's face. Relaina flinched, and Nadia rolled her eyes and motioned again.

"'Calm yourself' she says," Desiree translated. "'I won't bite.'"

Relaina sighed and allowed the healer to fix her swelling cheek and eye, standing there awkwardly for a few minutes as the others watched.

"Thank you," Relaina said, and Nadia smiled, gently taking Relaina's hand and forming it into a fist at her heart. The healer mirrored the motion and mouthed, *thank you*. Relaina understood, then, and made the motion on her own. Nadia smiled again and motioned back with a fist at her heart that swept downward into an open palm. *You're welcome.*

Just as the healer stepped away, satisfied with her work, Relaina blinked and the doors to the next room opened. King Fabian came forward in sweeping robes of red and gold, far more magnificent than what he'd worn in the inn cellar. In full light, his height was less intimidating. He was close to her uncle's height, though Jeremiah also towered over most.

"Welcome," King Fabian said. "I am pleased that you are here."

"We are grateful for your hospitality," Relaina said, inclining her head. The king smiled.

"My servants will show you to your rooms," he said. "Get some rest, and let us all speak tomorrow."

"Jacq, you go ahead," Bracken said. "I'll meet you there shortly."

He turned to Relaina and Darren.

"I know you're both exhausted, but we need to talk."

DARREN AND RELAINA followed Bracken down several corridors until they reached a door leading outside. The door led them not to the palace exterior but to a massive garden within the walls, so thick with flora they couldn't see the adjacent sides of Seacastle. The smell of jasmine, mint, and something else Darren couldn't place wafted through the air along a light breeze, pleasant and warm. Bracken led them down the stony path, weaving through trees and flowering shrubs. The sound of running water grew louder as they went, and as they turned a final corner, the source was revealed. Water flowed downward from a three-tiered fountain, splashing into the center of a rectangle-shaped pool lined with iridescent stones that shimmered and undulated in the light.

"I'm going to tell you both something," Bracken said, taking a seat on the pool's edge. "But I need you to promise me that you'll hear me out."

Relaina glanced at Darren, and he nodded once. They both sat and waited as Bracken closed his eyes and inhaled.

"I've been King Fabian's spy for five years. I know about Gabriel's plot to capture Relaina, and I knew who Darren was the moment he arrived in Parea."

Darren blinked rapidly. "You...*what?*"

Relaina and Darren sat silent and frozen as Bracken explained. He'd been on an extended trip to his home city five years prior when an envoy from Maremer approached him, offering Fabian's terms. Through Fabian's network of Shadows, Bracken had known everything—Gabriel's plot to capture Relaina, Darren's identity, the existence of the tenebrae.

Gratitude for Bracken's silence washed over him, but so did fear. He had never been truly safe, truly hidden, even with Camille and Maurice.

"Why didn't you tell my father?" Relaina asked, her voice quiet.

"Because my loyalty had shifted. King Fabian held your safety as a top priority, and he cares about not only his kingdom but Lyneisia and Terrana as well. I kept King Fabian informed, but I knew what King Stephan would do if he knew, especially after the rumors began that Darren was in Parea. I was so focused on keeping an eye on Darren that I missed something so crucial it almost cost us all our lives."

Darren waited, hardly breathing as Bracken gathered himself.

"Xavier's arrival," Bracken continued. "By the time King Fabian got my message, it was too late. Xavier had me framed for the work of another spy in Parea, someone who *was* selling information to King Gabriel."

"Who was it?" Relaina asked.

"We still don't know."

"But my family could still be in danger! Bracken, we have to find out who it is, we have to—"

"Relaina, you have been King Gabriel's target all along. Your family is probably in less danger now that you're gone."

It was true; Gabriel had never once mentioned any of the Gientys besides Relaina. Relaina gripped the edge of the fountain and fire filled Darren's lungs. He didn't know what his father wanted with Relaina, but Gabriel would touch her over his dead body.

"Five years of this, and you never told me?"

"I was sworn to secrecy, Relaina."

"Don't you think I deserve to know if it's *my* life that's in danger? I thought you and I didn't keep secrets from one another. I'm not some helpless doll sitting in a tower."

"I know you aren't, Relaina, which is why I couldn't tell you. You would've gotten in the way of your own safety. We couldn't risk it. Tell me you wouldn't have wanted to be a part of this and go after the man trying to kill you."

Relaina stood and crossed her arms. "So, what? It would have been my decision to make! It *should* have been my decision."

Bracken shook his head. "It wasn't just your life at stake. I'm sorry, Relaina. It killed me to keep this from you, but betraying your trust to keep you safe was a burden I was willing to shoulder."

Relaina's breath shook as her eyes welled with tears. She was a fighter, and a damned good one, but she didn't stand a chance against Gabriel. Only Darren had any hope of being his father's equal. He stared at his hands on his lap as they began to tremble, hating the darkness he knew was within.

"I'm glad you're safe," Relaina said, drawing him back to the conversation, "and I am grateful for King Fabian's protection and hospitality. But I...I need some time, and I'm not sure how to feel about you right now."

"Nothing that matters has changed with you and me, Laines. You're still my best friend. And I'm still yours if you don't despise me. I did what I did out of loyalty to *you*. I know trusting me won't be easy for a while, but I hope you can at least accept that I did it for the right reasons."

He squeezed her hand, and she nodded, looking down as tears fell from her eyes.

"Anyway...I wanted to be the one to tell you, before you spoke with King Fabian. I'll leave you both," Bracken said, standing. He pointed over his shoulder. "If you follow the path northward, you'll happen upon a glass door with two guards stationed outside. King Fabian tells me they were your mother's rooms, and he wishes for you to use them, if you'd like. Darren, your rooms are just across the corridor from Relaina's, as are mine."

Neither Relaina nor Darren spoke for a while after Bracken left.

"Can I ask you something?" Relaina said, turning to look at him. He nodded. "Do you think Bracken was right to keep everything from me?"

"I think that if Gabriel had any idea about this secret network of spies, they would all be dead within a week. Bracken's secrecy probably protected not only you but countless others."

Relaina's mouth twisted as she nodded. The nearby fountain bubbled, filling the silence that grew between them. He waited for her to speak again, but her eyes grew haunted, her knuckles turning white against the stone.

"Relaina?"

She didn't indicate that she heard him. The color drained from her face and she took a shaky breath.

"Relaina." Darren placed a hand on one of hers, and she met his gaze.

"Last night...you could have died," she said.

"But I didn't. You've saved my life twice."

"Are we keeping score now?"

"I've never wanted to win a game less."

The tightness in Darren's chest eased as she laughed, wiping her eyes. "I—shit, Darren, you're bleeding."

He looked down at the drops of blood on Relaina's hand and a growing red stain on his shirt. The wound must have reopened. "Gods damn it."

The doors and the guards were just where Bracken said they would be, stationed before two large glass doors with silver handles that led to an anterior room with a stone floor and wooden table. Atop the table was a vase of little white flowers, and beside it was Relaina's bag. She reached inside and grabbed a roll of bandages before assessing which door to try next. She opened the one on the left to reveal a small room containing several garments for swimming and a small stone basin with a tap for water.

They entered the next room and discovered the bedchamber. Light filtered in from the windows looking out on the garden. The ceiling was high, leaving ample room for the massive four-post bed in the center, boasting deep purple coverings and a canopy lined in gold. They both stared for a moment before returning to their senses and heading for the washroom.

Relaina had him sit on the edge of the large stone bath that was carved into the floor. She cleaned and rebandaged his wound with an expert hand. It was mostly healed, but a small sliver had reopened, persistent and deep, and it hurt like hell.

"Did that...tenebrae...use some kind of special knife?"

"They sometimes imbue their blades with dark magic." Darren closed his eyes. "It can be resistant to healing."

"Dark magic," Relaina muttered, her voice soft and far away. "Darren?"

He lifted his head, eyes flying open.

"Sorry. I'll let you go to sleep."

"It's fine." She climbed out of the empty bath and helped him up from the edge. He rubbed his face and headed for the door, hoping his room was easy to find. His hand was on the silver doorknob when Relaina said, "Wait."

He looked back at her, sleepy but expectant.

"Will you...will you stay with me?" Her eyes sparkled with anxiety, and Darren blinked—she wanted him to stay? "I know it's just across the hall and there are guards, but I—"

"I'll stay."

Relaina climbed into bed after she'd found a suitable nightgown, pulling a blanket over herself. Darren, who had at first attempted to sleep on a nearby couch until Relaina insisted the bed was fine, winced as he shifted on his back.

"How is it?"

"Better. Who needs a healer when you're around?"

Relaina turned over so she was facing the wall, but not before Darren caught her smiling.

"Sleep well, Relaina."

Chapter 13

Seacastle

Relaina blinked at the figures before her, contemplating the deep green of the forest clearing and the fire in the center. The figures —nymphs, she realized—touched closed flowers and made them bloom, whispered to birds and beasts, and brought dying plants back to life.

In the midst of them all stood a woman, tall and white-haired with azure skin, smiling as she lifted a hand to the sky and a gentle rain began to fall. The fire behind her burned brighter and shimmered as it turned blue. Relaina stood there, frozen, as the woman's silver eyes came to rest on her. Somewhere in the recesses of her memory, Relaina remembered the goddess's name:

Elenia.

The Queen of the Gods approached, bare feet padding silently on the grass of the lush grove, the fabric of her white dress fluttering in a breeze Relaina couldn't feel. Relaina knew she ought to bow, but she was still frozen in place. Elenia's gentle smile widened into a grin as she placed a hand on Relaina's head.

Don't fear the dark. Elenia's mouth didn't move, but Relaina heard her voice clearly. *We'd have no stars without the night.*

As quickly as the forest had appeared, it dissipated.

Relaina awoke, wondering at the dream before the memory of it slipped away, lost. Morning light streaming through the windows shone soft and gray on the tiled floor of her borrowed chambers. They'd slept the entire previous day and through the night, and she was well-rested for the first time in weeks. Beside her, Darren was still in a deep sleep, his chest rising and falling in a steady, slow rhythm. Scruff lined his jaw and had begun creeping down to his neck, which was smooth aside from a faint white scar below his left ear.

The scar on his chest stood out against the others on his torso, the jagged lines of the X running from his collarbone to his underarm, then from his shoulder to his sternum. Rage simmered beneath Relaina's skin. Whenever that wound had been inflicted, it was done with sadistic patience, intended to prolong suffering.

Someone knocked, and Relaina jumped violently, kneeing Darren in the side and narrowly avoiding his injury. He gasped awake and curled onto his side, trying to catch his breath.

"Oh gods, Darren, I'm so sorry." The knocking continued.

Relaina scrambled out of bed and hurried to answer the door. An older, cross-looking woman stood at the threshold, accompanied by two younger women.

"Good morning, Princess Relaina," the woman said, bowing her head. Her eyes darted over Relaina's shoulder. "Ah. Prince Darren."

Darren sat up slowly, grabbing at the blanket to cover his chest, and Relaina fought the urge to open a nearby window and dive into the foliage outside.

"I am Calliope. I am the matron of the servants here in Seacastle, and it is my duty to ensure that they all carry out their duties as they should. Girls?"

The other two women, who were much younger than Calliope, stepped forward, bowing.

"This is Pemma," Calliope gestured to a petite girl with silvery-blonde hair. "She is my granddaughter and has worked in this palace for several years now. And this is Selene." Calliope gestured to the other girl. She was tall, with shiny black hair that fell just past her wide hips, and freckles that rivaled Jacquelyn's.

"King Fabian has asked that all his guests join him for breakfast, but he wishes to speak alone with you first, Princess Relaina. Pemma and Selene will assist you with bathing, dressing, and fixing your hair."

Relaina glared at the matron, whose own hair fell in a white plait over her shoulder.

"As for you, Prince Darren, there are two servants waiting to assist you in your rooms across the corridor. Should either of you find their help unsatisfactory, I trust you will inform me. Good day."

Calliope turned on her heel and walked smartly from the room. Pemma and Selene remained where they were, waiting for Relaina to break out of her stupor. Darren slid out of bed and retrieved his shirt from the washroom. Relaina didn't move as Darren strode past, pulling his shirt on over his head as he went.

"I'll see you later," he muttered. *Praelia smite me.*

"We apologize for the intrusion, Princess," Selene said, inclining her head. "Our matron likes things done a particular way, and she does not waste time or care much for being tactful."

Relaina's heart ached desperately for Victoria as the girls scrubbed her skin and washed her hair in near silence. She tried her best to disappear within herself and focus on what she needed to do that day—meet with King Fabian.

A half hour later, Relaina was thoroughly clean and dressed in a simple, elegant gown the girls had found in the wardrobe. It was surprisingly comfortable after she'd worn nothing but loose shirts and trousers for two weeks. After clasping an opal pendant around her neck, they began to fix Relaina's hair.

"You have lovely hair, Your Highness," Selene said as she combed gently through Relaina's wet curls. "I brought a special elixir that will make it shine."

"Oh?" Relaina raised her eyebrows. Her curls had always been more wild than tame, and she'd given up trying to control them ages ago.

"My mother's hair is similar to yours. I'll show you how she does her own."

The process took a while, but when Relaina spied herself in the mirror, she could only stare.

Her hair had been styled for grand parties and balls before and looked stunning, but these dark, shining curls that cascaded around her face and down her back made her feel more like herself than ever before. They had not been forced into submission by brushes and pins, pulled and yanked into intricate knots. Relaina was and always would be grateful for Victoria, but this...

"Is there anything else we can do for you, Your Highness?"

Relaina blinked herself out of her trance.

"No, thank you. But please call me Relaina."

The girls exchanged a look, and Pemma giggled.

"As you wish," Selene said with a smile, and then they left.

Relaina walked over to the full-length mirror by the wardrobe to examine her appearance, shaking her curls behind her shoulder so she could see the gown fully. The fabric was made of white chiffon that crisscrossed and gathered over her chest, coming to meet at her waist where the color melted into lavender, then a deep violet as the skirt draped gracefully to the floor. Her back was entirely bare. Relaina looked again at her face and hair, blinking tears away.

She huffed a breath and wiped her eyes. If she allowed herself to fall apart now, she wouldn't be able to manage the coming day.

AFTER BEING GROOMED and dressed in a way Darren hadn't had to deal with in many years, he crossed the hall back to Relaina's room and knocked.

She opened the door, her neutral expression fading to unchecked awe as she beheld him in a black tunic with gold stitching. He kept his face smooth, but his thoughts mirrored hers. Her stunning hair and the way the gown hugged her breasts and waist made his knees almost give out.

"Did they dress and bathe you as well?" she asked.

"Yes." The small amount of facial hair he'd grown while traveling had been shaved back to neat stubble on his jawline, and his hair was no longer in his eyes. He tried to hide a smirk. "And they were quite confused when I walked up behind them as they knocked on my door."

Relaina groaned, covering her face in her hands as she stepped aside to let him in. "I don't like the idea of what I do or don't do in my private time being public knowledge or fodder for gossip."

"One would think you'd be used to that by now."

Relaina frowned, turning to look outside at the gathering clouds. "My father made many mistakes. But he was always very good at protecting me from potential scandal, even when I did something stupid. Our servants were always trustworthy, and our nobles knew better than to speak ill of me or my brother and sister, even if we deserved it at times."

"That makes him a hell of a lot better than my father. For what it's worth, I don't entirely blame King Stephan for imprisoning me. Had I been in his position, I may have done the same thing."

Relaina shook her head. "It was foolish. He is far too impulsive and doesn't listen to his advisors when they try to reason with him. He easily could have started a war over your death."

Another knock sounded at Relaina's door, and she massaged her temples. "How many *fucking* times..."

After speaking quietly to one of the servants from earlier, she closed the door and returned holding a cup full of hot liquid, blushing fiercely.

"What is that?"

"It's a...tonic."

"A tonic for wh—*oh.*"

He recognized the distinct smell of the pregnancy-preventing herbs and cringed. It conjured memories he'd tried to forget. Relaina set the tea down on a nearby table.

"We should probably go find the others," she said, striding to the door. "I don't want to keep King Fabian waiting."

"He seems like a reasonable man. I have a feeling it would be exceedingly difficult to offend him."

"Let's hope so." One door stood directly across from hers as they entered the corridor. "Is that one yours?"

Darren nodded. To their right was a dead end with a massive stained-glass window, so they set off in the other direction to locate Bracken's door. Bracken answered almost immediately, wearing a tunic like Darren's but bright orange. He smiled, a very guilty expression on his face, and Relaina let out a snort of laughter.

"What?" he asked, his smile fading.

"You have lip rouge on your face," she said, pointing to her mouth and chin. Bracken's eyes grew wide, and he touched his fingertips to his lips, and sure enough, they were reddish-pink when he studied them. Darren snickered.

"Damn it." Bracken opened the door wider, revealing Jacquelyn, dressed in a light green gown, now quickly wiping the lip rouge from her mouth. "Hand me that cloth, will you?"

Once Bracken and Jacquelyn had removed any incriminating evidence from their faces, Bracken led them to the Grand Hall. Darren laughed as Bracken said, "What if I just like wearing lip rouge?"

"Not your color at all," Darren said. "And it's usually not meant for one's chin."

"He's right," Jacquelyn said.

"Has anyone seen Connor?" Relaina asked, and Jacquelyn clicked her tongue.

"No, and I doubt we will for a while. He left me a note last night saying he was going into the city with a few servants that live off the palace grounds. He probably isn't even awake."

One of two guards came forward and bowed to Relaina once they'd arrived at the doors to the hall.

"His Grace wishes to speak to you alone, first," he said, his face impassive. Relaina inclined her head, and he opened one of the two doors for her.

The rest of them remained at the door, gazing at the walls or exchanging brief glances, an uncomfortable silence growing for several minutes. Darren cleared his throat, and Bracken and Jacquelyn looked at each other, evidently having a silent exchange of some sort. Had Jacquelyn known about Bracken's deceit all this time, or had he kept it from her as well?

The doors before them opened without warning, and a servant beckoned. The room was much larger than Darren had imagined. There were three huge tables, one at the back of the room by a massive fireplace, and one each on the left and right, both beneath banners of the Thereux and Evarian sigils. High windows rose on either side of the fireplace, bathing the hall in warm morning light.

"Join us, all of you!" King Fabian called to them from the smallest table by the fireplace. From another door on the opposite end of the room, Desiree strode inside, accompanied by a man Darren didn't recognize. He was a robust man with a coarse brown beard and tanned skin, wearing a lilac-colored tunic that fit snugly around his thick torso. He took a seat to the king's right, and Desiree sat on Fabian's left. Darren and Bracken sat on either side of Relaina.

"I hope you all slept soundly," Fabian said, smiling at each of them. Everyone gave general murmurs of assent. "Wonderful. The kitchen workers will be coming around any moment with food. After breakfast today you all are welcome to take your meals in your chambers and to venture to the kitchens at your own behest."

Darren glanced at Relaina and frowned. He nudged her gently with his elbow and she looked up at him, blinking rapidly to dispel gathering tears. She handed him a piece of paper beneath the table.

Fabian,

I write to you in great distress. You may have heard by now, but my daughter, Relaina, has fled Parea. The Terranian prince was captured and imprisoned here, but Relaina freed him, and they escaped from the Lynx Guard at the Evarian border. I don't know all of the details, but I do know that Prince Darren did not kidnap her, regardless of the rumors Stephan has sown. Based on a letter she left for me, I know that she felt she must do the right thing, and that she felt she had no other escape from a horribly matched marriage.

While I know she is in Evaria and will likely come to Maremer in pursuit of her friend Bracken, I have no knowledge of what will become of her. I ask you as an old, dear friend, to find her and to look out for her if

you can. I know she can take care of herself—she is
my daughter, after all. But it would put my mind at
ease to know that someone I trust is keeping her safe.
If you do find her, please tell her that I love her. Tell
her that I don't blame her for leaving, even if I wish
she hadn't.

I hope you are well, Fabian. I'm sorry I haven't
written to you very much as of late—we must make our
correspondence a regular occurrence once again.

I miss you dearly, my friend. Jeremiah remains
busy with his duties as the Captain of the Guard here,
but I'm certain he feels the same.

Love and Best Wishes Upon You,
Christine

Darren frowned, his head swimming. King Stephan was trying to spread a rumor that he took Relaina against her will? Darren desperately wished he could speak with Relaina alone, but Relaina reached for the letter and tucked it away into her bodice as a door to the left opened and servants flooded in from the kitchens. The last time Darren had smelled food so delicious was at the Harvest Festival in Castle Alterna. Servants brought out plate after plate of pastries and bacon and cakes, and Darren and the others took and ate what they pleased, making light conversation with one another. The man across from Relaina introduced himself as Lord Vontair, one of King Fabian's councilmen and advisors. When Relaina told him her name in turn, he blanched, setting down his goblet.

"Gods above, are you really?" Based on Vontair's physique, Darren had expected a deep, gravelly tone, but his speech was rather lyrical. He looked to the king on his left, his bushy mustache twitching. "My dear king, you didn't tell me we would be expecting such a royal guest!"

Fabian smiled, but it was unlike the smiles he'd given when he was greeting his new guests the previous night. It didn't quite reach his eyes.

"In truth, Lord Vontair, we weren't expecting her for quite some time. Our young friend Bracken guessed that she and the lovely Jacquelyn would both find their way to us eventually, but they arrived last night."

"Indeed? You must be Jacquelyn." He smiled at her. "Bracken described you in great detail, but I don't think he came close to the beauty I see before me."

Jacquelyn blushed and muttered an embarrassed thanks. Darren resisted the urge to grimace and roll his eyes.

"Oh, but where is your other companion?" Fabian asked. "I believe he is Jacquelyn's brother?"

Bracken finished chewing the pastry he'd picked up and said, "I'm afraid Connor is still missing after last night, King Fabian. He ran off after a servant girl once she'd shown him to his rooms."

Fabian chuckled.

"Ah, to be young. Let him have his fun. I'm sure we will see him at another time. Oh, but how rude of me...I neglected to properly introduce everyone to Lord Vontair. He is one of my most trusted advisors and the official Keeper of Coin."

Lord Vontair inclined his head to all of them. His eyes shifted to Darren, his pleasant smile still plastered on his face.

"I'm afraid I don't know who you are."

The sound of forks on plates stopped. Darren spoke before the silence became too pronounced.

"Darren. Darren LaGuarde."

Lord Vontair's smile faded. Relaina's knuckles had gone white on her fork.

"The elusive Prince of Terrana," the lord said, surprised. "Here in Maremer, with Lyneisians? How intriguing."

"My dear friend," Fabian said, clapping a hand on Vontair's shoulder, and the lord turned to his king. "I would be loath to make our guests recount such a harrowing tale. I will fill you in later. For now, though, we ought to get on with the reason we've gathered?"

"Of course, my king."

"I would like to be truthful with you all," Fabian said. Bracken set down the drink in his hand and shifted in his seat. Darren placed his full attention on the Evarian king.

"About twenty years ago, after King Gabriel's failed attempt to infiltrate Lyneisian defenses, I decided to create my network of spies, the Shadows of Maremer. If ever the Tyrant King were to set his sights on invasion again, I wanted to be ready. It was only two years later that I became king of Evaria. For many years I have watched, waited, and acted in an attempt to stifle the damage done by the Terranian Elite and the tenebrae."

Darren stopped breathing. Someone else *did* know about the tenebrae.

"Ever since your disappearance, Darren, Gabriel has been restless and foolish. We have caught and silenced more of his assassins in the past three years than we had during the previous decade. It was as if your absence made them weaker somehow. Normally, my Shadows stood almost no chance at survival if they came upon a Terranian Elite that was tenebrae. But soon, I received word of more and more of them falling. I took this as a victory."

Darren's heart filled with dread as Fabian heaved a great sigh.

"I was a fool, it seemed." His warm, golden-brown eyes found Darren's, setting him more at ease. "Or rather, I was simply ignorant of the true nature of the tenebrae. What I came to discover over the course of several months was that half of my spies had become tenebrae hosts without my knowledge. The tenebrae controlled them entirely, keeping up the façade of reporting to me just well enough to avoid suspicion for a while. Then violence began breaking out in the places where my Shadows were stationed. One of my best spies came to Maremer unannounced in the middle of the night, bringing the news that her closest friend and fellow spy had tried to kill her. Her description of the attack told us all we needed to know."

Fabian took a shuddering breath.

"A year later, half of my spies were dead at the hands of King

Gabriel. The tenebrae were summoned back to Lues, and we hadn't heard a whisper of them until this incident at the Gnarled Root. I am sharing all of this with you because I have a request."

All of them, even Bracken, waited with bated breath.

"Help me protect Esran. Let us share our knowledge about Gabriel and the tenebrae and help fill the void left by the people who died in the name of protecting the innocent."

Silence filled the hall, pressing down on Darren's ears and lungs.

"We will need time to think and discuss this," Relaina said. Darren exhaled. "If you don't mind."

"Of course. Enjoy the amenities of Seacastle in the meantime. You are welcome here as long as you would like to stay."

"There is no nobler path," Lord Vontair said, "than to join the Shadows. His Majesty has done much work in favor of the safety and prosperity of all of Esran."

"With all due respect, Lord Vontair," Relaina narrowed her eyes, "I did not know of the existence of this network and its apparent role in my own life until yesterday. As I said, we will need time to discuss this amongst ourselves."

"I encourage you to do so," King Fabian said, inclining his head. "And I wish for there to be no more secrets on my part. If you have any questions, I will answer them truthfully. Oh, but what now?"

A servant hailed Fabian, bringing a message from one of his nobles. He and Desiree lingered by the table as the others stood and walked around the room, admiring the statues, banners, and other various treasures mounted on the walls. Two golden swords were crossed beneath an expertly woven tapestry of the Evarian phoenix. Darren's gaze shifted back to Fabian and Desiree, who appeared to be having a whispered argument. She left in a huff, snapping her fingers and taking two guards with her as Fabian continued a hushed conversation with Lord Vontair. How long would someone live if they dared argue with King Stephan or King Gabriel? Not long, in Gabriel's court. But King Fabian simply listened and conversed.

"I think we should do it," Darren said to Relaina, his voice low. She looked up at him, eyebrows raised.

"You've already decided?"

"I know it's a risk, but I'm no stranger to risk. I spent a year in Parea in peace. If I can help them work toward eradicating the Terranian Elite, I might one day live in peace with permanence." And he might make amends for his past.

Relaina's mouth twisted the way it often did when she considered something serious.

"I'm still troubled by all the secrecy," she said, glancing at Bracken. "But I understand the necessity behind it. If you're willing to do it and share the information you have, I will do what I can to help."

Darren nodded, and Relaina beckoned to Jacquelyn and Bracken.

"Did you know of this before?" Relaina asked Jacquelyn without preamble.

Jacquelyn exchanged a glance with Bracken.

"Yes. Not the details, but I knew he worked for King Fabian."

"I'm so sorry about the interruption," King Fabian said, walking toward them. Lord Vontair had disappeared. "Now that we've all had something to eat, why don't I show you around the palace?"

As they traversed the halls and passed by servants who bowed hastily upon their king's approach, Darren got the sense that most noble guests did not receive a tour of the palace from the king himself. Natural light filled the different rooms, filtering in from the massive windows that existed in every corner of the palace. Darren's favorite room was the ballroom on the northern side—the massive hall made entirely of glass that they'd seen upon their arrival the night before. Like the entrance hall, numerous crystal chandeliers hung from its domed ceiling, giving off the illusion of twinkling stars, even against the clouds above. Outside was a magnificent view of the Great Sea, just beyond the cliffs.

Despite the magnificence and splendor of it all, Darren couldn't keep himself from taking note of the different escape routes he could utilize to sneak out of the palace without detection, if need be. He watched Relaina carefully as well, gauging her reaction to everything. She was distracted and subdued...until they reached the library.

Two floors full of massive bookshelves appeared before them as they stepped through the large oak doors. The far wall was, much like the ballroom, all glass, giving a full view of the palace's interior gardens.

Desks and chairs stood everywhere, some occupied, most empty. The railing of the spiral staircase leading to the second floor was a deep cherry wood color, polished and shining as it swept upwards. Numerous candles gave the entire cavernous room a golden, warm glow.

"I take it by your expressions that you are pleased with my library," King Fabian said with a grin. Beside Darren, Relaina nodded, still gaping at all the books. "You are welcome here any time."

Relaina looked like Fabian had just given her a puppy. Darren couldn't help but smile to himself at her unbridled joy.

"Oi! Jacquelyn, Brack—oh, gods." Connor had leapt up from a table and approached them before noticing the king. He stopped dead and sank into a clumsy bow. "Your Majesty."

"You must be Connor. Welcome."

Connor nodded, dumbstruck.

"It's here that I'll take my leave," Fabian said, addressing them all. "Let my servants know where you'd like to eat lunch. I'll be in several meetings this afternoon and evening, but I would like for you all to join me after dinner for a drink, and we can discuss your involvement further."

They all decided to dine in Relaina's rooms after bidding Fabian farewell and assuring him they would join him for the meeting later that night. Darren and Relaina noticed at the same time that the bed had been remade since this morning, and both of them quickly looked away from one another, cheeks burning as they sat around a table large enough for six. Darren chastised himself for being so ridiculous; there was no reason for him to feel so embarrassed about sleeping with her. It wasn't like he was *sleeping* with her.

"So, Bracken," Darren said as Relaina occupied herself with the food, "how does this all work? How was I trailed by Fabian's Shadows for so long without knowing?"

Bracken's explanation of locations and procedures took up most of the afternoon. As the already dull light grew dimmer, they each ended up in various lounging locations in Relaina's chambers: Darren and Relaina took the two plush, purple chairs by the fire, Bracken remained in one of the dining chairs but had turned it in at least three different directions, Jacquelyn sat by Bracken on a cushion on the floor, and Connor lay sprawled upon the largest couch, staring at the ceiling.

"So, we would be split up and expected to station ourselves in various locations around Esran?" Darren asked. The last thing he wanted to do was start traveling again.

"No," Bracken said, shaking his head. "King Fabian would never expect you or Relaina to execute a mission like that; you're both too important in this to risk. You'll remain here in Maremer and carry out missions within the city itself. Darren, I expect the king will want to meet with you quite a lot to find out as much as he can about the tenebrae."

"Understandable. What about you three?"

"We may be sent out on occasion, but there is much work to do in the city. King Fabian is worried after the attack last night; there's never been a tenebrae attack within the walls of Maremer. He's concerned there are more."

"His concern is not unfounded. When I fought Xavier over a year ago, I destroyed the tenebrae within him, and then killed him not two weeks ago. Most of them do not forgive the destruction of their kind."

"Why didn't the tenebrae possess me that night in the inn?" Relaina asked. She'd been quiet for hours. Darren looked at her in the firelight.

"I...I don't know. I've never seen that happen before, almost like it couldn't bear to touch you."

Silence filled the room. If Darren didn't know, none of them would.

After dinner, they returned to the banquet hall to meet with the king. Some of the ever-present worry in Darren's heart eased as Relaina told Fabian they would help him fight the Tyrant King.

"I am gladdened to hear that you're willing to help us." The king raised his glass of wine. "To your bravery, resilience, and continued health."

Darren raised his glass. *To my father's downfall.*

CHAPTER 14

IN THE CITY

Relaina had felt the beginnings of an emotional avalanche since that morning. She held it together all day and just long enough for Darren to shut the door behind them as they retired for the night, and then she sank to the floor and burst into tears.

Darren joined her on the floor and offered her his hand, which she took and gripped tightly.

"I-I'm s-sorry," she said, too embarrassed to look at him.

"Don't be." Whether or not he knew why she'd fallen apart, he sat there with her in steady silence while she cried.

"I can stay again, if you want me to."

"Please."

They sat for a while longer, until Relaina's breathing became more even again.

"I miss them," she said. "Everyone back home...I didn't expect it to be so difficult." Darren squeezed her clammy hand, and Relaina squeezed back before releasing him and wiping her palm on her dress. "But I don't regret it. I'd hoped for a new start here and that I could leave behind my title and past, but I don't think either of us are going to get away with that."

"It would seem not."

Relaina sniffled, finally looking at him. "I didn't intend for any of this to happen."

"Neither did I." His eyebrows scrunched together as he draped his arms over his knees. "I can't ease the ache of missing those you love, but if you'd like, when it's just us, we don't have to be Prince Darren or Princess Relaina. When we're alone, or with Bracken and Jacquelyn and Connor, we can just be ourselves. No pretending. No secret agendas. Just Relaina. Just Darren."

Relaina's chest eased a bit. "I would like that."

That night, Relaina stared at the bed hangings with tired eyes, yet still she could not quiet her thoughts enough to sleep. She listened for Darren's steady breathing as she sat up, looking through the darkness at the curtains concealing the windows. When she was certain that he was sound asleep, she slid out of bed and tiptoed to the wardrobe, grimacing as the door creaked, but he didn't stir. Relaina sighed in relief and removed dark, simple clothing from the deepest corner of the wardrobe. After lacing up her boots and placing a note for Darren on her pillow, she made her way to the door.

Her silent feet led her back to the glass ballroom, almost on the opposite side of the palace from her rooms. She found the narrow staircase she'd noted earlier, her hand gliding against the cool glass of the rail until it ran underground and turned to stone, and finally she happened upon a door. It opened with hardly any noise at all. The scent of baking bread lingered, ghostlike, in the air of the dimly lit corridor. Relaina stepped farther inside, assessing how long the corridor was by the number of intermittent lanterns she could count. About ten of them, each several feet apart.

Only a few more steps and she was inside the massive kitchens, standing in what appeared to be a servant's dining room. The wooden table appeared plain yet sturdy, and at the far end, sitting by candlelight with a book in one hand and a scone in the other, was King Fabian.

"Relaina," he said, setting down his book next to a cup of tea. "This is a pleasant surprise."

"K—Fabian. I'm sorry if I'm intruding."

"Not at all. Join me, please."

Relaina did, sitting in the chair to his left. He poured her some tea in an extra cup and offered her a scone from his plate, which she accepted gladly. It tasted like oranges and cinnamon.

"This is delicious."

"A favorite of mine. Ever since I was a child."

"I still find it hard to imagine that my mother and uncle grew up here. My uncle must have loved going to that library."

Fabian smiled softly. "Getting him to ever *leave* the library was almost impossible. I see you share his love of books."

"Very much so. Do you have any recommendations?"

"Hmm." Fabian took a sip from his cup of tea. "I may have a few I keep in my personal collection that you would enjoy. I'll have a servant bring them tomorrow."

Relaina took a sip of tea herself, letting the notes of hibiscus and orange peel wash over her tongue. Fabian was quiet and pensive, garbed in a deep violet robe, his head unadorned with a crown or circlet.

"Fabian, do you ever get to just...be yourself?"

Fabian huffed through his nose, his eyes suddenly heavy with responsibility.

"Not often. We royals have a duty to appear and act a certain way, to lead by example when the eyes of our subjects are upon us. It's not terribly often that the eyes of my subjects are not upon me."

Relaina frowned. "I know that feeling."

"You, Relaina, are still young, and not a ruler. You made a choice that may guarantee you never become one, a fact of which you are well aware and with which you may be content. But a circumstance of your birth, sovereign or not, is that people will look to you for guidance and leadership in troubling times. And I fear that troubling times are upon us."

Relaina sipped her tea some more, mulling.

"Take heart, though," Fabian said, his smile warm. "Here you will find less scrutiny than what you are accustomed to. I hope you will find peace in the presence of your companions."

Relaina nodded, struck once again by his sincerity.

"When will we find out what our assignments are?"

"Soon. You should know I do not plan to give you something easy because of your station. Are you certain you're comfortable with that?"

"I want to be useful, not burdensome."

Fabian closed his eyes and nodded once. "Then I will send for you all when it's time."

Relaina stared at what was left of her tea for a moment.

"Do you know why Gabriel is after me? I'm no spy or assassin. How could someone like me pose such a threat to the Tyrant King?"

Fabian shook his head. "That, I'm afraid, has always been the missing piece. I'd hoped Darren would know, but it would seem the Tyrant King keeps that secret close."

"Then I will await your instructions and aid you in fighting against him."

"I appreciate your help more than you know. But until then, enjoy the city, get to know its layout. It's quite beautiful here."

Relaina nodded again, yawning. "I'm sorry. I'm quite tired."

"Go get some rest. No one will wake you in the morning. If I may offer a suggestion, have Bracken take you all into the city in the morning to a café owned by Madame Follier. They have a most excellent bakery and the best tea in Maremer."

Relaina smiled softly. "Thank you, Fabian." She stood, heading back to her rooms and to Darren.

As FABIAN HAD PROMISED, there was no knock on the door the next morning, so Relaina and Darren didn't have to endure any further embarrassment. Darren went across the hall to his room to find clean clothes while Relaina struggled to find something inconspicuous to wear into the city; she finally extracted a modest tunic and pulled on a forest-green cloak.

"I wonder if Connor will want to come as well," Relaina said as she used some of the elixir to refresh her curls. They'd stayed mostly intact even through the night, and it took little effort to adjust the few that had become misshapen against her pillow. Darren leaned against her wardrobe, already prepared to leave.

"I'm sure he'll want to. I can't imagine he'd want to stay in this palace all day again, even if it does provide such extravagant amenities—and women."

Relaina moved away from her vanity and fastened the cords on her cloak. "That reminds me, I want to write a letter to my mother when we return. I can't remember how to get to the library, though..."

"I don't remember either, but I'm sure Bracken could show us."

They left the room and, like the day before, knocked on Bracken's door. He answered it promptly but gazed at them with drooping eyes framed by dark circles.

"Are you all right?" Relaina asked.

"Just tired. Jacquelyn's not feeling well. I slept on the couch to give her some space, but the coughing kept me awake all night."

"Oh no. I...well, we were going to ask if you would show us around the city, but I can understand if you would rather stay with her."

Bracken's eyes lit up. "Oh, I'd love to go into the city." He glanced over his shoulder. "I think she's finally asleep, and in all honesty, Jacquelyn is horrible when she's ill. Short temper and a real grouch since she's stuck in bed all day. Just give me a moment to put on some proper clothes."

Relaina and Darren waited outside for Bracken to change, Relaina growing rather impatient. She was eager to see more of Maremer...and also quite hungry. Darren, standing across the hall on the opposite wall, caught her eye.

"What?" she asked.

Darren smiled crookedly and broke her gaze, shaking his head. "Nothing."

"You find my impatience amusing."

"You get this look on your face as if you've just bitten into a sour grape."

"That expression scares most people."

"I'm not easily intimidated."

Relaina opened her mouth to fire back a retort, but Bracken opened his door and came striding out into the hall.

"Gods, do they make anything simple here?" he asked, fastening a belt around his waist.

Bracken dodged the pillow Connor launched after waking him and led the way to the stables on the eastern side of the palace grounds. Relaina was pleased to find that Amariah had been well taken care of and even groomed, her silky black coat gleaming and her mane neatly braided. They each mounted up and headed for the gate. The guards did not speak as they passed, staring straight ahead and holding their spears upright.

The city was far more crowded than it had been the night they'd arrived; vendors strolled about, hawking their goods, insisting that their prices and quality were the best; merchants dressed in garments of all shapes and sizes came in and out of shops to buy and sell what they had acquired on their trips abroad; parents held the hands of their children, who tried desperately to pull free whenever they saw something to their fancy. Relaina had never in all her life seen such vibrancy and diversity of life in one place. As much as she wanted to stop and look at everything around them, her stomach had other ideas.

Being on horseback made it easier to navigate the streets; they could see above the heads of most people, and even the thickest crowds would part to make way for three large horses carrying people that, despite their efforts to blend in, clearly appeared noble. Relaina sighed. At least she'd tried.

The harbor appeared, the masts of ships and their sails towering above the buildings before them. Though it seemed impossible to Relaina that the crowd could get any denser, they soon found the way impassable on horseback, and were forced to dismount and leave their horses with a couple of city guards standing by the entrance to a temple.

"As much as I hate to admit it," Bracken said, leading the way through the crowd, "having those guards crawling all over the place is quite convenient."

Soon they'd made their way out of the streets and into the fish market by the harbor. Hundreds of stalls surrounded them, roofed with different colored canvases. Relaina wrinkled her nose at the strong odor.

"You'll get used to it," Bracken said.

They shuffled through the busy market, headed for a tall building perched on a rocky outcrop overlooking the bay. They walked along the docks and up a flight of stairs before entering the café on the top floor. They were seated at a table by the balcony railing, vines hanging from the ceiling above to frame the view of the bay and sea beyond. Relaina had a hard time not staring at the clear blue of the bay and the trees that bordered it, which had just begun turning into brilliant shades of red, orange, and yellow.

They ate at a leisurely pace, enjoying the tea and baked goods immensely. Relaina had never gone to a place like this in Parea.

"I almost wish we could stay here in the city," Relaina said. Bracken had just taken a rather large bite out of a roll.

"Iz jus' no' az safe," he said, mouth full. Relaina rolled her eyes at him.

"Really?"

"Wha'?" He swallowed. "I don't have to keep up appearances for anybody anymore."

"Lucky bastard." Relaina smiled. He really was the same as he always was, ever her friend and supporter. He'd just kept a life-altering secret for five years.

As midmorning approached, they returned to the fish market, curious to see what fishermen and sailors were selling. There were shiny, silver fish, clams, oysters, shells made into jewelry, crabs, and one man was selling seaweed, trying to convince everyone within earshot that it was versatile enough to be both food and a headdress.

"Your lover will love it! They can wear it to a gathering, and then eat it when they get hungry!"

Relaina giggled. "Can you imagine if someone had shown up to a ball at Castle Alterna wearing a seaweed headdress?"

Bracken snorted. "All the nobles would've fainted."

Relaina looked at Darren, and her smile faded. His face had gone white.

"What's wrong?"

He blinked and shook his head. "I'm not sure. I'll...I'll be right back."

⁓

THROUGH THE DENSE CROWD, a woman nearby made very deliberate eye contact with Darren, paying no mind to the people around her. She wore a gray cloak, hood pulled up to obscure her face, but as she turned and began walking away, there was no mistaking that she wanted him to follow her. But how was she here?

He followed the woman out of the fish market and down the street, where she turned a corner after throwing him another glance. He walked after her, turning right at the end of the street and finding himself in an alley with a dead end. Buildings rose on either side of the alley with windows a few stories up, but no doors on this level. There was no sign of life here besides Darren and the woman standing before him. She lowered her hood, letting her long, honey-blonde hair fall loose over her shoulders, her dark eyes boring into him as she smiled.

"Hello, Prince Darren."

"Katarina. What are you doing here?"

She began walking toward him, smirking.

"You aren't the only one who fled Terrana when you had the chance," she said into his ear as she passed him, looking him over. She made a full circle and then stood in front of him again. "You've changed."

"You haven't," Darren said. She laughed throatily, brushing her hair over her shoulder. "Why did you leave Terrana? I thought your father was favored by the king."

Katarina frowned. "My father tried to force me to marry Lord Gerratt."

"My uncle." Darren grimaced.

"Your uncle. I've been living in Maremer for a few months now, passing as a common tavern wench and working for King Fabian as one of his Shadows. I stole enough money from my father to rent myself a place to stay in the inn where I work, and once King Fabian approached me, I didn't have to worry about making a wage. But enough of my tedious woes. I saw you today at the market and could hardly believe my eyes. They've been searching for you for years, and here I find you without even trying."

"I've been keeping well out of sight."

"Clearly. You look taller than when I last saw you. And stronger." She walked closer, so her mouth was close to his. "It's a shame you weren't this handsome four years ago. Any time you want to come by, my door's always open..."

Darren took a step back. "I'm not interested."

"Oh? That's too bad. Found some girl, have you?"

When Darren didn't answer, Katarina's eyes lit up.

"You *have*!"

Darren turned to leave.

"Who is she? How did you meet her if you were in hiding?"

"It doesn't matter." He tried to walk quickly, but Katarina kept up easily, persistent.

"If it didn't matter, you could tell me. Is she important? Some noble's daughter? Is she Evarian?"

"Katarina." Darren stopped before they reached the open street again, facing her. "Just because you and I once shared a bed doesn't mean you get to know everything about me and what I've been doing."

"Oh, please. You were in love with me."

"I couldn't have loved you, Katarina. Not when I was so broken."

"An intimate friend and confidant, then. I did you a favor by becoming your paramour. You would tell me anything."

"Things you were unable to keep to yourself."

Katarina frowned, her eyes wandering over to the fish market.

"I was just trying to tell them that you wouldn't be like King Gabriel," she said quietly. "I didn't know he'd find out and..."

Darren didn't respond. The last thing he needed right now was for those memories to surface when he had nothing to ground him. Katarina didn't seem to notice his sudden anxiety and kept staring at the crowd in the market. Her mouth popped open into a small *o*.

"That girl...she was the one beside you earlier. Is that her? I didn't see her face."

Darren blinked and followed her gaze, and sure enough, Relaina was standing just outside of the market with Bracken, her arms crossed and her green eyes sparkling with concern. Katarina looked back at him.

"She *is* noble! Those clothes are far too expensive for a common girl to afford. Trust me, I would know."

"It doesn't matter. She doesn't want me."

For a moment, Katarina and Darren watched Relaina scan the market crowd, brow furrowed.

"Seems to me like she's looking for you." She turned to face him. "Do you love her?"

Darren didn't answer, momentarily stunned.

Did he?

Katarina smiled sadly. "I'm sorry to pry. I want you to be happy."

Darren blinked. Perhaps Katarina had changed after all.

"You know, I really hated you when you left Terrana. *Not* because I was in love with you," Katarina said when Darren grinned wolfishly. "No, you ass, I was fooling around with General Roan prior to our arrangement and he intended to propose, but my father was determined to find a way to have *you* marry me. I knew you were kinder than your father, and I figured if my father was going to treat me like those Lyneisian prudes and make me marry someone I didn't choose for myself, at least you wouldn't hurt me. When you left, my father went mad. He was so disappointed that I'd lost the chance to be queen that he had Roan demoted to one of the training camps and forced me into an engagement with Lord Gerratt since his family is next in line after yours for the crown."

Darren's smile faded. "I'm sorry."

"Don't be. Your father's good intentions disappeared when he turned to the tenebrae. He made choices that nearly destroyed you and could destroy the rest of us. Now that I look back on it, I'm surprised you didn't leave sooner."

"I'm glad you got out of there, Katarina." She nodded and replaced her hood once more.

"I'll see you around, Darren. King Fabian often holds meetings in the palace for the Shadows that walk the city. If you need anything, let me know."

With that, she walked out into the crowd again and disappeared. Darren emerged from the alleyway and headed for Relaina and Bracken. When Relaina caught sight of him, the softening of her features made his heart ache. For a moment, out of all the people around them, her face was the only one he could see, beautiful in its relieved impatience.

He was doing rather poorly with the idea of just being her friend.

"Where did you go?" Relaina asked.

"I saw someone I recognized," Darren said. "Her name is Katarina. We were, uh, friends in Terrana."

It was immediately apparent in her facial expression that Relaina understood what kind of "friends" they had been. Darren's face flushed.

"*Gods*, would you look at that sun in the sky?" Bracken said. "I'd best be off to check on Jacquelyn and bring her some...herbs...or something."

Bracken hastened away through the crowd, and Relaina and Darren headed for the docks, walking by the moored ships. They said nothing for a while, a heaviness in the air between them that Darren wanted to dispel. A few times they dodged sailors that came running up the planks in a hurry, but as they neared the outer edge of the harbor where cliffs rose high above the sea to the palace, there were fewer people to avoid.

"Tell me about Terranian court," Relaina said. "I know that it's different from Lyneisia, but all I've heard is rumor."

Darren sighed, grateful that she had spoken first. "It's mostly a cesspool of corruption. The nobles either love my father or hate him, but they support him and do everything he wants regardless. But it wasn't always like that. I never met my grandmother, but I heard she was a wise and fair ruler."

"What happened to her?"

"From what I was told, she was prone to illnesses, and they took a steeper toll as she aged. My father ascended the throne when he was twenty-six."

"And we know what's happened since."

"It's unfortunate. My father burned all records of my grandmother's reign. The only reason I know these things is because my mother told me when he wasn't around."

Darren could still picture his mother's face as he gazed out at the sparkling sea; her smiling brown eyes and raven-black hair. He thanked the gods every day that he'd been graced with her eyes, even if he was cursed to resemble his father in every other feature.

"So what did Katarina want?"

"She wanted to know why I was here. She fled Terrana not too long ago, found a place to stay here a few months back, and has begun working for Fabian."

"Was she a noble in Terrana?"

Darren nodded. "She was a guest at the castle in Lues because her father was a favorite of the king, and her father pressured her to...seduce me so I'd marry her."

"Ah."

"Women are seldom forced into arranged marriages in Terrana. But Katarina's father was power-hungry and spent most of his time scheming in the Obsidian Keep. The Terranian Court is a vile place with my father on the throne. He would degrade me in front of the nobles regularly."

Relaina's eyes widened. "For what reason?" Darren shrugged and shook his head.

"Demonstrating his absolute control, showing his willingness to stoop to any level to get what he wants."

"Gods. Was he always so cruel?"

"I remember he was...better, at least, when my mother was still alive." An old, familiar weight settled on his heart. "Or perhaps she simply shielded me from him. When I was eight, she and my five-year-old brother died in a carriage accident."

"I'm so sorry." Relaina stopped as they reached the end of the docks.

"I didn't always hate him," he said, compelled by the vulnerable softness and compassion in her eyes. "I even admired him when I was younger; he could be harsh at times, but a good king needed to be unmovable and without self-doubt, I thought. But after I became one of his assassins, one of his...*tools*, I saw him clearly. He once spoke of a united Esran, but not for the sake of peace or harmony. He wished to rule over it all."

Relaina was quiet for a while. Darren hoped he hadn't somehow offended or frightened her. It was the first time he'd been able to speak of any of it without gut-wrenching fear and grief.

"That still doesn't explain what he wants with *me*."

Darren sighed. "No. It does not."

They headed back to Seacastle Palace, retrieving their horses from the same guards who'd taken them earlier. A stack of books waited for

Relaina on the dining table next to lunch, and she examined each one eagerly, running her fingers along the leather covers marked with titles in gold or silver and covered in beautiful symbols.

"Such lovely editions," she said, and Darren smirked beside her. Relaina picked up a stunning green novel, *The Sailor and the Songbird*. As she reached for a slice of bread, a small piece of paper slipped out of the middle of the book, landing just shy of a shallow dish full of marmalade. She picked it up and unfolded it.

"What's that?"

"I'm not sure," Relaina said, squinting at the faded handwriting. She read the note several times. "Oh."

"Oh?"

"I don't think Fabian meant to leave this here."

> Fabian —
>
> I particularly enjoyed this one, and I think you will too. Read it while I'm away so we can discuss it upon my return. I'll be back within the fortnight, and I'll come to you as soon as I'm able, as promised.
>
> I love

"He must look at it often," Relaina said. "Look how faded it is. What is that...an *I*? An *L*? I can't tell."

Darren frowned. "Strange. He must have forgotten it was inside."

"I wonder who it could be? If only I could tell what that last letter was..."

Darren leaned over to look at it more closely.

"It's so faded it could be anything. You could try to find out."

"It's none of my business, really," Relaina said, tucking the note back into the book. "I don't want people prying into my personal affairs, and I'm certain Fabian doesn't either."

They finished lunch and spoke of other things—training, the weather, their potential Shadow assignments. Darren found himself content in her presence, and wondered again about the question Katarina had asked him.

Do you love her?

And, if the answer was yes, what would he do?

CHAPTER 15

THE SCHEME

Snow was falling in Parea, and Jeremiah Andovier observed the annual winter preparations with an excess of melancholy. The temperature in Castle Alterna remained comfortable—even the king's chambers on the thirteenth floor were expertly sealed against the cold with hides that had been deemed unfit for leather armor. Even so, the atmosphere of the corridors rang hollow and somber with Relaina's absence ever on his mind.

Jeremiah left his study to join Christine in the seventh floor lounge, nodding at servants hanging hides against the open air of the sixth floor. The guards outside the lounge nodded, muttering, "Captain," as he entered the room.

"Brother." Christine stood from her chair and handed him a piece of parchment. His heart leapt at the sight of the familiar handwriting.

> *Mother,*
> *I read the letter you sent to an old friend. I am with him, and he is a kind host, with a large house. He's given me your old rooms to stay in.*
> *I'm safe here, or as safe as I can be. I want you*

to know that I miss you terribly, and I worry for your safety as well. I have found an old friend too, and while he knows many things, he is not a traitor. All of you at home should be vigilant—a traitor may still be among you.

The man Father mistrusts is not an evil man. He is, in fact, a better man than many others I know. I am safe in his company, and he is safe in mine. We have been working with your friend to help make our kingdoms safe once more.

I'll write again as soon as I can. Please give my love to my brother and sister, and my uncle. I have no idea how he ever could have left all of the books in this exquisite library behind.

    Love,

    Laines

Jeremiah handed the letter back to Christine, relief washing over him. Relaina was with Fabian. He covered his face with his hands.

"I'm so glad she's safe," he said. Christine reached over and squeezed his hand.

"As am I."

Jeremiah stared out the window at the flurries of snow falling against the night sky.

"Do you think she knows?" he asked. Christine shifted in her chair, sighing.

"No. I believe that letter would have been very different if she did. Or she may not have written at all."

"I wonder if she'll stay in Maremer a while."

"There's no way to know." Christine looked at him with those scrutinizing eyes he usually tried to avoid. "I wonder how it's changed. The last time I visited was more than ten years ago. And for you..."

Jeremiah frowned at the floor. "Twenty-one years."

"You know you can go back now."

"Can I?"

"Fabian lifted your banishment years ago. You don't have to stay here and serve a kingdom that isn't your own. You're the heir to our house. Stephan would understand."

"Lyneisia has been my home for half my life. I'll return to Evaria when Mother passes and I have no choice but to take the seat at Crestfall."

His sister frowned but did not press him further. It was the same conversation they'd had many times, and it always ended the same way —with Jeremiah insisting that he would stay, that he was happy here. And he was, or at least he had been until recently.

A knock came at the door then, and King Stephan strode through, haggard as he so often was these days. Jeremiah stood and bowed, and Stephan waved a hand for him to sit again.

"What's the news?" the king asked, sitting in a chair across from his wife and Jeremiah. He propped up his feet and pinched the bridge of his nose.

"A letter from Relaina," Christine said, and Stephan sat up. Christine handed him the letter and he read through quickly, his brow furrowed.

"It seems...it seems she is working with King Fabian." He looked at Christine. "So, she is in Maremer."

"We believe so," Christine said. They sat in silence for a few more moments while Stephan looked at the letter again.

"She seems well," he said, no ounce of kingliness in his voice.

"Are there still guards after them?" Christine asked.

"No," Jeremiah said. "They've all returned empty-handed. They await my next instructions, Stephan."

The king looked at him, weary-eyed.

"Send them back to their posts within the castle or city. It's time we move forward."

Jeremiah was both relieved and disappointed. He wanted nothing more than Relaina's happiness and safety, but he also deeply missed her.

Stephan's decision now made it official that Aronn was Crown Prince, and that Relaina was under no obligation to return.

"I'll make the announcement in the morning," the king said with a heavy sigh. "We'll need to send someone to wake Aronn."

For a while they all sat in silence, the weight of the decision to name Aronn heir hanging in the air. *As it should have been, anyway.* Aronn wasn't a natural leader like Relaina, but the Lyneisian crown was his birthright, and all three of them knew it.

"She would have been an exceptional queen," Stephan said, almost to himself.

"What will you do should Relaina return?" Christine asked. Stephan blinked slowly and looked up at her as the fire crackled behind him.

"I will beg her forgiveness. I...I have not been the father that she needed. I did not see...or I did not want to see how she began to struggle in recent months. Or was it years? I never...it is shameful to admit...but she is a stranger to me. Jeremiah is closer to her than I ever was."

Jeremiah wanted to reassure Stephan that he'd done his best with the circumstances, but he'd watched Relaina struggle, too, and Stephan had done nothing to help her.

"We will move forward," Christine said, reaching to take her husband's hand. "Relaina is safe. That much we know. Aronn is clever and has been taking his studies and duties much more seriously lately. He will make a fine king."

Stephan nodded absently, his gaze on his fingers, entwined with Christine's.

"What of the warning Relaina gave in her letter?" Jeremiah asked. "About a traitor in our midst?"

"That must be dealt with as well," Stephan said, sitting up taller. "I would have you call upon our Sacred Guard, Jeremiah. They will follow us at a distance and keep their eyes out for any eavesdroppers."

Jeremiah nodded, already thinking through the logistics.

"And from now on, all letters and messages sent must be ciphered," Stephan said. "Even within the castle. We'll need to teach Annalise the solution. Aronn has learned it already."

"Wise," Christine said, nodding. "I will teach her myself."

"I'll begin preparations tonight," Jeremiah said as he stood, palming the hilt of his sword. "If either of you receive a guard you do not recognize, send for me immediately but discreetly."

"We'll also need a fair amount of guards present tomorrow for my announcement."

Jeremiah nodded and turned to leave.

"I fear," he turned around as he reached the door, "we may now only be able to trust ourselves."

Christine smirked without an ounce of humor in her eyes.

"Then not much has changed, has it?"

"AND HERE YOU'LL find Lord Barlaye, he's rather fond of hunting," King Stephan said. "I've never seen him arrive anywhere without having just shot some poor beast to parade it through whatever city or village he's visiting. Gods, man, just eat it and be done with it."

Aronn yawned as his father continued talking and pointing out places on the map. He'd been awake since dawn, endured his father's announcement that he was the new heir, and now he sat slumped in a chair, cheek resting heavily on his hand as his father recited the familial habits and locations of every last noble house in Lyneisia. They'd been at this for hours, and he could no longer keep straight the difference between Lord Barlaye and Lord Howsen and the Green Valley as opposed to the Gold Valley.

"Father."

"Hmm?"

"Could we start again in the morning? I'm exhausted."

"Aronn, you must study diligently and make sure you know these things," Stephan said. Aronn looked up at him, his eyelids drooping. The king sighed. "But very well, you're dismissed. Be back here before midmorning."

Aronn nodded and stood from the chair at his father's desk, relieved to be headed for bed. He was half-asleep as he trudged to his chambers, yawning again, when he turned back and took a different corridor. He knocked on Annalise's door.

"Aronn!" His sister flung her arms around him. "You look tired."

"I am, but I wanted to come by before I went to bed. How was your day?"

"Not a bad day." Annalise flopped down on her white couch. She was the only person Aronn knew that wouldn't soil the upholstery with food or drink. "After Father's announcement, Mother and I went for a walk in the gardens, and Uncle Jeremiah gave me a book. Oh, and Lucinda fitted me for a gown for the winter ball."

"Gods, is that happening so soon?" The thought made him wearier.

"In about a month. She says she'll make my dress more extravagant than usual, since..."

She lapsed into silence, but what was left unsaid weighed upon him —*since Relaina is gone*. Annalise's eyes filled with tears.

"Why did she have to leave?" Annalise asked.

Aronn sat up from where he'd slouched in a chair.

"She had to do what was right. For herself, and for the Prince of Terrana," he said.

"Why is everyone saying that he captured her? I heard the servants whispering about it near the kitchens today."

"Father wanted to paint him as a villain to justify capturing him. It's not a terrible strategy. King Gabriel would have a harder time justifying attacking Lyneisia for his capture or execution if his son were the one to strike first."

Annalise's forehead wrinkled.

"But it's dishonest. And he was going to kill Darren anyway, even before Relaina saved him."

Aronn blinked. He wasn't aware that his sister knew so much.

"He was, and it is dishonest."

"I met Darren, and he was nice enough to me. If Father had spoken to him, perhaps he would've had a change of heart."

"Perhaps."

"If he had, then Relaina could have married him."

"I don't follow."

"Father would have spoken to Darren." Annalise held out her hands as she listed things off. "He would realize Darren is a nice person. Then Relaina wouldn't have had to leave, and since Darren is a prince, they could have married. Relaina obviously likes him if she gave up the crown to save his life. It would have been perfect."

Aronn could only stare at Annalise, his heart aching for this to have been the outcome of recent events.

"And," Annalise said, "if Relaina married him, it would have connected Lyneisia and Terrana. People would start to get along better. Well, after the Tyrant King is dead, at least."

"Hmm." Aronn's brow furrowed. "Gabriel LaGuarde would have certainly been a complication in that plan. I wonder what would've made him angrier with Lyneisia—killing his son, or marrying his son to the heir apparent of his rival kingdom?"

"I don't know. But I just wish Relaina was still here."

"I do too."

They sat in relative silence for a few more moments, Aronn staring out the window without seeing anything.

"Aronn, will you lie when you're king?"

Aronn frowned—could he promise he wouldn't?

"I will always aim to do the right thing. And I will never lie to you, Annalise."

"Good."

After bidding Annalise goodnight, Aronn trekked back to his own room, his feet heavy in the dark corridors. He was so tired he almost didn't recognize the figure walking past him.

"Zarias? What are you doing here?"

Zarias Conclave stopped, mildly startled. "Oh, Aronn! I was looking for you. I wanted to congratulate you on your new appointment as Crown Prince."

"Oh. Well, thank you, but it's nearly midnight. You ought to leave before the guards find you and kick you out. They've been far stricter lately."

"Right you are. I'll see you later then."

Zarias headed for the staircase at the end of the hall, and Aronn shook his head a few times. He hadn't spoken to Zarias in weeks, not since Relaina had fled the city, and he couldn't imagine who else would have invited Zarias into the castle. Aronn groaned—a mystery for another day when he wasn't so exhausted.

He arrived at his room, flung his shirt and shoes off, and fell into bed, staring at the ceiling until his eyes began to droop shut.

A thud startled Aronn awake. He blinked at the gentle pre-dawn light coming in from his windows, groaning and placing a pillow over his head to drown out the rapping at his door. Who in the name of the gods would call on him at this hour?

"Go away!" he said. The knocking stopped, and Aronn sighed in relief, already drifting back to sleep.

BANG!

Aronn nearly flew out of bed as his door opened with a crash and Zarias, Samuel, and Laviath walked inside.

"What the hell? How did you get in here?" Aronn scrambled out of bed as they approached. Zarias stopped directly in front of him, and as the fog of sleep cleared from his eyes, Aronn noticed what Samuel and Laviath were holding.

Rope.

Aronn ran but didn't get far. Samuel grabbed him by the arms, and Laviath dealt a blow to Aronn's stomach that had him on his knees. They began binding him by his wrists and ankles as he struggled to breathe. Zarias grabbed him by the roots of his hair, forcing Aronn's head back.

"You f—!" They shoved a piece of rope between his teeth, cutting off his curse. He screamed at Zarias and the others, the sound of his rage dampened by the gag.

"Don't take this personally, Aronn," Zarias said. "But in order for me to be king and establish my line, Lyneisia needs a crown princess, not a crown prince."

Aronn's eyes widened. *Annalise.* He kicked and pulled against his bindings but Samuel and Laviath held him down.

"Let's go," Zarias said. They placed a hood over Aronn's head, and Aronn lashed out once again, this time kicking Zarias in the face. "Gods *damn* it! Laviath!"

Aronn squirmed, trying desperately to get away, but a blow from Laviath caught him swift and sure over the head, and darkness swallowed him.

CHAPTER 16

SECRETS OF THE TYRANT KING

Relaina sat at the large meeting table, trying hard to keep herself from drumming her fingers or bouncing her leg as they waited for King Fabian and the rest of his Shadows to arrive. She hadn't met any of them yet, save for Bracken, and was unsure how they would react to her presence—and Darren's.

The doors opened for the fifth or sixth time that evening, and a woman walked inside who immediately made Relaina self-conscious about her own tousled appearance, hair and clothes unkempt after a day of training. The woman's blonde hair shimmered in waves down to her waist and there was kohl around her dark brown eyes, mysterious and striking. She smiled, and Relaina first thought that she was smiling at her, but all too soon she realized that this captivating woman's grin was for Darren. When he saw her, he smiled too, and stood to greet her as she approached.

"Katarina." Relaina's insides went cold.

"Glad to see you here, love," Katarina said, kissing his cheek. After that, Relaina had to look away. *This* was his former lover from Terrana?

"Do these meetings usually start on time or are people usually late?" Darren asked.

"It depends," Katarina said. "Sometimes there are Shadows out on a mission that keeps them longer, and we wait to begin so we can hear their report if their mission is crucial to moving forward with other plans."

Over the next quarter hour or so, Relaina sat silently, reaching for the flagon of wine and goblet before her on the table. By the time Darren took his seat next to her, she had downed two cups of wine and was pouring a third.

"You all right, Laines?" Bracken asked as he sat on her other side. Relaina pressed her lips together in a forced smile and nodded. If she opened her mouth, she might let out the internal scream that had started the moment she knew she was in the presence of Darren's ridiculously beautiful former paramour. She hadn't felt this inadequate since Lucinda's comment that she looked like a young boy during a fitting when she was sixteen.

The meeting began and, three goblets of wine deep into her own spite, Relaina struggled to pay attention to what King Fabian was saying. She knew it was unreasonable to fixate on Darren's friendliness toward Katarina, but here she was with a knot in her stomach and the persistent threat of tears behind her eyes. She was no longer worried about the other Shadows' perception of her and Darren—they were all rather unbothered, anyway, listening intently to their king, as Relaina *ought* to be doing. With the wine flushing her cheeks and numbing her head, she only comprehended pieces of the conversation. She poured another goblet.

"...And very soon we'll need to address some shady merchants in the richer parts of the city..."

Halfway through the meeting, Bracken ducked his head and nudged Relaina with his elbow.

"Laines, take it easy. I've never seen you down more than five cups of wine and still be able to walk straight."

"S'fine," she said, her tongue heavy and slow. *Gods in hell.* Perhaps he was right. How much had she had? She'd lost count after six.

The meeting ended sooner than Relaina expected. When she got up, she swayed, steadied herself, and marched from the room, unwilling to watch Darren with Katarina again. Others she scarcely noticed passed by in her periphery as she put all her focus into remaining upright in the corridors.

Darren arrived at Relaina's rooms moments after she did. As soon as he closed the door, Relaina turned, intending to say something to him, but instead she placed a hand on his chest, lost her balance, and inadvertently pushed him against the door.

"Relaina..."

She looked into his eyes, watched them dart down to her mouth and then back, his face flushing. Emboldened, Relaina leaned in and pressed her lips to his. Darren's hands traveled up her back and into her hair—the warmth of his touch and mouth made her head spin more than the wine. She slipped her fingers beneath his shirt, beginning to lift it off, but as soon as he inhaled, his lips parting slightly, he pushed her away as if he'd been struck.

"Relaina, please don't."

She blinked at his anguished face, tears forming in her eyes. "I'm sorry...that was...oh gods, I'm sorry."

He took her face in his hands. "You're drunk." A tear fell down her cheek, and he brushed it away.

"I'm sorry. I...Katarina is very pretty."

Darren's lovely, deep brown eyes grew wide.

"Is that what this is about?"

Relaina nodded, more tears falling. Her cares about protecting her heart had melted away. This was *Darren*, for Iros's sake—if she wasn't safe with him, she wasn't safe with anyone. Darren exhaled sharply and looked Relaina in her tear-blurred, drink-clouded eyes.

"I want this," he said. "I want you. But not like this. I want you to be fully in control of your decisions. I want it to be real."

"It *is* real." Relaina's words were still sliding together. "I'm just drunk enough to admit it."

Darren let out a laugh mingled with pain.

"As tempting and beautiful as you are, I won't be kissing you or doing anything else until you admit it when you're fully sober." He took her elbow and shoulder and guided her toward the bed. She flopped down on it, relishing the softness of the pillows and blankets and closing her eyes.

"We both know I'm too stubborn to do anything of the sort, Darren LaGuarde."

Darren got in bed beside her. Relaina opened one eye and found a pillow placed between them, and he was about as close to the edge of the bed as he could get.

"You really think I'm beautiful?"

Darren rolled onto his back and looked at her with tired eyes.

"Of course I do. But you're more than that. You're Relaina."

"Well, I'm glad you know my name," she flopped back down on the pillows, "but what the hell does that mean?"

"Nobody else is Relaina. And I want you."

"Oh...that's...that's really...really..."

Relaina's words tapered off, and sleep took her, swift and unnoticed.

DARREN LISTENED as Relaina's breathing grew slow and steady, staring up at the bed hangings, trying not to dwell on the ghost of her lips lingering on his. He'd been ready to give in, had desperately wanted to even after he tasted the wine on her lips and recalled the flagons at the meeting. He wanted more than anything for it to be real, as she'd drunkenly disclosed it was.

Because, as he'd recently come to realize, he loved her.

If she didn't remember in the morning, he wouldn't mention it. It was up to her to decide when or if she wanted to tell him how she felt. Still, even as sleep evaded him that night for several hours to come, a soft, glowing warmth settled in his chest. Perhaps he'd find the courage to tell her how *he* felt, but for now, knowing it was not one-sided was enough.

THE FOLLOWING MORNING, Darren slid out of bed and got dressed as quietly as he could while Relaina slept off the wine she'd consumed last night. He made sure one last time that she was sleeping on her side before he left, heading for the kitchens to grab a bit of breakfast before his meeting with King Fabian and Desiree.

With a piece of toast in one hand and a piece of parchment detailing the meeting's location in the other, Darren made his way up to the fourth floor of the palace. He'd expected to meet Fabian in the same secret hall where the Shadows met, but the king had instead elected to meet with him in a room closer to his chambers. The ceilings of the fourth floor were tall and carved in intricate designs, and every few steps soft morning sunlight illuminated the tiled floor through high windows. Darren no longer had to consult his written instructions when he spied the red double doors gilded in gold at the end of the corridor. Two guards stood at attention on either side, nodding to him as he approached. Darren took a breath and knocked.

"Enter."

The room's simplicity surprised him: the plain stone walls, single wooden table with only four chairs, and modest fireplace did not boast the same extravagance as the rest of the palace. Even the carpet seemed less thick in here, though still richly saturated in a deep red. Three arched windows rose to the ceiling, allowing in the morning light, shining in beams upon King Fabian's back. Desiree sat next to him, the circles under her eyes deep and prominent. She was wearing the same armored crimson dress with golden earrings and matching guardbraces she'd worn when they first encountered her in the inn.

"Good morning to you, Darren," Fabian said. "Please, sit."

Darren did so as Fabian shifted a few papers on the table and Desiree blinked, sitting up in her chair.

"These are the most recent documents I was able to gather regarding Terrana," Fabian said. "Maps, names of nobles, leaders in the soldiers' ranks." Darren glanced over a few of them. "What I'd like from you first is to verify this information, and to aid in filling in what's missing. I'd also like to know about Gabriel himself."

Darren looked up at Fabian, surprised.

"The more I know about him—what motivates him, what his focuses are, who he trusts most—the better I can find his weaknesses." Darren looked from the king's open, kind face to the documents, and then back. He took a deep breath and nodded.

"I know this won't be easy for you to discuss," Fabian said. "So please don't push yourself too far too quickly."

"Thank you, Fabian. Your concern is appreciated, but I'm here to help you put a stop to my father. Nothing is more important and urgent to me than that."

Fabian grinned. "Excellent. Then let's begin."

For the better part of two hours, Darren pointed out mistakes or important details on Fabian's documents, which Desiree corrected or made additions to, and a clearer picture of Gabriel began to form. Darren had not given much thought to his father's motivations and goals beyond simple selfishness and narcissism driving an insatiable need for power. But as he explained Gabriel's behaviors and habits to Fabian, in conjunction with the story the documents told and Fabian's own knowledge of Gabriel's reign, he began to see where there were holes or weaknesses in the Terranian court and military.

"Gabriel prioritizes finding those with the ability to host tenebrae at a young age," Darren said after pointing out the location of a secret training camp on one of the maps. "He sends a group of the more personable soldiers out on a rolling basis to scour villages and recruit. They are indoctrinated before they can begin thinking critically about anything. By the time they become part of the Terranian Elite, they are loyal to the core."

"Have any of them ever defected?" Desiree asked, pen flying across parchment as Darren spoke.

"I know of only one. And I only found out by chance. My father quickly silences those who turn against him and removes any and all evidence of their life."

"Is this defector still alive?"

"No."

"What led them to turn against Gabriel?" Fabian asked.

"He killed her father because her father had offended Gabriel by not coming to a council meeting."

"So, it may be reasonable to say we could elicit more defectors if they find out Gabriel's true nature is not something to be admired or supported?"

"I think it's more complex than that. There were other factors that led her to defecting, and it may not be possible to recreate her particular situation."

"Perhaps we ought to start searches for defectors that are still alive," Desiree said. "If any of them are."

Their conversation concluded shortly after with an agreement to reconvene in two days. Fabian grabbed a map and took it to one of the windows to study it more closely in the light as Darren stood from his chair, stretching before he began to leave.

"Prince Darren," Desiree called after him. He turned just as he reached the doors. "Thank you for your help. You don't know what this means to us, to Esran."

Darren smiled gently. "I know what it means to me, and I'm happy to assist."

With a gracious nod from Desiree, he left the king's study exhausted but energized, discovering with every step a feeling that was foreign to him. He was finally pursuing his own freedom with an attainable end in sight, a future he wanted so desperately it physically pained him to imagine not having it. For now, though, he walked back to Relaina's rooms with a strong sense of sovereignty over his own fate—for the first time in his life.

"He insisted that I say nothing of his departure, and when I told him I couldn't just let him leave, he became violent," Zarias Conclave said, sporting a spectacular black eye. "He told me he couldn't handle the pressure of being Crown Prince."

King Stephan sat so still on his throne Jeremiah wondered if he'd turned to stone. Christine had lost all color as soon as Zarias gave the news of Aronn's departure, standing to gaze through the wall of glass behind the thrones.

"He left no note?" Christine asked without turning around. "No farewell?"

"I'm afraid not. He wanted to leave without delay."

Jeremiah stood motionless at the base of the dais, eyes flickering between Zarias, Stephan, and the Sacred Guard stationed around the room. Annalise stood beside him, big, silent tears rolling down her cheeks. He put a bracing hand on her shoulder, and she sniffled.

One of his guards entered the room, disheveled. He glanced at Zarias before approaching Jeremiah. His whispered warning fell on Jeremiah's ears like tolls of a death knell: "The Conclaves are staging a coup."

"Annalise," Jeremiah said, voice firm, "please go with Boden."

The look on his face silenced his normally inquisitive niece. He gave Boden a pointed look, and the man went pale but nodded. He and three other sworn Sacred Guard would take Annalise to safety, to a place even Jeremiah didn't know.

"How many?" Jeremiah asked, his voice almost inaudible.

"We're outnumbered."

Boden took Annalise from the room, disappearing behind a tapestry out of Zarias's line of sight. Jeremiah sent up a quick prayer to the gods.

As soon as Annalise and Boden had gone, Jeremiah looked to his six other guards stationed around the room and drew his sword. The sound of metal singing as swords left sheaths made Zarias pause midsentence. King Stephan and Queen Christine stared at Jeremiah and his guards from their thrones.

"Is there a problem, Captain?" Zarias asked, his voice cold.

"Zarias Conclave, for acts of treachery against the Crown and the abduction of Prince Aronn, I place you under arrest in the name of the King," Jeremiah said, his fury scarcely contained. Behind Zarias, Stephan stood from his throne.

"You *bastard*, where is my son?"

Zarias appeared unbothered by the king's outburst and the six men and women facing him with swords out and armor on.

"I truly didn't want it to come to this," Zarias said, sighing. He whistled, and the doors to the throne room burst open as twelve members of the Lynx Guard flooded in. They were not wearing their royal uniforms: their surcoats were embroidered with the red fox sigil of the Conclaves. Leading them was Archan Conclave.

Jeremiah and the Sacred Guard closed ranks around the king and queen, swords raised.

"Please," Archan said. "We don't want bloodshed."

"You should have thought about that before committing treason," Jeremiah said.

"What is the meaning of this, Archan?" King Stephan asked.

"We've been planning a gradual, peaceful seizure of the Crown for a while now," Archan said as Zarias came to stand beside him. "Our original intentions were to have Zarias marry your daughter, and once an heir was produced, we'd have him declared Sovereign King. We are still open to that course of action if you will cooperate. Your family's blood will live on in the royal line, if not in name."

"Who is 'we?'" Jeremiah asked, eyes narrowed. *Keep them talking. Buy Annalise a little more time.*

"The Conclaves, the Norhens, the Tarods, and most of your guard." Archan smirked. "They know who pays them."

"With *our* gold! You traitorous *snakes*," Christine said. "We will never cede to you."

"The Queen speaks true," Stephan said, resolve in his voice. Jeremiah braced himself.

"Very well," Archan said, drawing his own sword. The traitorous guards behind him fell into formation, and Jeremiah struck. Chaos reigned in the throne room for some minutes as they battled their fellow guards, most of them evenly matched. Jeremiah had trained each of them, put his blood and sweat into the work of teaching them to protect the royal family. His rage fueled him: he subdued two of them and was attacking a third as Zarias fled the room. Behind Jeremiah, King Stephan picked up a sword from a fallen traitor-guard and joined the fray.

"Fall back!" Archan said, but it was too late; Jeremiah and his six had finished the last of the traitors, leaving Archan alone. He stumbled backward and ran from the room, calling for more guards.

Christine made her way to Jeremiah, brandishing a dagger she'd obtained from gods-knew-where. She grabbed him by the collar as he stared at one of the guards he'd killed, one of the guards he'd trained.

"Jeremiah, go!"

He'd never seen her so wild, eyes burning and blood splattered across her clothes.

"Go to Maremer. Ask for aid. Find Relaina. Tell her the truth, tell her everything."

"Everything?"

"If you want to, you are free to do so. Now, go, before they come back with more guards!"

"Christine—"

"Gods damn it all, Jeremiah, we have lost! Go, brother, or I will never forgive you."

"We will protect them, Captain," Cirene said, a Sacred Guard of eight years. The other five around her nodded. Jeremiah embraced Christine one last time and looked to Stephan, who bowed his head. Part of Jeremiah's heart shattered as he forced his feet to move, leaving his sister and the king to face their fates.

He ran faster than he thought possible, out of the throne room and down the corridor to the servants' staircase. He flew down the many flights of stairs, dodging servants and skipping several steps at once. It was a miracle he made it to the bottom unscathed. Breathing deeply to calm himself, he snuck past a group of traitorous guards wearing that awful surcoat as they headed for the main staircase. Finally, he made it to the stables. He mounted his horse and flew through the streets so fast he was certain he caused a cart or two to overturn and quite a few people to jump out of his way. Arrows whizzed past his ears as he rode through the city gates, but none found their mark and he headed north. North to Evaria. North to Fabian and Relaina.

PART TWO

CHAPTER 17

THE SHADOWS OF MAREMER

The full moon was a beacon in the sky as Relaina crouched atop a garden wall in the city's richest neighborhood, assessing the scene below. The manor belonged to a merchant prince named Quentin Eriver, a man she'd studied during the day at the market for over three weeks now. He was cunning and ruthless when it came to gold and a suspected conspirator in the city's recent abductions. Relaina took a deep breath, steeling herself. She would not fail her first task as a Shadow of Maremer.

Relaina only vaguely remembered the first Shadow meeting. She'd woken the following morning with no recollection of returning to her chambers and a raging headache, missing both training and breakfast. Whether or not Darren knew the reason behind her indulgence in the wine, she couldn't say; he hadn't mentioned it, and Relaina had avoided the subject ever since. He had been unusually quiet outside of their training sessions, and Relaina couldn't help but wonder with a sinking feeling if he preferred spending time with Katarina.

Relaina shook her head—dwelling upon the past few weeks would do nothing to serve her purpose tonight. Before apprehension could take hold, she gripped a nearby vine and began her descent.

Halfway down the wall, one of the vines holding Relaina's left foot gave out. She gripped the vines in her hands with all her strength and regained her footing, breathing deeply to steady herself and slow her heart. It wasn't a long way to the ground, but the bushes beneath her looked thorny and would not provide a pleasant landing if she fell.

And it would be exceedingly difficult to explain away a dozen tiny cuts on her skin that hadn't been there the previous day. The most important rule of the Shadows, she'd learned, was to avoid anything that could allow someone to trace her.

Relaina reached the ground, carefully avoiding the thorns of what she now saw were rosebushes. Light pricked at her vision from straight ahead; a line of lanterns burned along the garden path, and, eager to conceal herself from the light, Relaina darted out from behind the rose-bushes and took refuge by a flowering plant with large leaves. A hired guard dressed in all black walked past, right below the wall where she'd just been. He strolled through the gardens, whistling a lively tune and twirling the spear in his hands, oblivious to Relaina's presence.

Once the guard disappeared around a corner, Relaina left her hiding spot, running through the plan in her head one last time. She scaled the side of the manor house up to a balcony in less than thirty seconds—the precise amount of time she had before another guard would appear. Her feet lit on the floor of the balcony soundlessly, and Relaina was grateful that Fabian had commissioned the tailoring of these boots for her. Those, and the fitted pants, tunic, mask, and hood that made her look like...well, a shadow.

The lock on the door leading inside was easy enough to pick with a pin she'd kept in her hair. Relaina pushed it open gently and slipped inside.

The room was dark and quiet. This was Quentin's private study, lined with books and trinkets along every wall, and a desk and chair by a window on Relaina's left. She crept over to it and rifled through the papers scattered about the surface. *Where is it?* She'd avoided detection outside, but there was no telling if someone would walk in. She needed to move quickly.

"Aha!" she whispered, holding the paper up to the window, bathing it in moonlight. It was Quentin's schedule of patrons from the week before. Relaina looked for the name she'd memorized, located it, and pocketed the schedule, pleased with herself. She headed for the balcony door.

"Hey!"

Relaina whirled around, her heart flying into her throat. A man in his undergarments stood in the doorway. She sprinted for the balcony and hurled herself at the railing, preparing to vault over the side and hoping to the gods that her leather gloves would grip the stone long enough for her to grab hold of something else.

But she wasn't able to test them—a hand grabbed her ankle just as she jumped, and the momentum she'd built up sent her crashing to the floor. Pain seared through her head as her chin clipped the stone, and blood filled her mouth as she gasped for the air that was knocked from her lungs. Relaina rolled onto her back right as the man straddled her at the waist and grabbed her wrists, pinning them down at eye level.

"A mask?" he said, spying the black woven fabric that covered Relaina's face below her eyes. "You filthy coward!"

Relaina bucked her hips, forcing the man to fall forward. She twisted her arms out of his grasp and leaned up to wrap an arm around his neck, just long enough to knee him in the sternum. His moment of stunned surprise and pain was all she needed to throw him off her, jump to her feet, and fly over the balcony.

"Guards! *Guards!*"

Relaina hit the ground and ran before she could take a breath. The wall was only a few yards away, but if the guards had bows...

She had to risk it. If she were caught, she doubted Quentin would turn her over to the city guard. The wealthy merchant prince would have a more personal punishment in mind.

Relaina ignored the sound of whizzing arrows that plinked against the stone around her as she climbed, choking down her fear. Somehow, she made it to the top and disappeared over the edge, landing on the stones of the street below. She ran hard for several minutes before darting into a narrow alleyway to catch her breath, yanking the mask away from her face to gulp down air, her chest heaving. She spat the gathering blood in her mouth on the ground and winced; she'd nearly bitten through her lip.

"Damn it," she said, resting her head on the wall behind her. A dog barked nearby, setting all the others barking within the area. She'd ended up heading in the opposite direction of the palace in her haste to escape, and now she had to backtrack and avoid detection. With a great sigh, she spat out more blood and began her trek through the streets.

Maremer was peaceful at night, despite its dense population. Most people retired to their homes or spent time inside pubs, tea shops, or smoking lounges, leaving the streets fairly empty. The market bustled a few streets over, so Relaina made a point to avoid it, slipping in and out of shadows and around corners when people approached.

When Relaina finally made it to Seacastle, she placed her hands on her knees to catch her breath and winced again. Her chin and ribs were throbbing where they'd slammed into the stone floor of Quentin's study. She waved gratefully to the guards that opened the gates for her and trudged her way inside the palace.

"Gods, you look like hell."

Relaina stiffened—Katarina Delimont was gazing at her with a furrowed brow.

"I presume Fabian had you on some mission tonight?" Katarina asked, and Relaina nodded. "I was on my way to the meeting room, if you'd like to walk with me."

"I can find my way there well enough on my own, thanks."

"Hmm." Katarina frowned. "Well, I'll walk nearby just in case you collapse. Which seems likely."

Relaina's skin prickled, and she turned away again, heading down the corridor.

"I've seen you with Darren quite a bit," Katarina said, dashing Relaina's hopes of walking in silence. "Haven't caught your name, though."

Relaina's insides went cold. In all the times she'd seen them speak, Darren hadn't mentioned her name? Was she that inconsequential to him?

"I'm Relaina."

The footsteps behind her stopped abruptly before picking up again with increased speed. Katarina caught up to Relaina, placing a hand lightly on her shoulder.

"Relaina? As in Princess Relaina Gienty?"

"Yes—where have you been? I'm certain most everyone in the palace knows who I am."

Katarina gaped at her. "I'm only in the palace for meetings. Gods...you..."

Relaina blinked, her irritation forgotten amidst Katarina's awestruck gaze. "What?"

"You're the reason Darren was able to escape his father."

Relaina's heart stopped. "Come again?"

"I...I've said too much. If he hasn't told you—"

"He told me he was ordered to capture and possibly kill me."

Katarina's agitation subsided. "He went to Parea to see why his father wanted you dead. When he came back, he was an entirely different person. Whatever happened in Parea gave him the courage to finally fight back against his father."

Relaina could only stare at her. Katarina looked back at her with a slight smile before glancing out the nearby window.

"Oh, we're going to be late! Best hurry on."

Katarina scurried down the corridor, and Relaina followed at a slower pace, dazed. She'd known that Darren defied his father in his refusal to hurt her, but to know it was the catalyst of his escape... How the hell was she supposed to feel about that? *Gods damn it, Katarina.*

Every swirling thought in her head funneled into the certainty that she cared about him far more than she should, and she had no idea what she'd do when she saw him that night.

DARREN WAITED in the meeting room, leg bouncing beneath the table as people filed in. None of them acknowledged his presence, save for Katarina, who nodded and winked before taking her place several seats down from his. Bracken and Jacquelyn both greeted him as they sat, but they remained engaged in a whispered conversation with one another. King Fabian hadn't arrived, and many of the other Shadows stood around with cups of wine or ale, talking cordially.

Darren had spent the majority of his afternoons at Seacastle with King Fabian, Desiree, and Lord Vontair, explaining everything he knew about the tenebrae and his father. He'd even taught them the words for destroying a tenebrae, though he was not confident that they would be able to wield them. No one outside of the LaGuarde family had ever tried.

The door to the meeting room opened again, and Relaina appeared. Darren released a breath, but his relief was short-lived: as she stepped into the light, his heart sank.

"Shit, what happened to Relaina?" Bracken asked.

Darren stood and met her halfway to the table. Her lip was bleeding, and she had a massive bruise forming on her chin.

"What happened?" he asked, his voice low.

"Good evening, all!" King Fabian greeted them briskly as he entered the room.

"I'll tell you later," Relaina said.

The meeting was all the same again, listening to reports from various Shadows and Fabian planning their next moves. Darren hated sitting in the palace while everyone else carried out missions, though he knew his information and counsel was invaluable. The only true satisfaction he found was when he trained with Relaina. He'd watched her improve enormously over the last several weeks and worried for her safety less. She was a skilled fighter and, unlike most opponents he'd faced, made him work for his victory. Victory which now came less and less.

But beside him now, she was breathing roughly and shifting often, clearly in pain. She kept up appearances while she gave her report, confirming that she'd succeeded in her mission to obtain Quentin Eriver's client list. She pulled it from a pocket within her tunic and placed it on the table.

"Tridset's name is on it, just as suspected," she said, wincing, with one hand clutching her ribs.

"Hmm." King Fabian looked to another Shadow. "And have we confirmed Tridset's involvement in the recent abductions?"

"We have, Your Majesty," said Sayam, a young man originally from the Isle of Naráz. Fabian took the schedule Relaina offered and examined it. "Though we do not yet know if these abductions are related to the Terranian Elite."

"The sum of this exchange is quite large, and listed as a sale of whiskey," Fabian said, frowning. "We will need to trace where this 'whiskey' has been delivered. Relaina, this will be your next task."

Relaina nodded.

"Quentin will be on high alert," Relaina said. "He saw me and attacked me at his manor tonight."

Darren's knuckles turned white on the arms of his chair.

"Then we must exercise more caution going forward," Fabian said. "Darren, Jacquelyn, I would like you to go with Relaina on her next mission. Scout ahead and behind."

Darren forced himself to nod instead of racing out of the palace to find this Quentin and break his knees. Maybe a few fingers too.

Fabian adjourned the meeting, and Darren waited as Relaina rose stiffly. Bracken and Jacquelyn joined them as others congregated or left the room.

"Let's go find a healer," Jacquelyn said, and the four of them made their way to the healer's quarters, a place with which they'd become quite familiar after all the training they'd done. The young healer Nadia smiled when they appeared and had Relaina sit on a table as she began to work on her heavily bruised side.

"Gods, Relaina, what did he do to you?" Bracken asked.

"He grabbed me right as I jumped for the balcony railing—ah," Relaina hissed, wincing as Nadia touched her ribs. "I fell onto the stones pretty hard and bit my lip. Then he tried pinning me down, but I threw him off using one of the techniques Darren taught me."

Relaina threw an appreciative glance in his direction, and he nodded once.

"They never saw my face, but his guards were shooting at me as I scaled the wall to escape." Darren gripped the side of the table, anchoring himself. "I got away easily after clearing it."

"Nothing about that sounds easy," Jacquelyn said. "You're lucky you weren't shot and captured."

"I know."

Nadia moved to heal Relaina's lip, and everyone was silent for several minutes as she worked. Once she had finished, Relaina's injuries appeared several weeks old.

"Thank you," Relaina signed, hopping off the table and bending a little. Nadia nodded and signed, "You're welcome."

Darren kept his mouth shut and his hands balled into fists as the four of them headed for their rooms, ready for sleep. Relaina bid Bracken and Jacquelyn a good night and left the door open for Darren as she stepped inside. He closed it behind them.

They were silent as they prepared for bed; Relaina peeled off her boots, grabbed a nightgown, and headed into the washroom to start the water for a bath. Darren's movements were mechanical as he removed his weapons and stowed them by Relaina's bed, as he did every night.

"What's wrong?" Relaina asked, reappearing at the washroom doorway and fidgeting with her braid. She eyed him apprehensively.

"I want to hunt down that bastard and break his jaw."

"Quentin?" Her fingers worked to unbraid her hair. The bath faucet continued to run behind her.

"Yes."

"Oh, i-it's fine. I'm fine. I can barely feel the bruises anymore."

"That's not the point."

"Then what is?"

Emotion built in Darren's chest. "You could have been captured. Or killed."

"But I wasn't, so you can stop worrying."

"That's difficult to do."

"Why?"

"Because I love you!"

Relaina froze before him, her breath catching in her throat, but he'd said it, and it was the truth.

"It terrifies me to imagine you being attacked or hurt," he said. "And I don't care if it's irrational to feel this way. I've tortured myself these past weeks over how to tell you, *what* to tell you, but the truth is, I've been yours since the moment you defended the Prince of Terrana in Maurice's shop."

Relaina just stared at him as the water continued to run behind her. Darren's heart began to fracture around the edges.

"I know you feel *something*. A few weeks ago, you...the night you were drunk you tried to...you said..."

Her face did not indicate she knew what he was talking about. Darren exhaled, his breath faltering.

"I'm sorry. I'll go."

He was a fool. A complete, utter fool. Quite possibly the most foolish person to ever exist. He started for the door, needing to get as far away from there as possible. After it clicked shut behind him, he took another shuddering breath.

The door opened again.

"Darren, wait—"

He turned to her and found fire in her gaze.

"Tell me what I said and did."

Darren exhaled. "You kissed me. I pushed you away when I realized you were drunk, you apologized and said Katarina was pretty—as if you aren't, gods—and I said I wanted this, I wanted *you*, but not unless it was real and you were sober—"

"Darren."

"—and you admitted it was real but—"

"*Darren.*"

"—how am I supposed to know if you just completely lose it when you're drunk or—"

She took his face in her hands, her steely eyes searching his as he stopped talking, frozen.

"Are you done?"

He blinked rapidly. "I think so."

She studied his face, one hand gliding down his cheek, his neck, coming to rest at the scar on his chest. She pressed her palm against it and the cracks around Darren's heart fell away, the glow of an impossible hope replacing them.

"I thought," she said, wincing, "I just thought you didn't feel that way for me. I thought Katarina..."

"Relaina," he breathed, placing a hand over hers. "I want *you*. More than anything. More than anyone."

The last of the armor in her eyes fell away. Relaina closed the space between them, pressed her lips against his, and he was undone.

The warmth within him turned to fire as they stumbled back across her threshold and he shut the door behind them. He backed her up against the wall nearby and Relaina gripped the front of his shirt as her lips parted. The feathery-light brush of her tongue against his only made him more desperate to tear off her clothes, but he took his time kissing her, his mouth moving to her neck, her jaw. He relished the sounds she made, the reaction of her body as she leaned into his touch.

Relaina slipped her hands beneath his shirt, and he leaned back long enough to let her pull it over his head before whisking her into his arms and carrying her to the washroom. The large stone bath was filling with water that smelled of lavender oil and sandalwood. Darren set Relaina down on her feet, his lips lingering on the smooth skin of her neck, his fingers threading through her haphazard curls. She started peeling off her black garb, but he stopped her.

"Can I?"

Relaina's striking green eyes met his, and she nodded. He didn't break her gaze as he deftly unlaced her tunic, beginning just above her breasts until the fabric loosened down to her waist. Her breath turned shallow, and Darren kissed her chilled skin where he slid the tunic off her body slowly, his touch light, teasing. Relaina ran her fingers through his hair as he pulled the fabric of her trousers off her hips until she was wearing nothing but a white cotton band around her breasts. He kissed her sternum, her stomach, her abdomen, and Relaina's fingers knotted in his hair.

"Kiss me," she whispered, and he complied, standing once more.

"Relaina, you're certain you want to do this?"

"Yes. With you...yes."

"Are there certain things you like?" He slipped his hands beneath the white band and tugged it downward, patiently working it around her hips, and it fell down her legs and onto the floor to join her tunic and trousers. "Things I can do?"

"Yes." Her eyes flashed with mischief. "I enjoy humiliation."

Darren blinked. "Oh."

He'd never done anything of the sort before, but...

Relaina was grinning, and it dawned on him—their conversation months ago after the bonfire in Parea. He burst out laughing.

"You had me for a moment," he said, resting his forehead on hers. Relaina's own laugh faded as Darren kissed her again.

"Will you show me?" He pressed his lips to her neck. "Tell me what you like." A small whimper escaped her lips, and Darren had to quiet the carnality it drew out of him as she nodded. He traced her curves with his fingertips and she shivered again.

"Gods," he said, fully taking her in. Relaina hadn't heard him. Her eyes were glued to the massive scar over his heart. She ran her fingers along the raised, white-pink flesh, which was smooth and rough at the same time. Darren took her hand and kissed her palm.

"I understand your anger, I think," she said, voice shaking. "If I ever meet who did this to you..."

He took her face in his hands.

"For your sake and mine, I hope you never do."

Relaina nodded, placing her hand atop one of his and leaning into his palm.

"Now," he said, his eyes darting down to her bare breasts. "Can I continue?"

Relaina grinned and leaned forward, pressing her lips to his stubbled jaw before lightly biting his lower lip. *Gods in hell.*

"Do your worst, Darren LaGuarde."

She said his name without fear, without judgment, and he loved her for it.

The next hour passed in a blur of skin on skin and the slickness of warm water and the silken touch of bed coverings. Darren spent long minutes ensuring her comfort and revealing the depth of what he felt with his hands, his mouth, and Relaina writhed beneath his touch, back arching. She bit her lip as he positioned himself to enter her, her body tensing, and he paused.

"We can stop," he said, leaning down and searching her eyes.

Relaina kissed him again. "I don't want to stop. I want you. I love you."

She loved him.

She wanted him, and he was hers already anyway, so Darren gave himself to her. They laughed together as they fumbled and reconfigured positions multiple times. He'd never recover from the sight of her straddling him and gasping in pleasure as her muscles relaxed around him.

He closed his eyes and remained still while she adjusted, breathing deeply.

"I think I need more time," she said as she climbed off of him, flopping down on the bed. "It's mostly pleasant but I'm not sure...I'm sorry."

"You have nothing to apologize for. We can take as long as you need."

She propped herself on her elbow and started to speak, but hesitated.

"What is it?"

"...Can you do that thing with your fingers again?"

Darren grinned and kissed her, reaching between her legs. She closed her eyes and exhaled before gripping his shaft and stroking it with confidence he hadn't expected. He buried his face in her neck, his breath ragged.

"Is this good?"

He managed to nod. "Mhmm."

He focused on her as her thighs began to tense, her climax imminent, and his own release followed at the sound of her moaning and calling his name. They walked to the washroom together to wash up, all nudges and giggles and bare feet padding on the cool stone floor.

Back in bed, Relaina moved so her back was against his chest, and he draped his arm around her middle. Her breathing became heavy and steady, and as Darren drifted off himself, he held her close and breathed, "I love you."

CHAPTER 18

THE MESSENGER

W hen Aronn awoke, his head was pounding, his eyelids assaulted by the sun overhead. With a gag-muffled groan he rolled onto his stomach, propping himself up with his still-bound arms, and blinked, fighting the nausea raging in his stomach. The rope shoved between his teeth made his mouth feel like sand.

His eyes focused and he found himself lying in a wooden cart, surrounded by sacks of grain. The sun shone directly overhead—the culprit behind the pink, tender skin on his chest. His captors hadn't bothered to put a tunic or shirt on him after dragging him out of his bed.

Aronn craned his neck to look at whoever was driving the cart. He recognized Samuel, seated by an old man he'd never seen before. He hadn't noticed Aronn was awake yet and draped an arm around the crouched old man as he sang a bawdy tune with a knife in his hand. The cart rolled and wobbled along a dirt path through a field covered in yellow oilseed flowers. Aronn blinked again and winced at the throb of his head, reaching to press a hand against his temple. His hands and feet were still bound.

"Just up here, old man!" Samuel said, pointing his knife. "And then we'll be out of your hair."

Aronn peeked over the edge of the cart as best he could. The field yielded to a thick forest, with trees that belonged to regions of Lyneisia far from the mountains of his home. How long had he been unconscious?

The cart trundled along and Aronn remained silent—the more information he could gather without being discovered, the better. *Gods, why can't I have Relaina's skill in fighting, just this once?*

Soon the shade of the trees covered them, and Aronn wiped his sweaty forehead and tried to ignore his intense thirst. Just ahead was a tall stone structure, dark and foreboding as it grew closer, appearing like just another part of this lush forest. Aronn shivered, the hair on the nape of his neck standing on end. The cart came to a halt, and Samuel jumped down, walking around to the back.

"Ah, you're awake!"

He climbed up to grab Aronn by the arm. Aronn shuffled away from him, but Samuel dragged him down from the cart with little difficulty. Aronn yanked against his bindings and Samuel's hold. Samuel brandished his knife.

"Come now, let's make this easy on both of us, Aronn." Aronn glowered at him but stopped struggling. "That's the spirit! Let's go."

Samuel led him toward the ancient building, an old temple, fallen into ruin. Aronn squinted at the crumbling statues placed along the worn stone path leading inside. He recognized one as Iros.

The entrance no longer had a door, so Samuel dragged Aronn inside with little effort. Old benches made of limestone lined the perimeter, and above them were balconies where priests and priestesses would've once stood to pay homage to their patron god by singing. Shafts of sunlight filtered through cracks and holes in the roof. At the opposite end of the temple was a remarkably intact stained-glass window, depicting the day Iros blessed humans with his healing magic. Below it stood a stone altar also made of limestone, engraved with ancient runes and symbols whose meanings had been lost to time.

Samuel dragged Aronn toward the altar and fastened the bindings around his wrists to an exquisitely carved swirl on the corner of the stone. Aronn sat there on the ground, hands bound above his head, looking up at Samuel with equal parts hatred and disgust. Samuel took out his knife again and bent down, and Aronn flinched away.

"Gods above, calm down. Do you want me to take off this gag, or not?"

Aronn stilled, allowing Samuel to cut through the rope that had dried out his tongue and chafed his lips.

"What the *hell*, Samuel?" he rasped.

"Like Zarias said, it's not personal." Samuel shrugged and flipped his blond hair out of his eyes. "Several high lords of Lyneisia have decided that our kingdom needs new leadership. After Relaina fled Parea, we had to reevaluate our strategy."

"You think Relaina would've stood for a coup against her family? She'd have slit Zarias's throat in the night, or yours, or anyone else's."

"You really think she'd murder the father of her children? Not likely. She'd cooperate or never see her children again."

"You're sick. All of you. You're sick."

Samuel merely shrugged again. "Enacting change on this level can require unsavory measures. Relaina may have fled the kingdom, but your other sister is far more malleable and accommodating, I hear."

The next words Aronn uttered were foul enough to wilt every flower in the nearby field. Samuel patted his cheek once and then began to walk away.

"Are you just going to leave me here to die?"

Samuel turned mid-stride, walking backward toward the doorway. "I'm sure our next man is already on his way to retrieve you. He should be here by tomorrow."

"*Tomorrow?*"

"You'll live!"

Samuel was three steps from the exit of the temple when light flashed from outside, and he stumbled back as if he'd been struck. He pulled out his knife again, searching wildly for his assailant. Aronn stared, mouth agape as three women appeared in the temple, all of them clad in protective leathers and armed to the teeth with spears, swords, and various knives. One of them, brown-skinned with eyes lined in bright orange, stood just in front of Samuel, unarmed but crouched to attack. Samuel prepared to throw his knife.

"Watch out!"

Aronn's warning was unnecessary. The woman dodged Samuel's knife with ease and held out a hand that emanated a healer's light. Her light did not heal Samuel—it blasted him off his feet before wrapping itself in a tendril around his middle and slamming him into the wall. The other two women ran to him as the first let him drop to the ground in a heap. He didn't dare move as they held swords to his throat.

Holy gods.

"Please don't kill me!"

The woman who had flung Samuel across the room hurried toward Aronn, cutting through his bindings with the swipe of a dagger.

"Come, Prince Aronn," she said, helping him stand. They hurried out of the temple, and only when he and the woman had cleared the door did the other two, twins with fair skin and dark brown hair, follow. They helped Aronn onto a horse behind the healer-hand woman and then set off at a fierce gallop into the woods. Aronn held onto the woman's waist for dear life.

"Who are you?" he asked over the wind battering his ears.

"Nehma!" she said, her voice carrying over her shoulder. "A healer of the Caspian Forest!"

"The Caspian Forest? That's at least two days east of Parea!"

"Yes. Our sisters at the sanctuary near Parea told us they'd been forced to sedate you, and we've been watching out for you ever since."

Tears streaked out of his eyes in the wind. "Where are we going?"

"To our village. You will be safe there."

"Nehma, if you don't stop yelling, you're going to alert the whole forest to who we are," one of the twins called. After that, the only sound around them was galloping hooves and wind. Aronn was just beginning to think his mouth would never recover from the dryness when they began to slow, veering off the main path to follow a narrower trail through thick trees and brush. They went one after the other and slowed to a walk.

"We're almost there, Your Highness," Nehma said.

Aronn looked ahead as they turned sharply, spying a wrought-iron gate ahead, held aloft by two stone pillars on either side. They were covered in moss but looked sturdy as they passed through. Nehma stopped after they'd entered and motioned for Aronn to dismount. She followed, and Aronn couldn't help but gape at her graceful strength.

Nehma smiled brightly at him.

"Welcome to the Caspian Healers' Sanctuary."

THE OLD INN where Jeremiah decided to stop was a familiar one. During his last two years in Maremer, after Christine had married Stephan and moved to Parea, he'd made the trek between the two capital cities many times. On his last journey from Maremer to Parea, however, he had taken a different route, one that would alter his life forever, though he hadn't known it at the time.

After a nervous stable boy took his horse for him, he stepped inside, exhausted, greeted by the warmth of a roaring fire and the smell of freshly baked bread. There were quite a few people seated inside, talking happily amongst themselves. The inn's coquettish barmaids and barmen surrounded several young travelers in the corner as they told outrageous stories of their adventures. Jeremiah almost smiled as he approached the wizened old innkeep at the bar.

"What can I do you for, my good man?" Roderick asked, not even glancing at Jeremiah as he wiped out a glass with an old cloth.

"A room with a bath and a hot meal would do just fine." Jeremiah tapped a gold coin on the bar. "I won't be staying long."

The innkeep gaped at the coin and looked up from the glass he was attempting to clean. His old, gray eyes blinked, squinted at Jeremiah, and then widened with recognition.

"I know you!" He reached across the bar to grab Jeremiah's hand and shook it vigorously. "Jacob, weren't it? No, that's not right... er...Jaime?"

"Jeremiah."

"That's it! Jeremiah, of course. You've gotten old, my friend."

Jeremiah coughed a laugh. "And you've clearly become bolder."

Roderick cackled. "Once you reach my age, you can say whatever you like. If I insult some prissy little highborn to the point where they decide to run me through, I say that's as good a way to die as anything else."

Jeremiah smirked despite himself. Roderick had always been able to get a chuckle or two out of him.

"I suppose that's fair enough." He placed the gold coin on the bar. Roderick snatched it up and held out a key for Jeremiah.

"Second floor, last room on your right. We'll draw you a hot bath. You can go clean up a bit an' I'll have Beatrice prepare a hot meal by the time you get back."

"Thank you, my friend." It felt strange to speak Evarian again. He and Christine sometimes slipped in a few words out of old habit, and Relaina and Aronn would occasionally mix it with Lyneisian, but it had been a long while since he'd spoken it exclusively. A pang of grief and guilt struck his stomach. *Christine...what's happening to you now?*

As if he could outrun his own terrifying thoughts, Jeremiah wove his way through the inn's raucous clientele, the room full of the language of his homeland. He found his room easily enough. It was one of Roderick's nicer rooms, with two decently sized beds and a private washroom. He was glad to find that the beds were not the same as the ones that had been here almost twenty years ago.

Remembering those treks between Maremer and Parea brought back other memories for Jeremiah, memories that would fully resurface once he reached the Evarian capital city and faced the king.

The king. For so long he'd pictured King Tristan as the leader of Evaria, the man who'd led fairly when it came to his subjects, even if he'd ruled his own family with far less compassion. How strange it was to imagine Fabian in that role...and to imagine that their reunion, which would be uncomfortable at best, would be further shadowed by the news Jeremiah brought from Parea.

When he'd finally forced himself to stop for sleep and food the first time, he'd considered sending a messenger ahead, but he trusted no one else with such sensitive news. How had he missed this scheme brewing right under his nose? Archan Conclave was the last man he'd ever expect to formulate and stage a coup.

Before his thoughts could take him down more unpleasant paths, Jeremiah set down the pack he was carrying and went about washing up.

His hair took the longest—he'd been meaning to cut it for ages but hadn't gotten around to it. After stepping out of the bath he turned to face the mirror and tied his hair back with a thin piece of leather he'd brought along with him. It had once been a sandy-blond color, never quite as golden as Christine's, but now it was darker, peppered with gray, and had lost most of its curl. The stubble on his chin had always been dark anyway, so at least now it matched.

He judged himself reasonably presentable and made his way back downstairs, where Roderick gestured to an empty table in the corner with a bowl of hot stew and fresh bread waiting for him. Jeremiah nodded in thanks and wove around the other tables where the inn's livelier patrons were seated. He took his seat with a fair amount of stiffness but ate in comfortable solitude. He listened silently to an absurd story a man was telling about how he'd single-handedly taken on a snow cat in the mountains of northeast Evaria.

"Why are you sitting all alone, m'lord?" A very beautiful young barmaid appeared beside Jeremiah, accompanied by two other young women. The girl who had spoken had raven-black hair plaited over her shoulder, and her blonde companions smiled at Jeremiah. It took all of his self-control to keep from sighing in exasperation. Roderick must have sent them over.

"I rather enjoy being alone," Jeremiah said. The raven-haired girl smiled and pulled out the chair across from Jeremiah, taking a seat and gazing at him. He frowned at her.

"I can tell you're one of those deep-thinkers," she said, folding her arms to make her breasts appear larger. She looked up at him through her lashes as the two other girls leaned on the table beside her, pouting their lips in a ridiculous fashion. "You have such...deep eyes."

"Ah, they're just eyes," Jeremiah said, shrugging. He took a long drink from his cup of ale and set it back down on the table. "They work well enough. Nothing terribly special, I'm afraid."

"They're a lovely brown. What color eyes do *you* like best, m'lord?" one of the blondes asked.

Jeremiah looked away from them, a melancholy smile playing at the edge of his lips. "Brown, actually."

"Ah...does m'lord have a lady?" Observant.

"No."

They all smiled.

"Well, if you are in need of some company tonight..."

"I appreciate the offer," Jeremiah said. "But I'm not interested."

The girls all pouted simultaneously, as if they'd rehearsed the expression a thousand times, which they probably had.

"Are you sure, m'lord?" the raven-haired beauty asked.

"I'm quite sure. I'm far too old for you girls, anyway. Go have your fun. And be so kind as to remind Roderick that seducing his guests and then robbing them is, in fact, illegal."

The raven-haired girl's face went red, all pretenses forgotten. The three of them scurried away quickly after that, and Jeremiah gave a white-faced Roderick a friendly wave.

Jeremiah got up from his table shortly after, planning to retire quietly to his room upstairs. He had another day's hard travel ahead of him and would allow himself only this night to rest.

Sleep, however, did not come easily. No matter how many times he tossed and turned, he could not get comfortable. It wasn't until the very early hours of the morning that he finally found a restless slumber.

He awoke much later than he intended—the pattering of rain and the occasional rumble of far-off thunder brought him gently out of the sleep he so desperately needed. The thunder was so soothing, but he leapt out of bed and looked outside. It was raining so heavily he could hardly see ten feet in front of him.

"Gods in hell." He let his forehead hit the glass. He certainly hadn't missed Evaria's rainy season. He didn't have time for this. With a great sigh, Jeremiah walked back to his bed, the wooden floors creaking loudly beneath his feet as he put on his sword belt and boots.

Just as he was tying his hair back, a commotion broke out downstairs. Unintelligible shouting and chairs scraping loudly against the floor hurried his progress to the main room.

"...I need a *damned horse!*"

A woman was screaming at Roderick, who cowered as she gripped him by the front of his shirt. She was dressed in all black, but her tunic and armor were damaged at the shoulder, where a festering, horrible wound peeked through. Her silver-gray hair was unkempt and caked with dirt, and her skin was pallid. As Jeremiah descended the stairs, her head snapped up to look him over with a snarl, and he stopped in his tracks, recognizing her even amidst the bruise-like blotches on her face.

"Corinne?"

She blinked. "Jeremiah Andovier." She dropped Roderick to the floor with a *thump*. Her energy dissipated, and she swayed on the spot.

"Gods in hell, woman!" Roderick said, scrambling away from her. Jeremiah approached her, reaching for her as she collapsed. He knelt and cradled her head as she blinked at the ceiling, her breathing ragged. She was far older than when he'd last seen her, when they were both trainees for the Seacastle Guard.

"I have to get to Maremer," she said, her words bleeding into one another. "Urgent news for the king."

Jeremiah almost recoiled at the wound in her shoulder. She would never make it to Maremer.

"I'm going there now," Jeremiah said. "What news do you bring?"

Corinne wheezed as she inhaled. Her lips were white, her eyes sunk in.

"Terranian soldiers approaching the border."

Jeremiah's blood ran cold.

"Gods damn us all. I'll tell King Fabian, Corinne. I promise."

She grabbed his wrist, her eyes filling with tears.

"Jeremiah. You were always the best of us."

Jeremiah sobbed once, taking her ice-cold fingers in his. Her eyes rolled back into her head as she lost consciousness.

"Roderick," he said. He set Corinne's head down on the floor gently. The old man sidled up, having watched their exchange with apprehensive curiosity. Jeremiah reached into his pocket and flipped a gold coin onto the nearest table, the last of the money he'd had on him in the throne room days ago.

"Take care of her. I know healers are sparse around here, so if you can't find one...just make sure she's comfortable. Please."

Roderick frowned and nodded.

"Who is she?"

"An old friend of mine." Jeremiah blinked tears out of his eyes. He lowered his voice. "And important to King Fabian."

Roderick looked past Jeremiah to gaze at Corinne.

"She's not gonna...stab me or anything, is she?"

"No. She'll be too weak to do anything when she wakes. If she wakes again."

"Gods."

"Thank you, Roderick." Jeremiah donned his cloak and prepared to step out into the rain.

CHAPTER 19

A CONVERGENCE OF PATHS

Relaina didn't open her eyes when she awoke, reluctant to possibly find herself in a world where Darren hadn't admitted he loved her, where they hadn't spent a good deal of the night without clothing, where all barriers hadn't been shattered between them. It had been too perfect—awkward a few times, but he was so warm and beautiful and earnest and—*gods in hell, I'm in love with him.*

She remembered now her drunken episode three weeks back after seeing Katarina for the first time, how she'd thrown herself at Darren out of desperation and jealousy, and wished to disintegrate into the bedcovers. But if last night was real...

She had to open her eyes, then, and her heart leapt. Darren slept beside her with mussed hair and marks on his skin that were clear evidence of the night's shenanigans. Relaina sidled closer to him and propped herself up on her elbows so she could kiss his exposed neck and chest. He inhaled, disrupting the steady breath of sleep.

"Please wake me up like that every morning," Darren said, reaching for her as she grinned. He tucked a loose curl behind her ear and brought her face to his to kiss her. Relaina melted into his touch, heat gathering between her thighs as his fingers knotted in her hair and she recalled the things his hands had done last night.

Gathering every ounce of her willpower, she broke away from him, sitting back on the bed.

"I need to apologize to you," she said. He blinked at her, lost. "For that night a few weeks ago."

"Oh." He fought a smile. "It was very difficult for me to say no to you."

Relaina groaned and plopped her head into the pillow on her lap.

"It was foolish and selfish of me." She looked up at him, taking a deep breath. "I want my intentions to be clear. Drunk or not, I'm sorry that I acted then out of fear rather than a desire for you to know the truth."

Darren smiled at her, that same smile he'd given her months ago in Parea, a world and a lifetime away in Maurice's shop. Relaina knew him well enough now to realize that it was a unique mixture of grace and gentle wonder.

"And what truth was that?"

Relaina took his hands, brushing her thumbs along his knuckles. "I knew I would leave Parea the moment I heard you were imprisoned. It didn't matter whose son you were or which kingdom you belonged to, because even knowing you just a few weeks convinced me that this gods-damned world is better with you in it. My *life* is better with you in it. I love you, Darren LaGuarde."

Somehow it settled differently in the light of the morning. She could see every emotion that played across his features as she said it. He pulled her close, shoving the bedcovers and her pillow aside as his kiss turned into a smile against her mouth. Joy. Unbridled, overwhelming joy filled her at every angle, replacing the anxiety she'd harbored with a current of warmth. Perhaps this new brightness would give her strength to take on all the challenges they faced.

"Also," Relaina said as he kissed her neck, "I'm sorry I ruined it the first time we almost kissed."

Darren laughed. "I wanted to throw myself into the campfire. I thought I'd misread everything."

"You certainly hadn't. I just..."

"Relaina." He pulled back to look at her. "You don't have to explain. I knew you were struggling with everything that happened."

For a while after that they didn't say much at all, occupied with other things that made Relaina's skin tingle and her breath catch.

"We need to train," she said.

"This is far more enjoyable."

Relaina wrapped her arms around his neck, hitching one of her legs around his waist.

"You're just afraid I'll beat you again."

Darren leaned back, smirking. "Someone's cocky."

Relaina raised an eyebrow, glancing down at his crotch, and his face flushed. He got up and headed for the washroom.

"Where are you going?" Relaina got up, jogging after him.

"Don't know. Leaving the city. Leaving the kingdom. I can never show my face here again."

Relaina laughed as she caught up to him and he pulled her into his arms, kissing her again. "All right, let's get lunch and we can train."

"Don't you dare go easy on me from now on."

"Oh, you can be sure I'll make things more difficult."

Relaina laughed. "Good. You retain my express permission to hit me when we train."

"Noted."

After dressing, they headed for the dining hall, and Relaina sobered herself. Now that she was able to brush her fingers along Darren's arm or kiss his neck, not doing so proved challenging. She was so distracted by his proximity she turned a corner without checking and collided with a servant.

"Oh, gods, I'm so sorry," Relaina said, trying to regain her balance. Darren had jumped aside to avoid them.

"Oh, that's all right, Princess!" the servant girl said breathlessly, bowing. Several other servants appeared and followed her as she hurried on, all of them somewhat panicked.

"So, should I assume you'll just let me fall if I lose my balance while we're walking together?"

Darren held up his hands in surrender. "I was just trying to offset the damage. You falling on your own would prove much less painful than if I went down on top of you."

"You didn't mind being on top of me last night," Relaina muttered, striking at him playfully, but he grabbed her arm and spun her around until her back was pressed against the wall and his nose grazed hers.

"Is this revenge for what I did when we first met?" she asked, her lips almost touching his as her pulse quickened.

"Relaina, Darren!"

They sprang away from one another as Bracken approached from the direction the servants had come, jogging to meet them.

"King Fabian requests that we lunch in your rooms, Relaina," Bracken said, a little out of breath. "He just sent me to find you."

Relaina stared at him for a moment too long. "Oh! Well, that's convenient."

Darren subtly jabbed Relaina's side, and she remembered.

There were various articles of clothing all over her chambers.

Relaina cleared her throat. "Darren, why don't you go tell the servants they can clean my rooms later?"

"Excellent idea."

Bracken blinked, looked at Darren's retreating figure and back to Relaina, and a mischievous grin lit up his face.

"Relaina, did you...with him? I...you *didn't*."

"Shut up, Bracken."

"It was about time too."

Relaina glanced at him sidelong. "What in Ashima's name are you talking about?"

"The excruciating sexual tension we've all had to endure since your arrival is what I'm talking about."

"If you tell anyone about it, I'll end you."

Bracken laughed. "Best friend's honor."

Relaina fought a grin as they approached her rooms, and for a moment it felt like they were back in Castle Alterna, bickering back and forth in good spirits.

"So...was it good?"

Relaina smacked his arm as her face went violently red. She walked on ahead of him, dodging a few more servants as they hastened past. Darren's head appeared in the doorway to her chambers as they approached.

"Relaina, a moment?"

Relaina smiled sheepishly at Bracken as she stole inside, Darren shutting the door behind her and presenting her with a warm beverage.

"Oh, thank the gods," Relaina said, smelling the herbs in the tea. "Did Selene bring this again?"

"She did. I'm sorry I didn't consider it earlier," he said. Relaina downed it quickly, grimacing at the bitter taste. "Next time I'll be sure to take the herbs myself beforehand."

Relaina set the teacup down on a small decorative table by the door. "It's all right, Darren. I don't think either of us expected last night to go the way it did."

"Fuck," he whispered, grinning.

"What?"

"I'm so glad last night went the way it did." His lovely eyes were bright as they caught hers. An abrupt knock made Relaina's already fluttering heart skip a beat. She reached to open the door.

"If you two are finished reciting poetry to one another, I'd like to get out of the way of these servants."

Relaina stepped aside to allow Bracken entry. "Is it your primary aspiration in life to mortify me at every opportunity?"

"Of course. Didn't you know that already?"

"What's with all this?" Darren asked, gesturing to the servants scurrying by in the corridor beyond.

"I'm not sure," Bracken said, closing the door once more. "Fabian said he would explain at lunch."

"Where is Jacquelyn?" Relaina asked. "And Connor?"

"Jacquelyn is visiting a nearby village for the next day or two, and Connor decided to join her to get out of the city for a bit. Doing some work for the Shadows since your mission is paused for now."

"What?" Relaina asked.

"Oh, Fabian hasn't been able to tell you yet. There's a storm coming that'll prevent nighttime missions for a few days. Your best bet will be to try and locate Tridset during the Winter Festival."

"I see." Relaina frowned. It did seem like the wisest next move in her pursuit of Tridset and his mysterious whiskey, but that left her little to do for the next week.

After lounging around for a few minutes, Relaina directing the conversation away from anything related to her sleeping with Darren, King Fabian arrived. Lunch was served by far fewer servants than usual, all of whom looked haggard.

"Please tell Khorlana to just roast some fish and serve whatever fruit is on hand," Fabian said to his servants as they poured wine and asked for requests. "And then tell her to let you all sleep." They nodded and bowed, exiting the room swiftly.

"There are fifteen highborn lords and ladies of Evaria," Fabian said, rubbing his neck and looking outside the nearby window. Rain battered the glass, allowing for little visibility. Relaina grimaced at her food as Fabian explained the arrival of noble guests as the Winter Festival drew near. She'd met most of the noblemen of Evaria before, when they'd come to Parea to court her.

"You'll see more guests than that, but the others are lesser nobles. Most arrived last night, and some are arriving this morning, and I'll have to greet them once they're settled in. Arriving soon should be Lady Kerrith and Lord Swanson."

Relaina grimaced, and Fabian chuckled.

"I understand you aren't terribly fond of him."

Relaina and Darren made sounds of agreement.

"Ah, but we're all in for some entertainment," Bracken said, and the king raised an eyebrow. Bracken draped an arm around Relaina's shoulder, and she briefly considered biting it off. "Not only does Relaina despise Swanson, she has rejected half of the arriving noblemen as potential suitors."

Fabian turned to Relaina, a twinkle in his eye. "Yes, I'm well aware of that too. I have also rejected a number of marriage offers from families present, and while I don't wish you or myself distress, I must admit that this convergence of paths will provide ample entertainment for us all."

"If I don't kill them all first," Relaina said under her breath, so Fabian didn't hear, but she had to admit it comforted her to know she wouldn't be the only person who had snubbed visiting nobles.

A young woman entered Relaina's chambers unbidden and came forward to whisper something in Fabian's ear. Bracken began talking idly with Darren, but Relaina watched Fabian with interest. The king's smile faded, his expression changing from gentle, trivial exasperation to blank shock.

"Here? Now?" The girl nodded. "For what purpose?"

"He won't say to anyone but you, Your Grace."

Fabian's face traveled through several more emotions before he mastered himself. He stood slowly, and the chatter at the table died.

"I'm afraid I must meet with someone," the king said, and Relaina thought his eyes flickered to her, for only a moment. "I would request that you all remain in the palace until I send word."

He left swiftly, and the servants followed him. Darren looked at Relaina inquisitively, and Bracken merely shrugged.

"Sounds like someone important," Bracken said, chewing. "Could take a while."

Relaina took another sip of delightfully tart apple juice and frowned.

"I suppose we'll wait here," she said.

Bracken slumped back in his chair, settling down.

"Would you sing for us, Laines?" Bracken asked. "I haven't heard music in far too long."

"Oh," she said, taken aback. "All right."

KING FABIAN FELT as if someone else were controlling his legs as he walked down the corridor toward the entrance hall, unsure if this was some sort of elaborate, cruel joke. He approached the doors slowly but held up a hand as the guards on either side reached to open them. They paused as Fabian stood there for a moment, gathering himself.

But, gods, what was he supposed to do? Jeremiah was back after twenty-one years, apparently with news too important or secret to share with anyone but Fabian. He hadn't even asked for Relaina.

Fabian took a deep breath and nodded, and his guards swung the doors open wide.

The man standing at the far end of the hall was tall and muscular but bowed with fatigue. His bronze-gray hair was pulled back haphazardly from his pale face, his clothes were dirty from travel, and yet...there was still that same man Fabian had known, found in his dark brown eyes and the look of sheer relief that flashed across his face when he first spied Fabian.

The king's heart faltered. His usual careful control of his emotions evaporated as Jeremiah walked toward him.

"Fabian," Jeremiah said, though it sounded more like a sob. The sound ripped open a wound so old Fabian had to take another moment to gather himself. Jeremiah stopped in his tracks, waiting as Fabian closed his eyes and placed a hand over them. He breathed in once, twice, and exhaled sharply.

"Fabian," Jeremiah said again, his voice strained. "I know this is not ideal. But I fear I bring news that requires our immediate attention."

Fabian let his hand drop and looked at Jeremiah.

"Tell me."

Jeremiah's face contorted. "I come firstly from Parea. A group of nobles in Lyneisia have decided to stage a coup."

Fabian's breath left his lungs.

"Christine?"

"I don't know," Jeremiah said, clearly fighting back tears. "Our Sacred Guard defended them. Aronn was taken before we knew what was happening. I have good reason to believe Annalise has reached safety. But as for Christine and Stephan, I cannot say. The throne room was a bloodbath. Christine asked me to come here." Jeremiah dropped to a knee, bowing. "My King, Queen Christine asks for your aid, in whatever form you can give it."

"I will give all I can. Stand, Jeremiah. You do not bow to me."

Jeremiah looked up at him, a single tear cascading down his cheek. "Before you offer all, you must hear the other news I bear."

Fabian waited as Jeremiah stood, closer than he had been before. They were still of a height, Fabian noticed.

"One of your Shadows found me at an inn two days ago. Corinne Rochel. She had blood poisoning from an arrow wound and told me she'd seen Terranian soldiers marching for the Evarian border."

Fabian's heart seemed to stop altogether.

"So soon?" He looked at the wall behind Jeremiah and stepped away, one hand on his brow.

"You knew they would come?"

"There have been rumblings." Fabian braced himself on a nearby table decorated with orange lilies. He stared at the darker orange dots on the petals and allowed himself a moment to be bewildered. *I'm speaking to Jeremiah Andovier.* He shook his head. "I planned to put protections in place with my nobles while they are here for the festival, to speak with them all regarding the potential for attack. I see now we must act even more quickly than I anticipated."

"Are they here now? All of them?"

Fabian turned to look at Jeremiah again.

"Now they are. Your mother did not come."

Jeremiah grimaced. "I knew she was stubborn but didn't know she could hold a twenty-year grudge."

"I didn't know you could either."

Jeremiah looked as if he'd slapped him.

"That isn't fair. What they did to me aside, Fabian, you don't know what all has happened—"

"Because you never wrote me back!" This was the last thing he'd wanted to happen, but now that the old scars felt so freshly reopened, he couldn't pull back the tide. "How would I know what's happened to you when you refused to speak to me? When you refused to return even after I lifted your banishment? My parents had just died, and I'd just become king. You think a single day went by that I didn't feel the weight of what they did to you? To both of us? But then they were gone—and I begged you to come back. I needed you and you turned your back on me."

Jeremiah took a step toward Fabian, the skin between his eyebrows pinched together, his gaze desperate.

"I swear I will explain everything if you let me. But it involves secrets too dangerous to divulge anywhere we could be overheard. Now is not the time."

Fabian stared at him, begrudgingly willing to hear him out. After all these years, an answer to the question that had haunted him each night:

Why had Jeremiah stopped loving him?

"Very well. But you will tell me soon," Fabian said.

"I swear it."

"Thank you. I will call a meeting with the nobles present for tonight. Will you act as representative of Crestfall, as well as Lyneisia?"

Jeremiah nodded.

"Good. Let's go find your niece."

～

Keelie was the finest dove, the finest dove we knew.
She had wings of starry white and eyes like morning dew.
But she flew south through the storms and the snow,
And she never did return.
Yet still I hear, in the dead of the night,
Her song in the winds that blow...

DARREN HAD ALMOST FORGOTTEN that they were waiting on Fabian, lost entirely in Relaina's singing as it filled the room, the melody haunting and somber. Bracken had fallen asleep in his chair and now wiped away a small bit of drool as someone knocked, blinking his way back to consciousness.

Darren answered it and found a rather unexpected face peering down at him.

"Oh," he said.

Before him stood Jeremiah Andovier, the man who'd arrested him the last time they'd met. He let go of the door, letting it creak open of its own accord. Darren looked back to Relaina, who'd gone rigid with shock.

And then she was running. She barreled toward her uncle, and Darren stepped aside quickly as she nearly knocked Jeremiah over with the force of her embrace. The captain wrapped his arms around her in turn, and she burst into tears.

Neither of them said a word. Jeremiah held her tightly, his own tears falling on her hair. Darren knew, then, that his reason for coming was not for a joyous reunion. Relaina held onto him for a few more blissful moments before whatever tidings he brought diminished her happiness.

"Relaina," Jeremiah said. "There is much to discuss."

Relaina let go of him, and Darren glanced behind Jeremiah to find King Fabian standing there, a deep frown set in his face. Bracken had approached quietly, also wary of Jeremiah's presence.

"Let's go to the meeting room," Fabian said. "The five of us."

With every step through the corridors, Darren became more certain that something was very, very wrong, and it filled him with dread. The walls that had seemed so warm and safe only an hour ago now pressed in on him. Relaina reached for his hand, and he squeezed hers once before they let go.

When they arrived, Fabian dismissed the guards outside and locked the door from within. None of them sat. Jeremiah inhaled deeply as Fabian came to stand by them, closing his eyes.

"There has been a coup in Parea," Jeremiah said. Darren's veins froze as Jeremiah recounted what had happened and who was responsible.

"Those fucking bastards," Bracken said. Darren agreed, but his rage was too great for words. Relaina was meant to have married that smug piece of horseshit, and all along he'd planned to usurp her throne after having children with her—

"Aronn was taken by them in the night," Jeremiah said, his face tortured. "We don't know where he is, but I sent word out to the healers around the kingdom to watch for him, since we don't know which guards or nobles to trust. I had the Sacred Guard take Annalise to safety before Archan arrived. Stephan and Christine...I don't know what's happened to them now."

Jeremiah kept speaking, but Relaina had gone completely stiff and silent. Only Darren's sharp tap on her back brought her once more to the present.

"What will we do?" she asked, her voice hard.

"I will send soldiers and Shadows alike to restore order," Fabian said. "Given the Lyneisian people's love for the Gienty family, without Relaina or Annalise, the traitors have no feasible path to the throne. My people will make quick work of them and act as a stand-in guard for the king and queen while they handle the traitorous nobles. I will also send messages to my Shadows in Lyneisia to be on the lookout for Aronn."

"I want to go," Relaina said. "I want to help."

"As do I," Bracken said.

Darren started to agree and volunteer himself, but Jeremiah shook his head.

"There is more." He turned his gaze to Darren. "There are Terranian soldiers moving toward the Evarian border. They will be here in less than two weeks."

Darren's exhale was audible. *Oh, gods, no...*

"No," Relaina whispered beside him.

"Bracken may go to help in Lyneisia," Fabian said. "But it's too dangerous to send you, Relaina. If you fall into their hands, they could torture you into compliance or keep you locked up to ensure their coup is complete."

Fire flooded Darren's insides, replacing the ice. They'd have to kill him before they did anything of the sort to Relaina.

"We will send soldiers and Shadows to Parea tomorrow," Fabian said.

"Won't you need aid from Lyneisia?" Relaina asked.

"Perhaps. But my army is vast and my soldiers well-trained. We can manage Gabriel for a while, until your mother and father are restored to the throne. If we're lucky, that may be handled by the time the Terranian forces arrive."

"What happens if they're...if they're..." Relaina's lip was trembling too much to continue.

"We will come to that only when we must," Jeremiah said, before Fabian could answer. A strange glance passed between them, but Darren's head was swimming with too much information to be concerned with it.

"There will be a meeting held tonight with all visiting nobles," Fabian said. "We will discuss plans for defense. Relaina, your mission to expose Tridset and Quentin's true plans is imperative. If these abductions are in any way related to the Terranian army, we *must* know and uncover the truth. Darren, we will need your expertise now more than ever."

Darren could hardly hear what Fabian was saying over the buzzing that had begun in his ears but nodded anyway. Relaina reached for his hand and twined her fingers through his. The gesture shot a bolt of clarity through him. They would overcome this; they would help defeat Gabriel together. And once his father was no longer a threat, perhaps he could finally have a life of freedom and peace. And perhaps Relaina could be at his side.

"Just tell us what we must do," Darren said.

CHAPTER 20

THE EVARIAN NOBLES

By the time Relaina, Darren, and Bracken arrived at the banquet hall that night, there was a pervasive uneasiness within the palace. Every Evarian noble was there and had been called to this meeting. Relaina twined her fingers through Darren's as they waited to be admitted through the doors.

"Darren."

He turned to her, eyes full of anxiety.

"I'm with you."

His face softened, and he brought her hand to his lips, kissing her fingers. The two guards before them opened the doors with a flourish.

Most of the nobles were distracted. Many of them had already eaten, and they were gathered in little groups, laughing or scheming or pretending to listen to what was being said. Several heads turned as the three foreigners entered, and Relaina held her head high, refusing to be intimidated by any of them.

Relaina had elected to wear the same gown she'd worn on her first day in Maremer, since it was less conspicuous but elegant enough to boost her confidence. Even so, she ended up standing out a bit more than she'd intended: most of the other noblewomen wore fine gowns, but they were neither as colorful as Relaina's nor were they as finely made.

"Gods, there are so many of them," Bracken said. "Do you think they know who we are?"

"They know me, at least," Relaina said, making accidental eye contact with Lord Swanson. He was imposing his presence on two noblewomen, but when he caught her eye his face went slack with shock. Relaina boldly took Darren's arm and began walking toward the other end of the table. A servant appeared in their path.

"Your Highnesses," he said, bowing. Relaina cringed as several nobles heard him and looked over at them with interest. "King Fabian has asked that all of his guests from Lyneisia and Terrana be seated at the center of the king's table."

Relaina frowned. "Must we sit there just to eat?"

The servant shuffled their feet. "I'm afraid so. It's just to avoid confusion, Your Highness."

Relaina sighed and turned, towing a taciturn Darren along with her as she followed the servant to the center of the table. Bracken sat beside Relaina before reaching for the food already laid out in front of them.

"I wish Jacquelyn were here," Bracken said, glancing at the rain beading on one of the massive windows. "There are so many stuffy nobles in here I can feel my tunic getting tighter by the second."

"Your tunic is getting tighter by the second because you inhale your food instead of chewing it," Relaina said, reaching for one of those delectable pastries. Beside her, Darren relaxed slightly, smiling.

Relaina took his hand and leaned close. "Even if these nobles think they know who you are, you have time to show them that you are not your father."

Darren brushed his thumb over the back of her hand and then looked at her. His brown eyes were remarkable with the emerald tunic he wore. "You're right."

The doors to the hall opened again and silence swept across the room as King Fabian entered, accompanied by Desiree and two guards who remained by the door once it closed again. Everyone stood and bowed to their king, who came to a halt in the center of the room.

"I ask now that everyone be seated," King Fabian said. "There is much to discuss."

The sounds of feet shuffling and chair legs scraping against stone filled the room for a few moments as every noble found their place. Fabian sat at the center in the tallest of the chairs, with Desiree at his right and Lord Vontair on his left. The jolly lord was just across from Relaina and offered her a bright smile, which she returned halfheartedly. As everyone settled in, she took a quick count and found that there were twenty-one nobles and noble family members at the table—including six men she'd met before as suitors. The only one she didn't entirely dread seeing was Lord Mirnoff, though she was briefly nervous that he might've brought his personal guard along with him, whom she'd kissed in a closet more than a year ago. She located Mirnoff easily enough amidst the others with that shock of red, curly hair, and when she caught his eye, he gave her a friendly nod. She nodded in turn, relieved that his guard was not present.

"I'm certain you are all wondering why I have called you to a meeting tonight," Fabian said, and every eye in the room was trained on him. "The reason is—"

The sound of doors opening interrupted him. Everyone turned, and Relaina's uncle entered the room. He breathed heavily, as if he'd been running, and then he froze, letting the door shut behind him with a dull clunk. Relaina looked at him and then back at Fabian. The king had gone entirely rigid himself, staring at Jeremiah. Relaina felt as though she could reach out and pluck the tension like the string of a harp.

Jeremiah appeared to regain his senses as he came forward, taking his seat amongst the nobles on Relaina's left. She glanced at Fabian, who looked conflicted, as if he couldn't quite decide how to react to Jeremiah's late appearance. But then he gathered himself and put that smooth mask of his back in place.

"The reason I have gathered you for this meeting," Fabian said, "is so we can prepare for war with Terrana."

The room was dead silent for a half second, and then it erupted. Relaina, Darren, and Bracken sat in quiet observance as the nobles stood or shouted or whispered to their neighbor.

"War? Gods save us..."

"I doubt things will escalate *that* far..."

"King Gabriel has been planning this for years. To hell with him!"

"The Lyneisians have dragged us into this!"

Relaina's hands balled up into fists, but she retained her composure. Across the table, Fabian rubbed his face in his hands, looking as though he desperately needed a drink. Lord Vontair leaned over to whisper something to him, and he looked up and nodded with a sigh.

"All right," Fabian said, but the nobles continued. One woman had even gone so far as to leave the room. Fabian stood. "*Enough*!"

The king's voice echoed throughout the hall, and silence fell once more. Relaina glanced down the table and spotted her uncle sitting with an irritated expression on his face. It wasn't difficult to guess why—he was seated two down from Lord Swanson, who was still muttering to a noblewoman beside him.

"I know this is not what you want to hear, after we've had so many years of perceived peace. But Terranian soldiers have been seen approaching the border. They will arrive in less than two weeks. I don't want war any more than the rest of you, and I will do everything in my power to avoid the devastation we experienced all those years ago when war last plagued this land." Fabian returned to his seat, weaving his fingers together. "But King Gabriel is powerful and dangerous, and I want you all to be prepared for what may come. So...let us plan for the protection of the villages and people on your lands. Those of you who bear land between here and the southeastern border must evacuate all who dwell there, and you must fortify your holdings."

For the better part of an hour, King Fabian gave orders, answered questions, and made plans with his nobles. Relaina listened intently, curious to know which nobles were more cooperative than others.

"And we're certain that the people taking Evarians off the streets of Maremer are Terranians?" Lady Guerraine asked. She was wearing a powder-blue gown with extremely large sleeves and was sporting a hairstyle so elaborate that Relaina wondered if her neck was sore.

"We are investigating this currently, but we are fairly certain," Fabian said, glancing at Relaina briefly. "What we don't know is *why*."

"What could they have to gain?" Lady Guerraine asked, frowning.

"Slaves, of course," Lord Swanson said. "Every Terranian wants a slave if they aren't one." He snickered, nudging a lord beside him, who shuffled away, frowning.

"You don't know what you're talking about."

Relaina turned. Darren was staring daggers at Swanson, and everyone else in the room was staring at him.

"Most Terranians find slavery abhorrent. King Gabriel perpetuates the practice and no one opposes him because they're terrified, and rightfully so."

"So, you are Terranian," Lord Mirnoff said.

Darren looked him in the eye. "My name is Darren LaGuarde."

The room exploded again, and this time not even Fabian could silence them. Relaina only caught snippets of what was said—or shouted—and despite her revulsion of the nobles' attention, she could not sit there silently while a room full of nobles accused Darren of abducting her or of bringing the Terranian soldiers to their lands. She stood and waited as the uproar died down, her palms sweaty.

"There's something I'd like to say, if I may, King Fabian," she said. The last of the whispered conversations ended as Fabian nodded.

"If you don't know me, I am Relaina Gienty. You may have heard rumors about what transpired in Parea two months ago. Here is the truth of it: Darren LaGuarde did not abduct me. A Terranian assassin named Xavier posed as a reformed soldier to work for my father, got Bracken Averatt banished, and almost killed me. Darren saved my life and I freed him from the dungeons of Castle Alterna and fled the kingdom. I trust Darren completely, and he deserves the chance to earn your trust as well."

The nobles sat in gravid silence as Relaina took her seat once more. She allowed herself a glance at Swanson and found him staring wide-eyed at Darren, who sat with his arms crossed.

"If he knew how dangerous this Xavier was, why not come forward?" Lady Guerraine asked. "Why not inform the Lyneisian Guard that a traitor was in their midst?"

"There was no way he could have told them about Xavier without exposing himself and getting killed in the process," Relaina said, shaking her head.

"He told me," Bracken said. "I started watching Xavier, and that's why Xavier saw fit to get rid of me. Not that I blame you for that, Darren."

"I appreciate it."

"Of course."

"What I would like you all to know," Relaina said, talking over them, "is that not trusting Darren prevents you from achieving a great advantage in the upcoming conflict. When was the last time you spoke with anyone so close to the heart of the Terranian court?"

The corners of Lady Guerraine's mouth lifted ever so slightly, and she gave Relaina a small nod. Other nobles muttered as Relaina shifted in her chair. Darren made no verbal acknowledgement of what she'd said on his behalf, but he did take her hand beneath the table, squeezing once. King Fabian looked at her with a twinkle in his eye before he spoke again.

"Lords Harnow, Fennel, and Ladies Guerraine, Drennal, and Rhoe, you will all need to make your way back to your homes first thing tomorrow to begin evacuations. Evarian soldiers will accompany you. As for the rest of you, you are welcome to stay here, but you must send for the people on your lands who are part of our reserve fighters. We will press on with festivities for the Winter Festival in hopes that Gabriel will not suspect that we're preparing our defenses."

Fabian stood from his chair, and everyone else followed suit, bowing as he made for the door with Desiree at his side. The nobles began to disperse, and Relaina craned her neck to look for her uncle.

"Well, that was certainly the most interesting meeting I've ever attended," Lord Vontair said, appearing behind Relaina. He smirked at her, Darren, and Bracken. "If it were up to me, we would have you three at all of our council meetings."

He patted Darren on the shoulder and chuckled without humor before he sauntered off, greeting Lady Guerraine. One noblewoman approached them and nodded in greeting, dark tresses of hair falling over her shoulders and brushing against her round, pink cheeks that gave her a youthful air despite her age.

"I am Lady Kenna Granger. I reside over lands to the north, and I have heard very little about what you all have been through until today. I wanted to say that while your actions may not have been conventional,

Princess Relaina, they were certainly honorable." She looked to Darren. "I am glad you are here, Prince Darren. You strike me as an honest man, and you will be an invaluable contributor when we find ourselves at war with Terrana."

With a gentle smile, she bowed her head and then headed for the door. Several of the other nobles lingered, speaking to one another, including one man who was talking animatedly to Relaina's uncle. She slipped away from Darren and Bracken and approached Jeremiah and his companion.

"Princess Relaina," the man said, turning his attention from Jeremiah and bowing. "I have wanted to meet you for some time."

"Relaina, this is Edward Drivan, son of Lord Torren Drivan," Jeremiah said, and Edward smiled.

"And you'd think I'd be Lord Drivan by now, but my father is a stubborn old goat and isn't planning on dying anytime soon." Edward laughed and clapped Jeremiah on the back. The gesture looked a bit odd, since Jeremiah was at least a head taller than him. "I've heard much about you, Princess—"

"Please, call me Relaina."

"Oh, yes, yes, your mother was a good friend of mine, as well as your uncle here! If you're anything like Christine was at your age, then I suspect we will all be wonderfully entertained during our stay in Seacastle!"

Relaina felt the blood drain from her face as she thought of her mother. Edward laughed once more and looked up at Jeremiah. "Well, it was good to see you, my friend. I'm certain we'll cross paths again very soon."

Jeremiah exhaled as Edward walked away, his face drawn.

"When will you leave for Lyneisia?" Relaina asked.

"Not until the day after the Winter Ball. We need time to gather volunteers."

"I wish I could help."

"I know." He stared at her for a moment, and then blinked and shook his head. "I don't know about you, but I desperately need to hit something."

Relaina smiled, though it felt a little forced. "I'm up for a spar. I'm sure the others will want to come as well. We could all use a distraction... and a bit of fun."

"I'm not entirely sure you can call hacking at things with a sword, 'fun,'" Bracken said as he and Darren joined Relaina and Jeremiah. "But it will definitely help to ease some frustration."

"We'll have to use the indoor sparring hall," Jeremiah said, looking at the window. "Do you know how to get there?"

"Actually, yes. Darren and I go there frequently."

"Excellent. I'd like to see what you've learned," Jeremiah said. "We'll get changed, and I'll meet you there in twenty minutes."

After giving the three of them an excruciatingly forced smile, Jeremiah left.

"Perhaps everything will work out," Bracken said with a sigh.

"Perhaps," Relaina said, frowning. "I hope so. Let's go get changed."

RELAINA FASTENED the laces on her boots quickly, eager to meet her uncle and the others. While she waited on Darren, she pulled out her sword and studied the text on the blade again. The light from the candles glinted off the metal as she read:

Fearless, I rise eternal
Lifted in great heavenly truth

Jeremiah had told her that they were words belonging to an ancient family of Esran, but she hadn't studied the histories of those houses in years.

Darren strode out of the washroom, adjusting the sleeves on his tunic.

"Ready?"

Relaina sheathed her sword and put it back in the wardrobe, nodding. When they opened her door, Bracken was standing outside, staring at the wall. He smiled. "Shall we?"

Jeremiah was already waiting on them when they reached the sparring hall, garbed in some of the plainest clothes Relaina had ever seen him wear. More often than not he'd worn his guard uniform in Parea. He rolled up the sleeves of his undershirt as they approached.

"I forgot how warm it can be in Maremer, even in late autumn. When I left Parea, it was snowing."

"I miss the snow," Relaina said. "And the winter clothes."

"I am not the least bit offended by Maremer's weather," Bracken said. "Well, I could do without the storms, I suppose."

Jeremiah snorted, nodding. "The storms can get rather nasty here. The winter of my sixteenth year we had a storm so powerful one of the windows in my bedroom shattered." He turned his arm over to show them several lines of faint white scars on his skin. Relaina had never really paid much attention to them. Her uncle had multiple scars along his arms and hands, and she'd always assumed they'd come from battle or training. It occurred to her that she knew very little about his time here, about his childhood and adolescence.

"The healer in the palace at the time was only an apprentice, so the scars never fully faded."

"What about that one?" Relaina asked. "The one on your palm?"

Jeremiah closed his fist and let his arm fall back to his side.

"Oh, probably a sparring accident. It all happened so long ago...and speaking of age, your birthday is in a few weeks, Relaina."

Relaina stopped short. She'd completely forgotten.

"I suppose it is."

Bracken gasped. "Can you imagine the feast King Fabian would have for you?"

"*Don't* tell him," Relaina said, whipping around to glare at him.

"Relaina, if we've said it aloud in the palace, King Fabian will know," Darren said.

"Well then, I'd like to let any eavesdroppers know that I do *not* want any kind of extravagant festivities thrown for my birthday," Relaina said loudly, and Darren and Bracken laughed. "We have enough to worry about for the time being. Celebrating feels wrong."

The four of them made their way to the armory at the back of the hall, passing by sparring rings full of guards. As they approached, they ran into Saheer and another guard, who was wielding a spear.

"Back again?" Relaina asked.

"It's my cohort's day off," Saheer said. "But no one wants to look like a lazy shit, so we come here to train in the morning and evening anyway."

"Ah, yes," Jeremiah said with a chuckle. "And everyone gets absurdly competitive about who wakes up earliest to get here and who can stay out the longest?"

Saheer gave him a surprised half-smile.

"Yes. And between you and me, I've been winning for the past month."

They all laughed, and Saheer turned to her companion.

"Come on, Peter, let's get to work," she said, tapping his back with the flat side of her training spear. He flinched.

"Ow! Saheer, I told you to avoid touching my back for the day. Vehra isn't going to be happy if this tattoo gets infected."

"He just got his betrothal tattoo," Saheer said to Relaina, and Peter rolled his eyes. "He's taken every opportunity to mention it and his fiancée. Vehra this, and Vehra that..."

"At least I speak freely about my lover, unlike *someone* who just exchanges longing glances with the Captai—"

Saheer thwacked him on the back again, and he yelped. Relaina and Darren stared at her. Saheer winked.

"I'm sure I'll see you all around the palace." She walked off, the sound of her laughter following them as Relaina and Darren made their way to the armory. Bows, spears, swords, maces, crossbows, and shields hung on the walls and sat on shelves, accompanied by a few sets of vambraces and quivers. Relaina went straight for a set of twin daggers, having become rather attached to them after learning from Darren. She almost felt exposed without a weapon in each hand now.

To her right, Darren reached for one of the bows on the wall. He carefully removed it and stroked the smooth surface of the polished wood, which was so dark it appeared black. The arrows in its quiver were made of the same wood, snow-white fletching.

"A blackwood bow," Jeremiah said, nodding as he walked over, holding a longsword. "From the southeast of Terrana."

"Where did they get it?" Darren asked.

"It has been a part of the Seacastle weaponry for many years now. It was given to King Tristan as a gift, I believe. From Queen Arienne."

Darren's brow furrowed, and Jeremiah left to help Bracken pick out a proper sword. Darren took the quiver off the wall and slung it over his back.

"Queen Arienne," Relaina said as Darren drew the bow without an arrow, testing its weight. "Your grandmother?"

"Yes."

"It's a shame you never knew her."

"It is. My mother spoke so highly of her."

"Hmm."

"What?"

"Rulers can be so different, even parent and child."

Jeremiah and Bracken headed for the door, and Relaina and Darren followed, armed and ready.

"My father always had malice in his soul," Darren said, adjusting the vambraces he'd donned as they walked. "I don't know if his mother could have made him different, or if he was just an evil bastard through and through."

"Regardless of how it happened, he *is* an evil bastard," Relaina said. Darren's eyes darkened as he began to withdraw into himself. Relaina placed a hand on his shoulder. "Let's not think about him for now. I'll spar with my uncle and then kick your ass."

Darren smiled. "I'm up for that."

"Are you two coming, or not?" Bracken asked from up ahead, where he and Jeremiah were standing by one of the empty sparring circles.

Darren went to the archery enclosure on the other side of the armory while Bracken remained behind to watch Relaina and Jeremiah spar. Relaina's fighting style was different already—she fought harder, with more ferocity than before, and it showed in how Jeremiah responded to her attacks.

"Good," Jeremiah said, panting as he and Relaina both paused to rest. "You've improved immensely since I last saw you. It's been a very long time since I've fought someone with that style."

Relaina's brow furrowed. "You've fought Terranians before?"

"Many years ago," Jeremiah said. "Before Gabriel's reign."

"Oi, if you two are done chatting, I'd like to practice!" Bracken called.

"All right then, come on," Relaina said, and she flipped her daggers as Bracken approached.

"You wield those well," Jeremiah said, one corner of his mouth lifting. Relaina couldn't help but smile in return. "All right, Bracken, let's see your stance."

"My turn," Darren said, appearing at the edge of the circle. Relaina grinned and stepped into the adjacent circle, only to have her excitement tarnished by the sight of three noblemen approaching from the opposite end of the hall. Swanson and two others whose names she did not recall conversed loudly, making their way to the bench for spectators. Relaina rolled her shoulders and flipped her daggers in her hands again, settling into her fighting stance and bringing her focus back to Darren.

"Tired?" Darren asked, brandishing his own daggers. Relaina bit her lip and kicked herself for ogling his smooth, muscular forearms. *Get it together.*

"Not at all."

"Good."

Relaina blocked his blow just in time.

"You bastard..."

Darren laughed as he reset his stance, and their dance began. Relaina wove around his attacks, focusing on her breath, lunging for her own attack every now and then. Behind her, laughter floated through the hall, and she glanced over her shoulder to find Bracken flat on his ass before Jeremiah while Swanson and the others watched with glee.

"*Oof!*"

Darren landed a blow to her side, and Relaina stumbled back.

"Fuck," she said. Darren grinned.

"Ready to quit?"

"Not even close." She tuned out Swanson and the others.

It had only been a month of training, but Relaina felt more powerful than she ever had, full of confidence and tenacity as her body moved exactly how she wanted it to. Each time they'd fought recently, there was a moment when Darren's face shifted from mild amusement to absolute concentration, and Relaina reveled in it as it appeared now.

Just as Darren swiped downward, she dropped to the floor, narrowly avoiding his blade. He realized what she was doing an instant too late—Relaina was kneeling before him, daggers poised to eviscerate him. He dropped his own daggers to the floor with a clatter, conceding defeat.

"Ha!" Relaina sprang to her feet. "You haven't won once this week!"

"You've defeated me handily." He retrieved his daggers, smiling. Raucous laughter floated over to meet them again, and they both turned. Bracken was on the ground in the ring again, and the three lords were still watching and jeering. A few guards had stopped what they were doing to determine the source of the disturbance. Relaina's nostrils flared as she gazed upon Swanson's laughing face, and she was suddenly transported back in time to Castle Alterna. Bracken had been ridiculed on more than one occasion by the other sons of Lyneisia's lords for his friendship with Relaina. By Zarias, especially.

Relaina froze. Zarias.

Relaina was only vaguely aware of Darren's quiet footsteps behind her as she marched into the ring with Bracken and Jeremiah. Bracken, upon seeing her expression, brushed himself off and said, "Just leave it alone, Relaina."

"Don't do anything rash, Relaina," Jeremiah said, but she ignored him. He didn't know Swanson was friends with Zarias, and she hadn't pieced it together until just now. The Evarian lords all stopped laughing and talking abruptly when she reached them and grabbed Swanson by the front of his tunic.

"Were you in on it?" He blinked at her, too shocked to attempt to free himself. Relaina bared her teeth and snarled, "Were you working with Zarias, you smug fuck?"

"Get off him!" One of the others grabbed at her, and she released Swanson to elbow her assailant in the ribs, sending him reeling backward.

"Answer me, Swanson!"

"No!" Swanson said, his face pale as he beheld her furious expression. "I didn't help him. I wanted no part of it."

She could have incinerated him with her gaze. "So you knew what they were planning?"

He raised his hands, palms forward and pleading.

"I didn't want to be involved. He didn't tell me about any of it until after I arrived, and then that mess with the assassin happened and...I swear, I was only there for you."

Jeremiah managed to grab Relaina just as she lunged at Swanson, barely holding her back from ripping the man to shreds.

"You could have stopped it! My parents may be *dead* because you said *nothing*, you *fucking coward*!"

Swanson stumbled into the bench behind him, panicked as he met her ferocious eyes.

"Relaina," Jeremiah said in her ear. "You must calm yourself."

"He could have *stopped it*!" Tears burned her eyes but didn't fall. For a long moment there was silence in the hall except for Relaina's gasps for air. Jeremiah kept his arms firmly around her as she stilled, and Darren and Bracken stood close by.

"I think you ought to leave," Darren said, his icy tone directed at the nobles. Relaina slowed her breathing and heart, and her uncle released her as Swanson and his companions gathered together.

"If I find out you had a hand in any of it," Relaina said, "I will dismember you with a rusty butterknife."

Relaina stalked away, and Swanson's friends grumbled to one another as she approached Darren. He held out his hand for her as he threw a threatening glare at Swanson.

"I still can't fathom why King Fabian is housing them here and trusting the Terranian prince," Swanson said loudly. "Perhaps the king isn't mad like some rumors suggested, but he's certainly an incompetent fool."

Relaina whirled around, but Swanson was already on the floor, lying in a listless heap. The Evarian lords stared at the limp young man before slowly turning to look at Jeremiah, who was wringing out his hand.

"When he comes to," Jeremiah said, his voice menacing, "you tell him to keep the king's name out of his petulant mouth." He began walking away, and then turned back. "And if it comes to light that any of you had a hand in putting my family in danger, I won't discourage my niece from beating you all senseless."

The lords nodded, their faces pale as they hefted Swanson up and started to carry him off. Relaina and everyone else nearby gaped at Jeremiah. He noticed their stares after opening and closing his fingers several times to ensure he hadn't broken anything in his hand. He cleared his throat and looked at the floor.

"Well, *that* was overdue," one of the guards called.

Bracken burst into hearty guffaws behind Relaina, and as the sound filled the hall, everyone else began laughing too. Jeremiah tried to fight a smile as Relaina led the way out of the hall, the heavy atmosphere within Seacastle now somewhat lifted.

CHAPTER 21

THE GATHERING STORM

Aronn breathed in deeply, gazing at the ceiling above his borrowed bed as moonlight trickled in through the tiny window. The night air was cool, the forest crickets loud. He closed his eyes and tried to calm his mind, but it raced on as he waited for Nehma to return with the others, due back any moment now. They'd left two days ago to seek information about the coup in Parea. Sighing, Aronn got up and splashed his face in the nearby water basin. He'd spent two weeks sitting around in the Caspian Healers' Sanctuary, and he'd had more than enough time to brood upon how he'd ended up in such a place.

"You're a fool," he whispered to his reflection in the water. During the day, when he was with Nehma and the twins or exploring the village and forest, it was easier to ignore the growing certainty that his foolishness had contributed to the violence against his family. His knuckles turned white on the basin's edge. If he ever saw Zarias again, he would rip the bastard's heart out with his bare hands.

A call drifted through the open window, announcing the healers' return. The entire place was abuzz with whispers and activity. Aronn pulled on a shirt and stepped outside Nehma's little house to investigate.

Lanterns shone on faces that betrayed ill tidings as the healers dismounted their horses. Nehma spoke to another healer, Catrin, who swore loudly before jogging off, her red hair flying behind her.

"What's going on?" Aronn asked when Nehma approached. She gave him a pained expression.

"We were intercepted by agents of King Fabian's. Evaria has sent aid to Parea, but Terrana marches toward Evaria, set to arrive in Maremer in less than two weeks."

Aronn's stomach dropped to his toes.

"My sister is in Maremer."

"We will go. We must convene with the elders first, but I am certain they will send our warriors."

"I'll go too."

"No, Aronn—"

"Nehma. My *sister* is there. She's protected me my entire life. I must do what I can to protect her in return. Please, tell the elders that. Convince them to let me go."

Nehma's eyes bored into his. Aronn's breath hitched in his throat as she fixed him with that gaze.

"All right. I will make a case for you."

She turned to leave, braids flicking over her shoulder.

"Nehma—" She looked at him expectantly. He sighed. "Thank you."

She smiled at him and bounded off down the dirt road toward the elders' cottage, and Aronn stared after her, cheeks warm.

He'd never been so flummoxed by a woman before, never felt that odd flutter in his stomach that made him nervous to speak to her on most occasions. She was either oblivious to his befuddlement or apathetic, and Aronn wasn't sure which he preferred.

He sighed. *Get it together, Aronn.*

He traipsed back to the little house, gazing numbly at the trees above. He couldn't even wish that Relaina had stayed in Parea to take the crown, not after having learned of the Conclaves' plot. Two weeks and no word on his family's well-being or whereabouts, and now Terrana was bringing war to the continent.

"Aronn."

Nehma had returned.

"I think you should come with me. The elders would be more likely to allow you to leave if you are present when I ask."

Aronn stared at her for a moment, and then shook his head to clear it.

"All right."

He followed her down the dirt path toward the elders' cottage. Many healers moved quickly around the village, speaking to one another in hushed voices as they passed. Surely the elders would hold a meeting for everyone to discuss what to do, but when he and Nehma arrived at the cottage, they were the only ones present.

The cottage was a short stone tower, inlaid with polished stones of every color imaginable that sparkled when beams of sunlight filtered through the thick canopy of trees during the day. Inside was a large circular room with spiraling stairs that went up a total of five levels, according to Nehma. The first level was filled with flowers and plants, a kitchen, and several large basins for laundry. In the center of it all stood five chairs in a circle, one for each elder. Aronn's anxiety subsided amidst the glowing lanterns and the smell of burning incense.

When they saw Aronn and Nehma, the five elders left their tasks—healing plants, washing clothing, baking bread—and sat in the circle surrounding Nehma and Aronn. They were all garbed in dark blue robes, and their hair was identical in length and color, flowing down to their hips and snowy-white. The only way Aronn could remember their names was by their hair styles. Aaresh, the one with ringlet curls, waved an arm, and the lights within the large, circular room brightened.

"Maremer calls for aid," Nehma said as soon as they sat down. "I would take our finest warriors, and Prince Aronn is here to request that he go to help as well. His sister, Princess Relaina, is in the city."

She was met with silence that made Aronn outrageously uncomfortable as the seconds ticked by.

"Prince Aronn will not go with you," said Shiva, the oldest of them, who kept their hair in braids. "Because you will not be going."

A beat of silence.

"*What*?"

"It is far too dangerous," Aaresh said. "Your aunt sent you here to learn what you can do with your magic and to keep you safe, not to toss you into the middle of a war."

"My aunt is in the capital of Evaria!" Nehma said. "She could use my help, our help. Who better to face the tenebrae? We were meant for this!"

"Enough, Nehma," Tolera said sharply, pushing their curtain of hair back from their face. "It is not your decision to make. It has been thousands of years since the tenebrae were faced with our magic. They have grown and evolved where we have dwindled. We will not send our own to face them when we know little of their power."

Nehma's right hand lit up, her eyes filling with the same light, and in her palm she gathered it until it formed a glowing orb. She lifted her arm and launched it, sending it careening into the wall. The stone disintegrated where the light made contact, forming a clean hole that allowed them to see the village. The elders stared at it silently.

"*I* have not dwindled," Nehma said, her voice low. "Our magic runs true in my veins. I have trained harder and grown stronger than anyone else."

"Your pride clouds your judgment," Corin said, their voice softer than the other elders. "Come back and speak to us when you're calmer."

Nehma turned on her heel, grabbed Aronn by the elbow, and marched outside. She let out a growl of frustration.

"I was calm!" she said. "I was in full control back there, did you see?"

"I did."

"And they say it's too dangerous to go. What is our purpose as healers and light-wielders if not to help others in their hour of need?" Nehma was still gripping Aronn's elbow even after they'd made it halfway back to her house. His cheeks burned.

"Sorry," she said, quickly releasing him. "I'm just...frustrated."

"What would happen if you left anyway?"

Nehma whipped around, eyes wide.

"Shh!" She beckoned him inside her house and closed the door.

"Would you stop me if I told you I was planning to go anyway?" Nehma asked, fixing him with a hard stare. Aronn swallowed.

"Of course not. And I'm going with you." Aronn just stared at her as she narrowed her eyes, looking him up and down.

"I haven't said I'm going. But *if* I were going to go...I would need to be very quiet, and very secretive. We would have to leave in the night and avoid patrols."

"Ha! Finally, something I can be helpful with," Aronn said. Nehma raised an eyebrow. "I am an expert at avoiding guards. I used to sneak out of the palace all the time and—"

Aronn stopped talking abruptly, his face going red. He cleared his throat.

"I'm just...good at avoiding guards. Only my sister knew when I'd snuck out, or my uncle." He couldn't meet her gaze.

"Then you will be an asset to our escape."

"Nehma!" Someone knocked on her door. "It's Rhea and Thea."

Aronn started for the door, but Nehma grabbed him and pulled him against her chest, clapping a hand over his mouth.

"We saw you blast a hole through the elders' cottage. Let us in, you fool."

"Sorry, I'm busy at the moment," Nehma called, and Aronn remained frozen in her grasp. Nehma lowered her voice. "Sorry to manhandle you for the second time today, but the fewer people that know about our plan, the better."

The shutters in the nearby window burst open, and Thea leaned on the windowsill, grinning.

"Busy, eh?" she said, nodding to her and the restrained Aronn. Nehma released him and Thea climbed inside the window, shortly followed by her twin.

"I take it the elders don't want us helping Evaria," Rhea drawled, flicking back one of her two long, dark brown plaits and examining her nails. Thea plopped down on Aronn's bed and crossed her legs.

"Of course not," Thea said. "They haven't wanted to get involved in anything since the raids. They're too afraid."

"They're cautious, and rightfully so." Catrin clambered through the window and closed the shutters behind her. Her hazel eyes landed on Aronn before she addressed Nehma. "But there is a time for caution and a time for action. So...when are we leaving?"

Nehma gaped at them.

"I—y-you want to go to Maremer?"

"We heard the news, same as you did," Rhea said.

"We cannot ignore this call for aid when we could tip the scales in Evaria's favor," Thea said. "Besides, what would happen if the Tyrant King conquers Evaria? There would be nothing to stop him from exterminating us. We cannot abandon our brethren in Evaria, and we cannot sit here and expect to remain protected if we won't help protect others."

"So, I ask again," Catrin said, eyes flashing, "When do we leave?"

Aronn's chest swelled with hope at the four light-harnessing women in the room, all ready to go to battle. Beside him, Nehma's eyes filled with tears.

"We go tonight."

KING FABIAN LEANED on the stone railing of a third-floor balcony, idly watching the progress of a figure walking in the gardens below. Last night's storm had run its course, and now the gardens were soaked, dirt dribbling over the cobblestones. Puddles were illuminated on the balcony by the light of the dawning sun, iridescent and rippling in the breeze.

"So," a familiar voice said from behind him, startling him. He turned to Desiree, who approached him with kahvi in hand, golden earrings tinkling. She offered him a cup, and he took it gladly before glancing down into the gardens again, grateful for his friend's presence. "It's been an eventful few days, has it not?"

Fabian took a sip of the steaming-hot, dark liquid in his hands, frowning at the dampness that had seeped from the stone railing into the sleeves of his red tunic. "I don't even know where to begin."

"Well, your nobles are cooperating without much complaint. Most of the villages have been evacuated, and all but a few families have been accounted for and brought into various houses here in Maremer. I'll be off to Lyneisia to aid the royal family tomorrow, so Rael will take over the task of overseeing the city gates."

"Mhmm." Fabian was still looking down into the gardens.

"You're distracted."

"I'm exhausted."

Desiree looked over the edge of the balcony.

"Ah. The famous Jeremiah Andovier."

"I don't know if *famous* is the right word." He sipped his kahvi and breathed in the revitalizing scent. He'd had it for the first time about a year ago when the visiting Prince of Naráz had brought it, and now he drank a cup every morning as the sun rose.

"Beside the point," Desiree said. "Did you hear he punched Swanson?"

Fabian couldn't help the slight twitch of his lips. "I heard."

"Ah, but did you hear why?"

"Anyone would have a multitude of reasons from which to choose to justify punching Henry Swanson."

"Fair. But from what you've told me, I gathered that Jeremiah Andovier is not the type of man to punch another noble unless he were greatly provoked."

"What are you getting at, Desiree?"

Desiree shrugged, swirling the kahvi in her cup and lifting it to her lips. "I hear Swanson was insulting you just before Jeremiah hit him."

"Is that so."

"That's what I hear." She downed the rest of her drink.

"That's a perfectly acceptable response to have if someone insults your king."

Desiree snorted.

"Please just say what you want to say, Desiree."

"I may speak freely?"

"You are always welcome to do so."

"It just seems to me that Jeremiah is quite the same man you described from your youth, and I want to know if you still love him."

Fabian frowned and drained his cup.

"I don't know. And it wouldn't matter if I did."

"Wouldn't matter? Fabian, you've spent the greater part of the past twenty years alone. Look at all you've done, at the lives you changed for the better, mine included. You've worked tirelessly to strengthen Evaria and made it more stable and prosperous than it has been in generations, and you deserve some joy in your life."

Desiree glanced over the balcony's railing again. She shook her head and said, "Especially if Gabriel is on his way to kill us all. You've tried to hide it, but I've caught glimpses of that tattoo on your back, Fabian, and I can guess who has one to match it. If Jeremiah Andovier is someone who could make you happy then I would say it matters a great deal."

"I don't feel happy when I look at him," Fabian said, struggling to find the words to explain. "Well...that isn't entirely true. But it's tangled up with other emotions. I feel...sad. And angry. And hurt. And I don't want to feel those things, Desiree. I thought I had left that broken part of myself in the past."

"I know how that feels," Desiree said, looking into her empty cup. "But feeling sad or angry or hurt does not mean you are broken. It means you are alive."

Fabian allowed the weight of her words to settle on him for a moment.

"How is your niece?" he asked.

"The same, if her last letter is any indicator. Still learning more about her power and flashing it about any chance she gets. I sent her to Lyneisia so she would be protected, but she sounds reckless as ever."

"We'll keep her safe. As we always have."

"I know I don't say this often, but I am grateful to have you as a friend, Fabian. I don't know what we would have done without you."

"Your friendship is a treasure, Desiree."

Fabian left the edge of the balcony just as servants appeared. They placed cushions in the now-dry chairs and offered Fabian and Desiree food. Despite the fact that the storm from yesterday had ceased and the skies cleared, the smell of rain still hung in the air.

"Why now?" Desiree asked at length, sitting in one of the cushioned chairs. "What's Gabriel's motive?"

Fabian reached for a grape and stared at the pink sky in the distance.

"I don't know. I've known for some time that it could happen, and I've shared my concerns with you. Perhaps he has heard that Relaina is here and seeks to attack us and take her."

"Why does he want her so badly? The Shadows have reported for years that the Terranian Elite failed to get to her because their aim was capture, rather than murder."

"There is something darker at play. Something we don't know yet, something we are missing. A storm is gathering and I fear we are unprepared."

They sat in silence for a long moment.

"I hope to the gods we can figure it out," Desiree said.

CHAPTER 22

A WINTER BALL

Jeremiah had forgotten how extravagant the parties were in the palace. No expense had been spared—four banquet tables overflowing with food; ice sculptures at the top of the main stair and lined intermittently around the room, taking the form of phoenixes, swans, lions, and dragons; extra crystal chandeliers installed; a group of the finest musicians placed on a dais; and finally, the garments worn by the guests. Every gown was finer than the last, and in keeping with tradition, they were ice-blue, white, or silver. It could've been a royal Lyneisian banquet, were it not for the copious extravagance of every detail.

He stood at the top of the main stair, which widened as it descended to the dance floor and hundreds of guests, observing quietly as he waited for Relaina and her companions to arrive. Guards stood at attention on either side of the double doors behind him, scrutinizing each guest as they entered the ballroom.

He'd once enjoyed this sort of party, eager to have a night off of training to do as he pleased.

And eager to spend time with Fabian.

"Quite the celebration, isn't it?"

Jeremiah's entire body went rigid. Standing just behind him was

Lady Andovier, dressed in a sparkling silver gown that matched her hair. Her shrewd hazel eyes looked him up and down.

"One would think with war imminent, we'd forego all this pomp," she said.

"Hello, Mother. I see you've broken your vow to remain at Crestfall until death summons you. When did you arrive?"

"A short while ago. It had to be done. I never expected the Tyrant King to launch another attack during my lifetime, and I will not miss my opportunity to see him bleed."

"You seem confident that he will be defeated."

"Of course. If we lack confidence, we might as well hand Evaria to Gabriel on a plate."

"True enough."

She stepped closer to him and lowered her voice. "I read your letter." A few guests arrived and walked past them, and she waited until they were out of earshot. "Your sister is in danger. You'll leave soon with a host to help her and the Lyneisian king?"

"Tomorrow morning. A large host will depart the city, and a small portion of us will head south for Lyneisia, while the majority marches to meet Gabriel's army."

"Good. Now...am I to wait all night for you to introduce me to my granddaughter?"

"She hasn't yet arrived. I'm waiting for her."

"I hear she's quite a fighter," Lady Andovier said, a satisfied smile on her face as she looked at the dancing guests below. "And a beauty, as well. A shame she decided to relinquish her claim to the Lyneisian throne. Beautiful fighters make for excellent queens, in my experience."

"I beg you not to mention that."

"Fine, fine. But let us wait for her elsewhere, my son. I am famished."

Escorting his mother around was not how Jeremiah had envisioned his time at the Winter Ball, but it was as good a distraction as any. He was anxious to leave tomorrow, but his heart ached when he imagined leaving Relaina behind. At least she would be safe.

He had not yet revealed to her what Christine had asked him to reveal. He'd planned to do it soon after his arrival in Maremer, but with

Terrana marching on Evaria, he could not bring himself to do it. Not yet.

He also hadn't had a chance to explain himself to Fabian. Perhaps he would do so tonight if he could find him. Despite his height and grand attire, Fabian had always had a talent for blending in at royal events.

Several Evarian nobles greeted his mother, surprised as he was at her presence. Amidst the nobles was a mixture of the richest merchants and most talented artisans. The man who'd carved the ice sculptures flitted around, badgering the servants about keeping them away from the chandeliers' heat.

"Oh, gods above," Lady Andovier said, placing her plate of food down on the banquet table and hurriedly chewing a strawberry covered in cream. "Is that her?"

Jeremiah followed her gaze. Relaina stood at the top of the stairs, dressed in an off-shoulder cobalt gown and silver sandals that looped up her calves. Beside her stood Darren LaGuarde, who couldn't take his eyes off her. Her hair was braided to perfection and decorated with sparkling pins, falling gracefully over her shoulder.

She looked like a queen.

A queen she will never be.

Lady Andovier let out a short chuckle as Relaina spotted Jeremiah and made her way toward him.

"A beauty. She favors her mother, don't you think?"

Jeremiah blinked. Before he could respond, his mother walked ahead to greet Relaina, taking her hands.

"My dear, it is good to finally meet you." Relaina raised an eyebrow at Jeremiah. He sighed and joined them.

"Relaina, this is your grandmother, Lady Rhonea Andovier."

Relaina's eyes widened as she bowed slightly to her grandmother.

"I am glad to meet you, Grandmother Rhonea." Lady Andovier looked to Relaina's companions, and Jeremiah nodded subtly toward Darren, Bracken, and Jacquelyn. The redheaded young woman had returned to the palace earlier that day. Jeremiah wasn't sure what mission she'd been assigned, but knowing Fabian, it was essential to the coming war.

"Oh," Relaina said. "May I introduce Darren LaGuarde, Bracken

Averatt, and Jacquelyn Sader."

"Darren LaGuarde. How fascinating it is to meet you."

While his mother trapped Darren in conversation, Jeremiah took the opportunity to speak to Relaina quietly.

"What is your goal for tonight?"

"Keep watch on Tridset," Relaina said. "He won't recognize me, and neither will Quentin. If they speak to one another, I am to get close and listen."

Jeremiah nodded. "Be careful. I don't see either of them yet, but then there are hundreds of guests here."

"...And he lived here for many years," Lady Andovier said to Bracken, Jacquelyn, and Darren. She looked back at Jeremiah. "He was quite the accomplished lad. A talented fighter and a musician!"

"Really?" Relaina blurted.

"Oh, yes!" Lady Andovier said, beaming. Jeremiah's heart sank as she looked over his shoulder at the musicians' dais. "Musician! You there. Fetch my son a fiddle, would you?"

"Mother, please—"

"Oh, would you?" Relaina asked, her eyes alight. "I didn't know you could play, Uncle!"

"Play? My son wrote hundreds of songs when he was a boy. Sang them at festivals."

A fiddler came down from the dais, instrument in hand. Jeremiah hesitated. Relaina gazed at him with bright, hopeful eyes, and he sighed.

"Very well. But only if you sing with me."

Relaina stopped short. Bracken nudged her from behind.

"Oh, all right," she said.

Jeremiah took the fiddle and walked toward the dais with Relaina just as the flute and lute finished a tune. A few people who had been dancing applauded politely. He and Relaina stepped up and turned, facing the ballroom full of people. Jeremiah scanned the crowd, fighting nervousness, and all other thoughts flew from his mind as he spotted Fabian by the door leading to the gardens. The king was garbed in blue, white, and gray, with a silver circlet atop his braids, crafted to look like a crown of snowflakes. In front of him was a ruggedly handsome merchant who had said something to make him laugh and smile.

"'The Merchant Prince,'" Jeremiah said to the musicians behind him, who nodded and prepared themselves. He turned to Relaina. "Do you know it?"

Relaina looked at him uncertainly but nodded. She took a deep breath in. Jeremiah readied his bow and began to play.

KING FABIAN'S head snapped up to look at the musicians' dais as Jeremiah played the introduction to the tune he'd picked. Relaina swallowed. She hadn't sung in front of a crowd this large since she was thirteen, and after that she'd put her foot down with her father about making her perform at banquets. But she'd wanted to hear her uncle play...and gods, it was worth it. His fingers danced across the strings, the bow creating a warm timbre as he slid it quickly back and forth. The other musicians joined in, filling out the texture of the music as Relaina began to sing.

> *Four nights past as I walked through,*
> *As I walked through the city,*
> *The moon was high and the stars aglow,*
> *The night, it was so pretty.*
>
> *High above in a manor house,*
> *A merchant prince, he spied me,*
> *And he called to me with a wicked smile,*
> *"My darling, you've beguiled me!"*

Relaina paused as Jeremiah played the interlude. People began clapping and dancing in time with the song, and Relaina smiled. On her right, her uncle played expertly, but his eyes were not on the instrument. He was looking through the crowd, gaze locked on King Fabian. Relaina, puzzled, took a breath and began the next verse.

> *He came down to the city street,*
> *Where he grinned and kissed my hand.*

He was handsome and I was fair,
I admit, I was entranced.

There upon that city street,
He came and swept me off my feet, and
You know the rest of the night we had—
My love—the prince—and me!

Relaina's eyes narrowed as she watched Jeremiah play the interlude again. King Fabian stared back at him.

His eyes shine golden in the sun—

Oh.

My love, the prince—

Oh.

She glanced back at Jeremiah, who sported the faintest of sly grins as he held the king's gaze.

Gods above.

Relaina finished singing, and Jeremiah ended the song with a flourish. The crowd clapped vigorously, flushed with excitement. Relaina and Jeremiah bowed and stepped down from the dais.

"I had no idea you played, much less played like *that*!" Relaina said.

"Right," Jeremiah said, not looking at her. Relaina followed his distracted look to Fabian, who had turned to enter the gardens. "If you'll excuse me."

Jeremiah left Relaina there just as his mother approached, ignoring Lady Andovier completely as he set off after the Evarian king. Relaina glanced sidelong at her grandmother.

"Let us leave him be, shall we?" Lady Andovier said. "He deserves to spend his evening in comfort before setting off tomorrow. And so do you, my dear."

Relaina watched her uncle go with a bit of concern, glancing around the crowd for Tridset or Quentin. Neither had shown up yet.

"I suppose you're right," Relaina said, and she allowed her grandmother to steer her back to Darren and the others. Darren looked magnificent in a white jacket with silver embroidery.

"Evening," Relaina said as her grandmother excused herself to speak with a friend. "Does anyone else want food? I'm famished."

They approached the food table together, Bracken snatching two flutes of sparkling wine as they wove past servants and guests. Relaina picked out several savory pastries and thanked the gods her gown wasn't uncomfortably snug around her middle.

"You look wonderful," she said, nudging Darren as he sniffed a cup of strange, frothing liquid and frowned. He set it back onto the table.

"Likewise," he said, his eyes traveling down and then up again. Relaina started humming with the music, smiling. Darren leaned in so his mouth was close to her ear, his arm slipping around her waist. "It's really a shame your gown is so lovely. All I want to do is tear it off of you."

Relaina's humming cut off as she turned bright red and giggled.

"Have you seen Tridset or Quentin?" Bracken leaned against the table to her left, popping a grape into his mouth. Relaina shook her head.

"Neither of them. They were on the guest list. I wonder why they haven't come."

"Perhaps they're celebrating in the city instead," Jacquelyn said. "That's where Connor is. Couldn't even be bothered to come here to change his clothes after we returned."

"I'm a little disappointed I won't get to see him before I leave," Bracken said. "Especially since he'd make this ball significantly more interesting."

Jacquelyn laughed. "That he would."

Relaina frowned, her heart aching amidst the jaunty music and chatter. "Bracken...please be careful in Lyneisia."

"I will be."

She faced him, taking both of his hands in hers. "I want you to know that I understand. I understand why you became one of Fabian's Shadows. And I don't blame you for not telling me."

Bracken smiled, blinking as tears formed in his eyes.

"Gods damn it, Relaina, you're going to make me blubber like a fool in front of everyone," he said, lifting their entwined hands to wipe his eye. Relaina made a face at the wetness on her knuckles.

"Good evening, my friends." Lord Vontair approached the four of them with a plump, pretty woman on his arm. "I would like you all to meet my wife, Lady Clarisse Vontair."

They each inclined their heads. Lady Vontair's brown hair was piled on top of her head, giving her the illusion of being just taller than her rotund husband, but both were still rather short.

"Oh, I *do* love parties," she said, her small mouth turning upwards into a smile, lifting her rosy cheeks. "The dancing especially. I remember years ago, when I first met my dear husband, we were..."

Lady Vontair went on at some length, and after a while Relaina's eyes began to wander. Guests danced and drank and ate around the massive room as the musicians played upon their dais.

"...But oh, we must be off!" Lady Vontair said as Relaina's attention returned. "I see a friend I haven't spoken to in many months! Jiteya! My dear!"

She ambled off, Lord Vontair trailing behind her. Relaina sighed.

"Well, tonight has been unsuccessful so far. How am I supposed to find out more about Tridset and Quentin when they aren't even here?"

"Perhaps we ought to go into the city to look for them," Jacquelyn said. "There are so many people here, I doubt we'll be missed. And the city's festivities go well into the night."

Relaina looked around the ballroom at the people dancing, the servants bustling, the musicians playing. Her grandmother had taken a seat by one of the ice sculptures, engaged in conversation with another older noblewoman. Jeremiah and Fabian had disappeared.

"Let's meet in an hour."

JEREMIAH WAITED AS PATIENTLY AS he could while Fabian sat across from him in stunned silence, processing all he'd just heard. The fire crackling in the grate by their chairs was the only sound as the king stared at the floor. Fabian's private study was covered wall-to-wall in bookshelves that reached to the ceiling—a few titles glowed in the fire-light, but most were indistinct.

"This changes a great deal of things," Fabian said. Jeremiah felt as though a great weight had been lifted from his shoulders. Finally, after all these years, he was able to explain to Fabian why he'd never come back. Even if Fabian never forgave him, at least he knew everything now. "Does she know?"

"I couldn't bear to tell her," Jeremiah said, shaking his head. "Not when I can't be here to help her manage it all."

"And if you should not return?"

It was a possibility Jeremiah did not want to think about, but one he had to consider nonetheless.

"Would you tell her for me?"

Fabian frowned. "Jeremiah...this needs to come from you."

"Fabian, please—"

"So take care to come back alive." Fabian's eyes sparkled amber in the firelight. "This all began here, the day you left. The pain will end here, too, I hope."

Jeremiah stared at him. "It was good, wasn't it? What we had?"

Fabian studied him for a moment.

"I have not accepted a marriage proposal in twenty years because it *was* good. More than good. And the ink on my back is a permanent reminder that I have always been yours. To explain that to someone else when it came time for marriage would be...distasteful at the very least."

Jeremiah could almost feel the lines of his own tattoo—a phoenix rising along his spine, hidden carefully away for so many years. But did Fabian just say—?

Fabian stood from his chair and walked toward one of his book-shelves, running his fingers along the spines of a few before selecting one and walking back to Jeremiah, holding it out. Jeremiah looked at the title, slowly reaching out his hand to take it. *The Narázi Pirate.*

"Gods, this was—"

"The last book you gave me. I never finished it."

Fabian's hand dropped as Jeremiah took hold of the book, thumbing through the pages as he stood from his chair.

"I don't know how to feel about what you've told me. And I don't know if I will find myself able to accept it. All I know is that you are here, and tomorrow you will not be here, and I want you to stay."

Jeremiah looked up at the king, a lump forming in his throat. "Fabian, you know I can't—"

"I know you must go tomorrow. But stay here, right now. With me."

Jeremiah stopped breathing. Warmth crept through his middle as Fabian gazed at him, that same warmth he'd felt when playing the fiddle downstairs. He'd chosen that song to grab Fabian's attention, and it had worked, had given him the opportunity to be in this place, in this moment.

"I don't mean to pressure you," Fabian said, shifting. *Oh.* He'd taken too long to respond. "But if you want—"

Jeremiah answered his question by tossing the book over his shoulder and stepping forward to kiss him. Every worry, every conflict, every heartbreak fell from his mind as Fabian drew him closer and began undoing the buttons on his jacket. The king took several steps backward, until he bumped into his desk, all the while pulling Jeremiah along with him. Jeremiah reached for Fabian's waist and tugged upward, guiding him so he was sitting on the desk, his hands almost trembling as they pulled Fabian's shirt over his head. Jeremiah's hands traveled up Fabian's chest and glided along his neck until reaching the evening roughness of his chin. It was all different and new, yet still the same as it had been all those years ago.

"I'll come back," Jeremiah said between kisses, both of them now halfway undressed. He decided, then and there, that after fixing things in Parea and ensuring his sister's safety, he would leave his post and return here, to the place and the person he'd always held in his heart. "Fabian, I promise you I will come back."

Fabian leaned back to look at him.

"Dearest Jeremiah." He ran his fingers through Jeremiah's hair. "Just kiss me."

Jeremiah did that, and more. And, gods, it felt like coming home.

CHAPTER 23

THE TRAITOR AND THE VOW

Back in their shared chambers, Darren stood from the couch and walked over to Relaina, wrapping his arms around her middle and resting his chin on her shoulder as she looked in the mirror.

"This may be my new favorite gown," Relaina said.

"It's more than lovely." Darren paused for a moment. "How much time do we have before we meet Bracken and Jacquelyn at the front gate?"

"Maybe twenty minutes before we're missed," Relaina said, smirking. Darren sighed and placed his forehead on her shoulder.

"Damn."

Relaina giggled and turned to face him. She took his face in her hands and gave him a chaste kiss. Darren pulled her back and kissed her slowly, patiently, biting her lip.

"Darren..." Relaina's breath caught as he kissed her neck.

"Relaina, do you—?"

"Yes." Jacquelyn and Bracken could wait.

Darren turned her around and began undoing the laces of her gown, his fingers gentle and adept. He kissed her shoulders and back as the bodice loosened, one hand tugging at her abdomen and traveling upward to glide along her breasts. His touch sent thrills of salacious desire along her skin, muddling her thoughts.

"You," Darren said in a low voice, "looked incredible tonight. The most beautiful person in the room."

Relaina grinned and shifted her shoulders so the dress fell to the floor, and, completely nude, she watched Darren's eager expression as she made quick work of unlacing his trousers. He shrugged off his jacket and shirt and pulled her to the bed.

A bit longer than twenty minutes later, Relaina and Darren dressed in their Shadow gear, making sure they were outfitted with the proper weapons. Relaina was pleased that Fabian had gifted Darren the same slim, protective armor she'd worn the night of her confrontation with Quentin. It would keep them safe from physical attacks as well as searching eyes in the night.

"Darren? Relaina?" Jacquelyn knocked briskly on the door. "We need to get going while festivities are still underway."

Relaina looked at Darren as he stood and stretched his arms, double-checking his daggers and bow and quiver, which were all strapped to his back. Relaina checked the two daggers at her hips, both ready to draw in an instant.

"Ready?" she asked. He nodded grimly.

The trek into the city was not difficult; the real challenge began when they reached the bottom of the hill, where the streets were full of festivalgoers, performers, and vendors. Music emanated from every street corner, and bright, white-flame lanterns had been lit all over the place, casting a bluish glow that made the cobblestones shimmer after all the recent rain.

"How do they get the flames to turn white?" Relaina asked as they crouched behind a cart full of straw. The nearby stable's stench was overpowering, and Relaina wrinkled her nose and turned away from it, gazing instead at the lanterns in the square.

"Some kind of mineral turns it that color," Bracken said. "Moon-stone, maybe?"

"Fascinating," Relaina said. "They're beautiful."

"I really hate to be my brother in this situation," Jacquelyn said, "but we have other things to worry about at present. There's no way the four of us will be inconspicuous enough to remain unnoticed."

Relaina frowned. The crowds were indeed denser than she'd imagined. The fountain at the center of the square bubbled as children ran circles around it, chasing one another with folded paper dragons. And the *smell*... It was nearly as enticing as the smell of Seacastle's food.

"She's right," Darren said, bringing Relaina back to the matter at hand. "We ought to go in pairs."

"Relaina and I will go west," Jacquelyn said, gazing down the street in that direction. "The crowds are larger and we're both smaller framed than the two of you. Bracken and Darren, you'll go south?"

They nodded.

"Where should we reconvene?" Bracken asked.

"Here," Jacquelyn said. She glanced at the moon high above, offering its own glow to the city below. "We'll meet back in an hour. If one of us has found Quentin or Tridset, we'll all go in that direction. Otherwise, we'll have to form a new plan."

Now that they were all agreed, each of them pulled their mask up over their mouth and nose, obscuring the greater part of their face. Relaina glanced at Darren once more—with a wink, he set off with Bracken to dart behind a nearby pub. As Relaina crept off just behind Jacquelyn in the opposite direction, her mask shifted as she smiled.

They scaled the exterior stable wall and hopped from that roof to the roof of a house, slowly making their way west, parallel to a wide street full of people. Relaina scanned each face and searched every stall for whiskey. The minutes passed more quickly than she would've liked as they leapt their way across roofs and approached another square that would force them to return to ground level. They vaulted down balconies and gripped windowsills around the back side of an inn near the bay, the cries of gulls and the rocking of ships along the docks the only sounds accompanying them.

"Gods," Relaina said, brushing her hands off on her pants. "This is impossible. There are too many people—"

Relaina had just turned to face Jacquelyn when a sound unlike any she'd ever heard swept around her, impossibly loud and...*hot*? It was too enveloping and bone-shaking to be fireworks.

Relaina coughed and blinked, her ears ringing as she lifted herself up off the cobblestones. How had she gotten there?

"Jacquelyn!" she called, blinking in the smoke and fire that had ignited in the bay. A silhouette appeared by the nearby inn, holding a spear. *Thank the gods.* Warm blood began oozing from her right shoulder.

"Shit—Jacquelyn, I—"

Something hard and fast caught her on the back of the head, and blackness swept over her.

~

DARREN STOOD beside Bracken a few feet back from the cart that was their meeting point, far enough into the shadows that passersby wouldn't notice them.

"It's been over an hour now, hasn't it?" Bracken asked, pacing and looking down the wide street leading west. Darren looked to the sky. The moon was lower, almost hidden behind the buildings of the city now, and clouds were gathering. "They should be here."

"We'll give them a few more minutes," Darren said. "And then we'll go look for them."

In the distance, a loud *boom* shook the air.

"Fireworks," Bracken said. "Didn't know King Fabian had imported them."

With every passing second, Darren barely kept the creeping dread at bay. His neck prickled with uneasiness as he scanned the western street for any sign of Relaina or Jacquelyn.

"Fuck it, let's go find them."

"Thank the gods," Bracken said, almost sagging with relief.

"Don't thank them yet." Darren drew one of his daggers, and he and Bracken struck out west, darting in and out of dark corners and behind stalls. A shadow passed by in his periphery and he tensed, but it was only a cat dashing into a covered alleyway. With a great sigh he continued on behind Bracken. He was going to find Relaina, and she would roll her eyes at him and tell him he was an impatient fool.

But they walked down that street, and three others, finally ending up near the bay, and there was no sign of Relaina or Jacquelyn. Darren forced himself to breathe, every nerve in his body alight with anxiety.

Ahead of Bracken, standing huddled by a stall full of festival bread for sale, was a gaggle of people dressed like anyone else around, inconspicuous and unremarkable. Darren might not have spared them a second glance.

But he recognized one man's face.

Darren grabbed Bracken's collar and yanked him out of sight, barely suppressing his terror.

"Listen to me and don't say anything," Darren said. "By the bread stall there's a group of people talking together. The man speaking the most is—argh!"

It was like a blow to the middle of his chest, swift and hollow. He hadn't felt it since he'd killed Xavier, and even then, it had been unfamiliar—

The screams began then, tearing up the street like a devastating wave.

Someone had just been killed nearby.

"Thieves! Murderers!"

"Run!"

And the cry that rang out above the rest, "*Fire!*"

Festivalgoers scrambled and shrieked, parents scooped up their children, vendors abandoned their carts as the group of Terranian assassins fanned out, firing arrows and sheathing blades in flesh.

Darren threw himself into the fray, marking the nearest as his first target, a man wielding a blackwood bow. The same feeling of untethering pulled at Darren's chest as he buried his dagger in the man's neck.

Not tenebrae, then—easy to kill. But he needed at least one alive.

The five assassins were so intent on their spree of bloodshed that they didn't notice as Darren picked them off one by one, feeling their deaths each time, and feeling the deaths of every person they murdered —they appeared to be targeting guards. He'd never had to try so hard to ignore it before, had never been so close to so many deaths at once.

At the end of the street, several blocks back from the bay now, bodies were strewn on the cobblestones around the last assassin, who turned to face Darren as he approached. The man was corded with muscle that stood out as he wiped the blood from his blade onto his pants. Darren tore the mask from his face, breathing hard. The man grinned, his eyes filling with the light-devouring void of the tenebrae.

"Nephew," he said. Darren tossed his empty quiver and bow to the ground, drawing both daggers. Not another soul was on the street; screams echoed all around him, and the faintest smell of smoke reached his nostrils as Lord Gerratt stalked toward him. Darren trembled at the sight of him. He looked so like Darren's mother, but it was a cruel joke that he continued to live his wretched life when Kacelle had died so young. It filled Darren with agonizing rage.

"Where are they?" Darren asked.

"Of whom do you speak?" Gerratt was still smiling.

Darren struck, landing a blow on Gerratt's shoulder, but it bounced off, deflected by armor. In a breath, Darren had dodged an attack and dealt another, missing narrowly, and they were once again circling one another.

"Where. Are. They?"

Gerratt grinned, lunging at Darren again lazily. Darren parried and danced out of reach before throwing himself at Gerratt again. This time his dagger caught Gerratt below the armpit, slicing a deep cut in his flesh. Gerratt growled in pain and displeasure, but it was drowned out by the rising of more screams and the thundering of hooves. A dozen guards appeared at the square behind Gerratt, approaching on horseback.

Gerratt turned to Darren with a terrible smile upon his face, and before Darren could shout a warning, Gerratt projected the shadow within, sending it to envelop a guard on her horse. She writhed for a moment and then jumped down, sword drawn as she headed straight for Darren. Gerratt laughed as Darren adjusted his technique to fight them both. He needed to get close enough to the guard to touch her...

Gerratt's sword slashed his upper arm, and Darren hissed, tucking it away for a moment to dodge a jab from the guard. There was an opening in the way she handled the blade, and the next time she attacked him he swiped upward with enough force to knock it from her hands. He grabbed her arm and began to say the words to dispel the tenebrae, but Gerratt came at him from the side, and he had to release her. With a curse, Darren forced Gerratt back and dove for her again, this time saying the words fast enough that the tenebrae was destroyed, dissipating into the air while Gerratt shrieked his fury and pain.

Darren launched himself at a distracted Gerratt and grappled for a moment before he had him disarmed on the ground. A few city guards surrounded them as Darren held a dagger at Gerratt's throat.

"*Where are they?*"

Gerratt chuckled.

"You mean the Lyneisian bitch? I expect you'll see her very soon. Maremer will fall, and once you're returned home, perhaps your father will let you watch after we hand her over to the priests."

No. *No.*

Darren's iron grip on the darkness deep within loosened. Icy cold erupted in his chest as he buried his second dagger in Gerratt's hand, pinning it to the ground. Gerratt screamed and began breathing heavily through his teeth.

"Tell me where she is, you *fucking snake!*"

"You've lost, *boy!*" Gerratt spat. "Our agent did her duty—fooled even you into trusting her. The ship they're on has already left the harbor."

Darren yanked the blade out of Gerratt's hand and shoved the other one through his abdomen in the location that would deliver the slowest death. He left him there without a glance and sprinted for the horse of the guard Gerratt had possessed. He took off through the streets as rain began to fall, blinking the water out of his eyes as he pushed the horse as fast as it could go toward the bay.

When Darren turned the final corner that cleared the way to the docks, he came to a halt, his horse balking.

Every ship in the bay—at the docks and those anchored further out —had been set ablaze, the flames devouring the wood as sailors and merchants shouted and scrambled to abandon the vessels or put out the fire. One ship exploded, flying into the water in a spray of splintered wood. Sailors dove and swam for the shore, some with horrible burns that had people running out of their homes to help them. The rain did little to smother the massive fires that had ships groaning and cracking as they collapsed against the docks and into the water. Darren dismounted, running toward the harbor's edge in the futile hope that the ship he sought was still docked somewhere nearby.

"*Relaina!*" There was almost no chance she would hear him, but he cried her name anyway. He looked around wildly, blinking and coughing as smoke filled his eyes and nose. "*Relaina!*"

He spotted it. Out in the distance, lanterns flickered against the darkness, revealing a single ship sailing out of the bay, untouched by the flames and unable to be pursued. Darren ran for the dock's edge, the smoke overwhelming as he passed a burning vessel, but he didn't feel the flames even as they licked his skin. He was vaguely aware of attempting to jump onto the ship, but an unknown force pulled him back. He coughed again, blinking at the figure above him as they yelled, but he couldn't tell what they said, nor did he care. All that mattered was getting to that ship...

"*No,*" he rasped, and then went limp.

RELAINA AWOKE with her head throbbing so forcefully she thought she might vomit. She whimpered, opened her eyes, and reached to touch the back of her head, but found she was unable to do so. As the rest of her senses returned, a dark room appeared, lit only by two grimy green lanterns that swung slowly back and forth. Metal clinked by her ears, a chain between the shackles that were clasped around her wrists. For a long moment she stared at them, unable to remember how they'd gotten there and where she was.

The wooden floor beneath her creaked and groaned as she braced herself on her palms and forced herself to sit up. A wave of nausea overtook her, not helped by a pungent odor nearby, but after a moment, it passed, and she opened her eyes once more.

Two silhouettes appeared before her, standing by a door between the lanterns.

"What did I tell you? She's healing rapidly. She must have the blood."

"It proves nothing."

Relaina blinked just as the lanterns threw their faces into relief.

Jacquelyn! They'd been scouring the city for Quentin and Tridset. They must've been ambushed, and now Jacquelyn was here with Relaina in this grimy little prison cell...

"I know where I hit her," Jacquelyn said. "If it had been anyone else, they'd have at least vomited multiple times, but most wouldn't even be awake yet."

What in the name of Ashima were they talking about? And why were they speaking in Terranian?

"Jacquelyn," Relaina said, her throat raw. "What...what's going on?"

Jacquelyn and the man beside her exchanged a glance. He opened the door, casting a dim light into the room before shutting it behind him, leaving them alone. Jacquelyn walked up to Relaina and squatted down before her. There were no shackles on her wrists.

"You're a prisoner of Tridset's and the Terranian Elite, and we're sailing to Terrana, where you'll await King Gabriel's return from war."

Her words fell on Relaina's ears like heavy blocks of stone.

"I don't understand."

Jacquelyn frowned. "Perhaps you aren't healed enough yet to comprehend. I'll come back later."

She stood and started to leave.

"No," Relaina said, "I don't understand why you aren't a prisoner too."

Jacquelyn's face was a smooth mask of neutrality as she gazed at Relaina.

"Because I'm the one who brought you here."

Every syllable felt like a small knife pricking into Relaina's skin.

"No...no...you...you can't have..." Relaina said, rubbing her eyes with her knuckles and then immediately regretting it as her head gave a nasty throb. Her heart pounded forcefully in her chest. She looked up at Jacquelyn again.

"Bracken?"

For the first time, Jacquelyn's face cracked slightly.

"All part of the plan."

Relaina just stared at her, unable to believe it. "*Why*?"

"Gabriel is a worthy leader for us all. He will unite Esran, and my brother and I are glad to serve him."

Relaina's breath came more quickly now, her stomach like heavy iron as tears formed in her eyes.

"Those days you were gone recently..."

"I met with the Terranian host, and we prepared for this."

"But we're *friends*," Relaina said, choking on the word.

Jacquelyn shook her head.

"Perhaps we might have been, under different circumstances." She looked down at the dirty floor. "I...you should know I did come to care for Bracken. I still do. He was good to me."

Relaina's denial came to a staggering halt.

"Get out."

Jacquelyn looked up again but did not move.

"What?"

"Get out. Get *out*, you *fucking bitch*!"

Jacquelyn stumbled backward. Tears streamed down Relaina's face as she screamed her throat raw, cursing Jacquelyn to every god she could think of. The door shut and locked with a loud *click,* and Relaina was left there alone to rage in the darkness.

Bracken... He was going to be devastated. If he was even alive. And Darren...

He would hunt them down.

The thought both comforted and terrified her. Relaina could not bear to imagine him once again a prisoner of his father's, forced to do his bidding, and she was the leverage for Gabriel to make Darren do anything he wanted. Relaina sobbed once, trying to gain control of her own rising hysteria.

"No," she whispered, a vow to the darkness before her.

CHAPTER 24

THE HEALER'S DAUGHTER

Darren coughed and opened his eyes, blinking in the darkness. A dank chill seeped into his bones as he inhaled and recognized the room with a flash of horror.

"Ahh...you're awake."

Darren flinched so violently the shackles on his wrists cut into his skin. His hands were empty, his weapons gone, and before him stood his father, smiling beside an altar, atop which lay—

"*Relaina!*"

Darren stood and tried to run to her, but his ankles were also bound by shackles and bolted to the floor. He landed hard on his shoulder and cried out. A chuckle echoed throughout the chamber.

"All these years," Gabriel said. "I have tried to capture her, and these last three years tried to bring you home. To get you both at the same time is a victory I'm glad to savor."

"Don't...touch...her!" Darren gasped from the ground, his lungs still aching from the smoke he'd inhaled.

"Hmm." Gabriel gazed down at him. He walked slowly toward his son, the sound of each step making Darren's head throb. Gabriel leaned down and grabbed Darren's chin, yanking it upward.

"I don't think you've realized that I can do...whatever I want."

He snapped his fingers, and a nearby door opened. Four priests of Calixtos entered the room, their faces and eyes hidden by black hoods. Dread seized Darren by the throat as he glanced between them and Relaina, who had been strangely silent this whole time. How badly was she hurt? Gabriel chuckled again.

"You—"

The priests arrived at the altar, and one of them held aloft a knife wreathed in black fire. *No...*

"Can do—"

The priests began to chant.

"*Nothing.*"

The knife came down, striking Relaina in the chest, and she screamed. Darren screamed with her, fighting, gasping—

His vision blurred and shifted, and Relaina's screams faded away as a tall figure with black hair appeared, eyes first black like the tenebrae, and then changed to a deep violet. He emanated a hazy white glow, and his indigo-onyx skin was covered in pinpricks of light, like stars against the night sky.

Don't fear your darkness as I did. Find her before it's too late.

Darren's breath came out in a puff of hot air against frigid cold. "Who are you?"

The man studied him, frowning.

I am Calixtos.

Darren sat bolt upright, coughing as his body fought to gulp down air. He clutched his torso and looked around, blinking at the lanterns and wreckage in the bay.

"Darren."

Bracken was on his right, his face blackened with soot, and beside him was Shojen, the same healer-guard who had helped him after the tenebrae attack in the Gnarled Root.

It hadn't been real. They still had time to prevent the horrors he'd just dreamt.

"We have to get back to Seacastle," Bracken said, his voice trembling.

Bracken and Darren reached the palace in record time along the undamaged but nearly empty city streets. Smoke still obscured much of the bay and the western half of Maremer, but most of the flames had been stifled by the time they arrived at the gates.

The palace doors opened before them and light poured out, making Darren squint against the shimmering rain. The act of dismounting his horse had him clutching at his ribs as his lungs battled for air. He and Bracken took the steps up with excruciating slowness. Fabian and Jeremiah met them in the entrance hall, disheveled and half-awake. Jeremiah's eyes locked on Darren as the doors shut behind them, and the number of people standing there remained at two instead of four.

"Where is she?"

Even ten feet away, Darren could hear Jeremiah perfectly. The cold darkness was gone, returned to the recesses of his being, but something broke inside him. He sobbed and fell to his knees.

Jeremiah walked forward and knelt before Darren, placing a hand on his shoulder. Tears stung his eyes as Jeremiah's grip tightened.

"Where is Relaina?" Jeremiah asked, his voice hard.

Darren shoved his grief and rage down and gritted his teeth.

"The Terranian Elite have her on a ship," Darren said, forcing himself to meet Jeremiah's eyes. Jeremiah's breath came out in a shaky *huff,* and then Darren was on his feet, pulled aloft by strong hands that gripped his tunic. Jeremiah slammed Darren up against the nearby wall, knocking a porcelain vase off a decorative table. It shattered on the floor. Bracken swore.

"Jeremiah!" Fabian said.

"*What did you do?*" Jeremiah asked, his eyes burning with pain and fury.

"I tried to—"

"*What have you done to my daughter?*"

The last word echoed in the entrance hall, hanging in the nascent silence.

Darren's eyes grew wide. Oh, gods. Oh, *gods.*

"It was Jacquelyn," Bracken said quietly.

The white-hot rage in Jeremiah's eyes dimmed, and his grip on Darren's tunic loosened as he turned to look at Bracken.

Bracken's hands and voice trembled. "Fabian, have you been sending Jacquelyn and Connor on missions outside of the city?"

The king frowned. "No."

Bracken nodded bitterly and slammed a fist onto another table, nearly taking out another priceless vase. "I'm such a *fool*! I should have known something wasn't right, gods *damn* it!"

"Bracken, what are you saying?" Fabian asked.

Bracken turned to Darren, his eyes anguished. "Jacquelyn betrayed us and took Relaina to the Terranians."

Now Darren remembered Gerratt's taunting words before he'd killed him. *Our agent did her duty...fooled even you into trusting her...*

Darren would kill her too.

Jeremiah released his grip on Darren's tunic, stepping away far enough to let him breathe.

"I would sooner throw myself into the realm of Calixtos than see Relaina in the hands of my father," Darren said, clutching at his ribs again. He took a labored breath and stood upright, looking Jeremiah, Relaina's *father*, right in the eye. "If I have to dry up the gods-damned sea to keep that from happening, I will find a way to do it."

Jeremiah studied him for a moment.

"Then we are of one mind. We'll form a plan and leave tonight." He turned to Fabian, whose face was frozen in a mask of horror. "Can your soldiers go to Parea without me?"

The king nodded. "Yes."

"Good." Jeremiah looked to Bracken and Darren. "Tell me everything."

RELAINA WAS JUST BEGINNING to doze off at whatever hour of day or night it was when the door to her cell opened, waking her with its abhorrent creak. She opened her eyes just enough to see who had entered and repressed a groan.

Jacquelyn trudged to the stool below one of the lanterns and slumped down onto it, sighing. Relaina opened her eyes a little more. Jacquelyn was haggard and dirty, as if she'd been running the entire ship by herself.

"I know you're awake," Jacquelyn said, in the same tone she used when criticizing her brother. Connor was on the ship, but he had not come down to Relaina's cell. Remembering their treachery made Relaina's bones ache, so instead of responding, she turned over, chains clinking as she faced the wall.

"Really? Suit yourself. You've recovered fully now from your head injury."

"Oh, you mean the one you inflicted so you could bring me to a man who wants me dead?" Relaina sat up and put her back to the wall, crossing her arms in front of her knees. Her Shadow gear had held up well, but it was growing colder as they journeyed on. Relaina wondered what their plan was as they headed south; along the Granica, the only way for ships to pass would be to destroy the bridges connecting Evaria and Lyneisia or somehow drag the ship to shore and around. Perhaps they intended to transfer Relaina to another ship, the way merchants did with goods and livestock. "Just take my bucket and get out."

"That's not my job today. I'm just here to assess your health."

"I'm eating porridge and stale bread, drinking questionable water, getting terrible sleep, and no exercise. How do you think my health is?"

Jacquelyn shrugged. "Just doing my job."

"What does it matter, anyway? Gabriel's going to kill me, so why worry about my recovery?"

"He doesn't want you dead. If he did, you'd be dead already."

"Then what in Ashima's name does he want with me? Why have I been his target for so long?"

"You really haven't figured it out yet?"

"You've pretended to be my friend for years. The least you can do is not patronize me when I ask a direct question."

Jacquelyn sighed. "Fair. You have healers' blood."

Relaina stared at her. "What? How is that possible?"

Jacquelyn shrugged again. "All I know is that you have the blood, and the blood of a powerful line, at that. It's why the tenebrae disintegrated when it tried to possess you in the inn."

"I've never exhibited magic of any kind," Relaina said. Perhaps Gabriel had sought the wrong person. "I know of no healers in the Gienty bloodline. Or the Andovier one, for that matter."

Jacquelyn opened her mouth to respond, but someone knocked,

and she stood to open the door. The man at the threshold was someone Relaina had only seen from a distance, in the markets of Maremer.

"Is she fully recovered?" His slippery voice clawed its way up Relaina's spine. Jacquelyn bowed her head.

"She is, sir."

"Excellent," Tridset said, and even in the dim light Relaina could make out a smile. He beckoned, and two others entered the room and approached Relaina. She flinched as they reached for her wrists, but one of them forced her arms against the wall behind her as the other unlatched the chains from the floor. They transferred them to hooks on the wall, pulling them taut and forcing Relaina to stand with her hands at eye level. She'd expected this since her capture, but now that it was happening, choking down her terror was nearly impossible. Her heartbeat thundered in her ears.

"What are you doing, Tridset?" Jacquelyn asked as the two lackeys secured Relaina's restraints and left the room. Tridset took off his gloves and held them out to Jacquelyn, who snatched them and tossed them to the floor.

"She stole invaluable information from my colleague," Tridset said, eyeing Relaina up and down. "Now that she's in good health, it's time for her to face the consequences."

"We never agreed—"

"Oh, *do* shut up, dear. I'll do what I please. The king won't mind a few scratches and bruises, right?"

He reached for a knife sheathed at his waist, unbuckling the leather and pulling it out slowly, as though to emphasize to Relaina its wicked sharpness and length. The metal was so black it stood out against the darkness in the room.

"What is *that*?" The horror on Jacquelyn's face suggested she already knew.

"Oh, don't you know?" Tridset grinned and turned to Relaina. He stared into her eyes as he spoke two words in a language that grated on Relaina's ears, and the knife ignited. The black flames provided neither light nor warmth and moved slowly, wreathing the blade in sinister darkness. "I'm an anointed priest of Calixtos."

He stalked toward Relaina slowly, savoring the fear in her eyes as he brought the blade closer to her skin. He pulled the fabric of her tunic aside, ripping it at her shoulder to expose her skin.

"Just a taste," he said into her ear, and the blade touched her flesh.

Everything blurred before her; burning, sharp cold spread from her shoulder to her chest, and she gritted her teeth and choked down a cry. A moment later the blade was gone, and the pain with it, as if it had never existed. Curiosity and hunger filled Tridset's eyes.

"Interesting," he said, his face lit by a faint bluish glow. Relaina turned her head away from him as much as she could, pushing the side of her face into the wall. When she opened her eyes, her fear disappeared. Her arm was glowing, covered in markings that shimmered with warm, white light.

A healer's light.

She had only a moment to marvel at it. Her vision blurred again as lightning erupted in the place where her arm met her shoulder. The blade and fire might have been dark, but the pain was white-hot and blinding as Tridset made a deep cut from the top of her arm to the hollow at her throat. This time, when he removed the knife, a terrible coldness radiated along the line he'd cut, a coldness that seeped through muscle and sinew and into her bones. Relaina sobbed once, and her eyes found Jacquelyn's horrified expression as Tridset assessed where to cut her next. The next explosion of pain began in her abdomen as he sliced through her protective garment, carving a jagged cut from her navel to the base of her ribs below her heart.

Tridset stepped away as Relaina shivered uncontrollably at the bone-cracking cold emanating from her wounds. He grabbed her by the chin.

"That's enough for today, I think. I thought the shadowfire might bring it out of you."

Relaina spat in his face. Tridset cringed and wiped it away with his sleeve before grabbing her by the throat. He squeezed, and a small whine escaped as her lungs burned for air.

"Do that again, and I'll have you begging for death before we reach King Gabriel." He released her and Relaina gasped, gulping down the foul-smelling air. Tridset turned on his heel and marched from the room, followed by Jacquelyn, who glanced at Relaina before closing the door, leaving her alone to shiver and weep.

DARREN AND JEREMIAH stood at the crest of a hill, consulting a map on a large boulder. The wind made it difficult to keep it in place, but they'd come far enough inland that the rain had abated, and sunlight shone in the west. About halfway down the hill, Bracken sat in the grass, tossing rocks at the trees below.

"We're here," Jeremiah said, indicating the place on the map. "And this is how far we must go to reach the Narrow Pass before the first bridge. There should be a small village with docks along the bank. If the Terranians plan to destroy the bridge the same way they destroyed the bay, then we must hurry. The second bridge is too close to the Terranian border. It's too risky to try and stop them there."

Darren glanced at the sun, the map, and the forest below them.

"Would you say it's about a day's ride?" he asked.

"More or less." Jeremiah folded the map and tucked it into his horse's saddle pack.

"We'll need to sleep eventually," Darren said, though every part of him raged against the idea of staying in one place for more than a few minutes. They'd been riding hard for two days already, pushing themselves and their horses toward intense fatigue. "Taking on a ship of trained assassins will go poorly if we're exhausted."

"Agreed." Jeremiah mounted his horse, and Darren did the same; he'd taken Amariah for her speed and strength. "If we can make it to the Happy Stump by morning, we'll catch a few hours' sleep."

"And if we don't?"

"Then we keep going and figure it out."

They rode down the hill carefully, and Bracken joined them as they approached, heading for the thick foliage.

"So," Bracken said, his voice tight as they emerged onto the forest road. They were all within striking distance of hopelessness and had spent much of their time traveling riding so hard the wind drowned out their thoughts. "How is it that you're Relaina's father?"

Darren tried not to look too interested, equally as curious. Jeremiah sighed.

"Her mother is not Christine, if that's what you're concerned about," Jeremiah said. He didn't seem inclined to go on.

"Who is her mother then?" Bracken asked. Darren valued his life enough to not be the one asking these questions.

"She was a powerful healer and a seer. Her name was Talea. I met her when I...after I was banished from Evaria twenty-one years ago."

"Banished?" Bracken asked. "You? For what?"

"The king accused me of conspiring with a violent crime ring in Maremer. But the real reason was because I was sleeping with the prince. The Andoviers were often ridiculed at court for our lack of wealth and my late father's frequent foolishness, and the king and queen were already prejudiced against nobles of a lesser status."

"So you and Fabian...?"

"We were in a relationship for two years before King Tristan found out and had me banished."

"What a prick," Bracken said.

Darren's heart sank, imagining both Jeremiah and Fabian's past suffering. Was every king a horrible tyrant to their children?

"What happened after you left Maremer?" Darren asked, his curiosity and need for distraction getting the better of him.

"I drank heavily and cared little for anything but the easing of my turmoil. One night, that led to an encounter with a kind woman in a pub in the middle of nowhere and...well. Months later I was in Parea working as a castle guard, and Christine had recently lost a pregnancy, the second one in two years. Talea came to Parea after having escaped a raid on her village, told me the child in her arms was mine, and begged me to take her."

"And you passed her off as Queen Christine's child," Bracken said quietly. Jeremiah nodded.

"Christine, Stephan, and I agreed: if Christine was unable to bear children, this was the answer to both protecting the daughter I wasn't ready to raise and providing stability for the kingdom. There was no way for us to know Christine would safely bear two other children, but by then we could not return to the truth."

"And you were able to keep servants from gossiping?" Bracken asked.

"It had been a week since the miscarriage, but Christine had yet to leave her chambers, and no one besides the healers had been allowed inside."

Darren stared at the path ahead. Jeremiah's account explained why his father was so intent on Relaina's capture, why the tenebrae had been unable to possess her that night in The Gnarled Root...

Why every part of him was drawn to her. Relaina was a child of light. And Darren...he looked down at his hands. He was not tenebrae, but he was a LaGuarde, and carried some of that dark power within himself.

Do not fear your darkness as I did.

"We'll find her," Darren said, his voice hard. "We'll get her back, and Gabriel and the rest of them will know my wrath."

"And mine," Jeremiah said.

"And mine," Bracken said, his voice almost a whisper.

"The sun won't be with us much longer," Jeremiah said. "Let's get going."

They set off at a gallop, and Darren allowed the wind to carry his thoughts, praying to every god he knew that they would not be too late.

CHAPTER 25

ALONG THE RIVER

Relaina shivered on the floor of her cell, her knees tucked close to her chest, the tears on her face long dried. The new wounds Tridset had raked across her back yesterday still ached.

As the cold from the gashes faded, the cold in the air grew more potent; they must be on the Granica by now, feeling the chill of the Lyneisian winter from the mountains to the south. They had not offered Relaina any replacement for the clothing Tridset had slashed, and it had not been enough for warmth here in the first place. She might never feel warm again.

The door creaked open and Tridset stalked inside, startling Jacquelyn, who was on duty to watch Relaina and had fallen asleep on the stool. Tridset ignored her and approached Relaina, looking down at her with a satisfied smirk.

"It looks like you've learned not to trifle with me."

He nudged Relaina's shoulder with his boot, examining the black scar that the shadowfire had left behind. Relaina's body had lit up each time he'd dug the knife into her skin and tried to heal the cuts, but while the bleeding stopped quickly and the flesh repaired itself overnight, bitter cold crept through her veins and prickled along her skin for hours. The scars were as black as the blade and had not faded. She had five, now

—the two from Tridset's first visit, two across her back, and one on the left side of her neck, from her jaw to her breastbone. Relaina glared at him from the floor.

"I've learned that you're a spineless sadist that preys on unarmed victims in the name of a god that will ultimately destroy you."

Tridset stared at her for a moment, and then turned to leave.

"What the fuck was that?" Jacquelyn hissed. Relaina didn't answer.

Tridset returned promptly, accompanied by his two lackeys. They yanked Relaina to her feet and detached the chains from the floor, and she fell forward, feigning vertigo. She grabbed at the lackey's waist, reaching for the key tied to his belt, but her fingers fumbled and she hit the ground with a hard thud.

"Weak bitch," Tridset spat.

"What the fuck do you expect when you've tortured her for four days?"

"Mind your tongue, Jacquelyn."

Relaina braced herself to endure another session with Tridset's knife, but instead of fastening her to the wall as usual, they began dragging her out of the cell, following Tridset into a narrow hallway and up a rickety flight of stairs. When the night air hit Relaina's face, she shuddered and suppressed a sob. It was cold and crisp with the faint hint of pine—it smelled like home. Stars shone brightly above them, a sight of beauty that Relaina etched into her mind. *We'd have no stars without the night.*

She couldn't remember where she'd heard the phrase, but she repeated it to herself now as she resigned herself to whatever Tridset was about to do.

Much of the ship's crew was awake, either manning various sails or rope fastenings or drinking and gambling. As Tridset's men hauled Relaina toward the central mast, the Terranians gathered around, curious.

"You think you can disrespect me?" Tridset growled in Relaina's ear as they fastened the chains to the mast, forcing her chest against the damp wood. "Daughter of Iros, I will *destroy* you."

Tridset took out his knife and cut through the remaining shreds of

Relaina's tunic, baring her back to the cold night air and a dozen pairs of eyes.

"If you beg, I may minimize your punishment," Tridset said. Relaina pressed her forehead into the wood, sucking in cold air.

"Fuck you."

"A shame," Tridset said, grabbing her hair by the roots to force her head backward. His breath puffed against her cheek and she recoiled. "Prince Darren used to beg."

Relaina's mouth twisted into a snarl as Tridset released her hair and laughed. He began yet another cut in her back, and she screamed in anguished rage.

After what felt like an eternity of pain, the knife's bite disappeared, leaving behind only the throbbing cold. With tear-stained cheeks and glowing skin, Relaina waited for them to toss her back into her tiny, dark prison, but instead they walked off, leaving her chained to the mast.

Breathing hard, Relaina forced herself to think about anything other than the cold—Tridset's need to punish her more publicly had given her the opportunity to glimpse above deck for a few moments, exposing the Terranians' plans.

Hundreds of barrels were stacked on board, filled with the source of that foul smell that had become Relaina's constant companion.

Explosive crystals.

She'd heard of their use in warfare in far-off lands, but never before in Esran. It was how the Terranians had set fire to the Bay of Trade so quickly and how they intended to get past the bridges along the Granica. They would make their way to Terrana and sever the main connections between Lyneisia and Evaria in a few short, fiery hours. It was clever and ruthless.

Her teeth chattered. *Focus, Relaina.* The mountains in the distance told her she was a day from the first bridge, and there was a trunk overflowing with weapons at the top of the stairs leading to her cell.

By the time dawn broke on the horizon, Relaina's entire body ached, exhausted by the constant shivering. She'd collapsed some time ago, unable to support her own weight as the hours dragged by. She yearned for the sun on her skin as it climbed higher, but before it hit the deck, two of Tridset's men retrieved her, dragging her back to her cell. Relaina realized with a pang that one of them was Connor.

As they reattached Relaina's chains, something cold and hard pressed against her left palm and a warm hand closed her fingers around it. She looked up and locked eyes with Connor as the other man grumbled and left the cell.

"I'll be on watch abovedeck in an hour," he whispered. He stood and followed his companion.

Stiffly, Relaina lay on her side, curling up to try and retain what little warmth she had left. She gripped the metal object he'd placed in her hand, hardly daring to believe what it was.

A key.

A FEW MINUTES PASSED, and warmth enveloped her. Relaina opened her eyes; a heavy cloak lay over her battered body, providing the first real relief from the cold in days. A brief flash of red hair lit up as the door opened and closed, and footsteps faded up the stairs.

Beneath the cloak, Relaina reached for the key she'd hidden in her boot and palmed it, wincing at the pain in her wrists—the raw skin had split open in the night as she hung from the shackles on the mast. She sat up and took a deep, settling breath, trying to calm herself and ignore the lingering cold in her bones. She closed her eyes and tried to reclaim that feeling when Tridset's knife had forced her magic to come alive, tried to reach for that core of warmth within her that had fought against the sting of the shadowfire.

It was difficult to accept that she possessed healing magic, had felt it course through her as though it had been there all along, as constant as her heartbeat. But now, as she tried to access it voluntarily, there was only resistance and pain. Her black scars pulsed and ached, and the light snapped back to her core, present but dim. Her markings flickered before disappearing again.

"Iros—" she said, but then she remembered her dream from weeks ago, when a goddess appeared before her. *Do not fear the dark.* "Elenia... please." Tears welled in Relaina's eyes as she tried once more to reach her own inner light but failed. How could she not fear the dark after the cold power of the god of darkness had ripped into her and caused her so much pain?

Relaina took a deep breath, willing the tears away. She would simply have to withstand the lingering cold and the pain in her wrists. She could do that in order to get out of here.

The front of her tunic was still intact, but the back hung off her shoulders, exposing her marred skin. Listening for any indication of movement outside of the cell door, Relaina inserted the key into one of the shackles at her wrists and twisted.

It unlocked, and she stared at it for a moment. Had Connor truly had a change of heart? Did it matter, if this was a chance for her to escape?

She unlocked the other shackle at her wrist and the two on her ankles and donned the cloak. She tied the cords at her neck and winced as the rough fabric brushed against the cuts on her back. As quietly as possible, she shuffled the empty shackles and chains into a far corner of the room.

"...don't understand *why* it's taking so long..."

Relaina's heart jumped into her throat, and she quickly dashed to the spot she'd been chained to, huddling on the floor. Footsteps and voices approached the door and passed it, heading deeper into the ship's hold. Relaina released a breath. *Stay calm.*

Hardly daring to breathe, Relaina unfurled and crept over to the door, pressing one ear to the wood. The only distinguishable sound was the creaking of the lanterns as they swayed on their rusted hooks.

This was her chance.

Relaina palmed the key in her hand again, inserting it into the lock and twisting. With a faint click, the door unlocked, and she pushed it open, cringing as it creaked. She pulled the hood of the cloak over her head and darted outside, praying that no one had been silently waiting in the dim corridor.

It was empty. Relaina forced herself to breathe, shivering once as her breath appeared in a cloud before her. If she'd timed things correctly, they would be sailing through the Narrow Pass now, offering her the only plausible chance she'd have to jump ship and swim to shore. She forced her trembling legs to move, to walk up the stairs, to open the trunk at the top and grab a knife and a shortsword, and finally to push open the door and step outside into the day.

None of the crew paid her any heed as she walked through the door and closed it behind her, gripping the blades tightly in her hands beneath the cloak. Perhaps they thought she was Jacquelyn, or perhaps they were so engrossed in their own tasks that they simply didn't notice her at all. Relaina wouldn't wait around long enough to find out.

Her eyes locked on the ship's railing, facing the foliage-covered Evarian side of the Granica. A half mile ahead was the faint outline of fishing boats docked at a little harbor. *A fishing village...*

That would be her best course. She just needed to stay hidden as she approached the railing, to avoid detection for a few more minutes until she could vault over the side and into the water.

Halfway along her meandering path to the port side, Relaina came face-to-face with Connor.

"Don't run," he said, turning to examine a nearby lantern. He wiped at the salt that had accumulated on the outside with his sleeve. "You'll be found out if you do."

He removed the lantern from its hook and walked away, muttering about it needing a good cleaning, and Relaina thawed out, forcing herself to ignore her thundering heart and move on. Just a few more feet until she would be underneath the upper platform of the ship, a gathering place for any crew. It was open to the salty spray of the sea between its roof and the ship's railing but guarded from the sun and searching eyes.

Someone grabbed her wrist just as she stepped beneath it, and Relaina whipped around, knife in hand. Jacquelyn caught that wrist as well and pushed Relaina away, further beneath the veranda. Relaina regained her footing as best she could and took a defensive stance, but Jacquelyn didn't attack. Her hair blew haphazardly in the breeze as she stared at Relaina for a moment, her expression somewhere between anger and disdain.

Had she, like her brother, changed her mind?

"She's escaping!" Jacquelyn shouted, and Relaina's heart dropped. There was a beat of total silence as every crew member froze in place and

Jacquelyn backed away, heading to retrieve her spear from an upper deck. "Help me, you idiots, she's getting away!"

Chaos reigned as various Terranians stumbled into action. Relaina dashed for the ship's railing, blades in hand, but Tridset and one other burst out of the nearby doorway to the captain's cabin, blocking her path. Relaina brandished her weapons and attacked, Darren's voice in her mind.

No hesitation, no mercy.

Relaina let out a cry that raged against her lingering pain as her sword came down upon the man beside Tridset, slicing his abdomen open. Blood sprayed, and he fell to the deck, unmoving. Tridset danced out of the way and drew his own sword, as well as the shadowfire knife. Even out here in the sunlight, Relaina could feel its cold.

"You clever little bitch," Tridset hissed and struck. Relaina parried and dodged as his attacks came faster and faster, but exhaustion pulled at her, slowing her down. Behind Tridset, a man charged at her with an axe but went flying to the ground as a crossbow bolt hit him squarely in the chest. Relaina didn't have time to see where the bolt had come from before Tridset was upon her again. He was toying with her, trying to wear her out, and if she didn't finish this soon, she was going to lose.

While she was distracted by yet another crewmember falling to a crossbow bolt, Tridset managed to wound her with the shadowfire blade, a deep slash down her right forearm. She screamed and stumbled, losing her sense of determination to do anything but get away from that knife. Tridset stalked closer to her as she tumbled onto her back and scrabbled backward, barely keeping her blades in hand.

"Nowhere to run, Princess," he said, smiling, his oily hair falling into his eyes. He held the point of his sword to Relaina's throat as her back hit the railing, the steel just touching her flesh. "You will pay dearly for this. I am going to—"

His threat was cut off by a cry as a crossbow bolt lodged itself into his arm, forcing him to drop the sword. Relaina leapt to her feet and lunged, bringing Tridset to the ground and plunging her knife into his sternum. She watched his eyes grow wide as he choked on the blood that spilled from his mouth and wished she could savor the poetry of the moment more thoroughly.

"For Darren," she said, and the light left Tridset's eyes.

Relaina stood as another crew member ran at her, but his battle cry halted and he coughed once, twice—the third cough had blood splattering out of his mouth, dotting his sword and Relaina's face. A scarlet stain bloomed across his chest as the tip of a spear emerged through his flesh. His body convulsed as the spear was yanked out of him, and he slumped to the ground, revealing Connor, and—

"Jacquelyn," Relaina rasped. She was staring at the man she'd just killed and Tridset with a look of mingled shock and disgust. Crew members had noticed and closed in on the three of them.

"Jacq," Connor warned, aiming his crossbow again. Jacquelyn dashed forward and grabbed Relaina by the shoulders. Connor threw himself past the guards, retrieving the lantern he'd held earlier, now lit despite the hour.

"You'd better fucking survive," Jacquelyn said, and in the infinitesimal moment before Jacquelyn shoved her over the side of the railing, Relaina caught a glimpse of Connor knocking over a barrel as he grappled with another Terranian and shattered the lantern on the deck where it fell.

Fire erupted.

It blasted Relaina into the cold, murky depths of the Granica, and she lost consciousness briefly before inhaling a lungful of water. She choked and fought against a gasp, flailing toward the surface, her sword slipping out of her grip. She coughed and retched as she broke the surface and grabbed the nearest piece of flotsam, expelling the water from her lungs and stomach. There was pain along her abdomen, more than what she'd felt before from the shadowfire blade, but not enough to stop her from swimming for the shore, even as her vision faded in and out. She didn't look back until she'd reached the bank, dragging her body halfway out of the river before slumping on the muddy earth and gazing out at the fiery remains of the ship, floating in pieces along the river.

CHAPTER 26

THE SEARCH

Aronn, Nehma, and the others struggled to calm their horses as they reared, startled by the explosion from up ahead. Aronn nearly fell but managed to grip the reins and dig his knees in as Reo, the young stallion he'd been given, bolted down the path. It took Aronn nearly a minute to regain control and soothe him, and by that time the Granica river was visible through the trees ahead.

"Are you all right?" Nehma, Rhea, Thea, and Catrin came riding up to meet him.

"Fine. What in Praelia's name *was* that?"

"I don't know, but it can't be good."

"Do you think the Terranian army is nearby?" Thea asked, voicing Aronn's fear. They'd specifically come this way instead of crossing the western bridge to avoid running into the Terranians. "Here at the border already?"

"No, it wouldn't make sense for them to take this route. Let's get to the bank and maybe we can see what—oh."

Everyone looked up, following Nehma's gaze. A massive pillar of smoke rose above the treetops downstream. They led their horses through the thinning trees until they reached the bank, and Aronn jumped down, squinting against the bright sun.

"Oh, gods." About a mile downstream was the source of the smoke —the remains of a ship, still partly on fire.

"Can you see the sails?" Catrin asked, putting a hand to her eyes to block the sun. "Is there a sigil?"

"I can't tell from here," Nehma said, and Aronn shook his head. "Let's head in that direction, and maybe we can find out. Be ready to fight."

They all drew various weapons, Rhea and Thea holding their preferred bows, Catrin brandishing her halberd, and Nehma and Aronn with shortswords light enough to carry in one hand as they rode.

While the river's current carried the debris to the west, the wind blew in the opposite direction, bringing the scent of smoke along with it. Aronn coughed as they drew nearer and blinked as his eyes watered. The healers each glowed briefly, and Nehma reached over to touch Aronn's hand and his horse's neck. His lungs cleared and the stinging in his eyes receded.

"There," Thea said, pointing toward a heavy piece of canvas floating in the water. As if her discovery had triggered a gust of wind, the smoke cleared before them and revealed a scene of destruction. A piece of the ship's mast had been blown all the way to shore, and the rest of it floated in the water, charred and splintered, some of it still aflame. They approached the piece of the mast, and while Aronn and Nehma examined it, the others searched for a sign of whose ship it had been.

"The sail was unmarked," Thea said as they returned. "Some kind of merchant ship, more than likely."

"Who the hell would blow up a merchant ship?" Nehma asked. She shook her head. "Any sign of survivors?"

"None," Catrin said. "A few bodies in the water, burnt beyond recognition or blown apart."

Aronn's heart sank. Something in his gut told him that the Terranians had something to do with this, but there was no way to know if there were no survivors. He gazed past the wreckage; fishing boats floated downriver, and dozens of people had gathered on the opposite bank.

"You don't think that little village could've done anything like this, do you?" he asked.

"No," Nehma said. "We know those villagers. They hardly have access to standard weapons, much less...whatever did this."

"Wait," Rhea said from behind, halting the party. She jumped down from her horse and approached the water's edge, reaching into the mud to extract a soggy, black cloak. Aronn's eyes followed hers to the disheveled earth beneath it, leading to mud stains on the grassy bank intermingled with blood.

"Someone survived."

Darren raced ahead of Bracken and Jeremiah, taking full advantage of Amariah's speed as they headed for the riverbank, toward the sound that had splintered his bones with fear. Images of fire and devastation flooded his mind no matter how hard he tried to push them back, punctuated by hollow pangs in his chest as he sped closer to a place fraught with death.

Amariah's hooves hit the cobblestones of a street, and just ahead, all the villagers gathered at the docks. Darren jumped down as the crowd became too dense for him to continue on horseback, shoving his way through people until he reached the edge, Jeremiah and Bracken now not far behind him. Indignant voices rang out from the villagers as they were pushed aside, but Darren did not hear them.

The ship had been utterly destroyed.

From this vantage point there was no sign of movement, but smoke clouded much of the debris, some of which still burned. Darren winced as he felt another untethering of a life somewhere within the murky waters.

"A boat," he said, not taking his eyes off the wreckage. "A boat! *Please*!" So much death...he could almost smell it on the air. He looked to the people around him, who stared at him and Bracken and Jeremiah.

"Can someone take us to the wreckage?" Jeremiah asked, coming out of a daze. He stood a head taller than most of the villagers, and all three of them must look terrifying with all the weapons they carried. Still, a fisherwoman stepped forward, beckoning, and they followed.

Darren almost lost his footing and ended up in the river as they crossed the docks and headed for the woman's vessel.

Please. Please...

They clambered onto the small boat and set off toward the middle of the river, not far from the docks. The fisherwoman and her two sons manned the oars and rudder as they floated through the jetsam, searching for any sign of life. An iron grip took hold of Darren's heart as the minutes passed and yielded no sign of Relaina.

"Look," Bracken said, pointing toward a body floating facedown. They steered for it, Jeremiah reaching down to turn it over and grimacing at the sight of scorched, black flesh and exposed teeth. It was no one they recognized. Jeremiah dropped the body back into the water, and they continued on to find a cluster of more dead, and a few stray body parts here and there. Bracken leaned over the side of the boat to vomit, and then slumped to the deck with a heartrending wail. Darren and Jeremiah flew to the railing.

Floating at the surface was another facedown corpse, torn in half at the waist and distinguished only by the fiery red hair that flowed from her head.

Jacquelyn.

Darren reached down to grip Bracken's shoulder as he convulsed with sobs. He would never forgive Jacquelyn for what she'd done, but Bracken had loved her, and his heart broke for his friend.

That same horrible grief Bracken felt threatened to choke Darren as they rowed on without finding Relaina, emerging onto the other side of the wreckage. Darren blinked—a hazy figure appeared on the Lyneisian side of the bank, next to a horse. She was examining something on the ground, black hair fluttering in the breeze.

"Sail for the shore," Darren said, taking a seat at one of the oars himself. Jeremiah took up the oar from the other boy, and as quickly as their rowing would take them, they made their way to the Lyneisian bank and the mysterious woman standing there. When they were close enough, Darren stood and dove off the side of the boat.

"Wait here for us, please," Jeremiah said, placing a piece of silver into the fisherwoman's hand before following Darren into the water. Bracken remained behind, still crouched next to the boat's railing. The woman on the shore drew her bow at their approach, and Darren slogged out of the water with his hands raised.

"What brings you here?" the woman demanded in Lyneisian. Darren tensed but did not reach for his weapons—yet. "Who are you?"

"I am Jeremiah Andovier," Jeremiah said. "Captain of the Lynx Guard."

The girl's face went slack.

"Captain Andovier." She lowered her bow and bowed deeply. "The healers of the Caspian Forest are glad to serve the royal family and Lynx Guard."

"We are looking for someone," Jeremiah said.

"Rhea? Who are you talking to?"

Another woman emerged from the trees, identical to the first.

"Thea, this is Captain Andovier." Thea gaped. "He must be looking for Aronn."

Thea turned to face the trees.

"Aronn!"

Aronn?

Another figure appeared moments later, shoving brambles off of his tunic and grumbling about being interrupted before looking up and stopping dead in his tracks.

"Uncle?"

"Aronn," Jeremiah said, close to weeping. He approached his nephew, and Aronn ran the rest of the way, laughing as he threw his arms around his uncle. Jeremiah dropped his sword to the ground.

As they embraced, a third woman stepped out of the forest, wielding a gleaming halberd.

"Nehma and I found the survivor," she said. "It's a woman. She's— wait, who is this?"

"My uncle," Aronn said, turning to her. He looked to Darren. "And...you are Darren LaGuarde?"

The three women sprang into action, taking defensive stances and brandishing their weapons.

"No, stop! He's with my uncle." Aronn turned to Jeremiah for confirmation, and Darren's heart eased a bit as Jeremiah nodded once. The twins and the third woman slowly lowered their weapons. Aronn exhaled with relief and turned to the red-haired woman with the halberd.

"Is she alive, Catrin?" he asked.

"Yes, but gravely injured," Catrin said. "Nehma is working to heal her now, but it is proving difficult."

"Why is that?"

Catrin frowned, eyes darting to Darren.

"She has the healers' light, but she has been marred by a dark power."

"Where is she?" Darren and Jeremiah spoke simultaneously. Aronn looked at them, bewildered.

"This way," Catrin said, leading them into the trees. Darren kept himself from sprinting into the forest—he wouldn't know which way to go, anyhow.

The seconds felt like hours as they approached a crouched healer exuding beautiful warm light. She knelt before a large tree, tending to a slumped figure with a bloodied abdomen and skin covered in jagged black scars.

Relaina.

Darren ran for her, and only a few paces away a blinding flash of light stopped him in his tracks. It sent ripples of pain through him, calling to the darkness within, and he cried out as he crumpled to the ground, the light burning him as he tried to hold the cooling darkness at bay. He struggled to his hands and knees as the burning stopped and the healer approached him, her entire body blazing with light. A tendril of light reached for him, touching his skin before recoiling. The healer growled and sent her light to cover Relaina, blocking her from view.

"Stay away from her, death-bringer," the healer, Nehma, snarled at him, and she whipped out another tendril of light to strike him in the chest. The light resonated in his bones, and he gasped.

"Nehma! What are you doing?" Aronn asked. She whipped around to face him.

"He is a son of darkness."

"He's on our side!"

Nehma's eyes blazed brighter for a moment and then dimmed,

bringing her light back to herself and Relaina's wounds. She glared at Darren.

"Relaina," he said, unconcerned by whatever this combative healer thought of him as he tried to get up. "Is she alive?"

Nehma looked from him to Aronn, and then to Relaina.

"That's my sister," Aronn whispered.

Jeremiah approached now, falling to his knees by Relaina as Nehma focused on healing her once more. Darren stumbled to his feet and knelt on her other side, trembling as he beheld the vicious black scars carved into her flesh. He'd seen scars like that only once before, on the one healer his father had kept alive in the dungeons, forced to heal prisoners before they were handed over to the priests of Calixtos.

Relaina was a healer, and someone had used a shadowfire blade on her.

Nehma's light receded. Darren's heart stopped beating altogether as Relaina's eyes fluttered open halfway and she groaned.

"Darren," she croaked, and he sobbed, reaching for her face. She leaned into his hand, lifting her own to rest atop it and smiling faintly as her gaze shifted.

"Jeremiah... Aronn..."

"We're here," Jeremiah said, taking her hand. "You're safe now. You can rest."

Relaina nodded once, and then went limp again.

"What's wrong with her?" Aronn asked, his voice strained.

"She lost a lot of blood from the wound to her abdomen," Nehma said. "It was not deep, but her body was resistant to my magic. I had to be careful not to touch the black scars."

"What caused that?" Jeremiah asked.

"A shadowfire blade," Darren said, still gazing at Relaina. "That's what they leave behind on someone who wields light magic."

"Wait," Aronn said. "Relaina is a healer?"

"She is," Nehma said.

"We have much to discuss," Jeremiah said. "But I fear we must move, and with haste. Terrana marches on Evaria."

"We know," Aronn and Nehma said together.

"We were headed for Maremer when we heard the explosion," Aronn said.

Jeremiah nodded. "Good—Maremer will need your help. But Relaina will need rest tonight. We should stay in the village before we make our way there."

Darren reached for Relaina, lifting her into his arms. Her back was bare, the Shadow tunic in tatters, and she leaned into him even in unconsciousness, desperate for warmth. He held her close and followed the others to the riverbank, thanking every god he knew that she was alive.

Perhaps even Calixtos.

~

THE VILLAGE BURNED.

She stood on the hilltop, the heat from the flames reaching even here, screams riding on the wind as soldiers attacked, laughing at the people as they fled. Her hands shook, and she lifted them to her face and shuddered. Half of her fingers were blackened on the ends. She called to the light within her, and it answered, illuminating her body as she took off down the hillside and rushed into the village. Other healers were here, fighting against the tenebrae who attacked them. They had slaughtered so many already...

She let out a cry of anguish and guilt and rage that echoed around the streets, fighting and taking down tenebrae even as they converged on her and tore her apart.

"*You came back,*" one of them hissed, stalking her as she struggled to remain upright. Two others joined, circling, snickering. "*Fool, you got away and came back, and for what?*"

She drew in a breath, and the healers around her felt her summons. They thrust their power at her with the very last of their strength, and she took it all in, holding it for a moment...

For my daughter.

She exhaled and unleashed herself upon them.

~

RELAINA WOKE WITH A GASP, panic gripping her throat as she traveled between sleep and waking. Above her was an ordinary thatch roof.

"Relaina?"

She blinked, breathing deeply to slow her heart rate as she extended a trembling hand to touch the face that had appeared beside her. Her fingers were her own and fully functional. But along her forearm, a black scar remained.

"Darren," she sobbed. She pulled down on his shoulders, and he acquiesced, climbing into bed to hold her.

"Where are we?" she asked.

"A fishing village right along the Granica. We found you in the woods after the ship blew up."

Relaina blinked again and stared at the soft fabric of his brown shirt, the fog of sleep receding. She remembered now—her haphazard escape, Jacquelyn, Connor, the explosive crystals. Tridset was dead, and so was the man who had been with him, both at her own hand. Relaina gasped, clutching at her chest as sobs wracked her body, sitting up in an attempt to breathe. Darren sat up with her, and she gripped his hand as all her grief and fear and relief poured out of her.

"I'm sorry," he said, his own voice breaking. "Relaina, I'm so sorry."

"I killed a man. They tortured me and humiliated me, and he deserved it. Why do I feel this guilt?"

He took her face in his hands gently, his brown eyes swimming with tears. "Even killing the evil ones can make you feel like you've forfeited part of yourself. I'll be here any time you want to talk about it. Nothing you can say, nothing you've done is too horrific or dark."

Relaina nodded and dropped her forehead onto his chest, shuddering.

"There was one...I killed him and would kill him again without a moment's hesitation."

"Who?"

"Tridset. He was a priest. He...he spoke of you."

Darren wrapped his arms around her, one hand threading into her hair, and they sat there for a long while in silence.

"I'm so sorry I didn't anticipate that this would happen. I'm sorry I wasn't able to protect you."

Relaina lifted her head, placing a hand on his beautiful, tormented face.

"Don't blame yourself for the treachery of someone else. I'm just glad you're safe."

"Me?"

"If I'd been brought to Terrana, you would have followed, wouldn't you?"

Darren frowned.

"My father is more cunning than we thought."

Relaina exhaled slowly, her gaze resting on the nearby window and the darkness outside.

"Darren." She fidgeted with the hem of his shirt before mustering the courage to look him in the eye. "I...I'm a healer."

He nodded, and a small smile touched his lips. "So I've heard."

There was a weight in his voice she didn't understand, but for now there were more pressing matters.

"Can I take a bath here? I smell like shit."

Darren laughed. "Of course. They drew one just a few minutes ago. I'll make sure it's still warm."

The washroom was not far. Darren returned shortly and helped Relaina stand, half carrying her from the bedroom. They were staying in a two-room inn that had a shared washroom, Darren explained, and Bracken and Jeremiah were in the other room.

"What about my brother? And those other people?"

"A family was kind enough to put them up for the night." Darren pushed open the washroom door with the hand not supporting Relaina. "They aren't far."

Darren locked the door behind them and helped Relaina to the large basin full of hot water. She sat on the edge and began peeling the tattered remains of her tunic from her body, wincing as it reached her abdomen. As the cool air hit her skin, she began shivering and could not stop. Darren knelt before her and took her hands.

"Can I help?"

Relaina nodded, teeth chattering. He gently removed the remainder of her tunic before setting to work on her trousers. Stiffly, Relaina wriggled out of the fitted pants as he pulled them down her legs. Darren's face changed from worry to menacing fury as he finished helping her undress and saw the scars that now totaled six, with the addition of whatever Tridset had cut into her back. Relaina sighed as she lowered herself into the water, reveling in the warmth that enveloped her.

"I know the bite of that knife," Darren said, sitting on the floor next to the basin and resting the back of his head on the edge. "The cold lingers for days."

"What did he carve into my back?"

It took Darren a moment to answer.

"It's a symbol representing imprisonment. The way mine represents detachment."

Relaina closed her eyes. Another obstacle to overcome, but not today.

"Connor gave me a key."

"What?"

"This morning." Relaina opened her eyes and swallowed hard. "After he...after using the shadowfire blade they left me chained to the mast for hours and then threw me back in the hold. He slipped a key into my hand."

Darren didn't, or perhaps couldn't, form an audible response. Relaina shivered as cold pricked at her skin again, even in the heat of the bath.

"Then he helped me escape." Darren turned around to face her. Relaina drew her knees to her chest, resting her chin on top of them as she recounted her escape. He remained silent for a few moments after she'd finished.

"We heard the explosion before we'd even reached the river," he said. "We searched the wreckage. Jacquelyn and Connor are dead, along with the rest of them."

A lump formed in Relaina's throat.

"I don't know how to feel about it all," she whispered. "They betrayed me, betrayed us all, but in the end, I survived because of their help."

"You don't have to feel a certain way. If you feel hatred, then let it come. If you feel gratitude, then feel gratitude. As for me, I'm glad they experienced a brief development of a conscience, but fuck them both."

"I wonder if it was just brief. Or if they truly had a change of heart."

"We'll never know." Darren tucked a limp curl behind Relaina's ear, the gesture so normal and comforting Relaina almost wept. She looked at him, *really* looked at him, for the first time since she'd woken, and noticed the circles under his eyes, the tension in his entire body.

"How long was I on the ship?"

"Five days."

"It felt like weeks." Relaina reached for the cloth on the basin's edge and began scrubbing at her skin. It was cathartic, as if she were scrubbing away the stain of the shadowfire and Tridset. Darren took over when she couldn't reach her back, and his familiar, gentle hands running along her skin helped to cleanse her of that stain as well, putting her at ease.

His hands began to tremble as he put down the cloth and traced the scars on her back. He leaned down and kissed her shoulder.

"I'm so sorry."

Relaina grabbed his hand and kissed his knuckles.

"I'll wear them with pride. A reminder that I survived. As you wear yours."

Darren squeezed her fingers.

"I never wanted you to have to do that." His voice broke, and Relaina grabbed the sides of the basin and slowly lifted herself, turning to face him. She reached for his face and wiped a tear from his cheek as it escaped. He reached to help steady her as she stepped out of the basin, and Relaina leaned into him as the warmth of his body touched her skin.

"Will you...will you just hold me a moment?" she asked, her voice constricting as her stomach lurched, a sudden fear rising in her chest. Darren didn't answer; he folded her into his arms until her trembling subsided.

"I love you," she said finally, her voice muffled by his shoulder.

"I love you, Relaina," he said, kissing her hair.

"If ever I meet your father, I'm going to *fucking* end him." Her fingers gripped his shirt above his scar. Darren shuddered.

"I truly hope it won't come to that. But if it does...may Calixtos guide your hand."

Relaina breathed slowly, the remainder of the panic and fear in her chest fading. *Calixtos*...there was something she almost remembered, something gentle and soothing, but it evaded her. She put it from her mind for now, changing into fresh clothes provided by the inn before leaving the washroom.

"I'm famished," she said.

"There's a small pub nearby. The others were there earlier."

"Let's go."

She desperately wanted to see Jeremiah and Bracken, but her heart leapt at the prospect of seeing Aronn for the first time in months, evidently safe from his Lyneisian captors. Darren led the way across the street, one arm around her to provide walking support and warmth in the chilly evening air. With every step, Relaina grew a little steadier.

"Relaina," he said, stopping before the door to the pub. The sound of clinking plates and cutlery drifted outside. "You should be prepared to learn some things that may be...shocking to hear."

Relaina frowned, her heart beating faster.

"What sort of things?"

"Your—Jeremiah will explain."

Relaina nodded, took a deep breath, and stepped into the pub with Darren.

CHAPTER 27

PREPARATIONS

Wind and rain whipped at Fabian's cloak as he stood upon the balcony overlooking his city. A massive storm approached from the west in the Great Sea, one that would rival even the worst storms he'd lived through, and despite the extra burden of evacuating citizens to the catacombs beneath Maremer, Fabian said a silent prayer of thanks to the goddess Oara for sending it. The unforgiving winds and rain had delayed the Terranian host by a day or more, giving them time to rein-force Maremer's walls and gates in preparation for a siege.

Based on information from his Shadows, the Terranian army had decimated the holdings along the way to Maremer. While the five lords and ladies were grief-stricken over their land and homes, their families and their people were safe behind Maremer's walls. The Terranians were near, even if they were not yet visible from Seacastle, and once the storm ceased, it would only be a day, perhaps two, before they mounted their attack.

Fabian looked to the southern gate, the only gate still allowing people to enter the city after a fierce vetting by Desiree or other high-ranking guards. It was there that he'd instructed Jeremiah and the others to return once they'd found Relaina. His heart ached as he watched sheets of rain pummel the gate, knowing that it could be long weeks before Jeremiah returned.

If he returned at all.

Any number of things could prevent Jeremiah from fulfilling the promise he'd made in Fabian's study. Jeremiah's banishment had nearly destroyed him all those years ago, and he was determined to protect his heart this time, even as he remembered Jeremiah's unrestrained kiss, his hands on him just the other night...

"Your Majesty!"

Fabian turned, blinking against the rain as one of his guards beckoned him back inside. He treaded carefully over the stones and into the hall while that guard and another fought to close the door against the wind. It slammed shut, and they latched it with a heavy iron bar, breathing heavily as Fabian wrung out the water in his cloak.

"Fabian." Desiree stood before him in a deep-blue dress reinforced with armor, one hand on the sword at her hip. "No one else is coming through that gate. Anyone left outside has taken shelter by now."

Fabian nodded. "Is it secure?"

"As secure as it can be without being sealed—like the other gates already are."

"We will keep it unsealed until the rain lets up. I won't bar people from getting inside, even if there's only a slight chance of that happening. Let us hope that the storm continues for another day, or more."

"Normally I would disagree." She matched step with Fabian as he headed for the door to the stairwell. "But since all our ships are already destroyed, let the rain and wind come."

"Is everything in place? The other gates? The evacuation? Food stores and supplies?"

"We are as prepared as we can be for a siege. We can survive here for several months on the stores we have, if necessary. Henry Swanson is a little shit, but at least his lands yielded a bountiful harvest this year. The only thing we lack is soldiers. Or rather, quality soldiers. We have them stationed along the city walls, some our own, many from various Evarian lords' houses, but few of them have seen battle. I fear for their resolve should the walls be breached."

Fabian rubbed his face. "Curse my ancestors for not having built higher walls with better defense mechanisms. When this is over, that will be our first project after rebuilding the docks and ships."

"That will take years."

"And years from now we will all be glad it was done."

A crack of thunder sounded from outside, shaking the lanterns in the stairwell as Fabian and Desiree descended.

"This is going to be a nasty one," Desiree said, holding the door open for Fabian at the bottom. "We'd better hope the glass holds up in the western wing."

"If it doesn't, we've already moved everyone out of that section, yes?"

Desiree nodded.

"Good. If it fails, it will just be another thing to add to our list of repairs. I think it should be fine; that glass and all the windows in the palace were tempered by expert craftsmen shortly after I ascended the throne."

"Were there many accidents before then?"

Fabian glanced at her sidelong. "Not too often, but a broken window almost killed Jeremiah when he was sixteen. That should not have happened."

"Ah, I see." They approached the entrance to the kitchens. "What would you like me to do next?"

"Have a drink. Eat something." Fabian smiled wryly. "Go find Saheer."

Desiree coughed, gaping at him as he smirked at her.

"As you know me, Desiree, I know you. She's always stationed near your chambers when you're off duty. And you've been smiling more lately."

Desiree scowled.

"I haven't done anything that would encourage her to shirk her responsibilities. Nor have I given her any special treatment."

"Relax, Desiree," Fabian reached for the door to the kitchens, "I know you haven't. Now, take a deep breath and go take care of yourself before this battle begins. I will need all your energy and strength."

Desiree exhaled, closing her eyes.

"I don't know what I did to deserve the kindness you offer me every day."

"You showed incredible potential as a trainee, and exceptional leadership as a guard. But most of all, you were a friend to me when I was most alone in this world."

Desiree's features softened, and after a moment's hesitation, she stood on her toes and kissed his cheek. Fabian gazed at her, delighted, and she bowed and scurried off.

Fabian's smile faded as she disappeared, and he sighed, his breath full of all that weighed on him. After retrieving a bit of food, he found his way to his private study, nodding at the guards before shutting the door and locking it. The fire burned brightly, warming him as he removed his sodden clothing and sat in the large chair behind his desk in a pair of fresh trousers. He stretched, rolling the soreness out of his shoulders before reaching for quill and ink. Something shimmering caught his eye as he began to write—the book Jeremiah had tossed to the floor five nights ago, facedown upon the carpet by the fireplace. Fabian smiled.

I, Fabian Thereux, King of Evaria and Servant of the People and Kingdom, do hereby name my heir, and bequeath my titles and lands to her in their entirety…

~

RELAINA STARED AT JEREMIAH, whose face and eyes were full of trepidation. Her thoughts moved so quickly she couldn't keep up—she might laugh or cry or scream or swear, and as these different impulses pulled at her, she sat in a chair in the little pub, frozen in place before Jeremiah.

Before her father.

Jeremiah was her *father*. The man she'd always loved like a father; the man who had trained her, who had encouraged her to find strength and done everything in his power to protect her, and taught her to protect herself.

But what about her parents? Christine was her aunt, and Stephan... she'd been happier without him in her life, but she still held a place for him in a small corner of her heart. To know that she held no blood relation to him...

She was not a Gienty.

The throne, the crown, the pressure, the suitors, the shouting matches, the tears—by every right and rule of law in Esran, she was never heir to any of it.

Relaina stood from the table and walked out of the pub, fighting the rising hysteria in her chest. Rain battered her face, but she didn't feel it.

"Relaina?"

She whipped around to face Jeremiah.

"How could you do this to me?" A crack of thunder echoed her cry. "I never was... I could have had...but you...you damned me to this life of heavy responsibility and horrible suitors and always feeling inadequate. I...I would have been so happy—*so* happy with you as my father, Jeremiah."

Relaina's legs gave out as she broke down into sobs. Jeremiah came forward, knelt, and pulled her into his arms. Relaina wept into his shoulder as the rain fell harder.

"I'm so sorry, Relaina. If I could go back and fix it all, I would." He leaned back, gripping her shoulders and looking into her bleary eyes. "But you would have never led a normal life either way. I agreed to hide you under the guise of royalty because Gabriel was less likely to know who you were and what power you held if you were the daughter of two non-healers with little to no magic in their blood. Somehow, and I don't know how, he figured it out anyway. I curse the ground the Tyrant King walks on every day for taking away the life we could have led, for ordering the raids that took you from Talea and destroyed her."

Relaina sobbed again as images from her dream flashed in her mind. She'd somehow seen it from Talea's eyes, all the destruction and devastation and evil that Gabriel had wrought upon the healers.

Jeremiah sat with her in the rain until she had regained control of her breath and calmed enough to think clearly again.

"What are we going to do?" Relaina asked as he helped her stand, her voice rough. "Aronn is safe, and Annalise, but what of my—?" She stopped, uncertain now what to call them. Jeremiah placed a hand on her face.

"They are still your parents, Relaina. I know this is difficult and confusing, but I would not rob you of that. I know you love them."

Relaina nodded, sniffling and shivering in the rain.

"Let's go back inside," he said. "We'll dry off and consult the others on what to do next."

They stepped back into the warm pub, and as Relaina beheld the faces that awaited them, she no longer felt the cold of the rain or her black scars.

Nehma, the healer who had saved her life, sat nearby with the other healers as they gathered to discuss next steps. Relaina felt odd next to them, knowing now that she was a healer, but one who knew nothing of using her power.

"I think we should all go to Maremer," Nehma said. "You have warriors on their way to aid Parea, and from what you said, the king and queen are unlikely to be harmed by these spineless insurgents."

"There's no guarantee of that," Jeremiah said.

"They cannot do anything permanent or lasting without a Gienty heir. Besides, the Evarians have already arrived in Parea by now. It would take you two days to get there, and that's only if you push your horse to exhaustion. They are capable warriors. I know they are—my aunt trained them."

"Your aunt?" Jeremiah asked.

"Desiree Fontaine. She is the captain of the Seacastle Guard."

Relaina, along with the rest of her party, gaped at her. Nehma *tsked*.

"My point is, our priority must be Maremer, to help push back the Terranian forces as much as we can. If we lose that battle, Evaria is doomed, and Lyneisia with it."

Relaina frowned. She was right.

"I agree with Nehma," Relaina said. "We must make defeating Terrana our priority."

"Then we're agreed," Jeremiah said.

"Agreed," Aronn said.

Relaina sipped at the ale she'd been nursing for almost an hour now.

"Nothing to say, death-bringer?" Nehma asked, glaring at Darren.

"I figured it was obvious where I stand," he said coldly.

"Call him that again and I'll knock your teeth out," Relaina growled.

"I'd like to see you try—"

"Nehma, Relaina, *please*," Thea said, just as thunder sounded overhead.

"You don't even know him," Relaina said.

"I know he is a LaGuarde. He carries darkness within."

"And I fought against it even when you attacked me," Darren said, silencing everyone else at the table. "I didn't choose to be born with whatever dark power my family is cursed with, but I did choose to defy my father and help King Fabian understand how to defeat him."

Nehma narrowed her eyes at him but offered no retort.

"What time will we leave in the morning?" Catrin asked.

"Sunrise," Jeremiah said. "If this wind is any indication, I'd say we're headed into a sea storm. The earlier we leave, the better."

Nehma and the healers retired soon after, headed for the home of whomever had offered them beds for the night. Aronn remained behind, sitting with Relaina while he finished his tankard of ale, not saying much as Darren and Jeremiah discussed getting back into the city if they found it besieged.

"Never thought we'd be here, eh?" Aronn asked. Relaina snorted.

"No, I did not." She turned to look at him. He looked so like Stephan, and Relaina...

"Cousins."

Aronn shook his head. "No, Relaina. You're my sister, always."

Relaina hugged him, wincing at the ache in her muscles. Aronn got up and gently patted her still-damp shoulder before taking his leave, and Jeremiah did the same soon after. Relaina looked to Bracken, who'd sat silently beside Jeremiah the entire time, staring at nothing. She exchanged a glance with Darren.

He leaned in close to her ear. "I'll be at the inn. Don't forget you need rest."

Relaina nodded as he turned to go. She left her own seat to sit beside Bracken, taking one of his hands.

"I'm sorry, Bracken."

When he turned to look at her, the expression on his face wrenched her heart.

"Did she..." he said, but gritted his teeth and squeezed his eyes shut, turning away. He shuddered. "Was any of it real?"

Relaina wished Jacquelyn were still alive, just so she could kill her herself. But her rage wasn't what Bracken needed right now.

"She said that she really cared for you. And in the end...she and Connor both made decisions that helped me escape."

Bracken sobbed, squeezing Relaina's fingers so tightly it hurt. Several times he started to say something else, but the words died on his lips. They sat there as the pub slowly emptied, watching patrons from their table in the corner. Bracken shifted and wrapped his arms around Relaina.

"I'm so glad you're safe, Laines. If I lost you, too, I...I don't know what I would do."

Relaina hugged him. "Oh, Bracken. You're stuck with me for life."

He laughed a little, a small step in the right direction.

"Good," he said. He leaned back. "Your clothes are soggy still."

Relaina smiled and stood up stiffly.

"Let's go get some sleep," she said. Bracken nodded, and Relaina thought he looked like the weariest person she'd ever seen. He stood and offered an arm to help support her as they walked back to the little inn.

"I love you, Laines," he said when they reached the door to his shared room with Jeremiah. Relaina would have teared up, if she'd had any tears left. She hugged him again.

"Love you too, Bracken."

Chapter 28

The King's Plan

The rain held out for three more days, and as Fabian had predicted, it was only a day after it dissipated that the Terranian host was visible from the balconies of Seacastle.

As dawn broke along the horizon, Fabian's first glimpse of the army sent him careening toward despair. The Evarians outnumbered the Terranians, but Gabriel's army was well-organized, and in their midst, pulled by oxen, were five massive wooden machines.

"What are they?" Fabian asked. Beside him, Lord Vontair had gone even paler than normal.

"Trebuchets," he said. "Siege weapons used to destroy stone and brick. Used in foreign lands, perhaps even in Artemia?"

"Then we will speak with Prince Dyami. He arrived last night, yes?" Vontair nodded. "Good."

Fabian didn't know how Gabriel had acquired these weapons, or the explosive crystals from before. Maremer's walls and the buildings within wouldn't stand a chance.

Fabian turned from the railing and swept back inside, accompanied by two guards who had trouble matching his pace.

"Ready my armor. And my horse."

He passed several nobles as he made his way to his chambers, ignoring Henry Swanson's attempts at bravado and silently nodding his acknowledgment of Lady Rhoe and her two children. An eerie quiet filled the corridors. Fabian's resolve only hardened as he passed by more people—*his* people—and saw the downcast expressions on their faces. He would find a way to protect them. It was the only option.

Fabian stood in his bedchamber with a frown as two servants helped him don his armor, a task usually undertaken by a family member or spouse, but he had neither. Desiree would be the obvious next choice, but she was already at the eastern wall.

The door creaked open as one servant struggled with fastening the left guardbrace, muttering near-silent apologies.

"I'll take it from here."

Calliope strode toward them. The two servants nodded and bowed before scurrying from the room, and she set about properly fastening his guardbrace.

"You look far away, my king."

Fabian sighed. "I have not seen battle for many years. And I was alone then too."

"You are not alone." She adjusted his armor in several places to ensure its integrity. "I know I am not your mother or father or even an aunt, but you have always been precious to me."

She looked up at Fabian, a gentleness in her eyes he'd seen only on rare occasions. He smiled softly.

"Thank you, Calliope."

"There *is* someone who should be here to do this. And if—gods forbid—there comes a day in the future where you must don armor again, I believe he will be at your side."

Fabian blinked back tears that threatened to form.

"You are precious not only to me, King Fabian," Calliope tightened the last of his armor fastenings, "but to your people. I know you will lead them in a way that will make them proud."

Fabian frowned.

"I was not expecting the trebuchets."

"You cannot save everyone. It is the way of war."

Fabian shook his head as he flexed his fingers in his fortified gauntlets. "I don't accept that. I will do whatever it takes to protect my people. Petty violence in the streets, sickness, hunger...I have done everything I can to stop even those deaths that seem inevitable. I will not lose lives to senseless war enacted by a tyrant."

Calliope pursed her lips but nodded and bowed to him.

"Even so, do not blame yourself for something that is not within your power to prevent."

Fabian nodded.

"I must get to Desiree," he said, as Calliope handed him a spear. He'd never been exceptional at fighting, but the spear was his favored weapon. The feel of it in his hands grounded him. "Do your best to keep the servants calm, Calliope. Many of them are young and have never seen an attack of this magnitude."

"Of course." Fabian made to leave, and she followed. "Take care, my king. We need you."

Fabian's answering smile didn't quite reach his eyes.

His horse was saddled and ready by the time he reached the palace entrance, after a quick detour to speak with Prince Dyami about the structure of trebuchets. Perhaps all was not lost.

With a group of ten guards, Fabian set off, riding into the streets of the city. It was quiet and empty, just as he'd ordered. Water still spilled from drains and rooftops and trees; the city would remain damp for several days, and much damage to the western side by the bay must be repaired. But there was no sense in putting energy into that when another attack was imminent.

The gray sky swirled above them as Fabian dismounted near the eastern gate, mirrored by the scurrying of soldiers on the street, up the steps, and along the wall. Many guards were dressed in their full plate armor, while fighters from his nobles' houses were dressed in surcoats with their various sigils and mail. Most of those dressed in mail were stationed as archers on the walls and intermittent towers. Fabian prayed that the stone would hold, and that their resolve would too.

"Your Majesty!"

Desiree approached him, wearing her full armor, bloodred tunic, and golden cloak, her visage cool and collected. She looked truly frightening.

"Our people are stationed and ready. The rest are additional warriors supplied by Prince Dyami."

"I just spoke with him." Fabian lowered his voice. "Desiree...the trebuchets."

His captain of the guard gave him a hard look, swallowing before she answered.

"We've moved civilians out of range."

Fabian looked at all the soldiers standing along the wall as far as he could see in both directions, and those standing on the towers.

"They will decimate us, Desiree."

She clenched her teeth. "We will fight back."

"The walls will fall. It will be chaos. We will all die."

"You don't know that—"

"Desiree. You are supposed to be the realistic one of the two of us."

Desiree's face crumpled, and she turned so that none of the guards could see. She closed her eyes, breathed in slowly, and exhaled.

"What do we do?" she asked.

"There is a way to prevent bloodshed, or to perhaps buy us more time to address the trebuchets."

"How?"

Fabian watched her eyes dart to the spear in his hand, and in a moment her expression changed from confusion to suspicion to realization to rage.

"*No*. Absolutely not."

"Desiree, it is the only way—"

"*No*, Fabian." Her eyes welled with tears. "You can't."

"They will kill everyone."

"*He* will kill *you*!" Several guards looked their way, shocked. "I'm begging you, Fabian, don't do this. There must be another way."

"It's already done, Desiree. I sent the messenger shortly after dawn."

"Fabian...we need you. *I* need you."

"You and the rest of my people need me to protect you in the best way I can. So that is what I'm doing."

Desiree was just shaking her head.

"When?"

"This afternoon, if Gabriel accepts my terms."

"Which are?"

"A full surrender if I win. A removal of Terranian troops from Evarian soil."

"And if you lose?" Desiree's voice broke.

"Then I will be the only one to die. The Evarian people will be allowed to leave or stay, but they will live."

"King Gabriel will never consent to those terms. And even if he does, he will never hold true to his word."

"Give me another viable option, Desiree, and I will take it."

Desiree opened and closed her mouth several times but had no response. Fabian smiled sadly at her.

"Your messenger hasn't returned?" Desiree asked finally.

"Not yet."

"Well then." Desiree rolled her shoulders. "I will hold out hope that your proposition has been declined."

She stalked away, snapping at a few guards who had been staring. Fabian gripped the spear in his hand so tightly the gauntlet dug into his knuckles.

"Your Majesty."

Fabian turned as a guard approached him. It was an older man, with gray hair and a strong jaw. He dropped to a knee before the king and placed a hand over his heart.

"May the gods shine their light upon you, my King." The guard didn't know it, but his gesture gave Fabian the strength he needed. His messenger would return soon, he hoped.

And then his fate would be decided.

A FIRE CRACKLED in the grate of the war tent, the first that had remained lit in days. Several Terranian lords and ladies were present, glancing sidelong at one another below King Gabriel, who sat upon a makeshift throne atop a small platform. He rested his chin on his hands as the Evarian messenger spoke, intrigued.

"So, King Fabian wants to settle this with single combat," Gabriel said. The messenger's face paled, but he didn't wince or whimper like most of Gabriel's own subjects did when he spoke.

The Tyrant King stood, his emerald-and-gold cloak sweeping across the various carpets placed on the ground. He looked into the fire, relishing the discomfort that permeated the room the longer he went without speaking. The fire hissed and crackled again.

"Tell me, sir," Gabriel said, still staring into the flames. "Do you think it wise for me to gamble the capture of a capital city? My trebuchets would have your walls crumbling before the day is out."

No one said a word. Gabriel turned to look at the Evarian man, who was now struggling not to tremble. The King of Terrana laughed and looked back to the fire.

"Fire—the source of warmth—and destruction, as I'm sure you are well aware. Tell me, how high did the flames get when we set fire to every last ship in the Bay of Trade? I hear it was a sight to behold."

Gabriel could almost sense the man's rage, but goading him to attack would only result in the man's death, and then the inconvenience of sending one of his own men back to King Fabian...

"You've caught me in a good mood," Gabriel said to the messenger, turning to face him once more. "And I admire King Fabian's desire to serve his kingdom and his people. I accept his terms, but our fight will be tomorrow at dawn. I need another day to rest without rain beating down on my tent."

"My King, are you sure this is a good id—"

Lord Forye's question cut off as he made a choking sound, eyes bulging. Gabriel waved a hand at the tenebrae guard nearby.

"Enough."

Forye's breath returned to him with a gasp, and a shadow darted across the carpets back to the tenebrae.

"Tomorrow at dawn," Gabriel said again to the messenger, who bowed and hastened from the tent. The king of Terrana addressed his nobles. "This victory will come for us more easily than I anticipated."

"Will we truly hold to King Fabian's terms?" Lady Delimont asked.

"Of course we will," King Gabriel said, making his way back to his throne. "I will not lose. He will die, and I will rule over both Terrana and Evaria. The Evarians that deny me will be quickly gathered and shipped across the Great Sea to be sold as slaves."

The nobles around the tent exchanged pleased glances and smiles.

"Tomorrow, Evaria will be mine. And soon after I will have the seer's daughter."

With Talea's daughter at his disposal, he would be unstoppable, even without his foolish son at his side. Gabriel smiled and settled into his chair.

Victory was imminent at last.

RELAINA'S EYES flew open and her pupils contracted in the sun, forcing her to shut them again. A thin sheen of sweat covered her from head to toe. With great effort she took several deep breaths to slow her racing heart and soothe the impulse to bolt into the nearby trees.

I'm safe now. She sat up and wrapped her arms around her middle. On the ground beside her, Darren stirred, reaching for her in his half-conscious state. Warmth bloomed inside her as he mumbled her name.

They'd sent the others ahead a day ago, insisting that Relaina's need for more rest should not prevent everyone from getting to Maremer as quickly as possible. Jeremiah had been especially reluctant to leave her, but he trusted Darren, and they were all reasonably confident that Gabriel would not find out about the ship and Relaina's escape for some weeks.

Relaina shifted and nestled herself in Darren's arms. He pulled her close and breathed in, eyes still closed. For a moment, Relaina wished to just stay there forever, wrapped in his embrace in the quiet of the woods.

"Relaina," Darren said. She leaned back so she could look at him. "What's going to happen to us?"

"What do you mean?" She ran her fingers through his hair, frowning.

"What will we do if Maremer falls?"

Relaina placed her forehead against his.

"Then we will regroup and fight to take it back. Do we have another choice?"

Darren laughed without humor.

"I suppose we don't." He moved to kiss her forehead, then her cheeks, and then her mouth. "One day, I'm going to whisk you to some faraway land, and we're going to stay there for weeks, eat our weight in food, sleep until noon, and go on adventures that don't involve near-death experiences."

"That will be a nice change." Relaina smiled. "No matter what happens, as long as I have you, I have hope."

"You've had me since the moment I first met you."

Relaina snorted. "Had you up against a wall, maybe."

Darren laughed, sitting up, and Relaina followed.

"Darren..." Relaina hesitated.

"Tell me."

"You came to Parea before, didn't you? Before you lived there?"

Amusement faded from his eyes. "I did."

"Katarina told me it's the reason you left Terrana."

Darren took a deep breath, staring at the trees.

"Is that true?"

He nodded. "I never had any intention of hurting you, so please know that."

Relaina brushed her fingers down his arm and took his hand. "I know. It's all right."

He sighed and nodded. "While I was in the city, there was a public event where your family appeared. You seemed irritated about something and argued with your father after it ended, and it terrified me for you. But nothing happened."

Darren's grip tightened on her hand and he drew his knees to his chest. He laughed even as a tear fell down his cheek. "It was such a small thing I don't even remember what you both said. And I realized my father had broken me so thoroughly that I didn't know until that moment how deeply twisted and wrong it all was."

Relaina's heart shattered at the look in his eyes.

"So then you left."

"So then I left. And even though I was in hiding and on the run, I was free. No more killing, no more rituals, and eventually I ended up in Parea. Camille and Maurice helped me more than they'll ever know."

"Did they know who you were?"

"Not at first. But they asked questions and I couldn't lie to them and allow them to unknowingly place themselves in danger for my sake."

Relaina nodded and traced the outline of his ear, her thumb brushing his cheek.

"I love you," she said. "Just in case you forgot."

"I could never." He kissed her hand, still intwined with his. "I love you, Relaina."

She moved closer to him, resting her head on his shoulder, listening to the birds and the wind in the trees. The underlying urgency of their journey caught up to her, then, and she sighed.

"We should go."

Darren splashed his face with cold water from a nearby stream while Relaina rebraided her hair.

"How are you feeling?" he asked, preparing Amariah for departure.

"Today? Like new," Relaina said, rolling her shoulders. "The soreness is gone. Well, the soreness from my injuries. Sleeping on the ground, however..."

"Not ideal. At this pace, we should only have to sleep out here for one more night."

"Good. I hope nothing terrible has happened."

Darren stepped into Amariah's stirrup and swung his leg over as Relaina secured their supplies and weapons on her saddle. "The storm will have slowed them down. If the fighting has begun already, hopefully we can slip inside the city the way Fabian instructed."

"Ow! Shit." Relaina yanked her hand back from one of the bags, assessing the fresh cut on her palm. "Gods damned knife, I forgot I put it in there."

"Did we bring bandages?"

Relaina opened her mouth to respond, but every thought vacated her mind as a sharp, agonizing pain lit up her entire body. She cried out, blinded by lightning crackling through her bones. When her vision returned, she was on the ground with Darren crouched over her, panic alight in his eyes.

"Relaina? Can you hear me?"

She let out a choked sound and curled up onto her side.

"Relaina!"

The terror in his voice made her open her eyes again, and she followed his horrified gaze to her arm, which glowed with her elusive healer's markings. But where Tridset's shadowfire blade had sliced open her forearm, the scar was moving, the blackness slowly spreading into the markings and replacing the light.

Darren grabbed her, his hands digging into her shoulders, and coolness shot down her arms, soothing the pain enough for her to catch her breath. But it froze in her throat a moment later—Darren's eyes had gone entirely black like the tenebrae, and up his arms a dark vapor coiled. He spoke something Relaina couldn't understand, in that same language Tridset had used, and the pain was gone.

She exhaled, but Darren did not release her.

"Darren."

He blinked, his eyes still black, and gritted his teeth. His grip tightened on Relaina's shoulders. She took a slow breath and touched his arm, and some of the cold, night-dark vapor swirled around her fingers.

"Darren."

With a gasp, he let go, and the darkness disappeared. Relaina sat up as he stared at his trembling hands.

"I'm sorry," he said. "Gods, Relaina, I—"

Amariah reared behind him, neighing as two figures shot out of the woods and tackled Darren to the ground.

"No!" Relaina lunged for them, but two sets of hands pulled her away.

"It's all right, Princess, you're safe now!"

"Get the fuck off me!"

Relaina elbowed one of her assailants in the stomach and twisted out of the other's grasp. The two holding Darren were glowing, and the darkness returned to his eyes as the healers' light grew brighter. Relaina dove at them, reaching for one of her daggers.

"Stop! Stop, Relaina!"

She looked up from the healer she'd attacked, her dagger halfway out of its sheath as she straddled the woman. Before her stood a girl with unkempt blonde hair, dirty clothes, and terrified gray eyes. Relaina's lungs deflated.

"Annalise."

CHAPTER 29

A CHANCE

Jeremiah drew his horse to a halt at the treeline and dismounted, pushing aside a branch to get a better look at Maremer. Black silhouettes of numerous tents stood by the eastern side of the city, made stark by the fires lit wherever possible.

"The fighting hasn't begun," Nehma said.

Jeremiah stood back and let the branch fall. "Then let's go. We'll free the horses. Take only your weapons."

They set off quickly and quietly into the open, crouching in the tall grass and pausing every few yards to ensure they hadn't been seen.

"The southern gate is sealed," Nehma said. "Where do we go?"

"There should be someone at the wall by the gate to instruct us," Jeremiah said, shuffling to the front of the brigade. He led them on, keeping one eye on the Terranian army to ensure no one came riding toward them. When they arrived before the gate, Jeremiah craned his neck and whistled softly, straining his eyes to locate a figure on the wall. Someone appeared soon after and called down to them.

"Identify yourselves!"

"Jeremiah Andovier! Accompanied by Aronn Gienty, Bracken Averatt, and four healers from the Caspian Forest, including Nehma Fontaine."

The figure disappeared without a word, and for long minutes they stood there, flattening themselves against the wall.

"Gods in hell, did the man forget about us?" Catrin hissed.

A loud crunching sound from Jeremiah's left startled them, continuing for a moment until a trapdoor flew open just in front of the stone of the wall, flinging dirt and mud and crumbling stone as a man's head appeared.

"Follow me."

They each climbed into the narrow hole, clinging to an old ladder that led at least twenty feet underground. Jeremiah's hands became ever more slippery on each rust-caked rung. At the bottom, a very short, narrow passage led them under the wall and to another ladder. When they emerged, they were just inside the southern gate.

Once the last of them had brushed themselves off and the guard had instructed three other guards to begin filling the passage with heavy stones and sand, Jeremiah approached him.

"What is happening? Have they attacked?"

"No. They arrived yesterday morning, my lord. With five trebuchets."

Jeremiah's blood ran cold.

"And they haven't yet attacked?"

The guard shook his head.

"King Fabian extended an offer of single combat, king to king. They say Gabriel accepted his terms. They fight at dawn."

Jeremiah forgot how to breathe as the guard's words punctured holes in his chest. He looked to the sky, which was lightening with cruel celerity. He grabbed the guard by the shoulders.

"Where?" The man mouthed silently, his face pale, and Jeremiah shook him. "*Where*, damn you?"

"A-at the ruins of the ancient kings, just outside the city on the cliff. Only a few guards were allowed to accompany each king."

Jeremiah released him and located a group of tethered horses by the guards sealing the gate's secret passage. He ran, mounted a horse in one swift motion, and took off down the streets, racing the dawn.

~

THE LAST OF the morning mist glided across the mossy stones of the ruins, dissipating as the sun broke the horizon. Fabian closed his eyes and breathed in the chilly air, drawing upon the undeniable presence of his ancestors and their strength of heart as he prepared to enter a fight that would be his end.

Desiree had not come. He'd insisted that she remain by the wall to lead the Evarians posted there and to watch the Terranian army. It was his final gift to her that she would not have to watch him die.

Fabian gripped his spear as five guards made a final check of his armor, and he hoped that the trembling in his hands was not visible to the Terranians across the courtyard. He exhaled and looked over the nearby cliff at the army squatted before his city's walls, and then glanced behind at the mighty palace that had been his home since he was born.

"It's time, Your Majesty," one of his guards, Peter, said quietly. Fabian loosened and tightened his grip on the spear and flipped it in his palm several times, mail clinking as he did so. He'd elected to wear a hauberk and surcoat emblazoned with the phoenix rather than full plate armor. It was less impenetrable, but made by the same tailors who'd fashioned the protective clothing for his Shadows.

As the sun began its ascent in earnest, King Gabriel stood from the chair he'd had brought up here, revealing that he, too, wore mail and coat. Fabian prayed that his was more old-fashioned, but it didn't matter anyway. Gabriel was a ruthless fighter and skilled swordsman, and Fabian had little training in comparison. But he only needed to last for a little while.

"It's not too late to save yourself and let me take the city by force, as planned," Gabriel said as they both stepped onto the mossy stone that would act as their battleground. His sword gleamed in the light of the dawn.

"Let's not speak of such absurdities," Fabian said, surprising himself with the steadiness of his voice. He entered a defensive position with his spear, flipping it in his hand. "Whenever you're ready, King Gabriel."

The Tyrant King grinned, his appearance unnervingly similar to young Darren. With no warning, he lunged, narrowly missing Fabian's left arm. Fabian danced back, already on the defensive and losing the strength of his stance. Gabriel chuckled. The Evarian king adjusted his grip and countered, and from there, the fight began.

The two kings attacked and parried, lunged and dodged, and for a while Fabian avoided the bite of Gabriel's blade, his reflexes sharp and his feet quick. A sharp sting erupted in Fabian's upper arm as the King of Terrana's sword sliced through his sleeve, but it was neither fatal nor unmanageable. Fabian continued to fight, and fight well, even managing to cut Gabriel's cheek with his spear. Gabriel darted back and touched his cheek, examining the blood as Fabian caught his breath.

"Impressive," Gabriel said. "But not enough."

Just as he finished speaking, a strong smell filled Fabian's nostrils, and his vision began to blur. He blinked, trying to clear his mind, but his eyes refused to focus.

You are a disgrace!

Fabian flinched at the sound of his father's voice, and that moment of distraction cost him—stars erupted in front of Fabian's eyes as the butt of King Gabriel's sword slammed into his face. Gabriel turned quickly and dealt a blow to Fabian's side, and the guards behind him gasped as Fabian swore, clutching at the gash, but despite the severity of the wound, Fabian marveled at the lack of pain he felt. *Oh gods.* He looked down at his blood-covered hand as his vision blurred again and slowly clenched it into a fist.

"Had enough, yet?" Gabriel asked, his voice garbled. Fabian ignored the shouts from guards on both sides.

"You...poisoned..." The earth beneath him wobbled.

Gabriel brandished his sword and began circling Fabian again. "So rather than yield and hand over Maremer, you will die, and I will take Maremer anyway. Seems like a poor deal for you."

Fabian moved to attack Gabriel while he was focused on pontificating, managing to land a hard blow on his left shoulder. It merely jabbed into the mail, but it was forceful enough to make Gabriel take a step back. Fabian gritted his teeth against the pain in his side and the throbbing in his head. He needed to last longer than this.

But his wounds throbbed, his head filled with fog, and he didn't know how long he could keep this up.

With unexpected force, Gabriel swung his longsword toward

Fabian, who narrowly avoided being decapitated. A momentary silence washed over the spectators, and then they erupted once more, the Terranians encouraging their king while the Evarians shouted in indignant fury. Fabian didn't have to hear what they shouted to know that they were afraid. He had to *focus*... He blinked, and for a moment he was not standing before Gabriel but before his mother, Queen Penelope.

Come now, Fabian. Be done with this foolishness.

Fabian squeezed his eyes shut and opened them again. Gabriel continued to come at him with the full force of his strength, and Fabian could feel himself weakening with every passing second. *Only a little longer.* Against his better judgment, he glanced at the horde of Terranian soldiers below, but they looked much the same as they had a few minutes before. His vision shifted, and the Terranian army turned into a large festival full of artisan tents. A moment later, reality returned. Sweat coated Fabian's forehead. *A little longer...*

Gabriel landed a blow on Fabian's dominant arm, followed by a quick kick to the knee, and Fabian went down—hard. Fabian gasped for air as his body came in contact with the aging stone.

"*Fabian!*"

Silence filled the air again, but this time it lingered, waiting. Gabriel walked toward Fabian slowly, standing over him with sword in hand. Fabian tried to rise, but his strength failed him.

It was over.

"It's a shame, really," Gabriel said, looking down at his sword, his face shifting in and out of focus, becoming Fabian's father, then his mother, and then once again the Tyrant King. "I had no quarrel with you until you began protecting the Lyneisian princess and my traitorous son. I would have let you live, even given you land and a title."

"Go fuck yourself."

Gabriel frowned, stepping on Fabian's forearm with his boot and pressing it into the ground. Gabriel leaned over him, digging the point of his blade into Fabian's shoulder. The sour smell of poison filled Fabian's nose, and warm blood began to soak the sleeve of the Evarian king's shirt as Gabriel drove the blade in deeper. Fabian clenched his teeth to stifle a scream.

"The last of your family's blood, spilling onto the very stones where the first Evarian kings and queens stood. Rather poetic, don't you think?"

Fabian said nothing. Even if he could focus on what Gabriel was saying, rather than the shifting images in his field of vision, he would not give him the satisfaction of showing weakness. Gabriel removed his sword, examining the blood on the end.

"Your bloodline will end, and I will be celebrated for years to come as the king who conquered Evaria."

"You'll be...a tyrant...who murdered...a king."

Gabriel pressed his boot into his arm harder, but Fabian was beyond feeling pain now. The Evarian guards had begun to shout again, like a distant ocean wave about to crash onto the shore. This wasn't the end. He would die, but Desiree would fight on, and Relaina would return... and so would Jeremiah.

The very thought of Jeremiah gutted Fabian more thoroughly than Gabriel ever could. *Forgive me.*

"*Fabian!*"

Gabriel raised his sword one last time, and Fabian kept his eyes firmly open as the metallic tang of blood coated his mouth. He would not meet death as a coward. The morning sun shone bright, glaring against the steel of Gabriel's blade. Fabian looked at the light without blinking—a symbol of fire and life, which would continue burning even when he was gone.

With a cry of victory, King Gabriel brought the blade down.

CHAPTER 30

THE BATTLE BEGINS

Another cry joined King Gabriel's, and something flashed above Fabian. His ears rang and steel sang throughout the ruins as Gabriel's sword violently collided with another, sending Gabriel's flying out of his hand and onto the stones, clanging several times before coming to rest on a small mound of moss. A figure stood defensively above him, blocking the Terranian king from Fabian's view.

"You broke the code of single combat!" Gabriel spat.

Someone had...saved him?

"*Fuck* you, LaGuarde."

Gods in hell.

It was Jeremiah.

JEREMIAH ANDOVIER STOOD before King Gabriel with fury in his eyes and fire in his blood, every fiber of every muscle fighting against the impulse to dispatch Gabriel where he stood. The Terranian guards stood poised to end him should he do so, already on edge after watching him sprint across the boundary into the ruins faster than they could react.

"That blade is coated in poison, and you accuse *me* of breaking the code?"

"You have no proof."

"The moss beneath your sword has died already." If that wasn't enough evidence, the distinct scent of the neriamnita was. "Our people and yours will know of your deceit."

Gabriel laughed once, harsh and cutting.

"Knowledge will not help your people now. Prepare your defenses. You're going to need them."

He turned to walk away, and Jeremiah lowered his sword and dropped to his knees by Fabian. The king's eyes were glazed over, his skin coated in a sheen of cold sweat, and blood seeped from the wound in his side.

"Fabian," Jeremiah said as he ripped a shred of fabric from his tunic to wrap around Fabian's middle. "What were you thinking? Gabriel never would have honored the terms you set."

"I know."

Jeremiah reached beneath him. "Grab onto me." With his uninjured arm, Fabian reached for his shoulders.

"Relaina?"

"She's safe, with Darren, a day behind. If you knew Gabriel wouldn't, why in hell did you do it?"

Just as the question left his lips, a thunderous crashing sound reached them from the expanse of land at the base of the cliff, followed by an earth-shaking explosion. Jeremiah watched the Terranian army descend into chaos as every last one of the trebuchets collapsed in a great cloud of debris, utterly dismantled and destroyed, and a quarter of the army lay scattered in the midst of a scorched crater left behind by their stash of explosive crystallized sulfur. For one immeasurable moment, there was absolute stillness as they took in what was happening. Jeremiah looked back to Fabian, who, despite his injuries, smiled.

"Gods," the king said, his grip on Jeremiah's shoulders weakening by the second. "They did it." King Gabriel turned slowly to look at Jeremiah, and then to King Fabian, who lay in his arms. Black vapor crept from the king's hands, swirling around his arms.

"You bastard," Gabriel said. He looked to his guards. "Kill them!"

Jeremiah didn't have time to let go of Fabian and pick up his sword, but the Evarian guards heard the order and came to meet the Terranians head on.

"Take the king and go!" one of them, Peter, said to Jeremiah and another guard. Jeremiah packed Fabian's wound with dirt from some nearby moss and, startled by Fabian's lack of reaction, lifted him as carefully as possible with the guard. There was no telling how potent the poison was, and judging by Fabian's condition, it might already be fatal. They had to get him to a healer.

The eastern entrance to the palace was close but seemed to take a lifetime to reach. Guards posted at the entrance caught sight of them as they approached and came to meet them. As much as Jeremiah wanted to stay with Fabian and personally ensure he got to a healer, he knew Fabian would never forgive him if he didn't do everything in his power to help Evaria win this battle.

"Get him to a healer *now*," Jeremiah said. "Tell them that King Gabriel's blade was coated in poison. It had a sour smell, and he seemed to be hallucinating. He's been unconscious for several minutes now."

The guards indicated that they understood, and Jeremiah turned and ran back toward the ruins. Gabriel and his one remaining guard fled in the other direction while the rest of them lay dead on the stones. Jeremiah swore and reached for his sword, which lay beside Peter's body. He muttered a quick prayer and closed all of their eyes before running back to the palace gates, skirting the perimeter to reach the winding road down into Maremer. As he drew closer to the eastern wall, the din of battle surged over rooftops.

He arrived at the eastern gate just as the healers entered the thick of the battle, unleashing their power upon the tenebrae that had begun wreaking havoc on the Evarians. Several of the archers on the walls merely stood there, staring as the violence unfolded beneath them, while others scrambled for more arrows and fired with shaking hands.

"Who is in charge here?" he asked a nearby guard, stepping just outside the perimeter of the gate.

"Captain Fontaine," she said, wiping blood from her mouth. "And then Syral, but she's dead...so next would be—"

"Jeremiah!"

He turned and nearly dropped where he stood. His mother approached, clad in armor inlaid with sapphires, wielding a shortsword.

"Captain Fontaine is being carried from the field by one of the light-wielders," she said. "I saw a tenebrae attack her moments ago."

"Gods in fucking hell. Do we know what her plans were? Do the soldiers know?"

"There was no plan for this. Once news broke that the king was going to fight Gabriel, we expected to wait and hear who had won and would decide what to do after that. When the trebuchets collapsed and the crystals exploded, Captain Fontaine led the charge, but now we are struggling to hold the line. I expect they will reach the walls before sundown."

Jeremiah swallowed hard, unsure how to respond. But he was spared as a shout came from behind them and several guards rushed to the aid of Captain Fontaine and her niece. Nehma transferred her aunt to the guards and dashed back to the battlefield, throwing herself between a tenebrae and an Evarian soldier.

As soon as Desiree reached the gate she grabbed Jeremiah by the front of his tunic and yanked him down to her level.

"The king?"

"He's alive."

Desiree breathed out, releasing him.

"He's badly hurt. Gabriel had coated his sword in poison. Fabian is with healers now."

"Oh, gods," Desiree said, her voice strained. She looked back to the still-raging battle, and Jeremiah knew she was thinking of her niece. She stared for another moment and then shook her head decidedly.

"I told Nehma not to waste her power on me. I must remain here for now if I am to live. I'll give orders on the wall. Take the command on the field, Captain Andovier."

Jeremiah stared at her.

"Don't make me repeat myself. You were trained as a guard here, and you've been captain of the Lyneisian guard for fifteen years. Do what you know how to do and *help* us."

She motioned for her guards to take her through the gate and up to the wall. Jeremiah's mother followed. The remaining guards looked to him.

"You heard Captain Fontaine," Jeremiah said. "Let's go."

"Jeremiah!"

King Fabian woke with a cry, his eyes flying open to greet the darkness of the night and a startled silhouette reaching for him.

"I'm here," he said, taking the king's face in his hands. Fabian was in his bedroom, gazing up at the luxurious gossamer canopy above his bed. He took a labored breath, wincing at the pain in his side, in his shoulder, in his head, and grabbed at the arm of the man he'd just relived losing in a series of horrifying, vivid dreams.

"Jeremiah..." Tears filled Fabian's eyes—they were both alive, and Jeremiah was *here*. He'd come back.

"I'm here, love." Jeremiah brushed his thumb across the king's cheek and took one of his hands.

"You stood against Gabriel."

Jeremiah tensed, the joy fading from his eyes.

"I don't regret it. I know I broke the code of single combat, and you had a plan and I interfered but I couldn't let Gabriel kill you, and I don't expect you to forgive me. I will do whatever it takes to protect you because you are the king Evaria needs, and selfishly because I am terrified to lose you. I love you, Fabian."

The last four words struck Fabian like a beam of sunlight appearing from behind a cloud. He stared at Jeremiah, at his tired eyes gleaming in the moonlight.

"Marry me."

Jeremiah blinked. A gravid silence filled the room.

"W-what?"

"Damn it, Jeremiah." Fabian winced as he sat up against the pillows behind him. "I've waited twenty-one years, and if we make it out of this gods-damned battle alive, I want you to marry me. Is that all right with you?"

Jeremiah only stared at him, his grip on Fabian's hand slackening.

"A-are you sure?"

They would need to work to move forward, to untangle the knots the past twenty years had created within them both, but Fabian was tired of denying himself a chance at happiness.

"I don't ask this lightly. I am sure."

Fabian's heart swelled as Jeremiah's eyes filled with tears. Jeremiah leaned down and kissed him.

"Yes. It's all right with me."

Fabian leaned back to look into those gentle eyes, hardly daring to believe that he was alive to gaze upon them.

"Well, now that that's settled," he said, wincing again as he shifted his weight. "Let's discuss how we're going to defeat Gabriel, shall we?"

CHAPTER 31

THE POWER OF CALIXTOS

Darren breathed slowly, eyes darting around the tent to the small brazier, the swaying canvas flaps, and each of the five healers. He'd memorized it all in seconds but couldn't stop checking and rechecking the entrance, the distrustful glances from the healers, Relaina's body language. She shifted beside him, Annalise's head in her lap.

"We set up camp here four nights ago when the rain stopped our progress. We planned to leave for Maremer earlier today but..."

But then they heard Relaina's screams and saw Darren crouched over her with shadowy vapor coiling up his arms. He'd spent years pushing it down, forcing it to heel, and the moment he touched Relaina he'd nearly lost all control.

"You can't take my sister to Maremer. It will soon be under attack by the Terranian army, if it isn't already."

Karra, the healers' leader, almost dropped the stick she was using to stoke the fire. She'd scrutinized him the least of the five, her blue eyes uncertain but not hostile when she looked in his direction.

"The Sacred Guard did not give us a second location."

"Karra," another healer said. "If there are tenebrae, we should go."

"Our duty is to keep the princess safe, Rael."

"Our duty is to Esran."

"Are you a trained warrior?" Karra stood, and the four others stared at her, wide-eyed. "None of us know the first thing about battle. We will find another place to take Princess Annalise and do what we swore we would."

Silence filled the tent as Karra sat once more.

"Can't I go with you and Darren?" Annalise asked, sitting up. The girl he'd met in Castle Alterna's greenhouse was nowhere in her exhausted face.

"No, Anna," Relaina said. "If the city is under siege, there's no guarantee we could safely get you inside."

Annalise's eyes filled with tears, but she nodded.

"Are you sure *you'll* be safe, Princess Relaina?" Karra asked.

"We have a plan. And I can fight if need be."

One of the other healers behind Karra shifted forward, his face unreadable. "Princess, those scars—"

"Were inflicted by a priest of Calixtos," Relaina said. All of their eyes darted to Darren, and his heart shot into his throat. Relaina tensed. "For the last time, it was *not him*. Listen to me. I was betrayed by someone I thought was my friend and ended up in the custody of Terranians as a result."

"And they did not follow you?"

"They couldn't, they're all dead."

Karra and the others shared another silent exchange.

"Very well. We will discuss a new plan."

"There is a village about a half day west of here," Darren said, and almost didn't continue when they all looked at him. He cleared his throat. "The people there are very hospitable and don't ask questions."

"That sounds ideal," Annalise said, offering him a gentle smile. "Karra?"

The healer narrowed her eyes but nodded. "We'll leave in the morning. You should both stay tonight and rest. We have blankets in the cart outside."

"Thank you," Relaina said.

They stepped outside, followed by Annalise, and the night air offered much-needed relief from the tension in the tent. Darren didn't blame the healers for attacking him, but the exhaustion of defending himself and easing their mistrust tore at his soul.

"I'm just so glad to see you," Annalise said. "But I wish you didn't have to leave again."

"I know," Relaina said, hugging her. Tears glistened in her eyes as a light wind rustled the trees overhead. "You have to stay safe. I'll send for you as soon as I can."

Annalise wiped her eyes as Relaina released her, turning to Darren. She smirked.

"I like you, Darren. Don't let my sister do anything stupid."

Despite himself, he smiled. "There's no way I can guarantee that."

Annalise giggled as Relaina smacked his chest. He lingered behind as Relaina and Annalise walked to the cart.

"I hope one day I'll find someone I'd stab a healer for."

Darren barked a laugh as Relaina said, "Oh gods in hell, Anna."

"You're so in love with him it's absurd."

"Please stop talking."

Annalise hugged Relaina again before returning to the tent, holding a quilt from the cart. Relaina sighed as Darren approached, her forehead falling onto his chest, and he held his breath. She drew back.

"What's wrong?"

"I—earlier, I...I'm sorry. I lost control." His voice broke as he stepped away from her, fear and shame reigniting in his chest. His father had used that vaporous power on him many times, holding him down, searing into his skin with that biting cold. To think that he'd let it surface for the first time in years and touched Relaina with it—

Relaina took his hand and squeezed it.

"Darren, look at me."

He tore his eyes away from the trees, meeting her soft gaze.

"Whatever you did earlier helped me."

The roaring in his mind staggered to a halt.

"...It didn't hurt?"

Relaina shook her head. "It stopped the pain. I don't understand any of this, but I know what I felt."

The pressure in his chest eased, relief washing over him. He hadn't hurt her. If his power was different from Gabriel's...

Do not fear your darkness as I did.

He released a breath. Relaina pulled him toward the cart, patting Amariah's flank before they climbed inside. A single small lantern stood at the back beside a pile of folded quilts.

"We've lost another day," Relaina said, plopping down and removing her boots.

Darren sat beside her. "We can make it there before nightfall tomorrow, especially if we're rested."

Relaina reached for a quilt, spreading it out on the narrow floor. Darren grabbed another quilt to place under their heads and lay down on his back, staring at the thick canvas roof of the cart. Relaina's face appeared above him, her eyes flashing in the lantern light.

"How did you know to do that? To stop the...the scars?"

Darren reached for her face, bracing himself to fight the pull of the darkness again, but it remained dormant. He tucked her hair behind her ear and traced the black scar that ran down her neck.

"I didn't know. I couldn't think of anything else to stop it, so I tried what I do to expel tenebrae. Normally that destroys the darkness entirely, but...whatever is happening with you is different."

Relaina took his hand.

"What is it, really?" she asked, staring at their entwined fingers. "Your power?"

Darren swallowed. "I'm not entirely sure. All I know is that it feels dangerous and difficult to control. My father wields it and uses it to hurt people, so I thought mine...I thought mine would hurt people too."

Relaina's face crumpled. She opened his hand and kissed his palm before settling down beside him, her fingers tracing soothing circles on his chest.

"I'm not afraid of you, Darren LaGuarde."

Darren turned on his side, wrapping her in his arms. She'd never know how much it meant for her to trust him so completely, to defend him without hesitation, to love him without condition.

"I'd stab a healer for you too."

Relaina laughed and leaned back, brushing her fingers across his cheek before pressing her lips to his. He wove his fingers through her hair and kissed her indulgently for a few minutes before Relaina pulled back, her face flushed and her hands gripping the fabric of his shirt. He shifted, adjusting his trousers to accommodate his inopportune arousal.

"If we weren't ten yards away from other people, I'd be straddling you naked right now," Relaina said, her breath tickling his ear. He groaned quietly.

"You're not helping."

Relaina giggled and kissed him once more before resting her head against the quilt, her hand on the scar above his still-intact heart.

"OUR LINES ARE FALTERING," Saheer said, wiping her brow with her sword in hand as she, Jeremiah, and Desiree gazed out over the battlefield from the city wall. The massive field had turned to silty muck, aside from the section closest to the trees in the southeast that was scorched and littered with bodies. Jeremiah and Teiran, a seasoned guard, had ridden back within the city walls to consult with Desiree, who gripped the ramparts so hard her knuckles were almost white. The healers and Evarian soldiers still fought fifty yards out, weapons flashing and cries ringing out as battle raged on.

"The sun is setting, but the Terranians aren't showing signs of retreat. If they push us into the night, we'll be done for," Jeremiah said.

"And the healers are weakening," Teiran said. "They have not ceased fighting since the moment they arrived."

Jeremiah frowned at the approaching night sky from the east. It was true that the Terranians had pushed them back toward the city walls—there were fewer and fewer Evarians on the field as darkness crept in.

"We will fall back," Desiree said, reaching for Saheer to help her stand as she stepped away from the edge of the wall. "Seal the gate and pack the walls with soldiers who have had time to rest. We need as many archers as possible, and we need fire-tipped arrows."

Saheer and Teiran nodded.

"I'll ride out and find our own," Jeremiah said. "A loud call for retreat will only encourage the Terranians."

"We will join you," Saheer said, and Teiran nodded.

"Jeremiah," Desiree said. "I'm going to report to Fabian. Take command of the wall when you return."

With a solemn nod, Jeremiah set off with Saheer and Teiran.

For the next hour they rode out beyond the wall, quietly sounding the retreat and ushering everyone to the safety of the city. The wounded and exhausted found their way back to the gates, and with the help of archers on the wall Jeremiah covered their retreat. The healers were the last to return, stumbling almost drunkenly past Jeremiah and another archer through the gate. The Terranians headed for the city walls in droves with ravenous, furious tenebrae in their midst. They had lost many to the healers today, and the bloodlust was strong in their shadowy veins.

With ruthless efficiency they shut and sealed the gate, and a deep darkness swept over them as the sun made its full descent and soldiers struggled to light the torches and lamps within the walls.

Jeremiah stood there as the scrambling unfolded—injured carted off to healers, grieving soldiers slouched against the stone wall, and all of them barely remaining upright. Jeremiah knew this battle exhaustion, had lived it before, when all that kept him going was the will to survive and defend what was precious. Bits of hope peeked through as he walked around, amidst the chaos and the tears and the soldiers who were nodding off on the stairs: the clapping of shoulders, the snorting of laughter at a dark joke, the relief that rest had come at last. Perhaps all was not lost.

A few minutes of riding later, Jeremiah dismounted his horse with a groan, his various cuts and bruises barking as he trudged to the entrance of The Gnarled Root and stepped inside. Desiree had come here the day before, doted on by her very worried brother, Josquin, who pounced on Jeremiah as he spotted him from behind the bar. The tables and chairs had been cleared to make room for cots where the injured could be tended.

"What news?" Josquin asked Jeremiah, who winced as he took another step.

"Nothing much yet. I came to get myself healed while there's a break in the fighting."

Josquin called for a healer nearby and had Jeremiah sit on a cot.

"When was the last time you slept?" Josquin shifted to make room for the healer to work.

"Last night. I slept for a few hours before King Fabian awoke."

"And you've been fighting since the sun arose?"

"More or less."

"You need rest, my friend."

"I'll rest when we push back those tenebrae bastards." Jeremiah moved his left arm around as the healer finished and started to work on his battered ribcage. "I trust our young healer-warriors came here a short while ago?"

"They did. Each of them barely made it up the stairs before falling asleep. My niece is strong, but we all have our breaking point."

Jeremiah's thoughts drifted to Relaina as another healer called Josquin away. He hoped that Relaina and Darren were close. They needed Darren's expertise on the Tyrant King, and if Relaina was well enough to fight, they could always use another sword.

But if Relaina was still weak...he'd be hard-pressed to keep her out of the fight, but he refused to allow anything else to happen to her. The sheer terror that had roiled through him at the sight of that ship in pieces on the Granica sent a wave of nausea through his stomach, even now. Jeremiah breathed in deeply as the healer finished mending the last of his cuts, and he stood and thanked her before leaving.

He would fight, and he would not allow the Terranians to win, not when he had such beautiful things within his reach, such hope for the future. He could not dwell on the ache of wanting it all so desperately when at any moment a Terranian soldier could cut him down, or a stray arrow could find his eye. So he tucked that glowing, beautiful future away, into his heart, and rode down the streets back to the eastern gate.

He traveled along the eastern wall to ensure the battlements were properly manned and well-stocked with arms, his movements and replies to soldiers becoming less coordinated as the night deepened. After almost tripping on a loose stone, two soldiers shunted him down a flight of stairs and into an old barracks with a separate room for a captain.

"Sorry, Lord Andovier, but Saheer gave us an order to make sure you get at least some sleep tonight. We'll have someone come find you if anything happens," said one of the soldiers.

Jeremiah sighed, looking at the resolute expression on the soldier's young face.

"Very well. But don't let me sleep longer than five hours. I want to be up well before dawn."

The woman nodded and nudged him toward the door to the captain's quarters. "I promise I will come find you if we need you."

An empty washing basin appeared in a small shaft of light streaming in from the door, feet away from a straw bed. Jeremiah stumbled forward and all but fell asleep midair as he slumped upon the mattress.

KING GABRIEL PACED in his war tent until a scuffle made him turn, and for the first time in two days, he was truly pleased. Two of his tenebrae tossed at his feet a girl of radiant beauty, battered but whole.

"Hello, Katarina," he said, and she flinched violently. Her eyes met his, and she scrambled, making a wild and fruitless effort to get away. He sighed and drew upon his power to drag her back to stand before him, a tendril of darkness over her mouth as she struggled to free herself. Gabriel's eyes flashed, and the darkness constricted. The girl let out a muffled scream. He let this go on for a moment and then relinquished his hold. The darkness receded from her mouth, and she gasped as tears streaked down her bruised face.

"I don't appreciate you forcing me to use my power. I think we can both agree that running is incredibly foolish, and if you do that again I won't be so forgiving." Katarina's breathing was labored as her terrified eyes bored into his. "Tala, fetch Lady Delimont."

Katarina sobbed and fell to her knees.

"Katarina!"

Lady Delimont rushed forward, but Gabriel held up a hand, and she stopped, several feet away from her daughter.

"Lady Delimont, your daughter has committed acts of treason against Terrana these past months," Gabriel said, clasping his hands behind his back. The woman dropped to the ground, prone before him.

"Please, Your Grace, she is but a foolish child. I beg you—"

"Do not fear, my lady. I may have a solution. To your shame, and to your daughter's current predicament." He turned back to Katarina, kneeling beside her.

"Tell me, Katarina...where are the secret entrances to the city?"

Katarina looked at him with pure hatred, and he stifled a chuckle. How foolish she appeared, a viper hissing at a lion.

Gabriel signaled to his tenebrae, and they unleashed their darkness upon her. She hardly had time to scream before one of them had possessed her, and now Gabriel looked at her, satisfied as her blackened sclera reflected the light of the fire and then receded. She smiled at him.

"At your service, my king," she said. Lady Delimont choked on a gasp.

"Do shut up, Ula. We don't have time to play games."

Ula, using Katarina's arms and hand, took the knife offered her by Tala, her tenebrae sister.

"Your Grace, *please—*"

"I gave her a chance, did I not?" Gabriel whipped around, and Lady Delimont recoiled. "Proceed, Ula."

The tenebrae selected a part of Katarina's thigh and drove the knife to the hilt in her flesh. A scream tore from Katarina's lips as the tenebrae relinquished control, and she fell to the floor, her hands trembling around the hilt of the knife. Gabriel approached her whimpering form and knelt once more.

"Here is what will happen. You are going to give me the information I seek. You will help me win this battle, and I will spare your life and even allow you a measure of comfort in a marriage I will arrange to an Evarian lord. Or I will hand you back over to Ula, and you will fight against your own friends, killing them or forcing them to kill you."

He reached down and poked the hilt of the knife, and Katarina cried out. Lady Delimont retched behind him.

"Your choice," he said, smiling.

Katarina looked at him with that seething hatred again, but he'd won, and she had no other choice but to tell him what he—

"Fuck you, Gabriel."

Katarina yanked the knife out of her thigh and then buried it again in her own heart. She twitched, and then was still.

For a long moment, Gabriel stared at her as blood pooled beneath her, hardly noticing Lady Delimont's agonized screams. It had been a long time indeed since someone had thrown him so utterly, had done something so unpredictable that the anger within him built slowly, brick by fury-hewn brick.

And then it broke the surface, and he was screaming in a rage, drowning out Lady Delimont's cries. Dark power filled him from his center outward, and he let the darkness consume him in a swirling cloud that blotted out all light. Ula and Tala cowered in a corner as the tent flapped and surged around them, caught up in the dark wind now emanating from their king.

With this dark power and incredible rage, Gabriel exited the tent and made his way toward the eastern wall of Maremer.

～

THE STONE around Jeremiah shook as a deafening crash rocked through the eastern wall. He fell off of his mattress and clambered to his feet, blinking the sleep from his eyes as best he could before donning his sword belt and running for the door. Another crash sounded, and the walls shook in the barracks. Soldiers ran around in a panic. Saheer appeared at the other end of the narrow path between bunks.

"They've begun attacking the wall!" she called. "They...the tenebrae...they've somehow grown stronger!"

Jeremiah ran. Atop of the battlements of the eastern wall, he had full view of the violence taking place as dozens of tenebrae threw themselves repeatedly at the wall by the eastern gate. It was beginning to falter.

"Get everyone ready near that part of the city," Jeremiah said. "Send as many soldiers as you can. Preferably those proficient with spears or swords."

Saheer nodded and darted away. The sun was at least an hour from rising, none of their soldiers had gotten ample sleep in days, and they had not planned for this. Jeremiah braced himself and forced his mind to focus on the task at hand. *I will not fall into despair.*

Jeremiah stood at the top of the stairs leading to the barracks to address the panicking soldiers below.

"Get your weapons ready and head for the eastern gate! They are going to breach the wall, and we will *not* allow them to get further into the city!"

After barking more orders at archers still along the wall to stay put, he hastened down the battlements to a set of stairs that would take him into the streets. Every nerve in his body was alive with urgency as he drew his sword and ran to the eastern gate, headlong into what he knew would be the battle for their lives.

CHAPTER 32

THE KING OF TERRANA

Darren held fast to Relaina as Amariah balked just past the treeline, frightened by the cloud of darkness swirling several hundred yards from the eastern wall. It grew steadily, gathering strength, and Darren gritted his teeth against its pull. They dismounted and Relaina led Amariah back into the trees.

"Darren," she said as wind picked up, standing beside him, "what *is* that?"

"I—"

Before he could answer, the wind went still, the massive orb of darkness suspended above the ground. As easily as a sigh a beam of it shot out from where it had gathered, pummeling into the eastern wall of the city. The sound of the blow was loud enough to indicate that the stone had failed, and the wall was breached.

"*No,*" Relaina said.

He looked at the place where he knew his father stood amidst the settling darkness, and looked to Relaina, and he raced through a scenario where he took her and ran far, far away from this place. They could remain hidden, they could stay safe, find a ship to take them away from Esran—

No.

He would not run anymore.

"We have to find the others," Relaina said, and Darren blinked himself back into reality. "We have to make sure they're all right and see what we can do to help."

Darren nodded. "You'll need to move quickly."

The moon shone in her eyes as she assessed him.

"And you?"

His voice almost failed him.

"I'm the only one with a chance at stopping him." The darkness within him pulsed and shimmered, as if it knew what he planned. Relaina's gaze pierced right through him, just as it had in the moment he'd met her.

"Relaina, I—"

And like the moment he'd met her, Relaina grabbed him, but instead of pinning him against a wall, she kissed him, hard.

"I love you. I love you, Darren LaGuarde."

He reached for her, pulling her so close it almost hurt, tears pricking at the backs of his eyes as he kissed her, held her beautiful, ferocious face in his hands.

"More than anything," he said. "More than anyone."

"Promise you'll come back to me."

"Relaina—"

"Promise me."

Her face scrunched up as she fought back tears.

"I promise."

"Good."

She kissed him one last time and then let go, sprinting for the gate.

Darren blinked at her shrinking silhouette. With a breath that might very well be one of his last, he took off, heading for the place where the cloud of darkness had been moments before. Tendrils of darkness floated along the ground as he drew near a figure surrounded by a dark, foreboding fog. He slowed to a walk and drew his daggers. They provided a small measure of comfort, steady and familiar in his trembling hands as he forced himself forward. The figure before him turned, and Darren was glad for the darkness as he stopped several yards away, inhaling slowly as the power within him fought to be released.

A low chuckle shot fear through his heart, and he almost lost his hold on the power just beneath his skin.

"So this is how we meet again, Son?"

Darren steeled himself as he stood face-to-face with his father. His eyes adjusted to the darkness, and the king's face was just as he remembered it—cold, calculative, and scornful. Gabriel's dark power swirled around him and began to strengthen again, and Darren's responded, leaping within his skin. *Not yet.*

Moonlight glinted off the sword Gabriel drew from his belt. Darren brandished his daggers and took a defensive stance. His father chuckled again.

"Let us begin, then."

RELAINA LEFT every part of her that felt anything outside the walls of Maremer as she arrived at the gate and threw herself in the fray, taking down two Terranians before she'd even entered the city. She cut through her opponents quickly, the gore that covered her white-steel daggers and the warm blood that splattered on her face fueling her. A Terranian ran at her after cutting down an Evarian archer, and she blocked him before twisting to slice a dagger across his throat. He went down. She kept moving.

Through the clashing of blades and screams and curses she spotted Jeremiah defending a staircase leading to the wall. A gash at his hairline trailed blood down his face, but he fought on despite his injury and exhaustion. Relaina pushed and shoved her way toward him, slicing at figures that attempted to stop her.

She was yards from him when a Terranian soldier appeared on the stairs above, raising an axe.

"Behind!"

Jeremiah turned just in time to catch the axe on his blade and send the soldier tumbling from the stairs to the ground. His body fell right by Relaina, and Jeremiah's weary face lit up when he saw her. Relaina dodged a blow sent her way and kicked the woman in the chest, sending her careening to the ground. A moment later an arrow went through the woman's head.

"Are you badly hurt?" Relaina asked Jeremiah over the clamor.

"It's not deep. A piece of stone clipped me when the eastern wall exploded. Others were less lucky."

"Where is Aronn?" Relaina threw a knife into the leg of a man attacking an Evarian. "And the healers?"

"Aronn remains in the palace with Fabian. Desiree was badly hurt, and we tried to give the healers as much time to rest as we could, but they're choking us here." He took down another soldier, narrowly dodging a slice to the neck. "I've been given command."

"Gods." Relaina rolled to avoid an arrow. The Terranians just kept coming and coming, pouring through the collapsed wall and into the streets of Maremer. Relaina and Jeremiah caught their breath as the archers above them loosed a volley of arrows into the tide of Terranians headed for them, taking down dozens.

"*Lord Andovier!*"

Jeremiah and Relaina whipped around. The panicked face of an archer beckoned to them from the stairs. They darted up to the wall battlements and looked where the archer indicated.

Relaina's breath froze in her throat.

Closer to the eastern gate than she'd expected, the king and the Prince of Terrana battled with inhuman ferocity. The light from the city's lanterns glinted off their weapons as they flashed and swung, but the darkness emanating from Gabriel swallowed it soon after.

And that darkness was growing once more.

"They've pushed too far into the city," Jeremiah said. "We have to push them back as far as we can and hold the line."

Relaina was moving before he'd finished.

DARREN STAGGERED BACK and fell into a roll to dodge Gabriel's next attack. He faltered more and more, battling on two fronts at once —his father, and his own power roiling in his blood, thrashing for release. He needed to summon it to beat Gabriel, but terror at his lack of control gnawed at him.

"You feel that power, Darren?" Darren flinched; it had been years since Gabriel had used his name, instead of *Son* or *boy*. He clenched his daggers tighter. "If you had stayed...if you had listened to me and come into your power properly...you and I would have been unstoppable."

A tendril of darkness shot out and struck Darren in the shoulder, throwing him off balance just before a larger one struck him in the chest. He landed hard on his back, nearly losing his grip on his daggers, and as he coughed and dragged himself into a kneeling position, his father laughed again.

"You are *weak*, and you always have been. That weakness was always bound to destroy you."

Darren panted, digging one of his blades into the dirt to steady himself.

"I am not weak."

I am not weak.

He let go of the iron grip he held on his power.

Darkness engulfed him, exploding from the center of his being outward, swirling around him and his father. But unlike the darkness Gabriel wielded, Darren's was a shimmering ribbon of night, reflecting the stars amidst the dark. The familiar cold, the blackness filling his eyes, the heightened sensitivity to death all settled within and around him; but there was more. Strength filled his arms and legs again, soothing air swept into his aching lungs, and the pain from his injuries disappeared.

There was fear in the Tyrant King's eyes as Darren rose to his feet.

"You never understood," Darren said, his voice guttural, somehow larger, deeper than it had been before. "I don't want to be unstoppable, to be so powerful that people tremble in my presence."

A new feeling grew within him, a sound at the back of his mind, like the roaring of a crowd. His power spread around him, but it did not smother him; it remained tethered, obeying his will.

"If you want anything other than power, you are a fool." King Gabriel began circling again, and Darren watched his every move, each muscle in his body ready to defend. "You have no idea how this works. Allow me to teach you."

Darren braced himself and raised his blades.

WITH JEREMIAH AND THE EVARIANS, Relaina fought to push the Terranian horde out of the eastern square and back to the gate. They had to hold the line, had to—

Darkness entered the world, and her shadowfire scars glimmered and pulsed. It called to her, cold and lustrous, like a river in the dead of night. Fear gripped her and she froze, nearly losing her head to the swipe of a curved sword. Relaina cut the Terranian down and pushed her way to higher ground, clambering up a large fallen stone to peer over the heads of those fighting, but a tenebrae woman accosted her, grabbing her ankle and slamming her into the rubble below. Relaina managed to catch herself on her palms, cutting one on a jagged piece of stone.

Fuck.

The woman paused for a moment as Relaina scrambled to her feet, considering, assessing. The tenebrae's probing darkness invaded her body, and she, in turn, felt into their dark energy, and something inhuman in her recoiled, shoving against it. The tenebrae flinched back, emitting a menacing hiss, and attacked. Strength filled Relaina's bones, but this soldier fought with a rage Relaina did not match.

The initial surge of strength waned quickly, and as the tenebrae pushed her farther and farther back, the exhaustion in her arms was stayed only by her determination to figure out what was happening to Darren.

The tenebrae lunged at Relaina one last time, slicing into her upper arm before she could dart out of the way. Relaina cried out and swiped her blade upward, catching the woman's unguarded abdomen. The tenebrae fell.

Relaina scrambled away from the woman and ran to the stairs on the wall, weaving around archers both alive and dead to peer over the battlements.

Out on the field, visible even in the pre-dawn light of the morning, two opposing forces of darkness wove together in a violent dance that obscured the fighters within. Relaina's panic subsided—Darren was alive.

A blossoming warmth began to push against the cool darkness coursing through her veins, her body attempting to heal itself. *No...*

"*Arrrgghhhh!*"

The healer's light had spread just enough to reach the black scar on her chest, and she was in agony. Stars erupted in her vision, and she collapsed upon the stone. She blinked, trying to see past the pain. Blurry figures above her on the wall backed away or looked on curiously. More pain shot through her as a Terranian soldier appeared, grabbing her by the throat and hauling her to her feet. He was speaking to her, but she couldn't make sense of anything besides the anguish in her bones.

He tossed her to the ground, and the mundanity of the stone scraping her side and shoulder edged her toward clarity again. She sobbed and dragged herself to a half-seated position.

"Are you trying to get away?"

Relaina looked at the face of a Terranian soldier, and behind him at the slew of dead Evarian archers. Every part of her skin was on fire as he reached down to grab her and then threw her against the ramparts. Relaina barely registered the impact and the warm blood that began to trickle down her face. Her vision dimmed. *No, I have to fight...*

But her body had betrayed her, warring against itself.

Relaina...Relaina...!

Two blurry figures appeared, overtaking the Terranian soldier and kneeling before her.

"Oh gods...her eyes...what happened?"

She fell into darkness.

DARREN WAS WIND, more graceful and swift than he'd ever thought possible of himself. The power and darkness grew steadily, and that same chorus of whispering voices grew louder, stronger. But his power plateaued as he fought Gabriel, and the exhilaration that had filled him at first began to wane as his father grew stronger still.

"Now, do you see?" Gabriel asked, nearly landing a blow to Darren's chest. "You are only as strong as those who pledge themselves to you." His father's voice had become warped, strange—terrifying. "I give them death, and darkness, and conquest. You...you are young and tainted by the light."

Gabriel's void-like darkness lashed out, striking at Darren's, and a piece of his power ripped away. He gritted his teeth and lunged, grazing Gabriel's leg with one of his daggers. The king danced back and laughed.

"You'll never win this. Submit to me, and we'll be done with all of this foolishness."

Darren miscalculated Gabriel's next blow and received a wicked slice to the hip. He growled and swore and settled back into a defensive stance.

"You're a fool for ever having gone against me!" His father's jeering faded into nothing as Darren's attention shifted, to a voice in his mind that echoed in painful familiarity.

No...no...I have to fight...it hurts...please...

He cried out as if someone had struck him, and the moment of distraction cost him—Gabriel carved another gash in Darren's flesh along his forearm, which he'd raised just in time to avoid a fatal blow to his neck. Darren snarled and pushed Gabriel back a few paces before staggering a step to the side, fighting with every bit of his will to stay upright and in control of his power. He had to finish this, had to end it soon. Relaina was hurt.

Darren didn't know if Relaina could hear him in return, but in his mind he screamed at her to *fight,* even as Gabriel landed more and more blows and pushed him farther and farther toward the eastern gate. His body took a battering like none he'd yet endured, even as his power bolstered his strength and lessened his pain. *Please, even if I die...please, Relaina...* He wasn't even sure to whom he was pleading. The gods. The wind.

Darren's power continued to lessen, the swirling darkness slowing until it became more of a mist that hung around him as they fought. It shouldn't be possible for a man at his father's age to beat him, not with Darren's training, his determination...and yet, Gabriel was winning. Gabriel's power forced him to back down, to lose precious space between their fight and the city walls with each passing moment. Darren

chanced a glance backward—the intensity of the fighting at the demol-
ished wall had increased, and Relaina was in there somewhere, mortally
wounded.

Please, Relaina...

Gabriel relieved him of one of his daggers, and soon after, Darren
was on his knees, the upper thigh of his right leg pooling hot blood onto
the ground. His father stood above him, his blade pressing into the thin
flesh at Darren's jugular.

"How very disappointing," Gabriel said.

Instead of striking with his sword, darkness shot out from his hand,
choking Darren, suffocating his own power. One moment he was
looking at the triumphant face of his father, and the next he was swept
into darkness so complete all of his senses were smothered.

Nothing—he felt nothing.

~

RELAINA...PLEASE, fight it...

Relaina blinked, and shapes began to take form beyond blurry
circles, faces appearing in the pink light of the dawn. Two Evarian
soldiers crouched nearby, studying her, but their looks of concern meant
nothing as Relaina recognized a voice in her mind.

Even if I die...please...Relaina...

She closed her eyes again and saw darkness unlike any other, and out
of it appeared the face of a man that looked startlingly like Darren, but
far older. Her skin still boiled with pain, but a powerful pull cut
through it, allowing her to think, to move.

Darren. She had to get to Darren.

Relaina staggered to her feet, ignoring the protests of the two Evarians, and pushed past them toward the stairs. None of the fighters in the
crowded square paid any mind to the staggering girl with an unhinged
look in her eyes. She managed to avoid the path of any swing or slash of
a weapon and clambered her way over the broken stone and bodies that
littered the ground. She pressed on until she was once more outside the
city walls, a short distance away from Darren and Gabriel. A fierce wind

picked up from the gathering darkness that would soon conceal them both.

Relaina gritted her teeth and stumbled in their direction, eyes glued to Darren's kneeling form as his father held a sword at his throat. *No.* Gabriel said something she couldn't hear. More darkness erupted from the king, and it choked her, forced her back, but still she pressed on. She would crawl to Darren if she had to.

Gabriel's darkness grew, covering an area even larger than it had before. When she was mere yards away from him, she forced her legs into a clumsy run, despite the pain that raked down her skin. She screamed at Darren in her head, unable to speak. *You promised me! Don't you dare give up!*

The Tyrant King noticed her presence. His face went blank with shock at first, and then his mouth turned upward in cruel amusement.

"How interesting you are," he said, his voice almost swallowed by the darkness. "No matter. I'll deal with you as soon as I'm finished with my son."

Driven by pure instinct, Relaina continued forward. She cried out as Gabriel's darkness enveloped her, and she fell, her palms digging into the muddy earth. The shadowfire was warm compared to the all-consuming cold that filled her lungs, her eyes, her mouth, and covered her skin. She sobbed.

"Darren," she croaked. She couldn't see, but she dragged herself toward the pull of his power. "Darren!"

Her voice broke and didn't return. *You promised, you bastard!* Pure darkness closed in around her, and still she clawed her way forward. An eternity passed, accompanied by Gabriel's laughter, before Relaina's desperate, grasping hand took hold of Darren's arm.

Both Gabriel and Darren's powers froze, suspended, and then the cool, soothing darkness within Relaina raced down her arm and into her hand. The cold disappeared, replaced by a core of warm light in her chest, erasing her pain as it spread, and her body healed itself. Her mind cleared.

Darren inhaled and looked up, both of his irises his natural brown, but his left sclera remained black as night. He stared at Relaina for a moment, and then his iridescent darkness strengthened again. His power intensified even further as he got to his feet, and Gabriel fought to remain standing, but to no avail. The Tyrant King sank to his knees, covering his eyes with his arm against the wind, bellowing his fury. Darren looked from Gabriel's crouched form to Relaina, who gazed into his startling eyes, heart swelling with courage and pride as she beheld a crown of darkness that had formed atop his head, burning like black fire inlaid with diamonds.

CHAPTER 33

THE PRICE OF POWER

Darren's power was near limitless, but his body was not. A strange dance took place within him, a balancing act, and if he let the power slip too far out of his grasp, he would tumble into it headfirst. It was like an abyssal well of darkness, a gaping maw that yearned to swallow him whole.

He kept a firm grip on it as he and Relaina fought his father. Gabriel got up after the initial shock of Darren's newfound strength and attacked them both, full of wild rage. Whatever had happened when Relaina touched him had given him more power than Gabriel.

She was a viper, dealing and dodging attacks with incredible speed and strength, bolstered by the darkness within her that moved and shone along her scars. Her voice was clearest in his head, but others were there, shadows drawn by his darkness, not his father's.

Amidst her scars, Relaina's whole body glowed with the healer's light, but she wasn't in pain like she was before. Now she was focused, and—

Darkness lashed out at him and almost hit him in the chest. He kicked himself. He ought to be as focused as Relaina.

Attack his left.

Darren did, and whipping out his arm, directed a slash of darkness into Gabriel's side. The king's darkness faltered. Darren's grew.

On your right. Relaina dodged a stray tendril of Gabriel's power. On it went, Gabriel fighting both magic and blades until he had trouble moving.

Relaina slowed her own attacks as Darren's power grew even more. She stood back as Gabriel sank to his knees, and when he was nearly nose down in the dirt, Darren hit him over the head with the heel of his dagger. The Tyrant King slumped over, his power dissipating into the air.

Time was difficult to track, and irrelevant anyway, as Darren pulled the last of his power back to himself and the dust settled around them. Dawn had broken, gleaming off of Relaina's bloodstained daggers as she lowered them and relaxed her stance, and the two of them snapped back into themselves and a normal sense of the present.

Sounds and smells became clear again, and the voices were silent once more. Relaina looked worn and heavily bruised, with a few new cuts peppering her skin, though none of those fresh injuries stood out amidst her black scars. Those were as prominent as ever.

And, somehow, they carried a fragment of the power of Calixtos and the tenebrae.

Darren turned as shouts sounded behind them, and running full tilt in their direction was Nehma, along with Rhea and Thea. They were haggard and blood-splattered, but mostly unscathed.

"Relaina, Darren," Nehma said as she got closer. She stopped in front of them and wheezed once. "We need your help back inside the city. There are tenebrae everywhere, but some of them have turned—watch out!"

Darren whipped around. Gabriel staggered to his feet and opened his palm in Relaina's direction, and darkness exploded in a concentrated pillar toward her. Darren took the brunt of it directly to his back as he grabbed her and put himself in the line of fire. He held her fast and unleashed his own power once more.

It exploded out of him, fueled by rage and fear this time, unchecked and wild. Gabriel had taken everything from him—his childhood, his freedom, his dignity, his soul—he would not take Relaina.

The sharp darkness at his back was killing him slowly, despite his own power coursing through him and attacking Gabriel, and Darren forced his senses to engage again. He released Relaina, who was screaming his name.

The darkness at his back cut off, but the pain remained. Darren blinked at Relaina's terrified face.

"Relaina," he said, but that was all he could manage. With an exhale, Darren gave into his power, diving into that abyss, Relaina's voice echoing in his ears.

THE THREE HEALERS put every bit of their strength into restraining the Tyrant King after Darren's darkness had cowed him once more, their light glowing brightly. Relaina watched in horror as Darren's magic slowed and then fell back into him all at once. He collapsed, his eyes rolling back into his head. She grabbed for him and stooped beneath his weight to slow his momentum to the ground, careful to ensure he didn't hit his head on a bit of rock or a fallen weapon.

"Relaina!"

She looked up. Rhea and Thea channeled their power into Nehma, who stood at Gabriel's back, gripping his arms. He laughed as Relaina clambered to her feet.

"Help!" Nehma said.

Relaina exhaled and retrieved one of Darren's daggers from the ground. Now that her light had returned to just the warm glowing orb within her, the fatigue in her bones plagued her every movement. She trudged to Gabriel, who looked at her scowling face with wide, demented eyes.

"You could have been great too," Gabriel said. "But you're all fools. Your mother especially."

Relaina paused. He knew her mother...could tell her about Talea, how he knew her, why he hadn't imploded the Lyneisian line of succession by revealing Relaina's true parentage.

"Spare me and I'll tell you everything." The Tyrant King's voice was calm and reassuring. Relaina stared at him, at the man who had abused and tormented her Darren since he was eight years old.

"If I had time, I would peel your fucking skin off," she said, cocking her head to the side. "But I don't. So may Calixtos send you to hell, you evil piece of shit."

She shoved her dagger into his chest and twisted it.

Gabriel's body lurched. Nehma, Rhea, and Thea jumped back, their light subsiding as Gabriel slumped to the ground, blood pooling in the dirt, wide eyes unseeing.

The Tyrant King was dead.

Relaina turned away from Gabriel's body and staggered back to Darren, falling to her knees beside him. She moved aside the fabric by his neck to feel for a pulse. The presence of that gentle beating nearly made her sob as she placed her forehead on his chest and gripped his shoulder. He was alive, even if he didn't stir.

Darren. She reached out to him with her thoughts, unsure if it would work now that his power was dormant. *Darren.*

Relaina shook him gently, but still he remained unconscious. Just to be sure, she placed an ear to his chest. His heart was beating steadily.

The healers approached, and Relaina looked up at them, the morning sun shining on their dirty, tired faces. Behind them, the city fell quiet.

"It's over," Nehma said.

~

"THE FIGHTING HAS CEASED, but now we have prisoners we don't know what to do with," Jeremiah said.

Relaina sat by Darren's feet on the bed, facing everyone who had gathered in her borrowed chambers. She'd done little else but remain by his side. Jeremiah visited her a few times, and Bracken and Aronn, but she found herself with nothing to say.

She looked at each of the faces in the candlelight and breathed deeply. King Fabian and Desiree sat in chairs by the fireplace, still weak from their injuries; Jeremiah stood behind Fabian, both hands resting on the back of the king's chair as he spoke; Bracken and Aronn stood by a window, Aronn leaning on the windowsill with his arms crossed, half asleep; Nehma stood by the door, ready to bolt; and Rhea, Thea, and Catrin stood on either side of her. Catrin looked worse than anyone else in the room with a still-healing black eye and several knife wounds— she'd ended up fighting four tenebrae at once when they'd sprung on her in an abandoned alley after the fighting died down. It had been two days since the battle ended, but when a healer's power reached its limits, they could no longer heal themselves until getting ample rest. Sleep, they'd told her, was restorative when it came to magic.

Relaina could only hope that was why Darren had not yet woken.

"The tenebrae in the dungeons are watched every minute by healers. Many of the shadows claim loyalty to the 'true King of Terrana,'" Jeremiah said. "If we have Darren, I believe we can prove where their loyalties lie. But other prisoners aren't tenebrae at all, and that will be more complicated."

Relaina blinked, the image of Darren with the crown of darkness dancing before her eyes. *The true King of Terrana.*

"Can you help him?" Relaina asked, looking up at Nehma. The healers exchanged glances. "Please. He won't wake, and I...I can't..." She couldn't bring herself to say it. *I can't access my power.* She couldn't feel even a whisper of the warm orb in her chest.

"Nehma," Desiree said. "Please try. You're the most powerful healer we have, and we need him to mitigate the aftermath of this battle and the death of his father."

Nehma frowned but came forward. Relaina shifted out of her way and stood back, biting her lip. With a heavy sigh, Nehma placed her palm on his chest, calling forth the light. Her hand glowed for only a few moments before she lifted it away.

"What is it?" Relaina asked. Nehma looked up at her, her brow creased.

"He's...fine. Physically. But I can't sense...him."

Panic bubbled within her. "What does that mean?"

"I don't know. He's alive and healthy, but his...*self* is concealed from me. I can't sense it at all."

Relaina looked down at him again, tears welling in her eyes as she shook her head.

"I don't understand."

"I don't either, Relaina," Nehma said. "Perhaps he expended such an incredible amount of energy that he must sleep for a long while."

"I once slept for three days after I burnt myself out during training," Rhea said. "I lost control after getting really frustrated. I nearly injured the person I was supposed to be healing."

"And we have no way of knowing how his power works," Thea said.

"The bottom line is that we don't know," Fabian said, getting stiffly to his feet. Jeremiah offered his arm, and the king took it gladly, steadying himself. "We'll have to wait for Darren to wake, and in the meantime, we will need to each do our part in preventing chaos from spreading throughout the realm."

Relaina sat on the bed again, tucking herself back into her mind and letting the rest of them talk.

"Relaina."

She blinked and looked up. Everyone but Jeremiah had vacated the room. He approached her slowly, as if he were afraid she might flee like a frightened cat.

"What is it?" she asked.

He hesitated. "Relaina, I'm worried about you."

It rose again, that surge of fear and guilt and pain she'd tamped down deep into herself since the battle ended. She pushed it down, hard.

"My injuries were limited and are now mostly healed."

"You know that's not what I mean." Jeremiah sighed and joined her on the bed, placing a hand on hers. "I know what battle can do to you. And I know everyone copes differently. When you're ready to talk about it, if you ever want to, I'm here. For whatever you need. I love you, Relaina."

He kissed her forehead and got up to leave. She wanted to tell him that she knew he meant well, that she loved him too, but allowing herself to say and feel those things would open the door for her to feel other things she was not yet ready to face.

So she stayed there, keeping watch over Darren, holding on to the hope that at any moment, he would wake.

CHAPTER 34

THE BREAKING AND BUILDING

Aronn waited at the Seacastle gates for Nehma and the other healers to arrive from their shifts guarding the tenebrae, breathing into his hands to warm them.

Nehma was deeply mistrustful of the tenebrae, and Aronn could understand why; he'd seen from the balconies of the palace the horror of possessed Evarian soldiers attacking their own, controlled by the tenebrae that had stolen their free will. There were rumors, too, of a Terranian woman who sacrificed herself to guard Evarian secrets. All of that darkness and death—it was no wonder Relaina had hardly spoken since the battle.

"Have they shown up yet?"

Bracken strolled up the walkway, hands tucked into his cloak.

"Not yet," Aronn said, watching his breath puff out in front of him in the night air. "It's only a little past time."

"Are you going to tell them?"

Aronn's heart sank. He'd avoided thinking about it for nearly an hour now.

"I suppose I have to. You'll be going with us?"

Bracken gazed out at the city below, beyond the gate. "I don't think so. There's just...too much that's happened there. I can be of more help here."

"That may be. I'm sorry for what happened with my father. You didn't deserve any of it." He didn't deserve what Jacquelyn had done, either, but it was best to avoid that subject.

"Thank you, Aronn. Ah, here they come."

Nehma, Rhea, and Thea walked along the interior perimeter of the southern wall, a few dozen paces away. Catrin was still recovering from her last run-in with tenebrae, and instead spent her days helping the injured at the Gnarled Root.

As Nehma and the twins approached, Aronn's mouth went dry. He swallowed hard, his smile closer to a grimace.

"Rough day?" Bracken asked.

"Same as it has been," Rhea said. "I wish the Terranian prince would hurry and wake so we can be done with those bastards."

"Their magic saps the life out of me," Thea groaned. "It's so concentrated down there."

"Nehma," Aronn said, his face going red, "can we speak privately for a moment?"

Nehma nodded, leaving the twins to banter with Bracken. The two of them walked just far enough so the others were out of earshot, standing by a flower-covered trellis on the wall. Aronn was eternally grateful for the cool, gentle darkness of night as he turned to face Nehma and his blush crept down his neck.

"I'm leaving for Lyneisia tomorrow," he said. Nehma stared at him, her face unreadable, so he went on. "The Evarians are still fighting to subdue the coup, but they're optimistic. I want to be there to help how I can."

"Good," Nehma said. "Your presence will certainly boost morale."

Aronn deflated a bit. "Right. Anyway I...I wanted to thank you. For saving my life, and for protecting me, and for fighting in this battle until you nearly fell over. I was worried about you the entire time and..."

He was babbling like a fool, now. *Just tell her, you coward!*

"Nehma, I—I love you."

Nehma frowned. "I know."

"Y-you know?" Ashima smite him.

"I know. And I can't reciprocate."

Aronn's heart dropped to his toes. "Oh."

"You've been nothing but kind to me, but I'm not in a place where I can be that for you. I plan to stay in Maremer now that my aunt has seen what I am capable of."

Aronn sighed. "I understand." He shook his head. "You're right. I have to focus on helping my kingdom too. Can I write to you, at least?"

"Of course you can." Nehma smiled.

"Good. Well...I'm sorry if I made you feel uncomfortable."

"Telling a prince that I'm not interested in his affections is not my ideal evening." Gods in hell, someone just kill him now and put him out of his misery. Nehma placed a hand on his shoulder. "But you're Aronn first, and I do care about you, and I want to be your friend."

Aronn nodded. If he spoke, it would come out in a highly embarrassing manner.

"Thank you for telling me, anyway. Goodbye, Aronn. And safe travels."

He watched her walk away in the darkness, back to her friends, and a dull ache formed in his chest.

"Bye, Nehma."

JEREMIAH SHIFTED IN BED AGAIN, still unable to find a comfortable position despite the marvelous softness of the mattress and warmth of the blankets. He sighed and stared at the canopy in frustration. Gods curse him, why couldn't his mind stop racing for one moment?

The blankets beside him moved, and Fabian's hand blindly reached for him, landing on his chest.

"What is it?" the king asked. Jeremiah took his hand and kissed his knuckles.

"I woke you, I'm sorry." He shifted to his side to face Fabian.

"S'all right." Fabian breathed deeply, opening his eyes. "Tomorrow is going to be difficult, and you haven't slept these past few nights."

"You're right."

"Relaina?"

"Relaina. She's so quiet. During the battle she...gods, she killed at least two dozen. I've never seen anything like it."

"She was an integral part of our victory. Evaria, and Esran, too, will never forget that," Fabian said.

Jeremiah frowned, and Fabian placed a hand on his face, brushing a thumb across his cheek.

"She has been through much for one so young," Fabian said. "Our world was always brutal, but Relaina..."

Jeremiah blinked tears away. "I have no idea how to help her. I feel like so much of what has happened to her is my fault, and now I have no way to fix it."

"Jeremiah. You have been a father to her all her life, whether she knew who you really were or not. She adores you, as you do her. You will find a way to help her. I'm sure of it."

"I just can't stand to see her like this. She's not even in pain, she's... she's a shell. To leave her in this state..."

"It's only been six days since the battle ended. And you know I will watch over her as if she were my own. You're needed in Parea."

"I don't know if I'll be able to forgive myself for leaving her. I know it's only for a few weeks, but..."

"Relaina understands the importance of duty, especially in the wake of the attempted coup. She will not resent you for it, and she will have Bracken, me, and many others here to care for her. But to be honest, Jeremiah, I don't think she'll be able to fully process all that happened until Darren is awake again. We still only know what Nehma and the others told us. Who knows what mind games Gabriel played with them before he attacked Darren and Relaina killed him?"

Jeremiah would have liked to kill Gabriel himself for even looking in his daughter's direction.

"We will need to be very careful about how we handle that information," Jeremiah said. "At least at first as we try to keep control of the prisoners."

"I can still hardly believe she did it. She freed us all."

"She did. We have no idea what the extent of her power is. There are so many unknowns."

Fabian ran his fingers through Jeremiah's hair, and his racing heart slowed. "You're right. But for now, won't you try and sleep? You have quite the journey ahead of you tomorrow, and you cannot deal with all of this uncertainty if you're exhausted."

Jeremiah smiled, just a little. "At least I have one certainty."

The king leaned forward and kissed him.

"I love you," Fabian said. "And once things are resolved, I'm going to marry you."

Jeremiah grinned now.

"The only way I'm bringing myself to leave tomorrow is the knowledge that I should be back before spring." He stopped talking for a few minutes, devoting time to gentle kisses and gliding fingertips.

"Do you remember our plan?" Jeremiah asked.

Fabian rolled onto his back, chuckling.

"The waterfall at sunset, and swimming in the pool, then stargazing...then many less-innocent things." Fabian looked at Jeremiah again, grinning.

"Hmm." Jeremiah shifted closer to Fabian and kissed his neck. "I know we'll have to go through all the ceremonies and formal pomp, but one night we will do all of those things."

Fabian chuckled again.

"Who would have guessed? Jeremiah Andovier, a romantic." The king's golden-brown eyes glinted.

"And you are the only soul that will know that. I have a reputation to uphold, you know."

"I'm flattered to be in your good graces then. So, there we are: the jovial king and the stoic rock."

"Rock? I'll have you know that I played a rather jaunty tune in front of hundreds of your subjects only two weeks past."

"So, I'm to understand you've already ruined your own reputation?"

"I suppose I have." Jeremiah sighed dramatically. He blinked, his eyelids heavy. "I'm going to miss you, Fabian."

"It will be nothing compared to the years we've spent apart. And when you return, we will be together often."

Jeremiah closed his eyes, smiling. "So long have I dreamed of that."

"As have I." Fabian kissed his forehead. "Sleep, love. Whatever comes, we'll face it together."

"I SHOULD ONLY BE GONE a few weeks, but Fabian will be here for you, and so will Bracken," Jeremiah said, and Bracken nodded behind him. Relaina had a fistful of bedcovers bunched up in her hand. Jeremiah kissed the top of her head as he prepared to depart. Aronn approached her, frowning.

"Bye, Laines," he said, stepping forward to hug her. She couldn't find the will to lift her arms. "I...I'll see you soon, I hope."

He left, and Jeremiah followed. It was just past dawn.

Bracken sat beside her on the bed, careful to avoid Darren's blanket-covered feet. It had been a week now since the battle had ended, and still, he slept on. Each day a healer came in to ensure he wasn't losing weight or suffering from lack of water, but his body was sustaining itself perfectly.

"Relaina. Jeremiah is leaving. Aronn is leaving, and it may be a long, long time before you get to see him again."

His words fell on Relaina's ears and wound their way through her mind. They prodded at her, trying to get in, to elicit a reaction.

"I know things have changed, but he is still your brother, and he's headed into a potentially dangerous situation. You didn't even speak to him before he left."

Aronn is leaving. Aronn is leaving.

Relaina blinked rapidly as the words broke into the stone-cold casing around her heart.

"Oh, gods," she said, her voice hoarse. When was the last time she'd spoken? When did she last drink something? She shot up, scrambling to find her boots before realizing they were already on her feet, and then ran outside into the corridor. Her lungs protested as she sprinted through the halls of Seacastle, headed for the entrance hall, darting around servants and nobles and guards. She reached Aronn and Jeremiah just as they were walking outside, nearly knocking Aronn over as she ran into him and wrapped her arms around his neck.

She was sobbing then, and said, "I'm sorry, Aronn," over and over again until he interrupted her.

"Stop apologizing before I toss you down those steps."

She leaned back to look at him and smiled for the first time in days. "I love you, brother. Take care of yourself."

"And you, Relaina." Aronn pulled her into one more embrace. "It will be all right. I know it."

Relaina nodded, trying her best not to sob again. Everything that had fought to come to the surface for the past week was spilling over, her body barely able to contain the vastness and variety of it all. Aronn squeezed her hand and made his way down the steps to the horse and the eight Evarian guards waiting for him.

Jeremiah approached her, hesitant, and Relaina lost control again, burying her face in his tunic.

"Do your best these next few weeks, yes?" he said, holding her gently. "Try to sleep. Eat what you can. I'll write you from Parea, and when I get back, we'll talk."

Relaina nodded. "I love you, Father."

Jeremiah exhaled sharply. "You are my greatest joy, Relaina."

When she leaned back to look at him, there were tears in his eyes too. He kissed her on the forehead and wiped the tears from her cheeks.

"I didn't know Talea for long, but *erya dei rulo ey vi.*" *She would be proud of you.* Relaina stared at him, a question in her eyes, and he nodded once, confirming what she'd suspected since Gabriel had mentioned her birthmother's name.

She was half-Terranian.

As Jeremiah and Aronn mounted their horses, King Fabian kissed Jeremiah one last time and made his way up the steps to stand beside her. They watched until they could no longer see them, and still lingered a few minutes more.

"I will be glad every day for the rest of my life that you came to Maremer, Relaina Andovier," Fabian said, his eyes shining with tears of his own. Relaina's broken, battered heart swelled at the sound of that name. Fabian moved an arm, and then paused. "May I?"

Relaina nodded, and the King of Evaria wrapped an arm around her shoulders as they stared at the place where Aronn and Jeremiah had disappeared.

"I could use your advice and counsel these next few weeks," Fabian said. "If you feel up to it, I would very much appreciate your presence in my council meetings."

Relaina took a deep breath, and while a sharp pain lingered in her chest, the edge had dulled.

"I would be honored."

Fabian smiled. "Wonderful." He removed his arm and patted her shoulder. "Anything you need is yours."

"I think what I need most right now is a bath." Fabian laughed, and she couldn't help a smile.

"I'll have extra soaps and oils sent to your chambers. And food for you and Bracken."

Relaina nodded her thanks, and Fabian took one last glance at the city before walking back into the palace. Her insides were raw and broken, but the warm, gentle glow of healing light was present within her once again.

But gods, she really did need a bath. She returned to the palace and walked the halls this time, wrinkling her nose at her own stench. How the hell anyone with a working nose had condoned her presence this last week was beyond her.

Halfway back to her chambers, she shivered at a sudden chill. That's what she got for running outside with no cloak in early winter, mild Maremer winter or not. No matter—a bath would fix that too.

But the chill spread rapidly, until her entire body felt as if she'd just walked through a fresh Parean snow. Out of the depths of the cold an echoing voice rose, one that had her frozen one moment and sprinting the next.

Even in her mind, she knew his voice as he called her name.

Relaina.

Darren.

Epilogue

Darren drifted, until he didn't.

He sat up in utter darkness, each of his senses slow to wake. Water surrounded him, dark as obsidian—no, only as dark as the night sky. The shallow pool extended as far as he could see in every direction, reflecting the stars above.

Darren stood up, and shapes began to form in the vast emptiness. Shadows moved and disappeared, some slowly, others so quickly he wasn't sure he'd seen them at all. The stars shimmered in the ripples he created as he began to walk.

As the number of shadows grew, whispering reached his ears, indistinct—he only caught a word here and there, and the moment he recognized it, he forgot it. So he kept walking, and the shadows converged, some forming into the shape of a human.

A few more steps, and the world shifted until Darren stood inside the Obsidian Keep, in a corridor he'd known well. Shadows took on slight color now, revealing servants walking the halls with cleaning supplies or plates of food and drink. A small figure darted in front of him and he jumped back, watching as the shade of his younger self ran down the hall, his brother on his heels.

"Lucas," Darren said, and his voice echoed in an eerie whisper. The young boy—or shadow, or shade—stopped and turned, looking Darren up and down. He smiled. He was the same age he'd been when he'd died.

Lucas walked back down the corridor, and with each step he grew, becoming older until he reached the age he'd be if he were still alive. He stood before Darren with an easy grin.

"Hello, brother."

Darren fell to his knees and wept. Lucas knelt before him, bracing a hand on his shoulder, as solid as it appeared.

"Darren," he said, and Darren looked up. "You are in the realm of Calixtos, and you must find your way out."

"I... Am I dead?"

Lucas shook his head.

"Mother will explain it to you." Lucas began to fade, and before Darren could protest, he disappeared, along with the corridor. Darren stared once again at an endless pool of night.

Darren...

He jumped at the hoarse whisper, a sharp cold at his back, creeping down his spine.

Worthless...weak...

Darren stood and began walking again, trying to escape the voices behind him. They grew louder.

You could have been great...but you are a fool...

Darren broke out into a run, splashing water everywhere as he went, until he wasn't running through water anymore but through a garden he recognized as well as the corridor. It was the only part of the Obsidian Keep he'd ever found peaceful. The voices quieted, and he slowed to a brisk walk, glancing behind him as he trekked through the flowers and statues.

"Will you really leave without saying goodbye, my son?"

Darren whipped around at the sound of this new voice, and standing in the shade of an apple tree was Queen Kacelle LaGuarde.

His mother.

She was radiant, her dark hair shining and unbound, her bronze skin without a single blemish. She approached him and took his hands in hers while he stared and stared at her, trying to imprint the image of her into his mind.

"My son," she said, her voice full of deep joy. "My Darren. I am so proud of you."

"Mother," he said, his voice thick with tears.

"We don't have much time. Your extensive use of your power brought you here, and now you must get back before it is too late."

"Mother, I don't...I don't know what any of this means. Why am I here if I'm not dead?"

She placed a hand on his face. "Power exacts a price, my love. Use too much too quickly and you come here for a while. As the keeper of Calixtos's power you are able to leave, but you must not linger too long, or you will not be able to do so."

"Please...please tell me about this power. There is so much I don't know and don't understand."

"You will learn." She smiled at him. "I promise, you will learn. But you must go now. The shadows are coming. Continue the way forward, and don't listen to what they whisper at your back. You have come so far on your own, my son—don't give up now."

Tears fell down his cheeks again.

"I love you, Mother," he said, and she pulled him into an embrace.

"I love you, Darren. Now, go—leave the garden. Follow the voice that will lead you home."

"The voice...?"

"You have a promise to keep, do you not?"

His mother's embrace faded, and she disappeared as his brother had. Darren took a shaky breath, and then stepped forward, once more in the water. The whispers clawed at him again, but he closed his eyes, shut them out, and took another step.

Darren.

His head snapped up. He knew that voice.

The voice that would lead him home.

Relaina.

He broke out into a run again, knowing deep in his bones what direction he must go. The water receded until it was gone completely, and the night sky parted, pulling him up and out of the darkness until it was so bright he was almost blinded—

And then he opened his eyes.

Acknowledgments

An absolutely massive thanks to my editors/proofreaders, Sara, Holli, and Amie, who were professional, prompt, and thorough with this massive book and all its moving parts.

Thank you to my sensitivity readers, Holli, Shar, and Sydney, who were insightful, kind, and straightforward.

Thank you to my mom, Andrea, for listening to me read this ENTIRE book out loud and for helping catch those pesky typos.

Thank you to Madeline, Olivia, and Maggie, all of whom read the earliest drafts of this story, and whose spam-texts and investment in my characters' journeys kept me going even when I hit a creative lull or life got busy.

Thank you to anyone and everyone who came to see or streamed my opera, *Firelight*, in April 2022. Your feedback and encouragement is what really pushed me to take the leap into publishing this book, because you showed me that I could move and excite people with my creative work. Our gods and goddesses will have larger roles to play in subsequent books.

A huge thank you to Jenna and Iona for being the best author friends and writing cheerleaders a gal could ask for. I can say without a doubt that this book wouldn't have been published without your guidance, support, and humor.

Finally, from the bottom of my heart, thank you, reader, for picking up this book and taking the time to read about these characters and stories running around in my brain. It means the world to me.

ABOUT THE AUTHOR

Hayley Turner is a writer and composer from North Carolina. When she isn't furiously hacking away at her writing projects—both musical and prose—she can be found pounding cold brew and playing videogames while cuddling with her excessively fluffy dog, Leia, and chaotic void kitty, Nyx. *The Prince of Terrana* is Hayley's debut novel.

facebook.com/itrainsandhayls

instagram.com/hayley_turner_writes

tiktok.com/@hayley_turner_writes

patreon.com/hayleycomposer